"*The Dress Shop on King Street* by Ashley Clark is so much more than your typical romance. It's a rich, complex, and uplifting story of family lost and found that I won't soon forget. If you loved *Before We Were Yours*, you will love *The Dress Shop on King Street* as much as I did. Highly recommended!"

—Colleen Coble, *USA Today* bestselling author
of the Lavender Tide series and *One Little Lie*

"*The Dress Shop on King Street* is a novel that will sweetly tug you into a story line that flows seamlessly between two times, only to intertwine in beautiful ways. Page by page, secret by secret, moment by moment, a story is woven of love lost and found, and hopes and dreams restored. And each page was a gift I did not want to walk away from. Enter these pages only if you want to feel Millie's and Harper's stories deeply, and in the process, be reminded of how gentle God is as He guides us through dreams lost and found. You might just fall in love with a new-to-you author's writing. I know I have."

—Cara Putman, bestselling and award-winning author
of *Delayed Justice* and *Shadowed by Grace*

"A warm, inimitable voice and pure passion and heart underscore every carefully woven thread of this narrative's elegant tapestry. Impeccable research, touches of romance, complex characters, and dollops of charm inform *The Dress Shop on King Street*: the first offering from an author destined to make waves with her lush and immersive setting and powerful, resonant themes."

—Rachel McMillan, author of *The London Restoration*

"*The Dress Shop on King Street* weaves together romance, dreams, and adversity into a flawless time slip that will knock on your heart's door. With Ashley Clark's uniquely southern voice and southern charm, this novel will have the reader ordering a refill of sweet tea while eagerly turning pages."

—Betsy St. Amant, author of *The Key to Love*

"Hats off to Ashley Clark for this winning and moving novel! *The Dress Shop on King Street* is a full-of-hope story that readers won't be able to get enough of. From the gorgeous cover to the well-crafted writing to the tenderness and depth in every scene—*The Dress Shop on King Street* will linger even after readers turn the final page."

—Elizabeth Byler Younts, award-winning author
of *The Solace of Water*

HEIRLOOM
SECRETS
·ONE·

The Dress Shop on King Street

A NOVEL

ASHLEY CLARK

BETHANYHOUSE
a division of Baker Publishing Group
Minneapolis, Minnesota

389 8410

Published by Bethany House Publishers
11400 Hampshire Avenue South
Bloomington, Minnesota 55438
www.bethanyhouse.com

Bethany House Publishers is a division of
Baker Publishing Group, Grand Rapids, Michigan

Printed in the United States of America

Library of Congress Cataloging-in-Publication Data
Names: Clark, Ashley, author.
Title: The dress shop on King Street / Ashley Clark.
Description: Minneapolis, Minnesota : Bethany House, a division of Baker
    Publishing Group, [2020] | Series: Heirloom secrets
Identifiers: LCCN 2020029410 | ISBN 9780764237607 (trade paperback) | ISBN
    9780764237904 (casebound) | ISBN 9781493428281 (ebook)
Classification: LCC PS3603.L35546 D74 2020 | DDC 813/.6—dc23
LC record available at https://lccn.loc.gov/2020029410

Cover design by Kathleen Lynch / Black Kat Design
Cover image by Shelley Richmond / Trevillion Images

Vintage floral wallpaper by Mary Carver / Alamy Stock Photo

Author is represented by Spencerhill Associates

20 21 22 23 24 25 26   7 6 5 4 3 2 1

To my family—

To my husband, Matthew,
for always supporting my dreams
in every possible way.

To our son, Nathanael,
who brings joy to me every day.

And to my parents, Steve and Laurie,
for teaching me to dream fearlessly.

"Every shut-eye ain't sleep,
and every good-bye ain't gone."

—Gullah Proverb

PROLOGUE

Charleston, South Carolina, 1860

The candlelight sent a shadow of Rose up against the wooden wall. From the shadow, Rose looked taller. Stronger. Funny thing about shadows. They made even the smallest things into monsters or fairies or whatever folks wanted.

Even a caterpillar could have the wings of a butterfly.

Her daughter, Ashley, used to be scared of shadows when the girl woke to Rose fixin' their dresses by candlelight. Rose tried to teach her to find the familiar shapes of happy things—flowers or ribbons or the sea. But Ashley had never seen the sea. And sometimes she still woke up Rose when bad dreams made her kick her feet.

Rose pressed her own coarse hair back from her sweating forehead using her palm. She wrung her hands and paced the dirt floor of the little room where she and Ashley slept.

Sold. She could hardly think the word, much less speak it aloud.

Her daughter. *Her* daughter.

Only nine years old.

With all of life ahead of her, and none of it hers to live.

Rose swallowed back the bile in her throat. Her hands fisted, and she squeezed so tightly her fingernails soon brought drops of blood to her palms. That wicked, wicked man. Even from the grave, he ruined her.

First, ten years ago—when Rose herself was a child. And now, with his wife . . . who'd finally connected the dots about the girl.

The slave girl whose father was a white man.

That's all she was to them. A slave.

But to Rose, Ashley was a daughter. *Her* daughter.

Careful not to wake the little girl, Rose took a small blade from the table. For the briefest moment, she considered using it for another purpose, but shook her head. If God thought her life worth living without her daughter, who was she to question His timing?

Rose held the dull knife to the tip of her own braid, then cut slowly through the hair. She would put the lock of hair, a token of memory, with the rest of her daughter's things.

Her hands began to tremble as she looked over at Ashley, the braid still in her hand. In that moment, Rose's daughter was a baby all over again. Those sweet, round eyes and the hushed rise and fall of her breath.

And Rose would do anything to keep her like this forever, because her baby girl knew nothing of tomorrow's horror.

Rose reached for the empty feed sack and set the braid of hair inside. She folded Ashley's best dress with care, then put it inside too, along with three handfuls of pecans.

The candle flickered, and the shadows grew along the wall, and Rose knew this still wasn't enough.

She looked around the room at their meager belongings, then down at her own dress. Of course. The butterfly buttons Ashley had always admired.

The one thing Rose owned of beauty.

Rose snapped the two buttons from the cuffs of her worn cotton dress and dropped them into the bag. She closed the sack tight and set it down on the table beside her sleeping daughter.

She crawled into bed and slipped her arm around Ashley as she'd done every night of the child's life.

"The sack ain't much, child," she whispered. "But it be filled with my love always."

Rose held her daughter until the morning sun rose—an eternity between the night and dawn, and yet an eternity that passed in a moment. She memorized the size of the little girl's hands and the way she pulled the blankets to her chin.

And as Ashley stirred, Rose smiled—not for any joy, but these might be their final moments, and she wanted her daughter to remember them warmly.

She smiled because she'd no tears left to cry.

"Mornin', baby." Rose brushed her daughter's hair from her eyes. "Momma's got somethin' to tell you 'bout."

ONE

Downtown Charleston, 1946

Millicent Middleton.

That's the name Mama told her to give if anyone asked. Half of it was honest, at least.

Millie supposed her mama was being overcautious like all folks do when they've got an aching spot in heart or body, but she didn't mind playing along. She, too, still grieved for her daddy from what she remembered of him and sometimes wondered . . . if only they'd been more careful, well maybe he wouldn't have died.

Millie straightened the red cloche pinned to her bob-cut curls and peered into the window of the dress shop on King Street. The grey-blue of her dress complemented the deep olive of her skin, and her skirt swooshed a bit as she stood on her tiptoes to get a better look inside.

Ever since she first saw her mama's buttons, Millie had been fascinated by dresses and the stories of the women who wore them.

Mama collected buttons—said each had a hole to match—but there were two butterfly buttons in particular that she kept a close eye on and never saw fit to use.

Senseless, really. Buttons with that kind of beauty just lyin' around. Maybe they were waiting for just the right garment.

Inside the shop, a blond woman reached for a peach silk number on display. What Millie would give to go inside the store and let her own fingers graze the fabric of that gown.

Layers of peach silk draped down the back of the dress, then fell into a line of buttons along the fitted waistline and hips. The whole gown was like a summer dream.

Millie sighed.

Maybe someday.

Just as she was swooning, a young man tripped down the sidewalk and bumped into her arm. He righted her elbow immediately, and the two locked eyes.

He was handsome—Millie immediately noticed it—and he looked like just the sort who might've returned from war with Germany.

His blue eyes glimmered, his blond hair shone, and his pinstriped vest accentuated broad shoulders.

Millie smiled at him.

He returned her grin.

Her heart fluttered with all the possibilities of having been noticed.

"Looking for a wedding dress?" he asked, a glimmer in his eye. "My father owns the place, you know."

"Yes . . . I mean . . . oh no." Millie waved her hand, trying to clarify her meaning. "I'm looking, but no intent to buy." She held up her left hand for his inspection. "What I mean to say is I was daydreaming about the dresses. The fabrics. Sewing gowns like these."

He laughed at the response and seemed flattered to have flustered her. Then he took her hand in his own as if inspecting it more closely. "Now, you tell me—why does a woman as beautiful as yourself have such a lonesome ring finger?"

He was probably all talk, and Millie knew it, but she didn't care. She'd never experienced such blatant flattery from a boy before, and she was going to enjoy it while she could.

Millie pulled her hand from his, not wanting to draw attention to herself and this stranger, despite how she'd secretly enjoyed his touch.

She rubbed the sleeve of her dress where it scratched her wrist, and for a moment she wondered . . . didn't he know? Could he not tell what was different about her?

But it wasn't the sort of thing someone said. Not aloud, anyway.

And what did it really matter? It wasn't as if she planned to marry him.

"I'm Harry." The boy rocked back on the heels of his loafers. "Harry Calhoun. And you?"

"Millicent Middleton."

Harry nodded once. "Pleasure to make your acquaintance, Millie." He glanced down the street and gestured his head toward the soda fountain on the corner. "Don't suppose you'd want to get an ice cream, or maybe a Coca-Cola with me? My treat."

Millie gulped back the panic that began rising in her throat.

Speaking with this boy was one thing, but brazenly walking into the pharmacy with him? For all eyes to see? That was another.

She straightened the cloche on her head, though it didn't need straightening. "I appreciate the invitation, but I . . ."

Harry ducked down several inches to catch her gaze once more. "Aw, c'mon. It's just some ice cream."

She did love ice cream. And she hadn't tasted any in ages. Folks on the radio were always talking about the economic depression and the war and the country's recovery; but for Millie's family, growin' up in the decades prior hadn't exactly been rolled in luxury.

Actually, she couldn't remember the last time she'd had a sundae. Maybe a year? Her last birthday?

She could almost taste the chocolate fudge sauce dripping over the vanilla ice cream.

Millie sighed. She was set to meet Mama at five o'clock on the dot. So long as Mama and Harry didn't meet, maybe . . .

"Sure." The word left her lips before she had a chance to reconsider.

"Excellent." Harry sounded as if he'd never expected any other answer from her. His smile caught gleams of sunlight.

He started down the sidewalk and glanced over his shoulder, clearly expecting her to follow. "Have you ever been to this soda fountain?"

It was safe to say she hadn't.

Millie hesitated. "I don't think so."

"They make a great sundae. I always get coconut shavings on mine."

An automobile puffed a cloud of exhaust as it rumbled down the cobblestones of King Street. Harry waited for it, then checked both ways before crossing. Millie stayed close by his side, the skirt of her dress bouncing with each step.

Moments later, they'd reached the pharmacy. Harry held open the door for her, and Millie stepped through.

She'd never been on the other side of the glass before. A jukebox played a cheery tune from the corner, and patrons sat atop stools around the bar. It was everything she'd always envisioned, except alive. Real. And it smelled absolutely delicious.

Millie smiled.

This was going to be a good afternoon. For a few moments, she could live a different kind of reality.

"Welcome, kids. Have a seat." The man behind the counter scooped heaps of ice cream into fancy glass bowls and poured flavored syrups over them.

Harry chose a seat near the center of the bar, and Millie gladly slid onto the stool beside him.

Hand-painted signs for soda, chocolate milk, and ice cream hung on the wall behind the bar, and the checkered black-and-white tile floor brought an air of whimsy.

Millie swiveled right and left on her stool.

"What can I get you?" The man at the counter pulled a pen from behind his ear and a pad of paper from his apron.

"I'll have a sundae with chocolate fudge on top." Millie tried not to sound as enthusiastic as she felt—for she knew she was Cinderella in this dream, and she didn't want it ending a second sooner than it must. The last thing she needed was Harry thinking she didn't belong in a place like this.

Even though she didn't.

"You got it." The man tapped his fingers against the bar. "And you?"

Harry ordered the same, plus coconut shavings. As the man readied their orders, Harry turned to Millie with that dangerous grin again.

"So, if you aren't planning a wedding of your own, do tell me, Millie Middleton, what were you doing peering into a bridal shop? Spying on somebody?"

Millie laughed. "Don't be ridiculous."

"Then what?" Harry asked again. The man set both sundaes on the counter, and Harry plunged his spoon into the ice cream.

"You'll think it's silly." Millie felt her cheeks warming and wondered how much color might show. Not that she was embarrassed of it in the least, but she also wouldn't give Harry the satisfaction.

"Maybe," he said with a raise of his eyebrows. "But you never know until you say it out loud."

Millie took her first bite of ice cream. The vanilla melted sweetly on her tongue. Her dream was just as sweet—but also as much of a luxury.

"I want to own my own dress shop someday." Millie found boldness as she said the words aloud. "I want to be a seamstress."

Harry crossed his arms. "I don't see what's so silly about that."

No . . . you wouldn't, would you?

"Is it because you're a woman?" he asked.

Millie looked down at her sundae.

"Because no doubt, with a name like Middleton and a smile like yours, you'll marry well. I'm sure you'll find a man who will make it happen for you."

"What if I told you I want to make it happen for myself?" Her racing pulse defied the sass of her words.

Harry chuckled, then locked eyes with her. "Oh, you were serious."

"I was, and I am."

"Then I would say I admire your ambition." He hesitated a long moment. "But I would remind you that such idealism is precisely why we can't have women prancing around, running businesses. The idea may be alluring, but it will never happen in American society."

Millie clenched her teeth but managed a tight-lipped smile. Should've known better than to test him. She was normally not so foolish. Long ago, her mama explained why certain dreams and certain people were just not worth her time.

Millie took another bite of her ice cream, then mixed the chocolate fudge into the melting vanilla with her spoon. Blending the two together like a milkshake was her favorite part of a sundae—the hot and the cool, the rich and the sweet. Opposites blended deliciously.

"Tell me more about yourself. What brings you here this afternoon?"

Harry swept his blond hair back with his hand. "I'm studying at the College of Charleston so I can take on the family business someday. But with the pleasant weather today, I skipped class and took a walk down King Street. Perhaps it was fate that led to us meeting." He took a bite of his ice cream. "Do you live nearby?" he asked.

"Radcliffeborough."

"Really?" Harry sat up straighter.

"You sound surprised." Millie swallowed another bite of her sundae, determined not to let one drop go to waste. She ran her thumb beneath her lower lip to remove any traces of chocolate.

"I am, to be honest." Harry pivoted his stool to face her more directly. "I guess I just assumed you lived on Middleton Plantation or South of Broad. I'm surprised to hear you live uptown."

Oh, Millie. Why did you have to go and rattle that off?

"Despite that"—Harry inched ever so slightly closer—"I'd really like to see you again. Can I take you to dinner sometime?"

Millie frowned. "Did you just say *despite that*?"

"Did you not hear me say I'd like to take you to dinner?"

Millie simply stared at him. The clock had struck midnight, and it was time for Cinderella to leave.

"Thank you for the sundae, Harry." Millie stood from the stool and brushed the hem of her dress back into place.

"I . . . I don't understand." Harry dropped coins on the counter for the sundaes. In an instant, he was standing beside her, grabbing her arm, and turning her to face him. "I thought things were going well. Was I wrong?"

Heels planted firmly against the checkered tile, Millie raised her chin. "If you don't like persons from uptown, and you don't believe a woman can run a business, then I can tell you truthfully, Harry, you are *not* going to like me. Because you don't know the half of it if you find those things off-putting."

The ceiling fan above them pushed the air into a swirl.

"What does that mean, Millie?" Harry shook his head. "Are you trying to keep me guessing?"

Millie reached toward the door, but Harry wouldn't let go.

"Please, just tell me."

Millie's gaze scanned the pharmacy—the girls wearing beautiful dresses and the boys trying to impress them and the artwork that just moments ago, she'd studied so intently.

She'd never come here again. So what was the point of keeping it a secret, anyway?

She lowered her voice so as not to cause a scene. At least now, she might let go of the breath she'd been holding.

"Middleton was my great-grandmother's name. She was born a slave and had no other surname."

Harry blinked. Millie watched as realization slowly changed his expression from pleasantry to disgust.

He let go of his hold on her arm then, wiping his hand on the leg of his trousers. "Get away from me, you filthy girl," he hissed.

No one was watching them. No one was listening. Millie had made sure of it.

So no one saw when he pushed her on his way out the door, or when she righted her balance with her foot to keep from falling down onto the tile.

No one saw the tear on her sleeve from Harry's grip, the turmoil in her heart, or the resolve on her face as she left the pharmacy a wiser woman than when she'd come.

But most of all, no one knew Millie was a Black girl pretending to be white.

TWO

Charleston, Modern Day

Harper glanced up at the brick building on King Street and imagined what it must've looked like back in its prime. Streetlights cast a glow down the quiet end of the street as she took in the disrepair of the building.

Lucy looped her arm around Harper's elbow and nudged her toward the door. "Come on," her friend urged. "I know it's pretty, but the party's inside. You act like you've never been to Charleston before."

"I haven't," Harper admitted. Though now she wondered why she'd taken so long to make the drive.

"What? But it's right up your alley. A city that sings with beauty of all things restored." Lucy's long blond curls fell over the shoulders of her knee-length, open cardigan. She wore the cranberry sweater over a fitted floral pencil skirt and the lace-lined camisole that Harper had sewed for her from vintage fabrics.

Harper laughed. "You sound like a poet."

"I am an artist, and artists see magic wherever they go. Besides, it was Savannah College of Art and Design or Harvard, and who can resist pralines?" Lucy brushed her curls from her shoulders and reached for the door handle. "Now, are we ready?"

"Yeah, let's go inside." Harper grinned. "And you're right about the pralines." Though, pralines or not, Savannah was indeed a city for dreamers, and SCAD was their school. She would like to think that in between the years of studying stitching and design and cultural trends, she had finally earned the tools to transition her own dreams from the realm of fantasy to reality.

She was ready to open her own dress store as soon as she graduated and her designs made Senior Show. She needed to attract some attention to be taken seriously as a newcomer in the industry and finally get her career going.

Yes, the plan—the glorious plan that began as a dream in the heart of a girl taking sewing lessons from the old woman at the boardinghouse—was finally coming to fruition. And it felt good.

Harper followed her roommate into a large, open space that had been transformed for the wedding shower. Twinkle lights hung from the ceiling among a host of shiny balloons, and a banner that read *Mr. and Mrs.* was draped across the gift table. Gallon-sized mason jars held tea and punch, and the flower arrangements on the tables were mixed with palmetto roses for a touch that was uniquely Charlestonian.

The hosts had outdone themselves.

Of course, Harper didn't know any of them except the bride, Lucy's sister. Though they'd only met a few times, Harper had always found her to be a kindred spirit, so she took extra care with the gift—a sweet little vintage cardigan she had found at a consignment shop and repaired so the ivory flowers looked as good as new. She wasn't so brazen as to expect the woman to wear it on her wedding day, but perhaps the sweater would be the perfect bridal touch for their honeymoon.

Harper loved finding little gems like that, on the brink of disappearing into a landfill, and giving them new life. A second story.

She set her paper-and-twine-wrapped gift on the gift table and was scanning the twenty or so guests already in the room when Lucy leaned over. "Don't look now, but Mr. Darcy is standing over there."

Harper casually glanced toward the other side of the table and immediately spotted him. His dark, wavy hair and a button-down-with-khakis combo looked like it'd come from a Saks Fifth Avenue advertisement. "Whoa. You aren't kidding."

"Right? You should say hello. He looks fancy." Lucy grinned.

"You know I don't care about money," Harper said. And she meant it. She'd be happier in a one-bedroom apartment with fabric piled from here to high heaven than in a mansion with the wrong person.

"Okay. How about the fact he looks like the lead on that BBC show you like so much?"

Harper laughed. "Here's an idea. Why don't *you* talk to him?" She gently pressed the embroidered sleeves of her dress. She'd hesitated to wear it, but tomorrow she would take the dress for her department chair to judge whether or not the design deserved representation at SCAD's Senior Show. After months of watching *Gilmore Girls* reruns through the night, pulling out stitches to get the embroidery just so, wearing the dress tonight seemed appropriate. Like Cinderella's big moment. Still, she would be careful with it and stay away from all things chocolate.

"Maybe I will." Lucy straightened her crystal necklace and tucked her hair behind her ears. "How do I look? Any lipstick on my teeth? And by the way, you're coming with me."

Harper glanced toward Mr. Darcy and noticed for the first time that he was talking to someone else—a man wearing glasses and a tie that looked like it should've sunk with the *Titanic*.

She didn't mean to be ugly. He had a warm smile, and that was something. At least she didn't have to worry about him getting the wrong impression of why she was headed over there. "All right. Let's go make you sound enchanting."

"And what about the lipstick?" Lucy widened her grin for inspection.

"Not a speck." Harper gently pushed her friend onward. "Come on. Before you lose your opportunity."

Within moments, they had rounded the corner of the gift table. Harper took the liberty of starting the conversation before Lucy's nerves got the best of her. "Either of you know the story of this space? The building sure is beautiful." Slightly dilapidated, but beautiful.

Mr. Darcy grinned at his nerdy friend. "My cousin Peter can answer that one." His gaze moved to Lucy, and he held out his hand. "I'm Declan."

Lucy took his hand, then tucked her long curls behind her ear in one graceful movement that seemed to have Declan immediately entranced. Harper was always amazed at how she did that. After a moment's hesitation, Declan shifted his attention to Harper, and the round of introductions was made.

"I got suckered into buying the place." Peter took off his glasses and cleaned them with the hem of his shirt, then repositioned them back at the bridge of his nose. The frames were tortoise-shell, and though Harper was fairly confident the trendy flair was completely unintentional, still, she felt an unexpected wave of attraction toward him as she looked into his blue-green eyes for the first time. "And by suckered, I mean I'm a hopeless sentimen-talist," he added.

And articulate to boot.

Lucy could have the handsome one. Harper was more interested in an interesting conversation. A completely platonic conversa-tion.

"Decades ago, it was a dress store," Declan said. "Isn't that right, Peter?"

Harper's heart quickened. An old dress shop?

Peter nodded. "I'll need to find a tenant within the next few months. Maybe even weeks. But in the meantime, it seemed like a perfect place to have their wedding shower. What, with the ro-mantic history and all."

The Lord couldn't have been clearer had He opened up the heavens and dropped a banner straight from the clouds. This was

Harper's next step. She could feel it down to her bones. Coming to Charleston tonight, getting that invitation from Lucy's sister—it was all for a reason, a purpose.

By the time Peter got the space rental-ready, she would have all her proverbial ducks in a row. She would make Senior Show and get a little more money saved and graduate and get some inventory. . . .

Harper glanced over toward Lucy to see if she, too, recognized how perfectly this property aligned with Harper's long-term plans. But Lucy was too busy swooning to pay any mind. Harper would fill her in later.

"So you like old buildings?" Harper crossed her arms, careful not to pull any of the delicate stitching of the dress. Lucy and Declan were in the middle of a conversation about the bride and groom, so she'd give them a chance to chat.

Peter's eyes flickered with interest. "I've always been interested in the stories behind the walls. I think a large part of it comes from my own family history. My mom, she . . . uh . . . " With two fingers, he rubbed his temple where it met his forehead. "She passed away nine years ago. When she did, my stepfather gave away some things that didn't belong to him. Heirlooms that were once my mom's."

"I'm so sorry to hear that." Harper sighed. Should she tell him she, too, knew the grief of losing her own mother?

Peter met her eyes. "Thank you."

"So I take it you're looking for these family heirlooms?" Harper absentmindedly ran her thumb along the embroidery of her dress.

"I am. The difficult part is, I don't know what I'm looking for. They were in a box she kept, and I never paid it much mind until the box was gone."

Harper started to lean against the gift table, but one of the petite gift tags caught the side of her dress.

Panic rushed through her veins. She could not tear this dress . . . she could not tear this dress . . . she could not—

Peter closed the space between them and reached out to help.

Her desperate gaze met his and settled there. She took a deep breath. "I never should've worn this dress anyway. It's a showpiece I'm being graded on tomorrow."

"Tomorrow, huh? Sounds intense." Peter held the tag steady for her as Harper gently eased the embroidery free. For a brief moment, their fingers touched, and a flutter of magic traveled all the way down to her heart.

Such a strange emotion, almost like the feeling of coming home.

He leaned closer to study the fabric. "I don't see any damage done."

Harper freed the final stitch and sighed her relief. "I go to Savannah College of Art and Design and have this dream of owning my own dress shop."

"Really? That sounds interesting," Peter said. He secured the tag back on the gift and took a step back, but he was still standing closer than he had been before, and his nearness caused a whirl in her heart. He was tall—taller than she'd noticed before.

Harper didn't look away from his eyes. "Yeah, it's kind of a ridiculous dream, I guess. In the sense that most people say it's nearly impossible." She pressed the stitching of her dress. "But what fun is it to merely do the possible?"

A slow grin rose from the corners of Peter's lips. "I would have to agree."

From the other side of the room, the maid of honor clanked a glass and made an announcement. But all Harper could hear was the sound of her pulse and the echo of Peter's words in her mind: *"I've always been interested in the stories behind the walls."*

Yes, Peter. So have I.

When this space was ready for rental and she was done with her final push for the Senior Show, she would call him. Charleston wasn't so far from Savannah and might be a perfect spot to set up her store.

And after that . . . well, who knew what might happen.

Harper shifted her weight from one kitten heel to the other and waited outside her department chair's office. Daddy's words years ago still held just as much power as they did the night she confessed she wanted to attend Savannah College of Art and Design. Even though the two of them didn't have the money or the means.

"No matter how long it takes, Harper Rae, when your Jubilee tide comes in, make sure your nets are good and ready."

And look at her now. All the obstacles she'd overcome. Daddy would be so proud when she called him in a few hours and told him she'd officially passed this course and made it into the Senior Show. Her first several grades in the capstone class had been rough, but she'd done a slew of calculations and was confident that this dress was A-level work, which meant she could still get out with a B average. The start of the semester might have been grueling, but the challenge pushed her work to another level.

A soft sigh escaped her lips as Harper clutched the intricate gown in her arms. Yes, everything was redeemable. She had done the work and was now about to see the proof.

She traced the embroidery around the collar of the dress with her thumb—embroidery she had ripped out again and again because the stitches were never quite good enough. She had restitched it all so many times.

A student she recognized from her fashion aesthetics class stepped through the doorway and shook her head toward Harper.

"Not good?" Harper whispered.

The young woman paled, holding a garment bag closer to her chest as she hurried off toward the stairs.

Harper took a deep breath. Everything was going to be okay. She had worked years for this moment. Taken jobs making coffee and spent hours watching YouTube tutorials. Not to mention all the handsome men she had turned down as distractions.

Okay, so there weren't *that* many of them, and they weren't that handsome. But still. She knew what she was doing. She had more than enough experience, both knowledge-based and otherwise.

She was a confident person. A confident artist.

Yet her stomach turned this way and that, like the tide just before a storm. She swallowed hard, held the dress a little tighter with her sweaty palms, and stepped into the office before her nerves could take a stronger hold than they already had.

Her department chair glanced up. She wore a chunky pearl necklace that had to be heavy. "Harper." The woman nodded and used her pencil to scan a list of students' names, then checked a box. "Let's see what you've got."

Harper gently set her dress down on the desk. Months of work—years, really—ready to be evaluated in seconds.

The woman reached for the dress, taking in the embroidery and the organza layer of the skirt and inspecting the seams. All the while, Harper's fingers fidgeted, ready to get the dress back in her own hands.

What if . . .

Do not think about the implications. You are going to get into the Senior Show. This will be your big break. You're finally going to get your dress shop, maybe sometime next year. All Daddy's sacrifices to help pay for college will be worth it, and you'll never doubt your abilities again because you'll have a SCAD degree to your name—

"You are hoping to submit the dress to our Senior Show, yes?" The woman set the dress down.

Harper nodded feebly.

Her department chair continued. "This piece looks like the sort of thing I could get at any Anthropologie. Fine. But nothing unique." The woman put her pencil down and lowered her purple glasses so she could look at Harper eye to eye. "I'm sorry, but I question whether you've got the vision for this level of competition."

"You mean for the Senior Show?" Harper couldn't breathe.

"The Senior Show, yes . . . but also the fashion industry. It's a difficult business, even for someone who knows the space she wants to fill. As it stands, you're trying too hard to be too many things. You need to pick one thing, your thing, and do it well." The chair pointed to the multicolored embroidery and scalloped hemline of the dress. "Take this, for instance. These elements come across as if you are trying too hard. I need to see more cohesion in the piece."

"More cohesion?" Harper's mind spun. But the point was to evoke whimsy, opportunity. Did her department chair fail to see that, or the converse—was the woman right? Had Harper blinded herself to reality?

"You may want to consider other avenues."

The possibility that this woman was correct in her assessment and Harper had spent the last decade of her life pursuing the wrong dream struck her with the force of an anvil, hollowing out the spaces hope had filled.

But it all made sense now. The way she had to work twice as hard and twice as long as her peers. The awe she felt when she touched a stunning gown and knew down to her bones she could never sew so beautifully. The dream that drove her had become as elusive as a rainbow and ever out of reach.

My, what a fool she had been. So cheery and naïve.

The air gushed from the room in one fell swoop. Harper didn't know what to say, what to do. She thought she might pass out, as her vision began to blur into tiny black spots.

She reached for the dress and nodded.

A nod was enough, right? Her department chair would understand. Because words . . . well, she didn't have any right now. She stood to go.

The woman gestured with her glasses. "Don't take it personally. Some people just aren't cut out for all this. Forgive me for being terse, but I don't want you to waste your time doing something that's not a good fit."

No, we wouldn't want that.

Too heartbroken to cry and too disappointed to dream, Harper found herself paying for a sandwich she didn't really want from a quick service spot across from River Street.

She sat down on a park bench overlooking the water and unwrapped the sandwich from its paper covering. Her hands trembled, and she felt like a shell of herself—completely hollowed out.

Ten years. Ten *years*' worth of taking sewing jobs and studying her craft for this.

The persistence she'd once considered an asset had kept her blind to her own humiliation. And so she had continued all this time, thinking if she just tried hard enough, if she just kept going, she could make it. Be one of those rare and few people who actually caught their dream.

Harper brushed the sandwich crumbs from her lap as a little girl began doing cartwheels through the park.

So much for Charleston. The dress shop, and Peter. All the plans she'd made for her future. All of it, that whole eggs-in-a-basket cliché, had been built on this one goal.

And the only thing she could think, the only thing that made any sense, was to get out of this place. Up and leave. Before she made an even bigger fool of herself—a failure of a girl who'd chased far too big a dream.

THREE

Charleston, 1946

"Millie, go and fetch your hat—your uncle's gonna be here to pick us up."

"Be there in a minute, Mama," Millie called. She stifled a groan as she rushed to finish stitching up the tear on her dress sleeve. Then she situated her red cloche on top of her hairpins. The weather was beautiful, and sitting alongside the highway watching her aunt weave sweetgrass was the last thing she wanted to do today.

But she would do it for Mama, and she would be pleasant.

Millie took a long look at her reflection in the mirror.

This is for Mama.

Maybe if she told herself that enough times, the repetition would change her attitude. So far, it hadn't worked.

Two honks from the driveway suggested Uncle Clyde was here. Millie pinched some color into her olive-toned cheeks, straightened the waistline of her faded day dress, and walked toward the front door, where her mother waited less than patiently.

Mama took in the sight of her. "Slow as molasses, but at least you look the part." She winked in that uniquely mama way and all but pushed Millie out the door.

An hour later, Uncle Clyde's car rumbled down the highway toward the stands set up at the edge of folks' properties. When he reached

Aunt Bea's house, he pulled into the dirt driveway, careful not to run clear over her. She'd set up her stand so darn close to the road.

Mama doesn't like you using words like "darn"—

But thinking ain't the same as saying. Restraint had to count for something, right?

Uncle Clyde straightened his suspenders, slammed his own door, and reached for the handle of Millie's. Always so mannerly. No wonder he was Grandma Ashley's favorite. Well, that and the fact he was born in her youth. Grandma was always talkin' about how Mama had been a surprise baby, and when Millie asked how old she was when she fell pregnant, Grandma just said she could be her great-grandma but to hush up and stop asking questions. *"You get old enough and you don't need reminding how great you could be,"* she said.

Oh, her grandma never would've admitted liking Clyde the best. But Millie expressly remembered. On her deathbed a few years back, Grandma Ashley went on and on 'bout how Uncle Clyde had become the spitting image of her own mama, Rose, inside and out. And what could be a greater compliment than that?

Plus, she always snuck Uncle Clyde the extra benne wafers. She thought no one noticed, but Millie did.

Millie climbed out of the car and smoothed her dress with her hands.

"Millicent! Get over here, baby."

Aunt Bea was always saying that kind of stuff.

Millie was *sixteen*, for crying out loud. Old enough to marry, should the situation warrant it. Not that she had any solid prospects, nor that she was entirely sure she wanted prospects, but the point being, she was hardly anyone's baby anymore.

Nevertheless, Millie did as she was told. She linked arms with Mama and headed toward the little booth Aunt Bea had set up along the side of the road while Uncle Clyde—wise man that he was—headed toward the house.

Aunt Bea clutched an unfinished sweetgrass basket in one hand and managed to "hug" the living daylights out of Millie with the other. Millie had half a mind to think Aunt Bea could read her rebellious thoughts.

"Sit, sit." Aunt Bea pointed toward the wooden chairs she'd drug out to the edge of her property line. The little stand was crammed top to bottom with Aunt Bea's coin purses, fanners, Moses baskets, and every size basket in between.

Aunt Bea had a gift for sewing fibers together and seeing something when other folks saw nothing. She'd weave that sweetgrass with the longleaf pine needles to create the most intricate, beautiful patterns.

Millie and Mama took the two empty chairs at the back of the stand.

"Just you two wait and see what I've been working on. Finished it yesterday." Aunt Bea pulled a large woven box from underneath the table at the front of her stand and had to use both hands to pick it up.

Mama reached for it. When Aunt Bea lifted off the top, Mama gasped. Surprise flickered in her eyes.

Millie stood from her chair to get a better look inside.

Hmm. A little girl's dress?

Mama raised the tiny day dress out from the basket as if she were hanging her best linens on the line to dry. Her hands began to shake as Aunt Bea cried, and Millie frowned. She didn't know why Aunt Bea was crying.

Mama stroked the fabric for a while, then turned to Millie. "This dress once belonged to your grandma Ashley. It's a family heirloom. Her own mother gave it to her. . . ." Mama's words stuck like glue to her memory. She looked to Aunt Bea, unable to get the rest out herself.

Aunt Bea settled into her own chair, then jabbed the wooden handle of her spoon into the coil she was making. "The morning she was sold. Grandmama Rose never saw Ashley again, bless her soul."

Millie stilled. She'd heard this story about her grandma Ashley and Rose before, but seeing the dress . . .

Well, that was something else. The fabric of it carried a history, not unlike the baskets.

Millie imagined what her grandmother must have looked like, wearing that dress and weaving as a child. Imagined her grandma's grandma before that. Did they use old spoons for their sweetgrass sewing like Aunt Bea always had? Did their fingers callus from the sharp edges of the grass?

And what happened when Grandma Ashley outgrew the dress?

Aunt Bea was always sayin' how children needed to learn weaving because the baskets told an important story of the past. When the road was paved in front of her house, you would've thought Christmas came early for the way Aunt Bea was acting. She was sure this would mean more tourists, which would mean more customers, which—of course—would mean more sweetgrass baskets.

And as much as Millie begrudged giving up her Saturday afternoon to sit on the side of the road, she was transfixed watching her aunt. In and out, Aunt Bea wove the fibers, filling the spaces between the sweetgrass with a quality of workmanship that would cause her baskets to last for many generations.

Making baskets that would hold food and plants and dresses— stories, when it really came down to it—for the next hundred years or longer.

Mama set the little dress back into the basket and closed the lid, as though unable to look at it anymore.

Aunt Bea gave Mama's hand a long squeeze before picking up the large basket she'd been holding when they arrived.

"Want to give it a try?" she asked Millie. "You remember how I taught you, right?"

Millie reached out for the basket. She'd forgotten the pleasant smell of sweetgrass. Long blades stuck up sharply from the top, and Millie pushed the handle of the spoon right through the opening where the fibers needed to pass.

Not entirely different from dressmaking.

She heard the car approach but paid no mind. A customer, no

doubt, passing through. Aunt Bea would tell the story behind each basket as Aunt Bea always did, and the customer would purchase something, enchanted as she inevitably was by the stories, and together they would share that history.

"*See the way it works, yes?*" Aunt Bea had pointed out to Millie time and time again.

Millie heard footsteps but didn't look up from the basket she was weaving. She knew Aunt Bea could do a far better job telling the story.

Only, the footsteps stopped short.

"Millicent." His voice sent tremors down her spine.

Millie looked up. Harry wore that same confident smirk—or was it cocky?—only this time, his smile was ghost-like as he watched her and took it all in.

"Aren't you a sight for sore eyes?" he said.

Even without glancing at her, Millie felt her mama stiffen.

Harry reached out to touch the sharp tip of the sweetgrass sticking out from Millie's basket. He nodded back toward the car. "My mother is looking for a new bread basket and insists upon finding one like my grandmother used to own. Before the Late Unpleasantness, that is." Harry cleared his throat and raised the tip of his nose as he looked around the shop. He lifted a lid here and touched a handle there with no regard for the time or the heart Aunt Bea had invested in her craft.

Millie had half a mind to punch him square in the jaw. And if Mama hadn't been standing there, watching . . .

Harry crossed his arms over his chest and squared his shoulders. "Nothing here will meet my needs." His gaze, straight at Millie, violently turned her stomach. "But Millicent, it's good to see you've found a place where you belong."

He walked back toward the automobile, his frame growing smaller and smaller.

And Millie swore to herself in that moment, if it meant screaming or running or moving to Harlem, she would never lay eyes on the likes of Harry again.

FOUR

Charleston, Modern Day

The next morning, Harper hesitated on the step outside her favorite consignment store in downtown Savannah. She held the dress over her arm and stood beside two window boxes full of flowers whose once-dormant roots had survived the winter chill to nourish new blooms. Spanish moss dripped down onto the sidewalk from the oaks above.

Her heart had begun its prickly sting like a foot that's fallen asleep.

Did she really want to do this? Did she really want to sell the gown that represented all that work and all those dreams—the dress her department chair had called "fine" without so much as a blink?

Fine. The word settled down into her gut like a cup of tea that had been brewed too long.

Harper started to reach for the door handle, then hesitated. The chair's words echoed inside her mind with a haunting murmur. She straightened the hem of her favorite sweater, hidden by the dress she carried—the knitted cardigan was the dusty blue of clouds just before a good rain.

She stepped toward the door once more and lifted her chin

slightly before entering the store, careful not to snag her dress against the old brick building.

"Welcome!" The woman working the shop busied herself arranging a row of gemstone necklaces. Olivia was her name, if Harper remembered correctly. "Oh, I love those shoes." She pointed toward the ribbon bow of Harper's closed-toe, rosy heels.

"Thanks." Harper hugged the dress closer to her body. She'd paired the cardigan and heels with a floral-print skirt, hoping that wearing some of her favorite things would cheer her up. Vintage shoes were Harper's version of ice cream.

Olivia leaned down to straighten a stack of faded graphic tees before heading toward the counter. "Bring in an item to consign?"

Harper set the dress on the counter. A snag of thread from the dress caught against the button of her sweater. Harper tugged on it, but the thread just didn't want to let go. She had to loosen the button of her cardigan to detach herself.

"This is beautiful." Olivia reached out for the dress. "What's the label?"

"Doesn't have one." Harper looked around at the racks of dresses repurposed from vintage and antique fabrics, at the candles flickering. The scent of the place—the ever-so-slight dust of the old building, the espresso wafting from the coffee shop next door, and the from-the-box smell of new shoes, all mixed together. At once, Harper felt both settled and elated by the terribly deceptive feeling of belonging.

She always *had* been a fool for that feeling.

"Someone made it," Harper added.

Olivia held the dress up higher. "Truly, it's stunning. Why are you selling such a rare piece?"

Harper slid her hands into the pockets of her skirt and took a deep breath. "It doesn't fit me anymore."

She thought of the dresses all around, of the women who had worn these fabrics and sewed these seams. She thought of their stories and wondered why these dresses no longer fit *them*, either. Where had they gone, and what had happened to drive them away?

"I can give you eighty dollars of in-store credit—how does that sound?"

Harper nodded. "Works for me."

She swiveled on her heels and reached for a plum velvet dress that looked to be from the 1940s. Her fingers grazed the fabric, and she wondered for a moment if the department chair had been Mitchum-Huntzberger-level wrong in her assessment.

Because she did know fabric and she did know stitching, and she had spent years of her life practicing. She had drawn and studied every fashion trend in the last century, from Audrey's little black dress to Coco's pleated trousers. Whenever she got the chance and the fabric, she set to work practicing. Creating.

And her heart hummed to the tune of her sewing machine.

Harper pulled the hanger from the rack to get a better look at the dress.

"Stunning, isn't it?" Olivia crouched down to arrange more necklaces in a case on the bottom shelf. She gestured toward the velvet gown, several emerald necklaces swinging from her hand. "That one's from the forties. I actually kept the structure of the original dress—the shape of it still seemed relevant, you know? Just reinforced the ruching around the bust and sleeves."

"Timeless." Harper brushed the velvet with her thumb, then wiggled the dress hanger back onto the rack. The last thing she needed was to drop three hundred dollars on a dress. Especially today.

Who was she kidding? She would never make dresses as beautiful as these.

Olivia stood, then marched in place. Her thighs had to be burning after squatting so long. She wore fitted black leggings under an asymmetrical tunic, her hair pinned into a messy bun. "We've got some clearance shoes in the back. There's a pair you might like, actually. Navy with rhinestones. They're true vintage too."

"Say no more." Harper tugged the scarf at her neck and headed toward the back of the store.

When she found the shoes, it was love at first sight. She grabbed the shoebox before she could think better of it—clearance, right?—and headed to the register.

Olivia scanned the box, then looked through the windows as the register lagged. "Beautiful day outside, isn't it? Do you live nearby? I feel like I see you in here fairly regularly."

Harper took a glance over her shoulder as the sunlight scattered rays over the tree limbs, over the sidewalk, over the children laughing across the way.

"I used to." She slid her card into the chip reader and waited, tapping the toe of her shoe against the tile. "I'm actually moving today."

"Oh?" Olivia took a paper bag by both hands and waved it open. "Where to?"

Hope mingled with despair in the most unexpected way. Harper smiled, not because she was particularly happy, but because what else was there to do?

"We'll see."

Olivia's eyes widened. She hesitated a moment, then tucked a stray strand of hair behind her ears as she shook her head. "Sounds like an adventure. At least you've got the shoes for it."

I'll add them to my collection of therapy heels.

Harper reached for the bag and turned from the register. Then she took a deep breath of that dress-shop air in hopes it would sustain her, in hopes she could somehow remember, return to it, on the coming nights when she wondered what in the world she was thinking.

Because, really—what in the *world* was she thinking?

Harper spent the rest of the day as a tourist in Savannah because that was what she now considered herself—a woman passing through. She had the clearest sense of closure that her time here had come to an end, sad as it made her to admit.

She'd finally broken down and spent the money on a trolley tour and learned a surprising amount of history about the city. Then she strolled down River Street, watched the taffy roll through the old candy machines, and got ice cream at Leopold's before dropping off her new shoes in the apartment she shared with Lucy. Her friend was out of town for the next couple of days, so at least she could avoid a face-to-face retelling of the humiliation that'd come from her best-laid plans.

But there was one person she couldn't avoid calling any longer.

Harper adjusted her polka-dot umbrella as gentle rain fell, then settled onto a bench—crossing her legs at the ankles and using her free hand to take a sip from her to-go cup of mint sweet tea.

Before her stretched Forsyth Park in all its majesty. Spanish moss dripped from sprawling, long-settled oak trees, and Harper wondered why those trees seemed to have so little trouble planting themselves deep.

Muted sunbeams suggested the final hours of daylight as the streetlamps flickered on.

Harper set her tea down on the bench and unlocked her phone just as it began to ring. The name "Dad" appeared. His ears must've been itching. She took a deep breath as a few rogue raindrops slipped down her ankle toward her feet.

"Well, sweetheart, how'd it go? You left me hanging all day!" He spoke as if it was such a sure thing. As if he hadn't a doubt in the world she would succeed.

Harper held a little more tightly to the handle of her umbrella. "I'm afraid my update is pretty disheartening."

He waited a long moment before saying anything. She didn't feel the need to fill the silence. He would fill in all the gaps, as he always had, and simply knowing she needn't say more brought a sudden sense of relief.

"I'm leaving Savannah tomorrow. I'm sorry, Daddy." Harper

closed her eyes and bit her bottom lip. Her heart ached with the disappointment of her glorious, unfulfilled dream.

"Harper Rae, there's nothin' for you to be sorry about. Except talking about yourself like this."

"I was foolish to spend your money on such an expensive school." She opened her eyes and looked up as the clouds above deepened into a darker grey. But even the drizzle didn't stop all the passersby from posing for pictures in front of the fountain at the center of the park. "At the time, I thought this degree would make me more marketable—but what if I was being selfish? I should've done something more practical. I should've been an accountant."

"Sweetheart, and I mean this with love"—Daddy sounded like he was holding back a chuckle—"ain't nobody going to trust you with their finances."

Harper laughed for the first time all day.

"God's timing don't always match ours, and that's okay."

She slowly blew out a deep breath.

"Sometimes we believe a lie about ourselves is the truth because we've got its identity wrong. We trust it and give it far more than its fair share of our energy." He hesitated. Harper had a feeling she already knew what he was about to say. Was he waiting until she was ready to hear it?

"What about you go back to Alabama for a while? Stop by that inn you've always admired from the other side of the pier."

"No." Harper shook her head. "Not now. I'm ready to move on from dressmaking and find something new."

"I'm not saying you ought'a take sewing lessons with her again. I know you're not a kid . . . just go there, Harper. You'll feel better. You've always wanted to stay at the inn, haven't you?"

She pinned the phone between her shoulder and chin to reach for her tea. She *had* always imagined what it would be like to stay overnight at the place. And she did adore the owner . . . even if the woman had birthed Harper's love of dressmaking. The very love she was currently trying to forget. "I don't know, Dad."

"Just think about it, would you? Sometimes you have to look for the next good thing. Maybe this is yours. Give you something to look forward to."

The grassy square and old oaks took on a rosy hue, and Harper smiled softly. The world was always more beautiful after a good, steady rain.

FIVE

"Harper Girl, how many times have I told you to stop sewing when you're half-asleep? One of these days, you're gonna get hurt."

Harper blinked several times as the fishy smell of her father's clothes perked her senses, and the blurry outline of the Cranberries poster above her sewing machine came into view.

He flipped the switch of the lamp on her table, and Harper squinted. Too much light. Way too early in the morning.

She groaned. "Daddy . . . I have to do the dresses." Harper pointed toward the bed where ten formals lay in a perfect stack in the exact spot where she should be sleeping.

"Nighttime is for sleep. The dresses can wait."

"You should take your own advice." She turned off her sewing machine and stood to move the dresses from her bed to a chair by the window.

Daddy sighed. "You know it's Jubilee."

Harper shimmied under the worn quilt Mama had made years ago. Before their family became just her and Daddy.

"I can catch and sell enough to buy you that dress you want for the dance, Harper Rae."

Harper looked over at the dresses she had promised to alter for other girls at school. She'd carefully calculated how much she

41

would need for the fabric to make her own gown, and she knew very well that Daddy could use a nice pair of shoes now that he had a new job at the office. All the money from the extra fish caught during Jubilee should go to his shoes. She could manage just fine.

"You use it on yourself, Daddy."

"Nonsense." He tucked the edge of her sheets around her elbow as if she were six and not sixteen. Then he kissed her forehead and started toward the lamp. But her words stopped him halfway across her shag rug.

"I want to go to college. A design school in Savannah, Georgia. It's called SCAD."

Harper didn't know why she'd picked the three o'clock hour to blurt out the words she'd been holding inside for days. Maybe the tiredness took her filter, or maybe she knew he had to leave soon to beat other folks out to Jubilee. But either way, she'd said it, and there was no going back now.

He had always told her she could have the moon if she wanted it. But this . . . college and money they didn't have . . . it may as well be in a fictional galaxy.

Daddy sighed so long, it was a wonder he had any breath left in him. "Lord only knows where the money is gonna come from."

She clutched the seam of the bedsheet, soft from so many washings. He had never been one to give much advice, so when he did, she paid attention.

"But if God gave you a dream, you'd better listen. You just remember that God knows the how and the why, though the when may be frustrating. 'Cause, Harper, if I know one thing about life, it ain't always Jubilee."

Daddy switched the lamp off, and moonlight flooded the room. "No matter how long it takes, sweet girl, when your great tide comes in, make sure your nets are good and ready."

Daddy filled three nets' worth of crabs that morning. Plenty of provision to cover the price of her dress *and* his shoes, plus a nice dinner for the two of them that evening. Harper took the fancy lace tablecloth she and her mother once used for tea parties and shook it outside. It caught the wind, as if it had a message to send to anyone watching.

Mama and Harper *had* always loved that tablecloth, already an antique when they'd gotten it as a gift—already with a story to tell. The old fabric was woven from hopes and secrets that had endured for generations. Harper liked to think that now she was part of that larger story.

She gathered silverware and two cloth napkins to set up a real cozy spot on the patio of their home. The house was modest, to say the least, but waterfront property was never shabby, and Harper loved the view of the charming inn across the inlet.

The sun had just set over the water, dripping color in pinks and reds and blues from the heavens until the first star appeared.

Daddy was finishing up with the crabs inside while Harper poured tea into their glasses, staying as far from the kitchen as she could. She never could stomach the sight of crabs boiling, even after years of it. Daddy said her heart was sensitive. But truth was, she'd just never been comfortable with anything dying . . . not even crustaceans.

She started to put a napkin down in her mother's spot before she thought better of it, then blinked, staring at the chair. She would never get used to it, would she? Her mother should be here. Her mother had always loved Jubilee.

Harper looked up to find the twilight had deepened. She hadn't noticed as it happened, distracted as she was by readying the table. But she would need to turn the porch light on if she and Daddy wanted to see their food.

An outline caught her attention as she started toward the door. Harper squinted. A figure stood at the edge of the pier across the water. Though she couldn't make out many details, the man

43

seemed young and dejected. Oh, she was projecting the dejected part, but truth be told, something in the slump of his shoulders seemed particularly sad. No, that wasn't the right word. Hopeless, perhaps?

Harper frowned, the sight of him so unexpected. She'd never stayed the night at the inn herself, though Lord knew she wanted to if money ever allowed. But most folks who came through seemed to find peace and joy in the place, if the laughter that flitted across their pier was any indication.

Such wasn't the case with this man.

Harper stepped toward the back door and creaked it open just as Daddy appeared with a bowl full of crabs in one hand and an empty bowl for scraps in the other. She scanned the place settings for the salt and pepper shakers and made sure she'd remembered to put a paper towel over the top of the hush puppies to keep them warm.

Daddy set the bowl of crabs down and ruffled the top of her hair. "Hope you're hungry." He took a seat.

Harper pulled out her chair and followed his lead. She scooped a heap of hush puppies onto her plate and reached for the crabs.

"Careful," Daddy warned. "They're still pretty hot."

She opted for the old fork-and-knife-combo trick and safely moved a crab from the bowl to her plate. "These look delicious."

"Jubilee usually is." Daddy twisted off a claw and dropped it in the scrap bowl.

Harper's gaze traveled over the gentle pull of the tide between them, toward the young man on the pier. "Daddy, you know anything about that guy? Seems sad. Something about his shoulders."

Daddy looked up at her from his plate. "Imagine he is. Kid lost his mother."

Grief tugged Harper closer to the stranger. "How do you know?"

"Gary told me out on the boat today." Their neighbor Gary might as well be the town hairdresser for how well he kept himself updated on everyone's happenings. "Sad situation. I'm not sure how he knows the innkeeper—family friend, I think? Anyway, the boy's mother died tragically in a boating accident this year. Guess the stepfather thinks real highly of himself and can't be bothered since the kid isn't kin to him by blood. There's also some kind of drama about a family business and the young'un wanting to make his own way in life. It's a shame. Gary said he seems like a good kid."

Harper forced herself to swallow the hush puppy she'd been chewing. Poor guy. She knew the grief of losing a parent, but to be practically disowned by the other . . . that part she couldn't imagine. "How could he do that to his own family?"

Daddy seemed to sense there was more to Harper's empathy. He reached across the table and gave her hand a big squeeze. "Don't know. Some folks aren't worth their weight in salt if you ask me." Daddy glanced over his shoulder toward the boy on the pier.

Harper pulled a claw off her crab and used it to point toward the other pier. She'd never even met the stepfather and was ready to throw the crab claw right in his face.

"Sweetheart." It was a *your-compassion-is-acting-up-again* warning, not an admonishment.

Harper blinked, forcing herself back to the present. "You're right. This dinner is a celebration, after all. You caught enough this morning to feed the whole county." She smiled at Daddy, proud of how hard he worked, then looked back down at the crab and slowly broke off the other claw. She hesitated when it made an unexpected pop.

"You're thinking about that crab getting caught, aren't you?"

Harper set the food back down on her plate and let her laughter go free. "How did you know?"

Daddy grinned. "That's my girl. Always considering the oxygen-deprived crustaceans."

Harper took a long drink of tea and let her gaze move across the water once more. "What'd you say his name was?" She didn't know why she asked that, or why it even mattered. But for some reason, she wanted to put a name to the person—for she had already shared his posture on her own side of the pier.

"Who, the boy?" Her father scooped several hush puppies from the basket. "I think it was Peter."

"Peter," she murmured quietly, and the name of the net-casting disciple rolled toward the other side of the water, then back again once more.

SIX

Charleston, 1946

Mama paced back and forth along the skinny wooden slats of their living room floor. "You did *what*?!"

Millie's decision to explain what happened with Harry at the soda fountain had proven to be a slip in judgment, to say the least. But she did have sense enough to know she shouldn't answer that question. That another one would be forthcoming.

"Do you realize what could've happened?"

Millie was just going to let that second question slide by too.

Her mother turned to face her. The pacing stopped. She reached her aging hands toward the tear in Millie's dress, where the hasty stitches had now come undone.

Mama sighed. A deep sort of sigh. The sort of sigh that carries the weight of the world and sends it into the air, where the weight of the world can catch wings.

After a moment's pause, her mother touched Millie's arms gently. "I shouldn't have . . . " She cleared her throat. "If something had happened to you, Millie, I wouldn't be able to breathe . . . "

Too choked up to say any more, Mama simply folded Millie into her arms. Arms where Millie had always known comfort. Security. Safety. Arms that seemed to grow in reach as Millie grew in stature and need.

"It didn't, Mama." Millie pulled back from her mother and looked straight into her eyes. "You hear me? I'm fine."

But Mama's gaze kept trailing back to the tear on the shoulder of Millie's dress.

She was quiet—too quiet for too long. Mama wasn't usually one to hide how she was feeling.

"Mama?" Millie finally muttered. Her bare foot tapped against the floor, her body a bundle of nerves over the rebuke that was coming. Mama was clearly gathering thoughts, about to let her have it.

And she deserved it, didn't she?

Her mother was right. Any number of awful things could've happened to her because of what she told Harry.

Shouldn't she know better, after what happened to Daddy?

Millie swallowed. Her stomach turned when she thought of the men responsible. Men who hadn't even been prosecuted because they said it was self-defense, but really, they were angry her Italian father had loved Millie's Black mother, and especially angry the two of them had a baby. Angry Millie was playing with their own kids, and angry Daddy stepped in the way when they reached for Millie to teach her a lesson. So in their rage, they killed him.

And now both Mama and Millie were broken in pieces, and Millie couldn't imagine that sort of thing might ever be mended. That either of them might ever be the people they were before the violent grief had torn them in two.

Mama's full lips parted. "You said no one knew? Everyone thought you was white?"

Millie nodded. "You don't need to worry. I—"

Mama shushed her with a wave of one hand. "Now, hush up. You realize what this means?"

Should she?

"What'd you think would happen if you went back to that soda fountain?"

Millie shrugged. "They don't know the truth . . . They'd probably welcome me."

Mama paused. "Exactly." She held her darker forearm against Millie's. "You see this? You're lucky, Millie."

"Lucky?" Because she didn't quite belong anywhere? Black folks thought she was privileged, and white folks had to be tricked? Lucky when no one would accept her wholly, honestly, as one human being with two distinct parts of her heritage?

"Yes. Lucky beyond what you know. You've got options, sweet girl. Choices." Mama brushed her hand along Millie's face and held it there lovingly. Almost as if she was saying good-bye to something.

"If you don't belong somewhere, Mama, I don't either." But even as she said the words, Millie wondered—*what choices does Mama mean?*

Her mother continued as if Millie hadn't made that remark. "You've heard talk of folks passing for white all around the country. I've never mentioned it to you until now, but I've long thought you could do it, Millie. I was waiting for the right time to bring all this up." She shook her head and looked off, her gaze somewhere else. "I know this may seem like a lot to consider, but after what happened to your father . . ." Her eyes clouded, and she looked back to Millie. "Well, I don't want that happening to you too. Folks like that boy are the reason he's dead."

The memory of Millie's father flashed through Millie's mind with vibrancy.

Mama rubbed Millie's arms. "You remember that town your cousin was talking about, on the Gulf Coast of Alabama? Fairhope, it's called. What about that place? They're real accepting of folks. If you could just get there, Millie . . ."

"Then what?"

"You could have a different sort of life."

"I don't want a different sort of life." But didn't she? Why else would she pretend as she did with Harry?

Of course she knew the answer. It had nothing to do with denying Mama—Lord knew she was prouder of her family than a peacock of his feathers—but no. The truth was, Millie wanted to know what it might feel like to live without fear. To be given respect in an instant and to watch the world from inside the windows: to watch from all those spaces that same world wouldn't allow her passing through.

"Really?" Mama looked at her through eyes framed by long, beautiful lashes. "Even if it means you could own that dress store you always dreamin' about?"

"Not if it meant leaving home. Not if it meant leaving you."

"Hush, child." Mama swallowed visibly. "'Course I don't want to say good-bye to you. You're the reason I rise in the morning and the thing that keeps me breathing." She shook her head slightly. "But Millie, don't you see? I want more for you than this. I want you to have your dream."

It was at the word *dream* that the front window shattered.

A loud, violent crash.

And then deceptively melodic chimes as the glass hit the floor beneath their feet.

Mama shoved Millie hard onto the sofa and told her to cover her head.

Millie listened.

She should've been the brave one. She should've done the pushing to be sure her mother was clear out of the way, but instead she just cowered there with her hands over her head like Mama said to do.

Mama picked up a brick from the floor. With her free hand, she brushed the tiny shards of glass—the nearly invisible ones—from her dress before they could cut her, and she braved a long look around the windowsill.

When she stepped back over to the sofa and pulled Millie to standing, Millie's heart raced so fast she thought she might never catch it. But Millie knew then that whoever was responsible had fled, else Mama would've gone after them.

Her mother looked down at the brick she still held. "Harry is their son," she mumbled.

Millie couldn't seem to so much as blink. "I don't understand."

Mama met her gaze. "The men who killed your daddy. One of them is Harry's father and another is his kin." Mama moved the brick back and forth between her hands. "I didn't tell you before because I saw no sense in making you scared, but the boy clearly thinks like his father and is old enough now to be a problem." Mama never looked away. "They own the dress store, Millie. Don't you see? If you follow that dream here in Charleston . . . well, I'm not even sure you're safe, let alone that they'd give you the opportunity. You have to go."

Millie swallowed.

"Do it for me, Millie."

⁂

Charleston Train Station, 1946
Two Weeks Later

Millie listened for the whistle of the train as she gripped her carpetbag. The early morning air was already thick with August heat, and she moved her face from a bug flying past.

Mama and Millie stood outside Union Station on East Bay Street, the railway station's stunning architecture looming.

Mama'd insisted she wouldn't go inside. "Don't want any other passengers getting suspicious," she'd said. "Why would a white woman and a Black woman be out here socializing?"

But the thought of it turned Millie's stomach. What was she doing? Could Millie really up and leave her family, even if staying *was* dangerous? Was she doing right by them? She loved them something fierce and was so proud of them too. Mama knew that, didn't she?

It felt terribly as though she were pretending. Like the time she wore those handmade wings and tried to jump from the top of the shed in the backyard. That hadn't ended well. What's to say this flight would be any different?

But she'd hardly had time to process all that. Mama had been so sure, so convincing.

So here Millie stood. Carpetbag in hand—a photo of her mama inside as well as some benne wafers, and a few coins within a tiny sweetgrass container Mama wove years ago.

None of this was enough to get her by in Alabama, and they both knew it.

But none of this was enough for her life here, either. Millie was beginning to see that much plainly.

Mama straightened Millie's cloche and pressed the shoulders of her dress, the mended tear hardly noticeable. "Now you be careful, mind for strangers, and keep your talkin' brief. We don't want nobody asking questions, you hear?"

Millie nodded.

Mama's grip on her shoulders tightened. Her eyes looked tired. How long had they looked that way? "No matter what, you remember this, child. You got a place in this world. God gave you those big dreams, and you're gonna see them come into being. Don't let nobody tell you differently."

Millie breathed it all in. The comfort of her mother's words, the way her mother smelled of the soap they used on clothes, and the strong and very firm grasp of her mama's hands.

Just because Mama was strong didn't mean the same for Millie. Truth is, she was scared out of her wits and hadn't a clue what she was doing. But she'd pretend. Pretend to be strong, that is. For her mama's sake.

Then her mother did something unexpected. She opened Millie's right palm to face upward and dropped something into her hand. More coins, perhaps? But how would she have come by them?

Millie looked down and saw two buttons.

She gasped. "No, Mama. I refuse."

But Mama's response was simply to close Millie's fingers around the buttons. "Hush, child," she said.

That moment—that single moment—Millie knew she'd better leave or she'd never find the courage.

She kissed her mother's cheek and closed her eyes. Then Mama squeezed her arm once more.

Millie knew. It was time.

With a wobbly smile Mama probably saw straight through, Millie stepped into the train station and toward whatever was coming.

An hour later, she was sitting on the hard bench toward the back of her train car and watching for Mama as they pulled out of the station.

Mama's instructions had been very clear. She would wave, but Millie mustn't.

Everything within Millie groaned as one hungry for home, and the feeling nearly gave way to tears.

That's when she saw him. Chasing the train.

He wore black trousers rolled up at the hem, a white shirt, and a pair of suspenders. She couldn't make out his features, but he was a white man and about her age.

Nothing like Harry.

In an instant, he vanished.

Mama waved, and Millie smiled, and for some reason she couldn't quite explain, she was desperate to find out what happened to him.

The boy who was chasing the train. Just like she did. Albeit, in a different way.

SEVEN

Charleston, Modern Day

"Dude, I told you not to wear that tie. It screams *historian*," Declan said.

"Well, that's good, because I am a historian." Peter Perkins set his hammer down on the drop cloth he'd used to protect the original wooden floor. He was halfway through his renovation of the space above the dress shop and had big plans to convert it into another one of his short-term rentals. With the way tourism in Charleston continued rising, it should become a profitable property, especially if he could manage to brand it by preserving its history.

With the back of his hand, Peter wiped sweat from his forehead and repositioned his backward ball cap before glaring at his cousin Declan. "Look—if a woman writes me off because of something so innocuous, I'm not sure I have any interest in a second conversation."

Even if she looked like an angel. He knelt on the floor and worked to scrape cheap plaster from off the antique brick column he'd uncovered in the middle of the loft space.

"You keep wearing clothes that look like they belong on *Saved by the Bell* and even I am not going to be interested in another conversation."

Peter picked up his brush to wipe away plaster dust from the beam, choosing to ignore Declan's jab. "She left an impression. I'll give you that much." Truth was, he hadn't been able to get Harper out of his mind since the engagement party. Kept wondering what happened with that dress she'd made and if her professor liked it as much as he did. Although he imagined her professor might have different criteria . . .

Peter cleared his throat. "You think she really will call about renting the store?"

Declan rolled back on the soles of his loafers and groaned. "I just realized what you're doing."

Peter took the scraper to a stubborn corner. "What's that?"

"You're sprucing up this place in hopes she'll rent it from you. She said she'll call about the store below, right? You're hoping she rents it, and you can throw this loft in too."

"Don't be ridiculous." A large chunk of plaster fell to the drop cloth, sending a cloud of white dust into the air. Peter raised the hem of his T-shirt to cover his nose. "I had already planned out the renovations before meeting Harper. I've done this a few times before, Declan." He wouldn't mention how often he'd been thinking about her. Because then he would have to admit his buddy was right about his tie choice.

"So, are we going to lunch or what?" Declan asked. "I'm hungry for pizza."

Peter brushed the dust from his jeans and stood. "Yeah, just let me move these boxes over to the window." He reached down, careful to lift from his knees.

"Let me give you a hand." Declan unbuttoned the sleeves of his pressed shirt and rolled them. Then he took the other box and hauled it toward the window, setting it down beside Peter's. "What do you have in these things? Lead?"

"Leaded glass, actually."

Declan stood upright. "You're not kidding, are you?"

Peter laughed. "Actually, I'm not. I found these antique pieces, and I'm going to use them to restore the mosaic glass window." He shifted the drop cloth and moved the curtain he'd hung to protect the original piece.

"Only you." Declan looked at the damaged stained glass and whistled low. "Wow, that thing sure is beautiful."

Peter brushed more plaster dust from his shirt. He should be fine wearing these clothes—they were only getting pizza, not meeting the pope. Besides, he'd gotten used to feeling underdressed every time he grabbed lunch with his cousin. Declan had followed the wildly lucrative lifestyle of both his own father and Peter's stepfather, and he needed to dress the part to be taken seriously. Peter did not.

Peter patted the pockets of his jeans to check for his wallet, then realized it was missing. A phone he could do without, but he'd need a way to pay. He looked around the room as he tried to remember where he'd seen it last, then grinned as he took in the progress he'd made. This rental was turning out pretty great.

The long windows overlooked the comings and goings on King Street, and the loft was plenty large enough for a living area, small kitchen, and if he played his cards right, two bedrooms. He focused on the historical elements in all of his short-term rental properties because renters wanted to feel like they were being offered a story. And truthfully, Peter wanted the same thing.

"I saw your dad today." Declan started toward the stairwell.

Peter followed. "My stepfather, you mean?" Under regular circumstances, a person in Peter's position would probably ask, *"Did he mention me?"* But these were not regular circumstances, and Peter had long ago given up on being mentioned.

"I'm sorry." Declan stopped short on the top step. "I shouldn't have said anything. I know you left that life behind after what he did."

"It's fine, man." Peter blew out a deep breath and shoved his hands into his pockets. "And I wouldn't say I left it behind . . ." *More like I finally realized I never belonged there to begin with.*

The thought of his stepfather giving away that box full of his mother's heirlooms not even a month after her funeral—just up and giving them away, like a pair of worn-out shoes—still hollowed Peter out with loss.

Declan hit Peter on the shoulder. "I really do think you'll find her stuff someday."

"Thanks, but I don't even know what was inside that box. I wouldn't recognize it even if I did find it. I'd give anything to go back, to go through everything when I still had the chance." At least one good thing had come from it—Peter finally found the courage to uncover almost-forgotten stories, away from the scorn of his stepfather's elitist friends.

Declan took two steps, then looked back over his shoulder. "Do you think I'd be crazy to ask out Harper's friend Lucy?"

Peter shook his head and grinned. "Never a dull moment with you."

Radcliffeborough, Charleston, Modern Day

The next morning, a group of ladies with large beaded earrings and grey hair curled from here to high heaven clustered around a kitchen table lined with green Depression glass.

They had a saying around here. The higher the hair, the closer to God. And if that were true, well, the women of the Holy City would be a shoe-in when it came time for the rapture.

Peter maneuvered around them, straightening his glasses and turning to Sullivan, one of his buddies who worked part-time for him. This was not their first estate sale. Not even their first this month. And secretly, Peter loved the good-natured competition—swooping up artifacts before the minister's grandmother got to them. Some of the artifacts he would resell, while others he would use to furnish his rental properties. Rarely, he'd find an item for his own stash of historical treasures. "Let's head upstairs and see what furniture they've got in the bedrooms."

The oddity of estate sales could never quite escape him. Strangers coming into someone else's home as if they belonged, then evaluating what to keep, what to buy, what to sell. All in a bedroom or kitchen someone once called home.

But in cases like this one, where the old house would surely be demolished in the months to come and the lot developed from scratch, Peter would come in and save what he could because that's what gave him breath each morning.

An old chocolate Lab ambled closer, its claws clicking against the floor.

"Come 'ere, Billy girl." A man's voice from the other room called. The dog hesitated. Peter smiled, then reached out to briefly scratch the dog's grey-peppered ears. Satisfied to have received some attention, she rubbed her head once along the leg of Peter's jeans, then turned the corner back toward the owner.

Sullivan took the creaky stair steps two at a time. He always ducked a little when he climbed stairs, a habit Peter suspected he'd developed because his height kept him bumping into low ceilings. Peter was mid-step toward the landing when Sullivan whistled low.

Few other people had made the trek upstairs, so he and Sullivan had the space to themselves.

The wood-slat ceiling covered a room filled with old furniture. Peter watched the ceiling fan push a light haze of dust into a swirl, dust that fell upon decades-old pieces that were all remarkably salvageable.

Then his eyes widened. "This is a gold mine."

Sullivan stepped toward a few antique bed frames and pushed up his sleeves as he began to sort through the piles.

Peter skimmed the edges of an old writing desk with his thumb. A basket full of books next to the desk showed water damage, suggesting the house had flooded at some point.

But the desk was in immaculate condition. The no-nonsense frame of it made him guess it was over a century old.

Nervous energy had Peter tapping his foot among the dust as the morning sunlight streamed in. He was a twenty-eight-year-old grown man, for crying out loud, but he felt like a kid again whenever he found pieces like these. Every single time.

The reaction was enduring, probably pathetic, and a complete romanticization of history. But he couldn't help but wonder *who lived in this house* and *who did they care for* and a hundred other questions about their lives.

It was the entire reason he started his company—because maybe if a child used a century-old desk, something of the original owner would affect him or her, even if the memory itself did not. Like a heritage passed down, even if that heritage was never realized.

Sullivan cleared his throat. "Get a look at this." He stepped closer to the desk and held a bag toward Peter. "Found it in one of the drawers over there." Sullivan nodded to the other side of the room.

Peter frowned. He'd found plenty of items stashed inside drawers before—like cross-stitched bookmarks or broken cufflinks—but the items were typically small. Little reminders that the house had once been lived in and the items, used, long before the estate sale.

He took the fabric bag from Sullivan. A satchel, perhaps? Looked more than a hundred years old, easily.

Threads in brown and pink and green embroidered the time-stained satchel.

Peter read the inscription aloud.

"Rose, mother of Ashley,
gave her this sack when
she was sold at age nine in South Carolina.
It held a tattered dress, three handfuls of
pecans, a braid of Rose's hair,
and two buttons from Rose's own dress. Told her,
'It be filled with my Love always.'
She never saw her again.
Ashley is my great-grandmother.
—M.M. 1946."

Peter's hands trembled. He was holding a Civil War artifact. The weight of it so thin it could catch the wind and yet oh, so heavy.

He looked to Sullivan, who stood wide-eyed. "Man."

"Nine years old," Peter murmured.

"What are you going to do with it?"

Peter touched the embroidery with his thumb and hesitated a long moment. A discovery like this had profound implications. So few African American artifacts from the Civil War had been preserved, and this type of piece belonged either in a museum or with the original owner.

Surely this person, this M.M., wasn't still living.

"I'm going to find the story." His resolve grew as he heard himself speak the words.

Sullivan watched him, saying nothing.

"What? You don't think I can."

"Look, I know your persistence." Sullivan swept a streak of dust from the top of the desk. "But this may be a little outside your expertise."

"Not with some research." Peter looked up again, toward the ceiling fan. "We have her initials. How hard can it be?"

Sullivan's silence spoke for itself, but Peter wasn't swayed. When he set his mind to something, he would not give up. His mother, God rest her soul, had taught him that. And in this case, he was determined to find M.M.

Peter opened another desk drawer, searching for more. His hand caught against something tucked neatly into the drawer. A letter addressed to Rosie.

Peter stopped. *Rosie* was the nickname his mother went by.

Could these be *the* artifacts? His stomach leapt in anticipation, but with a deep breath he forced some sense back into himself. Ridiculous, at best. How many women of that time were named Rose? The name itself hardly meant these items were related to his mother.

His lips moved as he read the letter, but this time, he didn't dare speak the contents aloud. The sentiments seemed too sacred, too personal, spanning decades and generations through these inky words.

Dearest Rosie,

Moments ago, I held you for the last time. I cradled you, and I smelled your soft head full of hair, and I tried my hardest to memorize the feel of you in my arms—so angelic and so small.

These moments seem a lifetime past. And yet, my dress is still damp from the dribble of your mouth as it pressed against my shoulder.

Already, I feel I've made a terrible mistake, and I know I will keep this grief for the rest of my life. You have stretched first my womb and then my heart, such that I will always ache for your nearness. But I suppose all mothers learn to live with hollowed-out spaces, and over time, maybe come to appreciate them.

I wish I could tell you the circumstances. Why I must leave and you must stay. But trust me, child, when I say I wish this were not the case—for any of us.

My sweet Rosie, I hope you'll never doubt my love.

Your Mother

Peter reread the letter, then the satchel, again and again. But every time, the same line stopped him. *Two buttons from Rose's own dress.* He fumbled through the drawers once more, searching. His racing heart prompted him to move faster.

He had a hunch—and it was a wild hunch and completely unfounded—but after years of work with artifacts, you get a sense for these things. He had a hunch this somehow *did* connect to his mother. Not just the letter, but the satchel too. That they all came from the same place.

Now, where were those buttons?

EIGHT

Train from Charleston, 1946

Millie's cloche tipped on her forehead as she looked out the window. The train was approaching Savannah and slowing.

She bit her bottom lip, still looking for the man who had jumped the rails, but she saw nothing. Had she imagined him?

"Hello." The blond woman in the seat ahead of Millie turned to face her. She wore a red dress with yellow daisies that cinched at the waistline. "We're newlyweds. Starting our married life in Savannah." Her husband turned at this description. He straightened his flat wool cap and suit jacket.

"How nice." Millie nodded once at both of them and folded her empty hands.

"Enjoying the train ride?" The woman offered a rosy smile.

"I sure am." Looking first to her right and then left, Millie leaned forward. She lowered her voice. "Say, you haven't seen a man . . ."

The husband raised his eyebrows, waiting. When she didn't offer more explanation, his jaw tightened. "No one has offered you harm?"

Millie held up her hand. "Oh no. None at all." She hesitated, then decided she should trust them with a description. "It's just I saw a man jump the rails back in Charleston."

"And you're worried about him." His words were a statement, not a question.

"Yes."

"I wouldn't be." The train car jerked to a slower speed as they approached the Savannah station. The man's gaze went beyond Millie, out her window, and he frowned. "Freight hoppers are a feisty lot."

Millie started to look over her shoulder too, but a commotion to her left caught her attention.

Several people hurried over to the other side of the passenger car to get a better view. Millie stood from her seat and joined them.

An older woman who smelled of half a bottle of perfume pointed to the window, filling Millie in even as the artificial floral smell nauseated her. "Colored woman was jumpin' the rails and got caught by detectives."

Millie squinted to get a better view. "She's got a baby on her hip."

"Sure does. And the law in Georgia is thirty days in the chain gang for ridin' the rails. Don't know what the penalty is for women or Blacks."

Fire rose up in Millie. "But she's clearly just trying to feed her child." Millie had heard stories of folks following train lines in hopes of work they couldn't find at home. Northerners going south. Southerners going north. Nobody going nowhere better than the last, but everybody searching. For hope, much as anything else. The New Deal had helped a whole lot of folks, but not everyone.

Panic gripped Millie's chest. One of the train bulls approached the woman outside. He took the child, then raised his fist above the mother. In a blink, she collapsed to the ground. From inside the train car, Millie could see the child's wail.

"Somebody do something!" she wanted to yell.

But Mama had instructed her not to draw any attention to herself.

Surely she wasn't so defenseless. She needed to think fast.

63

A flicker of light caught her peripheral vision, and Millie turned to the window beside her seat, trying to make sense of the flash. What she saw quickened her pulse all the more.

The train jumper.

The boy in suspenders now wore a flat cap as he crossed near her side of the train car.

Everyone else stared at the commotion to her left.

For Millie's eyes only, his finger swept over the front of his lips, then back again, telling her to hush but also offering a wink that sent tingles dancing up her spine.

The newlyweds were gone. She looked around the row of seats to see if they'd already disembarked.

Nothing. And no more sign of the boy who'd jumped the rails.

But in his place, flames began to spark up from the ground.

"Fire!" Millie yelled, rushing into the aisle. The mixed-use train carried several wooden boxcars that could easily be engulfed. "Somebody help!"

In seconds, the rest of the passenger car erupted in screams.

The railway detective set the child back with his mother and ran toward the fire. The train bull had bigger priorities. A fire could endanger not only the passengers, but also the train's cargo.

"Close the station!" someone yelled with authority. "Don't let any new passengers on board until we put this thing out."

Everyone clamored. Several extinguishers quickly did the trick, but not for the passengers' rattled nerves.

Only then did Millie realize the Black mother and her child had vanished into the night.

Interesting.

"This seat taken, ma'am?"

Millie stared up at him, the boy she'd been dreaming about all the way from Charleston. Well, young man was more like it. Her heart skipped a beat.

Though she hadn't said a word, he tipped his hat to her and sat.

He smelled of pine and smoke and adventure. And the half grin he offered was far more dangerous than the train tracks.

Millie's mind reeled as she put the pieces together. Careful to keep her voice to a murmur for his ears alone, she faced him. "You snuck inside."

"Mhmm."

"You started that fire so the woman could get away."

"Mhmm."

"That man—that newlywed—gave you his hat and jacket so you'd blend in."

"Was he a newlywed? Good for him."

Millie gaped. "You do realize the penalty for riding the rails in Georgia is thirty days in the chain gang?" She spoke with authority and not as someone who'd just learned this information moments prior.

He raised his eyebrows, clearly humored. "I like you, Red."

"Red?"

"The color of your hat, of course." He bit down on his bottom lip. A beard framed his half grin. "And your cheeks, at the moment."

NINE

Charleston, Modern Day

The uneven floor creaked under Peter's feet as he shifted his weight back and forth. He set the satchel and the letter back on top of the desk and pocketed his hands. "These have got to be my mother's heirlooms." The ones his stepfather had given away like trash.

Ever since the day he came home to find the box of his mother's things gone, Peter desperately wanted more information. Felt like there was a gap inside of him with the heritage part left blank—a blank he might never fill now that his mother was gone.

He always knew it might be too late for those artifacts, but the curiosity had drawn him to old houses, old things. That day became the defining moment he finally gathered the courage to stand up to his stepfather's insatiable longing for prestige and instead take the path God had given him as a historian. In the years that followed, he'd begun to realize it was a lot easier to hear God's voice when he no longer allowed his stepfather's disapproval to scream inadequacy over his life.

But sometimes he still woke up in a cold sweat during the night, dreaming about empty boxes.

What if after all that time, *these* were the missing heirlooms? These could be the very clues he'd been trying to find.

"Mhmm." Sullivan shifted his weight on his Vans. Peter wanted to tell him to wipe that smug grin off his face. But they were interrupted.

"Right up here." A woman who looked to be in her seventies stepped into the room, while another woman followed closely behind. Her attention focused in on Sullivan, and she hesitated mid-step. Then her friend stopped behind her, nearly causing a pileup. "Dear me," she mumbled.

Peter pressed his lips together to keep from laughing. This was always happening to Sullivan—women young and old would notice his height and good looks and ask things like if he played basketball and whether he'd like to come over to meet their granddaughters, daughters, and friends. A slice of homemade pie was usually included in the offer.

Sullivan crossed his arms and smiled. "Sorry, y'all, but we're buying this room."

The woman moved her hand to the silk scarf at her neck. "Mercy. But you don't mean all of it?" She took another step toward them. "Why, there must be thousands of dollars' worth of furniture in here."

If they only knew.

Sullivan shrugged. "Sorry."

The woman turned to her friend, casting a clear frown of disapproval. After a long moment's hesitation, they left the room. "Let's take another look at the rose trellis we saw earlier." Her voice faded as she went down the stairs.

Sullivan looked at Peter and cracked his knuckles. "All right, stubborn fool—what are we searching next?"

Peter grinned. "Is that any way to speak to your boss?"

"That was the edited version, sir." Sullivan chuckled.

Peter stepped toward the closet of the bedroom. More dust clouded as he opened the door, and he started coughing.

"Delicate lungs?" Sullivan joked.

"You know what? You can just wait outside." Peter good-naturedly shoved Sullivan's shoulder.

Sullivan went back to the bedside table and opened the rest of the drawers.

"We have to find what this means." Peter shook his head.

A knock on the door interrupted them once more. A plump woman with grey hair and glasses, wearing an ample amount of his mother's old perfume, stood at the entry. "Excuse me, young men, but a very troubled customer told me you intend to purchase this entire room's worth of furniture. Y'all realize we don't offer any furniture transport?"

Peter tipped his chin. "Yes, ma'am. I own an architectural salvage business, and we acquire a fair amount of our inventory from sales like this one. I assure you, we won't have any trouble loading it ourselves."

Actually, he could probably haul half of this stuff by himself, since his own house was just up the block.

"If we do buy the entire room, could you offer us a bulk price?" Peter asked. Worth a try.

The woman shrugged. "How does a thousand sound?"

"Like a deal." Peter casually crossed his arms. "Now, would it be possible to close off this room to other customers until we can get it all paid for and loaded?"

"I don't see why not." She hesitated a moment. "I see you found the satchel."

Peter realized he was clenching his teeth and tried taking a deeper breath, but his heart was racing at the thought of this discovery and he was having a hard time playing it cool. "We did. What's the story?"

The woman looked over toward where it lay on the old dresser. "All I know is my niece lived here with her grandparents when they found it at a thrift shop. The box was labeled 'Radcliffeborough' and had an address on it. This satchel as well as some other items were inside. Seemed like fate, you know? To think, some of these artifacts may've been in a house like this one decades ago and then found their way back to the neighborhood." The woman smiled. "It's been—goodness—probably ten years or so. She was nine years old when she discovered it and said she'd offer it safekeeping. That a story like that needed protecting." The woman traced her finger along the edge of the door frame. "I think in reality, she probably liked that she shared an age with the girl from the embroidery. You're welcome to take it with the dresser set. It's just an old piece of cloth—not worth much."

Peter hesitated. He caught Sullivan's attention as everything within him hummed with the echo of her words. *Ten years ago.* It all fit with the timeline of when his stepfather gave away the artifacts. He knew, logically speaking, there were probably more letters to girls named Rosie than he dare count, but the fact that this one—this particular letter—was sitting in front of him made it different from all the rest.

This letter might be the key to the rest of the story.

"Ma'am?" Peter asked. "Do you happen to remember the number on that address?"

"Sure do. Six-seven-five." She turned from the doorway. "Why do you ask?"

Because that was his address.

Peter's throat burned as he swallowed. Sullivan stared at him, wide-eyed.

"Just curious," Peter mumbled.

He took another long look around the room where the sunlight came through the window, thinking about how the angle was the same it'd been for the past century as he breathed in the distinctive smell of old walls.

What did all of this mean?

An hour later, Peter and Sullivan had loaded nearly everything into their pickup trucks. Peter wiped the sweat from his forehead. He leaned against the faded blue paint of his truck, his arms crossed.

As he looked back up at the old cottage that'd be worth more as an empty lot than a house, he couldn't shake the feeling that the missing buttons held the answers he'd been searching for ever since his stepfather gave away his mother's heirlooms.

Sullivan put his hands in his pockets. "You are stubborn as a mule."

"Thank you." Realizing he'd missed checking one set of wooden drawers, Peter knelt beside the piece of furniture to search for the buttons. He pulled out the strong but sturdy drawers one by one.

When the final drawer resisted his pull, he gave it a tug, and all at once, the drawer released. Along with it came the contents.

An old wedding dress tumbled onto the ground in one discarded heap. But beyond the lace and the frills and the fabric, one tiny but significant piece of the garment arrested his attention.

The missing connection. The missing piece. The shimmering wings of an antique butterfly button.

He couldn't believe his eyes.

Sullivan stilled. "Maybe you're on to something."

As Peter reached for the dress, he was struck by its familiarity. He had never seen it before . . . at least, not in person. His jaw ached from clenching his teeth again, so he rolled his shoulders to loosen the tension.

Then recognition dawned.

Of course.

The fabric felt light as the dress slipped through his hands, and he grasped for it as one grasps for a shadow.

Peter *had* seen the dress before, in photos.

His mother had worn it on her wedding day to his father.

One Day Later

"Come on." Peter set the satchel down on his desk and leaned closer to his laptop. He sighed as he waited for his computer to load the search results.

So far, he'd determined the satchel had likely begun as a feed sack during the Civil War. In far too many cases, slave-related possessions had been destroyed during the Reconstruction, and slave stories were seldomly documented back then.

The embroidery, of course, intrigued him. Especially the skill of the work, which looked to be done by a professional seamstress. But who was she, this mystery woman?

"M.M.," he murmured to himself. Peter held the fabric closer to his glasses. Each stitch was precise and consistent, and the different colors of the embroidery made the story visually interesting. This woman knew her way around a needle and thread.

He had the strangest feeling he had seen these particular threads before.

"Who are you, M.M.? Who *were* you, and what is your story?" And maybe most importantly, why was his mother's wedding dress with these belongings?

Peter rubbed his eyes with the palm of his hands. It was nearly two o'clock in the morning, and even he could recognize he was far too immersed in this mystery.

But the whole thing gripped him, and sleep evaded his best efforts. He found himself staring at the ceiling fan and imagining that woman, grieving for her child. Nine years old and sold as if she were worth no more than a bag of flour.

He looked inside the empty satchel and pictured how it might've looked when it was once filled with care by a mother for her little girl. Whatever happened to the two of them? Was their story lost to the whim of history as the contents of the satchel had been?

Not if Peter had anything to do with it. He stood up from his chair to stretch his neck, then did twenty jumping jacks.

He sat back down.

Because his search had only just begun.

TEN

Train from Charleston, 1946

A sliver of the moon shone through the cloudless Alabama sky as the train rumbled down the tracks, and Millie wasn't sure of anything anymore.

Dawn was fast approaching, but Millie hadn't slept a wink. The same could not be said for the man seated beside her.

She took a long look at him as he slept, his head resting on the jacket he'd folded and propped up against the window.

Somewhere between Savannah and Atlanta, she'd realized he was jaw-droppingly handsome, and she imagined with a haircut and a shave, he would turn heads.

But what really struck her about the train jumper was the spark he carried. His presence was so different from the other boys she'd known.

As much as she'd enjoyed their conversation before he nodded off, the sleepless night had now sent her into every manner of doubt—so much that she didn't feel safe on this train anymore. Unsafe in what she was heading toward, unsafe in whom she was sitting beside. Maybe she liked him a little too much, when he was really still a stranger.

For it was all—the grand sum of it—an elaborate plan for a dream she now considered to be childish. She had left everything she loved and knew behind in Charleston, for what? A mere chance at a dream?

And what if she was found out for her real self—if a slip of the tongue gave her away—what would happen then and what would her mama think?

And, perhaps more terrifying—what if she was never found out? What if all went completely according to plan, and for the rest of her life she lived as if the first part of her life had never happened at all?

The handsome train jumper shifted in his seat, still asleep. Millie envied the ease with which he found rest.

Every time she closed her eyes, she saw her mother at the station, holding those buttons. Now, Millie clutched them inside the pocket of her dress, knowing the buttons should bring her comfort but instead feeling every manner the prodigal daughter.

She never should've left her mama.

No matter what her mother said that day with the sweetgrass and Harry, or every night since, or at the station.

How could a heritage half-denied bring a life fully lived?

Millie's stomach turned in grief. When would she see her mother again? *Would* she see her mother again? Lord only knew how long it would take to save enough money to visit Charleston. The dark circles under Mama's eyes had been there far too long. Why had Millie paid them no mind until today?

A hollowed-out space inside her heart first jabbed then ached, like the space between a broken bone—a space the rest of the body must work hard to heal until the throb subsides. The pain, the swelling, must be absorbed before the break can be mended.

Millie looked out the window.

Who are you, Millicent?

In a voice altogether separate from her own, she sensed the response.

Adored.

The word came as suddenly as a rainbow appears in the sky, and was so very startling she sat back for a minute.

And something—not quite joy or even peace, but perhaps it was purpose—began to fill that empty space to the brim, until a bone-weary Millie fluttered her eyes closed and gently grinned.

"The Lord gives, and the Lord takes away. Blessed be the name of the Lord."

She murmured the words to Mama's favorite verse under her breath, the familiarity of them a blanket against the chill of unfamiliarity that blew inside and out.

Adored.

Adored by the One who created the stars and knew her before she was born. Adored by her mama, who thought she could win the world if she tried hard enough.

She traced the outline of the buttons in her pocket. Yes, she mattered in this world. How and why and when, she had yet to find out.

But here on this train between home and new ground, God settled how very deeply she was loved, even as her grandparents before her had been, and the generations before them.

She would embroider Rose and Ashley's story on the satchel when she got situated in Alabama. Maybe that would bring some closure about the life she had to leave for the future she wanted to live. The hidden heritage that still caused her to ache with pride, regardless of where she called home.

Millie sighed, a blending of hope and grief all mixed into one.

The train jumper shifted once more in his chair, only this time, he opened his eyes. A sleepy grin tugged up his lips.

"How long have you been staring at me, Red?"

Her heart stirred with longing.

Not long enough.

Franklin Pinckney tightened the worn laces of his shoes.

His entire body ached.

You'd think a few hours' sleep from inside the train car would've done him good, not worrying about rolling off the top of the thing or being caught by train bulls. But, while he appreciated a moment of rest and safety, he'd gotten used to the sounds of the night. Like a country boy to a cricket lullaby.

His stomach growled aloud. Had the woman beside him heard it?

Franklin smiled slightly, hoping another growl wouldn't give away the timing of his last meal. Then he yawned, covering his mouth with his hand. "Where are you headed?"

The beautiful woman—and she was *beautiful* with those green eyes that danced in the sunlight—raised her chin ever so slightly. "I'm visiting my aunt in Fairhope, Alabama."

Her words were sheer confidence, but Franklin saw something else in her eyes. A flicker of uncertainty, perhaps, though her jaw locked with tenacity.

She was clearly not as experienced on the rails as he.

"That will be nice."

The woman nodded.

"You're close with her, then? Your aunt?"

She hesitated. "Not exactly."

"Thus the need for a visit, I suppose." Franklin rubbed the inside of his palm. He had the sneaking suspicion no such aunt existed and that Millie had rehearsed this line for safety's sake. His mother used to do the same thing. He should stop jabbering and let the poor woman be. But she was just so magnetizing. And he hadn't had real conversation with a woman his age in weeks.

She looked at him a long moment, taking in the sight of him. Franklin need not wonder what she noticed—for to someone the likes of her, he probably looked filthy.

"What about you?" she asked finally. "How did you get started, you know . . ." She seemed to falter on the phrase *train jumping*.

He locked on her gaze. If he was going to answer openly, he would need her honest response in return. Franklin was surprised when a sweep of her eyes revealed no hint of condescension, only interest. She leaned toward him almost imperceptibly.

But he sensed it, all right. He sensed her slight movement closer all the way down to his toes.

Might as well come out with it. "My father was never around, just my mother and me. My uncle tried to help us as best he could, but then the Depression came and he struggled to make his own ends meet, so my mother and I took to train jumping. She'd sneak on the trains with me in tow. It was the only way she could think of to keep us fed." He shook his head. His stomach turned at the memory of huddling close to his mother in those cold train cars, protecting her from strange men.

Millie's gulp was visible. "What happened to her?"

"She fell off the train one night as it was pulling into the station. I jumped after her, but not quick enough. She got hurt pretty badly." Franklin rubbed his thumb against his unwelcome beard. "Some women at one of the churches in that little town helped fix her up, but her arm never healed correctly, so her days riding the rails were over."

He shrugged. "I'm just glad she's all right, you know? For a while now, I've been sending money back to her whenever I can. It's not much, but it helps with food. I'm faster on my own anyway."

He hoped Millie wouldn't feel too sorry for him. He didn't look away from her eyes. He couldn't if he tried. "You probably know this, but riding the rails isn't so common as it used to be. This is actually the last train I plan to jump. Figure I can do better for myself now by settling down. Heard there's a lot of work to be had in Mobile, over in the shipyards. Or I may hitch my way over to Fairhope. I was down this way a few years ago, and folks were kind when I was good near starving, so I'm hoping they'll still be kind now."

Millie nodded. "That's why you helped the woman back in Savannah. She reminded you of your mother."

Franklin scratched above his eyebrow. "Suppose she did, but that's not why I helped her." He took a deep breath and brushed some dirt from the knees of his pants. "I helped her because it's the right thing to do."

"You didn't care that she was Black?"

"Of course not."

At this, she had the most surprising reaction of a slow and steady grin. The gesture was supremely rewarding, and he longed to earn another.

"I don't suppose you'd like the company of a stranger in Fair–hope?" It was a bold question and one that he probably shouldn't have asked. But nevertheless, he would regret not taking his chance while he had it.

She studied him. He could only imagine she was weighing the option. And he reminded himself he might not want to know what she was thinking. "Truth is, I don't have an aunt in Fairhope, though I do have some distant kin around there. I've never met them, though. My mama just heard Fairhope is friendly to people looking to start over. And, Train Jumper, I am awfully desperate for some company."

At the words *train jumper*, his heart skipped a beat.

"In that case"—he extended his callused right hand—"I'm Franklin."

When her delicate fingers met his, Franklin found himself trans–fixed. Sparks flew like coal embers after a long simmer in a train engine. All by the simplest touch. He wondered what he would do with himself.

"I'm Millie." Her smile was as sweet as the hum of bees.

ELEVEN

Fairhope, Modern Day

Harper Rae was tired of almost.

A hummingbird used to appear outside her bedroom. Sometimes it would perch at the feeder there, and for a few moments, she could watch it hover. Wings so fast, they blurred color and movement and space. In the blending came the flight. But invariably, she would blink, and the bird would be gone.

She always thought of that little bird on days like today.

Days where she had blinked.

Harper didn't know when the giving up came, exactly, or even if there was one singular moment. Maybe it came before the department chair's words, in a series of late-night assignments, poor grades, and misguided passion. But regardless of the moment, that didn't matter anymore.

Harper was moving forward. She had just watched the glorious Georgia sunshine become an Alabama sunset from the driver's window of her daddy's old Ford, and she was determined to find a new beginning.

She tapped the steering wheel, searching for a new rhythm, then shifted the gear and turned off the ignition. She hesitated to open her truck door—instead letting the April air settle over her as she closed her eyes.

What was so wrong with her designs that no one would give her a chance?

What was so wrong with *her* that no one would give her a chance, either?

Harper shook her head and went back to tapping the steering wheel. That was another question entirely.

But now, she needed a new dream. She was ready to bid her final adieu to the possibility of ever owning her own dress shop. And that's exactly what brought her to the boardinghouse along Mobile Bay.

It was as close as she could get to her old house without trespassing, since her father moved years ago to care for her grandmother. But the bay view was just the same.

Harper had wanted to spend the night here for as long as she could remember. Maybe Daddy was right. Now was as good a time as any.

Harper looked up toward the heavens. She had been so sure she'd heard from God. Wasn't stepping out in faith all it took to come into God's blessing?

Surely, for the One who held the stars and knew her brown eyes before she came into being, this wasn't such a big thing.

So why—*why*—had God given her such an out-of-reach dream?

Harper opened the door of her truck and hopped down to the dirt below. She walked past a slew of sprawling oak trees encircled by azalea bushes, and stepped toward the porch, where several rocking chairs greeted guests of the B&B. Glimmers of daylight landed along the porch steps as she took them purposefully.

An old sign had been suspended above the doorway of the historic inn. In cursive letters, it simply read *Millie's Boardinghouse*.

Blue-grey shutters framed the wide front porch. White rocking chairs had been situated in groups of two and three. The rest of the place was an uncommon yellow, like muted sunbeams filtered through trees.

It was the sort of place you'd see in one of those lists by *Southern Living*. Best this or that . . . small town, chocolate cake, you name it.

This place had Best Porch down to a T.

Harper let out a long sigh and set her heavy carpetbag down on the stairs as she looked up at the boardinghouse. How did she get here? Twenty-six and far too old to be stuck at a crossroads, yet twenty-six and far too young to be giving up.

She knocked three times on the front door.

Probably didn't need to knock, but she didn't feel quite comfortable stepping inside, either.

The door creaked open, and an elderly woman with red lipstick and a head full of thick, white hair stood at the entry. She looked exactly the same as Harper remembered, right down to the way she clipped up her hair beneath a red cloche. "Harper Rae, as I live and breathe."

Millie hugged Harper with surprising strength for a woman her age. Her posture was still straight. Only her pace had been slowed a little by time. But time will do that to all of us, won't it? In one way or another.

The screen door slapped shut as Harper came in. She took a look around the room. Coming here was like stepping into a dream. In this case, a dream she hadn't seen from the inside in well over a decade.

The brick fireplace caught her attention first, then the antique radio in the corner. Plush gingham couches with floral pillows provided a splash of whimsy. A chandelier hung from the ceiling, and a vase full of camellias perched on the coffee table between the sofas, the fragrance wafting around the room. At some point since Harper had last been inside the inn, the tongue-and-groove beadboard had been painted the color of a Tiffany's box. All the little cottage-style details were practically screaming for Pinterest.

"This place is amazing," Harper said under her breath. "Even cozier than I remember."

Millie smiled, deepening her laugh lines. "As I recall, you were much more interested in the snickerdoodles last time you came. I trust you're still sewing?"

Harper switched the handle of the carpetbag to her other hand. How could she explain to Millie that the very reason she'd returned home was to gather her thoughts before starting a new venture?

Millie studied her while Harper searched for something to say. Finally, she broke the silence—her few words speaking volumes. "Do you need a room, child?"

Harper bit down on her bottom lip. Her bag was starting to feel heavy, so she set it on the ground. "Yes, ma'am. Actually, I wanted to ask what your nightly rates are. I couldn't find anything online."

Millie waved her hand through the air. "I don't put anything online. If customers want to come, they'll find me the old-fashioned way. Besides . . ." She looked straight into Harper's eyes. "The Internet is nothing but a fad. Someday, society is going to wake up and realize the value of talking to each other again."

Harper opened her mouth to reply, but Millie wasn't done.

"How much do you have, sweetheart?" She studied Harper and seemed to be cataloging the details. Did she notice the sparkle in Harper's eyes had dulled? Could she read Harper's racing thoughts from too much caffeine, consumed in an attempt to stay alert while driving? Did she recognize the little wrinkles and forced smiles and signs of a hollowed-out dream?

Harper cleared her throat and glanced down at the wooden floor, which she knew to be original to the inn. "Probably a whole lot less than your nightly rate."

"And how long are you looking to stay?"

The woman didn't hem-haw around, did she?

"That depends on your nightly rate too." Harper tried to soften this part with a laugh.

Millie didn't laugh back.

"Well, maybe it's fate, you coming here now. I could use some help around the place . . . if you're interested."

"What kind of help, ma'am?"

"Helping *me*, actually." Millie swept a stray piece of white hair behind her ear. The woman radiated life like sunbeams. "I want to do some renovations to the honeymoon suite, but if you haven't noticed, these old joints aren't what they used to be. I need practical help getting things done around the place. Heck, I need practical help getting *around* the place." Millie's eyes danced with that.

Harper tugged at the hem of her denim jacket, completely overwhelmed by the offer. "I'm not sure what to say. I'm honored, but I don't know the first thing about innkeeping."

"Only seamstress work? Got to say, I'm flattered the sewing lessons I gave you all those years ago obviously stuck." Millie raised her chin slightly.

Harper hesitated. "How'd you know I was still making dresses?"

"You're wearing a vintage Dior, child. You are quite literally wearing your skills on your sleeve."

Harper pressed the fabric of her dress. She felt unraveled by Millie's accurate assessment. Beyond the front room where they stood, she saw a simple staircase leading up to more guest rooms. Millie walked past them all, and Harper followed.

"Where are we going?" Harper hauled her carpetbag and wished in that moment she'd opted for luggage with wheels rather than a true vintage piece. Millie was surprisingly tough to keep up with. The woman probably still walked a mile every morning even though she had to be in her nineties by now.

"We're taking the long way to your room," Millie said over her shoulder. She opened the back door, and a stunning garden came into view. Beyond it, a V of pelicans flew over Mobile Bay.

No thought or description seemed quite enough to capture the colors. Or the serenity.

From this angle, the edge of Millie's pier seemed to touch the edge of that pier on Harper's old property, and the familiarity of the place soothed a wound she didn't know it could heal.

Daddy was right, as he usually was. She needed to return and remember where she'd come from. Maybe then she could figure out where she was going.

TWELVE

Fairhope, Modern Day

Several days passed, and while Harper's sore heart hadn't begun to heal, exactly, she *did* find herself piecing the seams together—and after all, wasn't that the first step toward mending?

Harper's phone rang. She shut the door to the inn's library before accepting the call. Not that she expected her old roommate to say anything incriminating, but Millie . . . well, Millie, as it turned out, was nosy. If she was going to explain herself, Harper wanted to do it in peace.

"Hello?" Harper ran her fingers along the ornate edge of the writing desk.

"What were you thinking?" Lucy scolded. "Why did I come home to find two months' rent?"

"Because that's how much we have until the apartment lease—"

"That's not what I meant, and you know it." Lucy harrumphed. "I'm ripping it up, by the way. Your check."

Harper stepped behind the desk and took a seat. The wooden chair was so old, she feared it might crack under the weight of modernity. "You will do no such thing."

"I would say *watch me*, but you aren't here to do that, are you?"

Harper swept the hair from her eyes. "I realize you're upset—"

"You think?"

"And it was probably wrong of me to leave just a note and a check behind." Harper ran her hand along the edge of her vintage red sweater and noticed a gap in the seam. No matter—she could fix that later. The piece was one of her favorite recent finds, and a little tear was not going to stop her from wearing it. "But Lucy, you can't tell me that you wouldn't have tried to talk me out of it."

Lucy sighed. "You didn't give me the chance, did you? Besides, since when do you up and leave when things get difficult? Harper, you've been working toward this thing for years. Long before I met you. It's all you've ever wanted."

Harper would rather not discuss this further, but it seemed she had no choice at the moment. She hesitated. "And I have learned, after all these years, that sometimes we fail."

She imagined her roommate pacing back and forth through their kitchen as Lucy always did when confronted with a problem.

"So you're quitting."

"Not exactly." Harper tugged at the loose thread near the hole she'd found. *What if Lucy's right? Am I quitting?* "I'm stepping out into the harsh reality of the world, that's all. I'm not giving up my interest in vintage clothes or sewing. I'm just . . . personalizing it."

Yes, that was the best way to explain.

"Personalizing it? Give me a break, Harper. You've got a better eye for design than anyone I know. Surely you believe that."

"It's kind of you to say, but . . ." But she had already made herself look like a fool.

"So that's it, then?" Lucy waited.

"Friend, I'm out of options. It's time to start something new."

Harper fiddled with the knobs of the office desk and absentmindedly opened the drawer. A framed photograph inside caught her eye. When she took it out of the drawer, her heart stopped.

The man in the photo was achingly handsome. He wore a seersucker jacket over a pinned, chocolate-brown tie, and his neatly trimmed hair had that perfect *I'm not trying, I just woke up like this* vibe that could only be achieved with really expensive hair products. His jaw was tight, his eyes were kind, and his trimmed five o'clock shadow spelled trouble for all sorts of reasons.

But none of that was the reason her pulse was racing. The picture looked like the man she'd met in Charleston—the one who had purchased the space that once held an old dress shop.

She flipped over the photo, and her suspicions were confirmed. In scripted letters, the words *Peter—2012* were written.

Harper couldn't believe her eyes. Why would Millie have a picture of Peter?

"Lucy, I'm sorry. Something's come up," Harper said.

Millie's voice echoed down the hallway. Sounded like she was talking with a family who had just checked in.

Harper shoved the photo back inside the drawer and flew out of the office faster than a purple martin after a mosquito. She didn't want to get caught snooping.

Even after all the time they'd spent together over the years—mixing biscuit dough and straightening quilts and welcoming guests on the long front porch—Millie had never mentioned anything about her personal life. So why did she have a framed picture of this guy in her drawer? And why was he dressed like his outfit belonged in a different lifetime?

Harper pocketed her phone as she stepped out into the hall, and Millie turned, gesturing to the folks beside her.

"Harper, dear. Great timing. These are the Dickens, visiting us from chilly Iowa."

The young mother smiled, while her son waved. "Nice to meet you," the husband said.

Harper waved back to the little boy, hoping this family didn't sense her urgency to get rid of them and talk with Millie. "Pleasure is mine. Please let me know if there's any way I can make your stay extra memorable."

"Thank you." The woman put both hands on the young boy's shoulders. Millie's gaze lingered on the maternal gesture.

Harper's determination for answers skidded to a halt. Come to

85

think of it, Millie always paid extra care to the littlest visitors at the inn—offering coloring sheets and opportunities to bake cookies and even an old DVD collection of animated movies that were about twenty years from still being relevant, but it was sweet.

What if there was more to Millie's story? Did she have her own children? Grandchildren? Why would she have that picture of Peter?

"We'd better get to our room and freshen up." The woman patted her son's shoulders. "But it was nice meeting you, Harper."

"You as well." Harper offered the most welcoming smile she could manage, hoping the guests wouldn't notice her distraction.

Then they were gone, leaving Harper and Millie in the hallway together.

"Harper, are you okay?" Millie frowned. "You look as if you've seen a ghost."

Maybe I have.

Before she could respond, Millie started toward the door of Harper's bedroom. "Now, don't you get in a tizzy over it, but there's something I want to ask you about." Millie opened the door. The cottage decor of the room was true to the original style but also delightfully on trend.

The dress Harper had made for Senior Show was hanging from the closet handle, bold as a lighthouse in the middle of a storm. She opened her mouth, but words wouldn't come.

"How did you . . . where did you . . ." Harper just kept staring at the dress.

Millie pointed to the piece as if it stood on trial. "You made this, didn't you?"

Harper dropped her head and closed her eyes. She did not want to have this conversation right now. She sold that thing for a reason and didn't need it out in broad daylight. The rejection was still too fresh in her heart. Slowly, she nodded.

Millie closed the space between them and set both hands on

Harper's shoulders. At the touch, Harper met her affirming gaze. "You've really got something special."

Harper ran her tongue over her teeth to bite back her words. She had plenty of examples ready that would assure her own insufficiency. Her last days in college would attest to that.

She couldn't even manage to pass her capstone class. How did she ever dream she might manage an entire store?

But Millie would hush her if she admitted any of that, so she kept her explanation brief. "I appreciate the thought, Millie. Truly. But I tried that path, and it didn't work out."

Millie dropped her hands from Harper's shoulders and crossed her arms. "So you quit. Is that why you came here?"

Not waiting for a reply, Millie reached for the hanger and set the dress down on the bed. "Have you ever thought about shortening the sleeves?"

Harper tilted her head, studying the dress. "Actually, no, I hadn't . . ."

"Maybe raise the hem a little too. After all, this isn't Victorian England, is it?"

Harper's laugh was soft. "I suppose it's not."

"No matter. We all need adjustments, sweetheart."

Harper wasn't sure if "we" was supposed to mean the dresses or people generally, but she supposed the sentiment worked well either way.

Speaking of adjustments . . .

She started to ask Millie about the photograph, but her courage dwindled as Millie stepped closer to the bed and leaned over the gown. What if she'd stumbled upon something personal? Now was not the time to ask.

Millie picked up the dress to inspect it more closely. "Just as I thought. You've got a small tear here." She waved her free hand. "No matter. I can fix this up in no time."

Harper smiled and moved to stand beside the older woman. Side by side, they both studied the rip in the fabric and pieced the seam back. "I actually like your idea of shortening the sleeves. Maybe we could do that together."

Millie took her time handing back the dress. "Oh, don't look at me as if I'm going to keel over any minute and you've got to make a play for my fine china."

"Let's just get started on the sleeves, shall we? And besides, we both know your dishes came from Target." Harper started laughing. "Really though—how did you even know about this dress?"

Millie hesitated, her hands clutching the fabric, then looked toward Harper. "How would you feel about another houseguest?"

THIRTEEN

Mobile, Alabama, 1946

Steam puffed up from the engine as the train sputtered to a stop. The conductor announced their arrival in Alabama, and Franklin hopped from the passenger car. He set down Millie's carpetbag, then held out his hand to help Millie jump from the last step.

She hoped he didn't see her blush, for she wasn't accustomed to riding locomotives or taking a gentleman's hand—even if he was a freight hopper and just helping her for a moment. The whole thing felt like a dream rather than real life.

The dust and scrape of the tires against the rails stirred in Millie's nose, and she covered her sneeze with her free hand. For a moment, she wondered what Mama was doing right about now . . . but she stopped herself. Mama made her promise not to think thoughts like that. Wouldn't do nobody no good. So Millie looked up and scanned the small gathering of folks waiting to meet passengers. Then she put one hand to her hat to keep it from blowing off and glanced over at Franklin.

Hours ago, she had feared him. My, how things had turned around. Now, the planned part of her journey was over, and she had no idea where she was going next, save toward Fairhope. She'd been frettin' so much over the details of the train that she hadn't paid much mind to the obvious—what she would do after.

Millie was silent as she searched Franklin's expression. For what, she did not know. Strength, perhaps.

His voice softened with concern. "Don't worry, Red," he said. "We'll figure it out." And with that, he picked up her carpetbag once more. "The town you mentioned is a good place to start . . . for both of us."

Millie drew in a deep breath that pushed against the fitted waistline of her dress. "Seems as good a plan as any, I suppose." She tried not to let on how relieved she was that he'd be accompanying her. They had settled into an easy rhythm with one another, like friends rather than the strangers they actually were.

Franklin waved his hand. He walked over to the front of the station, to where the cars were parked. "Fairhope is a good ways from Mobile, so we'll have to drive."

Millie's eyes widened. "You're not planning to steal one of them?"

Franklin put one hand on his hip and leaned against a rusted white truck. "Now, do I look like that kind of man?" He washed her heart with relief, however short-lived, with his confident half grin. "For the record"—he lowered his voice—"I could hot-wire this thing in a pinch, but I'm no thief, Red. I answer to the Lord." His grin widened. "Besides, my mama would have a conniption if she ever caught wind."

"Young man, wha'dya think you're doin' leaning on this here truck?" a man said.

Franklin jumped, clearly startled. But when he got a hold of himself, he held out his hand toward the stranger. Millie was beginning to realize Franklin always had a plan. So what was he up to now?

"Fine truck you've got here, sir."

The burly man wore coveralls and puffed hand-rolled tobacco. "Worked mighty hard for it."

"Sure shows. What model is this thing?"

What followed in the next five minutes was more detail about vehicles, makes, and models than Millie ever wanted to know.

She nodded and smiled like a woman in these situations ought to, but inwardly breathed her relief when the conversation dwindled.

"Where y'all headed?" the man asked.

Millie put the dots together then. Oh no. This could *not* be Franklin's plan.

Please, God, do not let hitchhiking with this man be Franklin's—

"Fairhope." Franklin didn't miss a beat.

"You got yourself a ride?"

"No, sir," Franklin said. Millie fussed with her hat.

"I'm headin' east of Fairhope. Be glad to take y'all that way." And then, before they had a chance to so much as respond, he opened the bed of his truck for them to climb aboard.

Bless it! Millie wanted to say. She'd have to hitch up the skirt of her dress to even get in this thing. What was she, a head of cattle? She wasn't difficult to please, but goodness me. He couldn't have picked an actual car?

Franklin helped her into the back of the truck, settled in beside her, and set her bag down. Then he reached his arm over her shoulder and braced himself against the frame of the truck—a move she quickly realized would insulate her from being jarred around.

Two potholes and one sharp turn later, he seemed to read her thoughts. "Beggars can't be choosers." His charming grin made a reappearance. "I said I'd help you, Red. Didn't promise how. But I can promise you one thing. With me, you'll always have plenty enough adventure to go around."

You could say that again.

Millie had moxie. Franklin had seen enough of life to recognize it. A woman traveling by herself across the States? He had to respect her. But she was running from something. He'd noticed that too. She didn't keep a close enough watch on her bag and was too free with details about where she was going. Somebody could up and follow.

He'd learned these things the hard way, growin' up on the train with his mother. Who, in her own way, was maybe growin' up too.

But Millie watched him start that fire in Savannah while everybody else watched the ruckus.

And he couldn't get that out of his mind. Nobody had ever watched him before.

It's how he became so good at train jumping. Franklin was an expert when it came to being invisible. He looked over at Millie as the truck lurched down the bumpy road, then offered a smile. She was making the best of it. He had to hand it to her.

Franklin told himself he was helping her get settled safe and sound—it's what his mother would want him to do. But maybe it was the other way around, if he were being truthful. He suspected Millie might be helping him, seeing him, in a way he was not yet ready to admit.

She was also as beautiful as the dawn over the water.

Slowly, Millie shook her head. "You must think I'm foolish," she muttered under her breath. "Starting out on a new adventure with such a fragile plan and barely two pennies to rub together."

The road dipped, and he tightened his grip on her shoulder to keep her from falling into the cab of the truck.

"Not at all."

"Truly?" Her eyes widened.

"On the contrary, I was just thinking how brave you are. Traveling all this way alone."

She fidgeted with something in her pocket and studied him.

"What are you fiddlin' with?" he asked.

Millie pulled both hands out and opened her right fist to show a couple of buttons. She was quick to snap her fingers shut when the truck hit another pothole. Then she slipped her hands back into her pockets, the perfect covering for her treasure.

"You sew?" he asked.

"I do." There was something in her eyes, though, something akin to a haze.

"What aren't you telling me?" He didn't mean to prod, but her reaction left him curious.

"The buttons are my mama's."

She didn't say any more.

He knew the feeling. Didn't matter why she'd left home. The feeling was the same. Part of your heart, hollowed out.

"A gift." He nodded his understanding. Slid his hand into his own pocket and showed her the penny. "I always travel with my uncle's old coin for the same reason."

This seemed to open that invisible door between them.

"I want to own a dress shop," Millie blurted out. She looked him straight in the eye, the haze lifting as dawn pierced the fog.

He tugged at the back of his cap.

"You realize you're a woman, and a single one to boot."

"I do." She spoke the two words with the ease that comes from steady determination.

"So be it, then."

"You really think so?"

Franklin shifted slightly closer, getting her full attention. "Listen, Red. I'm of the mind that anybody can do anything if they work hard enough."

"Anybody?" She didn't so much as blink. "Women, and Blacks, and . . . well, you do mean anybody?"

"I'd be a hypocrite if I didn't." He brushed a piece of hair behind her ear. He didn't mean to reach out. It was an instinct, but it held a mighty grasp over him. And from the looks of it, her as well. She seemed to like him fine enough, at least.

"Look, why don't you let me help? A buddy of mine stayed at a boardinghouse in Fairhope once. Has views of Mobile Bay, and the people were real generous to him. We can go together, and I'll stay long enough to get you settled." Or longer, if she'd let him. He'd been growing weary from riding the rails, and she was the sort of woman he would gladly settle down with if the Lord allowed. "It's as good a place as any to get work, and I can send some money back to my mother."

"You would do that?" Her shoulders relaxed with her relief, and he was quite satisfied.

"I'd be happy to." He brushed a smear of rust from his trousers. He had the truck to thank for that.

"So we . . . what? Pretend we happened to arrive at the same time?" Millie straightened her collar as the truck began to rumble down a dirt road with huge oak trees on either side of the path.

"I think it'd be best if we give the appearance of being together. More sympathetic that way rather than two total strangers showin' up all at once."

"And I guess we aren't strangers, exactly." She looked into his eyes. "Not anymore, at least."

Franklin bit down on his bottom lip and adjusted his suspenders. Mercy, how he was already attracted to this woman. "No, Red, I guess we aren't."

FOURTEEN

Fairhope, Modern Day

Harper followed Millie through a hallway of open doors, each leading to another charming room with patterned wallpaper, eclectic light fixtures, and handmade quilts. Together they took the stairs toward Harper's favorite room of all—a loft with cathedral ceilings and windows overlooking Mobile Bay. The space looked like an English teacup had exploded, scattering the queen's rose garden all over the walls. And could there be a greater compliment than that? Harper liked to imagine if the room could speak, it would sound like Hugh Grant.

Harper trailed her hand along the stairwell. "Why are we going upstairs? What do you mean, another houseguest?" And when was Millie going to explain about the dress?

Millie reached the loft and turned to watch Harper take the last few steps. "I see your patience hasn't improved since you were a child and wanted first dibs on my sequined fabric."

Harper stood beside Millie and crossed her arms. "I was a lot more dedicated to my craft than any of those other kids."

"You keep that dedication, sweetheart." Millie thwacked Harper on the shoulder. The strength in her hands caught Harper off guard every time.

A clattering sound came from the closed door of the loft. Harper frowned. That was the only vacant room in the inn for the next few nights. "Millie, tell me you did not adopt that baby goat your friend told you about and put him *inside* the boardinghouse."

"First of all, I will have you know his name is Hank. And second, it's my inn, and I'll do as I like." Millie put both hands on her hips like a defiant teen.

"You had the new maid put the thing up here until you can get a shelter set up outside, didn't you? I already told you yesterday that was a bad idea . . ." Harper turned the door handle, ready to expose the baby goat adoption in progress.

But what she saw instead of Hank was a woman with silky blond hair, earth-toned makeup, and outstretched arms. Her laughter floated through the room and down the stairwell.

"Tada!" Lucy yelled. "You two were cracking me up, and I had the hardest time keeping quiet."

Harper's jaw dropped. "Lucy! What are you doing here?" Harper pulled her best friend into a tight hug. The smell of Lucy's coconut shampoo took Harper right back to their apartment in Savannah, but she determined not to let her mind wander. That chapter in her life was done now.

"I'm surprising you!" Lucy's grin was wide. She glanced over toward Millie. "Please tell me that whole baby goat thing is an option because I'm all over it," Lucy snapped, and her eyes widened with a new idea. "We could make goat's milk soap for the inn!"

"What a charming idea." Millie shook her pointed finger toward Lucy and looked at Harper. "I like her. You keep good friends."

"We all know we are not making our own goat's milk soap. And even if any of us *did* know how, do you really think one goat is going to provide enough milk to supply the entire boardinghouse? Imagine how tiny those soaps would have to be. Maybe we could mold them into miniature goats. Miniature goats are a thing, right?" Harper laughed freely—her joy, as joy is prone to doing, had snuck up on her. Even though she hadn't been at the boardinghouse long, her heart was finding healing here. Her dreams might be another story, but maybe that too would come in time.

Then a thought occurred. "Wait a second." She turned toward Lucy. "Did you just call me from upstairs?"

Lucy beamed, clearly proud of herself. "Sure did. I'm surprised you didn't hear the echo." She'd been too busy drooling over that picture of Peter to notice anything else . . .

Harper pivoted on her polka-dot heels toward Millie. "So this is how you got the dress? Lucy brought it."

"You've been reading a lot of Sherlock Holmes lately, haven't you?" Millie moved to stand beside Lucy. "Jokes aside, you've got a great friend here, Harper. Lucy tracked me down through your dad yesterday and called the boardinghouse."

Harper shook her head. "I don't understand. How did you know about my dress?"

"You're kidding, right?" Lucy raised one perfectly plucked eyebrow. "Harper, you're pretty predictable."

Relief washed over her in unexpected waves. Despite her rash choice to leave the dress behind, she was covered by her sweet friend's understanding. And as much as she hated to admit it—as adamant as she'd been that selling the dress had been the right decision—Lucy was right. That dress was still important, even if it represented the end of a youthful dream.

When the shock had worn off, Lucy reached for Harper and engulfed her in another hug. "Just be glad no one had bought that thing yet. The store owner told me multiple people tried it on."

"Really?" Well, that was flattering. And surprising.

"Really." Lucy responded as if this information should be obvious. "I've been telling you all along, Harper, that it's a beautiful piece. Why do you think I went looking for it before driving down here? I knew someday you would think back and see what the sting of disappointment has blinded you to now. You have a gift." Lucy simply smiled.

She said it with so much conviction, Harper almost believed her. But of course Lucy would say that. Lucy was an eternal optimist who saw beauty in everything.

Still, Harper was thankful for a friend who valued her dreams.

Millie straightened her red cloche. "I'm going to check on the guests downstairs and give you two a chance to catch up."

Thank you, Harper mouthed, and she knew Millie would understand she meant *for hiding my best friend and letting her stay here.* She had no doubt Millie was charging Lucy less than the regular rate, if anything at all.

Lucy waved Harper into the room and started toward the cushioned window seat with a giddy skip. The reality that her friend had searched for the dress and driven all this way sunk deep into her heart, like a seed planted into rich soil. And the comfort she found in that resonated deeply, despite the ache of her recent disappointment.

"Catch me up on what I missed since I left Savannah."

Lucy took a seat and hugged a floral pillow to her chest. "Things are going well. I had dinner with Declan, who, as it turns out, is not the one for me."

Harper sat on the other side of the window seat and chuckled. "Sorry to hear that."

"But he *did* tell me more about that guy you met, Peter."

Harper sat up straighter. "Go on . . ."

"Apparently, there are some buttons or a satchel or—I don't know, I wasn't following all of it—but the point is, Peter found something he believes once belonged to his mother. Clues."

"About the missing box he was looking for?" The framed image of him dressed like he was ready to attend a charity dinner— looking good enough to model for a charity *calendar*—flashed through Harper's mind. She cleared her throat.

"Yeah. Declan said he's doing historian things to figure it out."

"Historian things?" Harper reached for the handmade wooden train that Millie kept on the windowsill. She took it by the engine car and trailed it back and forth. No telling who made this thing or the little hands that once played with it.

"He's a historian and does walking tours—did he mention it to you when y'all talked back in Charleston?" Lucy must've had an eyelash in her eye because she swiped at her lashes. "I think he uses his history specialization to flip and rent out old houses. He also rescues old stuff and calls it something clever . . . architectural salvage? Is that a real thing?"

Harper looked through the windows as three pelicans flew over the bay. The pelicans dipped down, one by one, scooping water from the bay into their large beaks until a fish jumped. Harper looked away from the window and met her friend's questioning gaze. "Sounds like a real thing to me."

Only problem was, Harper couldn't go there and tell Peter what happened at the Senior Show. Their conversation in Charleston had enchanted her—filled her with longing and flutters of excitement for what could happen next—but that dream was gone now, and she had no reason to rent the shop from him.

She turned her attention back to the window just in the nick of time to see one of the pelicans grab a fish that was a little too big for its bill. At first, the pelican tried to flop the fish into the air and try again, but the fish just kept getting stuck. Finally, the poor little pelican gave up and set the fish back into the water.

Harper felt for him. Because she understood as well as anybody how it felt to have a dream that had simply and unceremoniously gotten stuck.

FIFTEEN

Fairhope, 1946

Franklin reached for Millie's hand to help her from the bed of the truck. She tried to maintain as much dignity as she could while crawling out of the thing, but Lord knew that was good near impossible.

A chorus of some kind of bug—like a cricket, only louder—grew with a timber Millie had never known back in Charleston. "What *is* that?" she asked Franklin.

"Dog-day cicadas. They come out every five years or so. Make a beautiful racket, though they'll scare the wits out of you if you ever see 'em up close."

Millie liked to think she wasn't particularly fussy, but she knew a little about cicadas, how they hid underground until the time was right years upon years later, and she had no desire to see one up close. As far as she was concerned, they could hum their song from the branches of the oaks.

Once Millie's feet hit the gravel, she straightened her dress and her hat. Absentmindedly, she slipped her hands into her pockets to check for the buttons.

The driver leaned out the open window of the truck. "Need any help?"

"No, sir." Franklin walked over toward him and shook the man's hand. "Thank you again."

"You kids take care of yourselves. And congratulations." He waved once and then drove off.

"Congratulations?" Millie murmured to herself, frowning.

Franklin carried her carpetbag toward the front door. "Look at us, Red." He shrugged. "The guy thinks we're hitched."

Millie's eyes widened. To keep Franklin from noticing her fluster, she turned her head toward the boardinghouse. But the view just behind it nearly knocked her senseless. Sunlight glittered over Mobile Bay, and large oaks with sprawling limbs stretched toward the water and the heavens all at one time. Who could blame them?

"My, my." She breathed the sweet air deeply. Gardenias, if she wasn't mistaken. She once had a gardenia bush back at home, and sometimes when it was blooming, she'd crack open her bedroom window to get whiffs of the smell all night, then wake up sweaty because gardenias always bloomed in May, except every so often, when a deep-summer flower would bloom well past its season.

Funny how memories could be.

"Beautiful place, isn't it?" Franklin started up the stairs of the wide porch, fitted for somebody living an entirely different type of life than Millie. But it sure was stunning. Had she said that already?

Millie took her time climbing the steps, allowing her hand to fall softly and graze the wooden porch rail. For a fleeting moment, she felt as if she were royalty, and the steps were air.

"It's like a dream." She stood beside Franklin. He opened the screen door, but before he could knock, a June bug buzzed past them, having escaped the space between doors.

Millie shrieked. "Is it a cicada?"

Franklin folded his lips, no doubt hiding a grin. "What am I going to do with you? Nothin' but a harmless June bug."

"It buzzed at me." She pretended to play coy but couldn't contain her giggles. Truthfully, with its loud warning sound, she'd thought the bug a much more menacing creature than it turned out to be.

Millie heard shuffling from the other side of the door. Franklin must have heard it too, because they both went rigid, waiting.

An older woman opened the door and smiled. She was plain, really, but still beautiful, and had a kindness in her eyes, a gentleness in the slight bend of her sloped shoulders, as if she had spent many a night with a needle and thread and a candle for company.

"May I help you?"

Franklin spoke up. "We just came in on the train from Charleston, ma'am."

The woman waved her hand. "First things first, I never let anyone call me ma'am. Makes me feel like an old woman. Understood?"

Franklin nodded. "Yes . . . yes."

She took a closer look at them. "Why don't you two come inside, and let's get you comfortable."

Several minutes later, they were seated on the velvet settee beneath the entryway chandelier, across the way from a large radio. Seemed to be the sitting room, from what Millie could tell, and she supposed this was where they served tea and that sort of thing. She hoped the rest of the place wasn't nearly so fancy, or she would be a nervous wreck.

"We haven't much money but heard this is a generous place for folks who are down on their luck." Franklin wrung his hands and took a visible breath. In that moment, in that expression, he looked as if he belonged somewhere on King Street rather than as a hobo riding the rails. Millie saw it in him and knew, somehow and against all logic, he could become whatever he wanted to be.

The innkeeper watched them, her gaze moving from Franklin to Millie, then back again. Millie froze under the scrutiny, her hands in her pockets with the buttons, not quite sure what to do with herself.

"Why, you two don't look much older than children." The woman hesitated. "You do honest work?"

They both nodded. Honest? Yes. What kind of work would still have to be determined. But it seemed as good an opportunity as any for the time being.

"Let me explain my situation." The slender woman raised her delicate shoulders. "My husband has recently passed, and I could use some help around the place. We have many tenants, but some folks can't afford to pay much." She straightened the little cat-shaped pin at her collar. "And I can't afford to send them away, not knowin' if they'll have food or shelter. Especially the grief-stricken young women who've lost husbands to the war. Seems everybody knows somebody like that nowadays. Anyhow, what I mean to say is if you two will agree to work daily—and it will be honest work—you can stay in a room free of charge for a while. I've only one room left."

"Oh, but we're not—" Millie started to point between herself and Franklin, but his glare stunned her clear into silence.

"We would be most grateful," he said.

The woman reached out her hand. "I'm Eloise Stevens, by the way. For better or worse, I own this establishment." She looked up to the ceiling then down to the wooden floors. "But the boarding-house has been good to me. It really has. You'll get room and board and a little stipend. Not much, but enough to start a mea-ger savings or to send back home if you've got somebody there in need."

Franklin and Millie took turns shaking Mrs. Stevens's hand and followed her toward the hallway. She reached for a key hanging from a tall rack.

Millie started down the hallway, but the woman called out. "Just a minute, honey."

She pivoted to find Mrs. Stevens pointing toward the back door. "Your room is actually detached from the rest of the house. Though modest in size, the little porch shows a mighty nice view of the sunset over Mobile Bay." She dropped the key into Franklin's hand. "The honeymoon suite," she added with a smile.

The *what*?

The next four months brought a new sort of rhythm. And though Millie was no closer to owning her dress shop, she was a lot closer to something else she had always wanted—having a best friend. And she'd found that from the first day she'd spent with the train jumper.

Franklin, as it turned out, was a class act. He had been a gentleman about the sleeping arrangements, going so far as to sleep on the floor while Millie took the bed to herself, night after night. Last month he was sick, and when she insisted he sleep in the bed beside her, he set two well-placed pillows between them. She suspected this was his way of honoring what little virtue she had left after continuing on with this marriage charade. Not that she had lied . . . per se. No one had asked about their marriage outright, after all. And say Mrs. Stevens questioned them—then of course Millie would admit the truth.

But Mrs. Stevens hadn't. No one had. And so the guise continued. Because, as Franklin was always saying, "These are hard times." First the economic depression and then the war. What other boardinghouse would waive the nightly payment in exchange for help? One dared not look a gift horse in the mouth, after all.

And so here they were. The boardinghouse was unusually busy on account of the holidays. Millie watched Franklin hang garland from the fireplace. The two of them had been buzzing this way and that in preparation for the Christmas party tonight, sweeping the front porch and pulling cinnamon tarts from the oven.

Families and singles alike were staying for the holiday. Millie found most of them pleasant enough, keeping to themselves, except for the incorrigible Mr. Danes. She had been eagerly awaiting his checkout date. The man hadn't so much as nodded to acknowledge her presence. But Millie hadn't the energy to worry over it. He'd be gone soon enough.

Mrs. Stevens had given Millie an early Christmas gift—some money with which to buy fabric for a party outfit. Day and night for two whole weeks, Millie had dreamed up what to sew. Finally, she decided on a red and green floral fabric that she ruched at the bust, with a full skirt and a trail of buttons along the neckline.

And of course, her favorite cloche. She never went anywhere without it.

She'd used the last of her money on the fancy buttons, so she had to wear her scuffed-up black Mary Janes. But the goal, of course, was that the guests might be so enraptured by her dress they wouldn't notice her shoes.

And by *guests*, of course she meant Franklin.

Two hours later, everyone had eaten their fill, and Mrs. Stevens played her new Benny Goodman record for anyone who wanted to dance.

Franklin wore suspenders, the new hat Mrs. Stevens had given him, and a grin that warmed Millie more thoroughly than the crackling fire beside them. He held out his hand. "Want to dance?"

He knew he needn't ask. Millie had been less than subtle in expressing how perfect the skirt of her dress might be for dancing. A girl only got the opportunity to dress as a princess once in a blue moon, and Millie had every intention of enjoying her moon before it passed.

The vibrant beat of "Sing, Sing, Sing" began, and Franklin rock-stepped so fast, he'd do his Charleston family proud. If only his mama could see him now. Of course, it could be years before he saw the woman again. At least the letter last week said she was doing okay, thanks in no small part to the checks he'd been sending.

Their plan to work at the boardinghouse for a few weeks had turned into more weeks, with no end date in sight. And Millie wasn't complaining a bit. She had a feeling she was going to be okay. That they were all were, eventually.

Franklin spun Millie around so fast, she was glad she could trust the soles of her Mary Janes over a slick pair of evening heels. He held tight to her hands and moved her arm over her head, nearly knocking her hat clear off. The next thing Millie knew, they were side by side, the waist of her skirt touching the seam of his white button-down.

She had never been so close to him, not in four months, and she didn't entirely dislike it. He smelled of the same soap she used, and the wood he had chopped for the fire, and a little bit like coffee, and she was entranced by the kick-kick-kick, rock-step pattern of his feet as he led her around.

She didn't know where he had learned to dance like that, but for a few moments, Millie found herself suspended between the past and the future, skipping her way through the dance. Her skirt spun, his eyes twinkled by the firelight, and she laughed in freedom, unafraid of what might come. Laughed as a woman having her blue moon moment.

The music ended as abruptly as the enchanting dance had begun, and Franklin dipped her low to the ground. Millie's arms sprawled toward her hat, trying to reach it before gravity did its work on her hat pins. She scarcely caught it in time. Her heart continued spinning though the music had ended, and she longed for another dance.

But when Franklin righted her feet back on the sturdy floor, his form was not the first to come into her vision.

Instead, Everett Danes stood steadfast, a little too close for comfort. He extended his hand toward Millie, but it was Franklin to whom he directed his words.

"Mind if I cut in?"

As if Franklin were the one to mind.

Millie stifled her inner *hmmph*, for she was always remembering her mama's words: *"We don't want nobody asking questions."* The phrase had become a mantra Millie used regularly to subdue her own behavior, responses to men like Everett Danes, who seemed to think that the women of the world hadn't brains by which they might be capable of any sort of decision making.

Franklin reached for both of her hands to fill them before Everett could. "My apologies," he said. "But I'm afraid this beautiful woman has promised the next dance to my two left feet."

Relief came over Millie, and she hoped Franklin could sense it in their touch.

But Everett didn't budge. "You mean to say she's your wife, then?" He straightened his bow tie as a teasing grin slipped up his otherwise handsome mouth. "Funny how the little lady doesn't have a ring."

Millie stilled.

Why had she thought their pretend marriage was safely hidden away at the boardinghouse? And why did it have to shatter on this magical evening, of all evenings?

Mrs. Stevens watched from a couple of steps away. A solemn expression washed her warm features, and she stepped forward when she saw the look of panic on Franklin's face.

"Mr. Danes," she said, calm and yet stern, a combination to which she held unique mastery. "Miss Sarah is looking mighty lonesome over by the piano. I trust a dance with you would provide the remedy, yes?"

Everett turned his attention from Franklin toward Mrs. Stevens. He hesitated a long moment, and Millie held her breath as he did.

"Yes, ma'am." In a snap, he was gone. Millie could breathe once more.

But the subject was not over.

"Follow me." Mrs. Stevens took Millie by the hand, but the command was clearly meant for Franklin too. She ushered them both into the dining room.

Mrs. Stevens wrung her hands, then pressed them against the shimmering fabric of her dress. When she finally did speak, her voice was hushed. "I don't mean to be a busybody, but . . . well, it's true, isn't it? You two aren't married. I've long wondered about the rings but just assumed you didn't have the money for somethin' like that."

Millie's stomach turned with emotion—anxiety and panic and even a little relief the secret was out. So much emotion, she felt sick.

"Obviously y'all love each other. Some couples have been married twenty years and don't look at each other the way you two do." The woman shook her head, deep lines now etched upon her forehead. Millie tried to read the space between words, the space between her frown and furrowed brows. She didn't like what she saw. "But if you're not married, I can't allow the two of you to continue sharing a room."

In desperation, Millie looked to Franklin. The roar of the ocean tide splashed from his silent eyes. He was sad. Just as sad as her. And he didn't know what to do, either. She could tell from the way he blinked as his eyes searched her own. She had never seen such a quiet plea. Both of them looking for answers from the other but finding none. Yet he centered her with the strength of his gaze, and he became the current she wanted to follow.

And she realized in that moment, she had to come up with something because she couldn't live without Franklin, plain and simple.

"Now, understand—I've come to love you both dearly these last few months, and it'd break my heart to think about you on the street. So here's my proposal." Mrs. Stevens's gaze was gentle yet stern as she looked back and forth between them. "I'll see the two of you married. I'll help with the arrangements. We'll have a nice little ceremony out back, overlooking the bay. Make an honest couple out of you."

Okay, Millie was definitely going to be sick now.

"What do you say about your boarding here?"

Millie looked over at Franklin, who slid his hands into the pockets of his trousers and gave her that same half grin she was getting used to now, but what was more, she was even beginning to like a little.

Maybe a lot.

How could he be smiling at her as if he were actually considering the idea!

Not that a marriage of convenience was an entirely new convention. It happened all around the world, for more histories and cultures than not. And Franklin was pleasant enough. Handsome enough. Kind enough.

What's more, he would support her in her dream to open the dress shop.

And he wouldn't ask any questions about her past. She could tell that much about him. She wouldn't have to risk the deception of falling in love with any ordinary white man, or falling in love with any ordinary Black one, for that matter.

Of course she wanted to find someone she could share all her secrets with, her pride of her mother's heritage and her father's heritage as well. But Mama had made it very clear that could never happen.

If she married Franklin, Millie wouldn't have to risk falling in love at all. And perhaps . . . yes, perhaps this was an opportunity she'd not yet considered. A partner who would also be her friend.

This way would be safest for everyone.

Their chances of finding another sympathetic innkeeper or even grocer were next to none, especially given the measly amount of change in her carpetbag. She could probably buy a dinner roll with that much.

They were out of options. *She* was out of options. She could try to get back to Charleston, but with what money, and to what end besides a reunion with Mama?

Millie imagined the arrangement would benefit Franklin and his own mother for the same reasons.

It was radical, yes, but also practical.

"You're shivering," Franklin said. He rubbed her arms with his hands. "It'll be all right, Red. Let's think this through. It could be an option for us."

Millie inched closer to Franklin and whispered. "You mean it?"

He touched the tip of his thumb to her chin and lifted her face closer to his own until their eyes met. "This arrangement could help us both. I could send money back to my mother, and support you—your sewing and all." If it were possible, he looked even deeper into her eyes. His lips moved in a quiet whisper, inches away from her own. "Let's be clear, Red. I don't have any expectation beyond that."

Millie caught another whiff of his coffee smell mixed with dirt from the rose garden. She blinked, and the kitchen candles glimmered down, and for some inexplicable reason, it was magic.

"Take the adventure with me? Say you'll consider it, at least. Sleep on it." He swept his thumb from her chin to her shoulders.

And before she could consider the why or the how or even the possibilities, the simple word—*yes*—was all she could think.

Still, she needed time to mull it over.

Tomorrow. Tomorrow she would give Franklin an answer.

SIXTEEN

Fairhope, Modern Day
One Month Later

Having just finished tidying all the guest rooms, Harper slid the lemon cake into the oven and made herself a cup of tea. She took the warm mug to the back porch, where a strong breeze at the right angle carried the scent of magnolia blooms.

Millie would give her a lecture if she caught Harper looking at her phone instead of breathing in the view, but Millie was taking an afternoon nap, and, after all, there was only so much breathing a person could do.

She tapped an app to see if she had any notifications and discovered a new message from Lucy, who had gone back to Savannah three weeks ago.

The message contained a screenshot from Peter's social media account. Harper held the phone closer. His hair curled at the edges just above his ears, and his eyes—

She blinked. She had no business staring into his eyes.

He looked different in this picture than in the one she'd found inside Millie's drawer, less classically handsome but in a way, more attractive. Almost as if he had traded the rules of how he was supposed to dress for simply being himself. She wondered about the story behind the transformation.

Lucy's message read, "This guy is right up your alley. Look what he said about his mother."

Harper mumbled as she read the text from the screenshots. *"Made some progress today in the search. I became a historian because after my mother died, I had some gaps in my own family history, which gave me a desire to find the gaps in other histories as well. After years of searching, I finally found something.*

"These heirlooms. An embroidered satchel signed M.M. and a wedding dress my mother wore when she married my father. The dress is old, and I have to wonder if it once belonged to my grandmother. Maybe my grandmother's still alive. If she is, I want to find her. Find her story. And discover the story behind the satchel as well. In the meantime, here's to all the other untold stories."

Harper hesitated.

A wedding dress? Something about that detail grabbed her, shook her, and wouldn't let go. She thought of the photograph that she never did have the courage to ask Millie about. She'd been too worried she'd stumbled across something that might make Millie uncomfortable, especially given the way Millie had avoided any and all conversations about the past.

But what if the letters M.M. stood for . . .

Harper's blood ran cold, despite the warmth of her tea and the summer air.

It was a shot in the dark, but the possibility of the connection screamed to be known—above the calm coo of the birds and the swoop of the pelican above the bay.

What if his grandmother was her Millie? The quirky old woman with a smile like the sun and a penchant for changing the subject any time Harper asked about her family. That woman had a secret. A photo of Peter.

Harper set down her teacup. She needed to wake Millie up.

Harper was careful to rap gently against the bedroom door. She didn't want to startle Millie. After a moment's hesitation, Millie appeared, wearing fuzzy slippers and a silk robe over her nightgown.

Millie glared at her. "Why did you interrupt my nap?"

Harper whipped her phone from her back pocket.

Millie frowned, narrowing her eyes. "You know I hate those contraptions."

"You might change your mind." Harper took Millie's arm and led her to the antique settee positioned by the bay window of Millie's bedroom. Millie called the place the honeymoon suite.

"Why are you guiding me by the elbow as if I am a child?" Millie swatted Harper's arm and sat down on her own accord.

"Because you need to sit for this." Harper brushed the velvet of the sofa and took a seat herself. She opened Lucy's message so Peter's smile filled the screen.

Then she watched Millie's expression shift from indifference to something else entirely. Recognition, perhaps? Longing? The expression was so strong, Harper could almost feel it in her own heart.

"I know your feelings about the Internet, and I know I was snooping, but several weeks ago, I found a photo of Peter in your drawer. I never had the gumption to bring it up, but now I feel like I have to." Harper inched closer. "Millie, is Peter related to you?" The question hung in the air. "Is he your grandson?"

Millie gripped the fabric of her seat. Her wrinkled hands moved to cover her mouth. Slowly, Millie nodded. "Yes."

Harper couldn't believe this. Her stomach leapt for Peter's sake, knowing how happy this news could make him. She couldn't believe she'd been right about the connection between them.

But as Harper reached out to brush Millie's shoulder, she noticed the far-off look in Millie's eyes. Was stirring all this up a good idea? She hadn't meant to traumatize Millie. But Peter was searching far and wide for answers and wanted to know her. Surely she'd done right by showing Millie. Surely Millie would want to know what he was doing.

"He still lives in Charleston?"

"He does." Harper clasped the strand of pearls at her neck. A ginger candle—*such* a fire hazard to use at naptime—flickered from across the room on Millie's nightstand. She kept watching it ebb and wane and spark, casting shadows against the wall until finally, she broke the silence. "May I ask you something? If the two of you know one another, why do you think it hasn't occurred to him the initials on the satchel are yours?"

Millie's eyes met Harper's above her trembling hands. "Because he believes I'm a white friend of his mother's, and no doubt imagines the woman who did the embroidery on the satchel to have a darker skin tone."

"Millie." Harper couldn't believe what she was hearing. "Surely you don't think your heritage is something to hide? Because from the little I know of Peter, he strikes me as the kind of person who'd want to know about all aspects of your story."

Millie shook her head. "No, you misunderstand. He doesn't know . . ." Her voice trailed off. "He doesn't know about the half of my heart that I had to leave behind."

Harper's heart ached at the tears forming in Millie's eyes. "Why don't you tell him, then?"

"I couldn't just show up on his doorstep and admit who I am." Millie's voice warbled, and she looked down into her open hands. "Not after all this time." She shook her head. "No, it wouldn't be the proper way to do things."

What Millie meant was *I'm terrified*, and they both knew it.

Harper moved closer and took Millie's hands in her own. "Believe it or not, I considered renting space in an old building from him to use as a dress shop."

Millie seemed lost in another world. "A dress shop, did you say?"

Harper took her time with her reply. "I could drive you there and tell him I'd like to see the space once more. That would give us a reason to meet up. Then, after a nice dinner and maybe some tea, you can ease him into the news that his grandmother can probably beat him at chess, movie trivia, and gardening."

"Harper, sweetheart, one does not 'beat' another person at gardening." She hesitated. The beginnings of a smile—whether sad or happy, Harper wasn't sure yet—pulled at the corners of Millie's painted lips, deepening the well-formed wrinkles like parentheses around her grin.

"Do you think Peter will believe it? That we're starting a store?" Harper asked.

"Of course he will." Millie turned a ring 'round and 'round her finger. "He knows I'm a trained seamstress, after all."

"Perkins Salvage. How may I help you?" Peter leaned back in his office chair and propped his feet on the desk in front of him. A stack of papers fluttered down. *Note to self*—it was way past time to clean his desk.

"Hi! This is Harper. We met several weeks ago. I'm calling about the space you have for rent."

His heart shot up in his chest. This was the moment he'd been waiting for. He'd all but given up it was coming. "Harper, yeah. Of course." *Play it cool.* Peter kicked his feet back down on the ground. "The apartment or the store?"

Harper hesitated. "Both. The loft is a short-term rental, right?"

Peter didn't know what made him more excited, the prospect of renting the space or of seeing Harper again. "Sure is. I was able to keep some really cool details from the original architecture. Windows and bookshelves and that kind of thing. It'll also be furnished. You'll be the first tenant." Did that sound desperate?

"Actually, *we'll* be the first tenants." Harper hesitated. "I'm traveling with an elderly friend of mine, so the two of us will be renting it together."

"Is she any trouble?" Peter joked.

"Only if you hate watching old movies. I've personally seen *Sabrina* fifteen times."

A pencil began to roll from the desk, and Peter caught it with his free hand. "Well, considering the tenant in one of my other properties spends his free time making audition videos for reality TV shows, I think I can handle it."

Harper laughed. The sound was more melodic than he'd remembered.

So Harper—beautiful Harper—was coming here at last. He tapped the pencil against his desk. "As long as we're talking the Bogie version."

"Of course we're talking Bogie. Is there anything else?"

Peter grinned. "As you know, the space downstairs needs some sprucing. Cosmetic, mostly. But it was abandoned a while and pretty badly neglected. I've been working hard on it, and it's storefront-ready, but you will want to do some polishing of your own." Peter swiveled in his chair. "Are you still interested?"

"I'm always up for a challenge," Harper said. "Though there is one more thing I should mention."

So long as it had nothing to do with his tie the night they met.

"Oh yeah?" he asked.

"Turns out, I'm practically a friend of your family."

Please tell me she's not a second cousin I never knew about.

"You don't say?" Outside the window, a couple hurried across King Street.

"I'm originally from Fairhope, Alabama," Harper added. She seemed to be waiting for him to connect the dots.

"But Fairhope is where Millie's from. Tell me you're not talking about Aunt Millie!"

Just when he thought Harper's arrival couldn't get any better, she was bringing along his favorite aunt? Well, honorary aunt, at least.

"Sure am. She said she's always dreamed of owning a dress store and wants to do this with me. She also said she thinks it'll be—and

I quote—a 'real hoot' to see you. Apparently, you haven't visited her as much as she'd like."

Peter chuckled. If it were up to Millie, he'd be living in Fairhope rather than South Carolina. "Please tell her I can't wait to see her and that she'd better be prepared to make me a batch of her biscuits. Can't find any like hers in the entire city of Charleston." He reached for a small notepad. "Tell you what—since it's Millie, I'll give y'all the first three weeks on the loft for free while you set up the storefront."

"Wow." Harper hesitated. "Are you sure? That's very generous."

"Absolutely. That woman is like family to me." Peter pinned his phone between his ear and shoulder while he scribbled down the specifics Harper gave about their arrival. "In fact, why don't you both plan to stay in the loft for a few days regardless of what you decide about the store? That way I can catch up with Millie."

"Sounds wonderful. So I guess I'll talk with you next week," she said.

"If not before." Peter grimaced and hit the palm of his hand to his forehead. Why did he have to say that? How was he going to spend all this time around the woman without acting a fool? Maybe she would be less enchanting than he remembered. But he doubted it. He would have to do his best to keep things professional. If he didn't, and Millie caught wind, he'd never hear the end of it.

Peter hung up the phone and caught himself humming "As Time Goes By" from *Casablanca*. He leaned toward his computer, ready to do some market research on the antique tiles he'd pulled up yesterday, and noticed a pristine envelope lying on the stack of papers that had fallen. Somehow, he must've missed this envelope when he got the mail earlier.

He shimmied his index finger under the flap and pulled out the letter.

Then the envelope fell from his hands.

Code enforcement?!

His eyes flew over the words, only able to process bits and pieces.

Thirty days to correct. Major electrical violations. Discovered in the wall adjacent to the neighboring building. Mechanical and plumbing violations also discovered.

Well, wasn't that great?

He'd just come into some money on one of his rental properties, but enough to rewire his side of the building? In a way that was up to code on the oh-so-regulated side of King Street? Hardly.

He just *had* to go and buy this property to save it from demolition, didn't he?

Peter groaned and ran his hand through his hair. What was he going to do now?

SEVENTEEN

Fairhope, 1946

The next morning, Millie was in the garden pulling weeds when Franklin returned from town. In place of the formal gown she showed off last night, she wore her faded day dress, which pulled a little at the seams.

Yet the air between them still jumped with the beat of "Sing, Sing, Sing," and it was everything Millie could do to pretend her growing feelings toward him were nothing.

Franklin carried several heaping sacks of flour over his shoulders. All the bags featured the same floral percale Millie wanted. She grinned up at him as he set the sacks down.

"I'll have you know, I had to lug whole stacks of these things around to get all the prints matching. The salesman gave me a time. Said he's thrilled packaging is changing to paper sacks 'cause he won't have to help customers match flowers much longer."

Millie laughed, imagining Franklin's relentless pursuit for the print she'd requested. "Your hard work will pay off when I wash 'em and make a new day dress out of the fabric. Just think what I'd look like wearing four different prints at once."

"I think you'd still be pretty as a peach." Franklin winked. He was such a troublemaker sometimes. "Red, might as well tell you now. I've been saving up to take you out to that theater they've got in town."

Millie's heart skipped. The prospect of a true-to-life date with Franklin stirred her nerves even more than the thought of a marriage to him.

She knew the reason why. But she could not admit it.

"Theater?" she mumbled.

"Magnet Theater, it's called. I met a real nice guy a couple weeks ago who works at Clay City Tile and built the construction materials for the place. He says it's something."

Something, all right.

"I have always wanted to go to the theater . . ." Millie looked down at her day dress. "Of course, I'll need to change."

"Wait—" Franklin caught her by the elbow. "You mean to tell me you've never been to the movies before?"

She froze, even as a little orange butterfly fluttered about the flowers.

Would he suspect her reason? How her upbringing and her mama's skin color factored into the equation?

Franklin released her arm and grinned. Millie's breath instantly eased. He'd been teasing. Of course he was teasing.

Still, she'd been wondering lately if she should tell him. Mama would hate it, of course. But Mama hadn't met Franklin.

Millie could trust him. She was nearly sure of it.

And it sure would certainly make things easier. The thought of getting hitched without him knowing the truth . . .

"Really haven't seen a movie on the big screen, have you?" Franklin watched her. "That's okay, Red. Nothin' to be embarrassed by. Times have been hard for everybody." He slipped his hands into his pockets, and he rose slightly from the heels of his loafers. "Nevertheless, I'd be honored to take you." His grin softened the promise, and she caught her heart before it grew wings and floated away like the butterfly.

Two hours later, Franklin parked Mrs. Stevens's car on Church Street and straightened his suspenders as Millie traipsed under the strong arms of a sprawling oak tree. She caught herself wondering what that tree might look like in a century.

"We're here." Franklin gently touched the back of Millie's freshly pressed floral dress, and she startled.

"Little jumpy, aren't we?" He grinned from ear to ear. "I promise you, Red, you'll love this place."

If he only knew the truth. That Millie was terrified someone might look too closely and see the brown rim between the whites of her green eyes.

"What's the movie called?" She hadn't thought to ask before. It hadn't mattered.

"*Notorious.*" Franklin walked up to a vendor selling popcorn and pressed a coin into the young man's palm, then took the heaping bag into his own hands. The smell of butter and fresh popcorn drifted toward Millie as she and Franklin entered the theater and found two seats together.

"Why are there so many people here?" she asked.

Franklin took a handful of popcorn from the bag. "Because we're talkin' about Cary Grant and Ingrid Bergman directed by Alfred Hitchcock. What else could you ask for?"

Millie began to chuckle. She had a lot to learn.

Franklin settled back in his chair. "She was great in *Casablanca.*" He caught Millie's gaze and pointed to emphasize his statement. "Mark my words. Someday, folks are gonna look back and say she was one of the greatest actresses that ever lived."

"Oh, are they?" Millie shifted in her seat to face him, crossing her legs at the ankles. "And you know this because . . ." Millie's cloche tipped catty-corner from where it sat on her head.

Franklin reached out to gently right it. "I recognize a gem when I see one."

Millie's heart beat so fast that she hoped Franklin didn't notice the pace of her breathing. She blinked repeatedly, wishing her eyes would adjust to the dimming lights of the theater so she could see him more clearly.

It was then that she knew.

She was going to marry this man.

And there was a great likelihood they would actually be wildly happy.

"None of my family married for love." He reached for another small handful of popcorn, then turned toward her. "What about yours?"

"Just my mama, and that didn't end well for her." Well, as "married" as they could be, considering it was against the law. They did find a preacher, though, who helped 'em say vows. Millie shook her head, hoping he wouldn't ask for details.

"It's not such a crazy idea, you know."

"What's that?" But she knew. She knew as her pulse sent her blood pushing through her veins.

"Marrying for reasons other than love." He watched her as if this were the most diplomatic, natural discussion in the world.

The projector flickered on. God bless that dear projector. Millie willed herself to breathe, willed herself to look straight ahead at the movie while she tried to think of something to say in response. Franklin, for all intents and purposes, had just proposed. Again. Only this time, without Mrs. Stevens hovering over and the threat of incorrigible inn guests, it felt real. Very real.

And Lord help her—she was going to say yes.

But he needed to know the truth.

Franklin reached over to squeeze Millie's hand once. She glanced toward him, and he smiled gently as if to say, *"Take all the time you need."*

One hour later, Millie gripped the armrest of her seat as Ingrid Bergman's character slipped the key to the wine cellar beneath the sole of her shoe. Such a bold move for a woman to be a spy, unable to tell the man she loved the truth.

And Millie wondered—didn't Ingrid want to tell him everything? And if she had, surely Cary would have come for her sooner. They could've avoided the whole poison-by-tea, climbing-a-sprawling-staircase portion of the movie. If only they'd put the pieces together about the bottle sooner. If only they'd worked together.

Millie turned to face Franklin. She rubbed her palms against the skirt of her dress, took a deep breath, and willed herself toward honesty.

"Franklin—"

"Hmm?" He leaned his ear closer to her, never taking his eyes off the screen.

My father was murdered for loving my mother. My grandmother was a slave, and she was sold as a child. I own the satchel her mother sent along with provision for her journey, not knowing where her child— her own child!—would sleep. They never saw each other again, and this—this—is the blood you don't see in me. You need to know it if you want to live with me. But mostly, you need to know it if you ever suspect yourself in love with me. Because I am proud of my heritage, no matter what the law and society think. I am proud of my mother and my mother's mother and all the rest who came before me. Without them, I wouldn't carry these dreams.

But the world doesn't see them as heroes. Not yet, at least.

Looking at his sharp silhouette, all the courage bound up in her heart whooshed away from her lips, and she moistened them as if that would make a difference, her hands now trembling.

"Nothing."

"Sure?" He turned his attention to her then. "For a moment there, I thought you might have an answer." He cleared his throat, and even in the dark, she could see him shifting in his seat.

"About the marriage, you mean?"

Franklin's gaze swept her eyes, down the tip of her nose, to her lips and back again. He seemed to be waiting for something. Waiting, perhaps, until she was ready.

"Yes," she blurted, quite confident she wouldn't change her

mind. "Yes, Franklin. I will marry you." She was a traitor to her own values, to her resolution of telling him about her heritage. But how would he respond if she did? Why, it wouldn't even be legal. She didn't want to lose him. Didn't want to lose all they already shared.

"It's settled, then." He inched closer and placed his hand over her own. She pretended to play coy, as if this gesture hadn't prompted the tickle in her toes. "We'll marry as soon as possible, obviously."

Millie's heart spun like the newlyweds she once watched dancing down King Street on Christmas Eve. Back at home. Back when she was a girl.

"One day, this movie is going to be a classic." Franklin removed his hand from hers and reached for another bite of popcorn.

"We'll see," said Millie.

He smiled back, and her very breath shook with the ring of his offer, with the ring of the woman she had promised to be.

When Mrs. Stevens said she'd bring some fabric by the honeymoon suite that afternoon, Millie never expected what the woman had in mind. Mrs. Stevens, hair perfectly pinned, stood in the doorway with a pile of clothing stacked higher than her hairstyle.

Millie hurried to help, taking several garments from the woman's arms, then spreading them on the bed quilt made from scraps of old dresses and flour sacks.

"This is too much." Millie's heart swelled with each glimpse of lace and silk.

"Hardly, Millie." Mrs. Stevens set the rest of the stack down. "None of it fits me anymore. Don't know why I kept it, but for fancy's sake. I'm sentimental to a fault, always remembering when I wore this or that."

Millie smiled and stilled. "I do the same." Her gaze traveled to the top of the stack as Mrs. Stevens continued.

"I'm just sorry I can't afford to help you buy a proper gown."

Why are you being so nice to me? she wanted to ask. But she knew the answer. Mrs. Stevens was just the sort of person to always be kind, and she reminded Millie of all the Bible stories Mama used to tell about Jesus.

In utter awe, Millie reached for the peach silk dressing gown.

"That one was a gift from my mother. I thought you might use it as a lining."

Millie nodded. She didn't know what else to say. Words failed the tug of gratitude she felt.

So instead, she turned to Mrs. Stevens and simply hugged the woman. Caught off guard at first, Mrs. Stevens relaxed and began to laugh softly. "You really are excited, aren't you? I hope you can make something lovely from these old fabrics. Bring a new life to them. A new story."

"I will," Millie said. "I promise you, I will."

With every seam, with every layer, with every button, for the rest of her life.

EIGHTEEN

Charleston, Modern Day

Why does a river change its course, and how do creeks turn into streams? Harper had been wondering this all day as she and Millie traveled through the Lowcountry, filled as it was with tall grasses and lazy waters and waving leaves.

A week after her phone call with Peter, Harper gripped the steering wheel and looked over at her ninety-something-year-old passenger. The other employees at the boardinghouse were looking after things, and it seemed Harper had talked Millie out of adopting the baby goat for the time being.

"Harper Rae, be a doll and mind the road." Millie's focus never left the path ahead.

Harper smiled and shook her head. Fields and fields of sweetgrass rustled beyond the car windows, as Lowcountry waters snaked through the mushy ground.

Though Harper was looking forward to seeing Peter again, she was no fool. The woman who'd met him just weeks ago was no longer a person she recognized. She still felt lost in many ways, like she was driving in circles. The trip would be for Millie and Peter's sake.

And maybe a little bit because Harper couldn't seem to get Peter out of her head. But no one needed to know that.

Harper drove over the Ashley River and into what Millie called the Holy City. It was nothing short of magical. She watched the buildings through her window—reading them, in a way, as she would read a beautiful gown. Wondering what age-old stories and secrets they had to tell.

"Are you sure you don't want to tell him who you are when we first meet up?" Harper slowed to a stop at a light on King Street. She snuck a glance at Millie, whose wrinkled lips were pursed together as she rapped her painted fingernails against the car door.

Millie shook her head, the pearls about her neck shifting ever so slightly. She settled in her seat and locked eyes with Harper. "Dear, I just need you to mind my wishes. You won't utter the word *grandmother* until I say so. Understood?"

"Understood. Just make sure you find a way to bring it up sooner rather than later. We don't want to owe him rent on a dress store that we're just using as a façade to soften the news." Harper checked the light, still red. But Millie didn't chuckle as Harper expected, so she turned her attention again to the woman. "You *are* still planning to return to Alabama rather than starting an actual store, right?"

Millie waved away the question. "How ridiculous you sound. Starting a shop at my age?"

Harper raised an eyebrow. Why did Millie's tone sound less than convincing? She decided not to press the issue for the time being. She was tired and probably imagining things. "How are you feeling? About all this, I mean."

"I'm feeling . . ." Millie's voice warbled, and she took a deep breath. "This strange intersection between a woman in the final stages of life, and a young girl suspended by choices." Millie sighed, straightening her pearls first, and then her pintucked blouse. "Choices that determined the course of . . . well, everything, really . . . and yet, have brought me back here again." She looked out at King Street as a sunbeam pierced past the clouds. "Back home."

Just for a moment, Harper recognized a different sort of Millie. A Millie who, despite this time working together, had never appeared to Harper before. A Millie who seemed the slightest bit vulnerable after all.

The light turned. Harper put both hands back on the wheel. "I never knew you had a history anywhere but Fairhope."

"No, few people do." Millie's voice was stronger now.

"Why, Millie?"

The aged woman patted her curled hairdo. "I suppose you'll know that soon enough. But for now, just mind the road."

She had spunk. Harper would give her that.

Two blocks later, GPS directed them to a courtyard behind a stunning old building on King Street. Harper immediately recognized it from when she'd been there weeks ago.

The two-story structure boasted long windows, and a cheery awning with antique scrolls along the roofline. Though it certainly showed its age, it also showed its charm, nestled between adjacent buildings with equal amounts of character. She parked and dialed Peter's phone number. He'd told them to call when they arrived.

"Harper," he said, slightly out of breath. "Great timing. I'll walk down now."

She directed him to where they'd parked, and then it hit her. The full weight of all this. Here she was in a strange city, driving around a woman who was the picture of health, but—let's face it—still in her nineties. If you'd told Harper several months ago that this was the direction her life would lead, she never would've believed it.

And now she was about to take a short-term rental from a man who was practically a stranger, and just pray he wasn't a psychopath or one of those people who is too eco-conscious to crank up the air conditioning.

Then she saw him, climbing down the external stairs at the side of the building and heading toward their car, and in that moment, she panicked. What had she been thinking? This was real life, not a dream. Suddenly she was thirteen again, at her first boy-girl party—back when they called them boy-girl parties—hiding in the bathroom in the era before cell phones and waiting, *waiting* until eight thirty.

Peter was several paces away from the car when Harper opened her door and stepped toward him, jitters abounding.

His loose curls slipped just behind his ears, short enough to maintain professionalism yet long enough to stir within Harper the most ridiculous desire to touch them. His glasses gave the appearance of being bookish, though he seemed the sort to wear the style before it was trendy. The hem of his faded T-shirt skimmed just below the waist of his well-fitting jeans.

Something about him drew her, and she found herself insensibly attracted to him. Harper had never made a habit of being attracted to strangers, especially not strangers she was supposed to be keeping secrets from.

The sunlight softened, the colors of the sky deepened, and Peter closed the space between them by holding out his hand. His smile, framed by that well-trimmed beard, bewitched her. His hold on her hand was gentle, and she allowed her fingers to linger a moment longer than she normally would've. Did he notice?

"Harper. Pleasure to see you again."

"And the same goes for you." She returned his grin, wondering what might be going through his own thoughts.

"Don't mind the old woman in the car." Millie opened the passenger side door. Peter chuckled, his laugh warm and almost familiar, like the aroma of a coffee-scented candle that instantly takes a person back home.

He stepped toward Millie, and his grin widened as he engulfed her in his arms. "My dear Millie."

"My dear boy." She looked up at him and returned his affection with her own radiant grin. "Our bags are in the back. You can manage them both, can you not?"

Harper cleared her throat. "That won't be necessary, Millie. I can carry my own."

"Nonsense, sugar." She waved away the notion. "None of that feminist rubbish. The man has offered to host. Let him host us."

Peter met Harper's gaze, sending a current of anticipation through her. "The luggage is really no trouble."

"If you're sure." Harper smiled, eager to see the space where they would be staying. Equally eager to talk with him more. Reflections of the setting sun lit the clouds every shade of pink, and Harper breathed a *thank You, God* because after years of professional and relational disappointment, the tide finally seemed to be turning, here in the Lowcountry.

This night, as it turned out, had already far exceeded her first party at the age of thirteen.

Later that evening, after leaving Millie and Harper to settle into the loft rental, Peter met up with Declan and Sullivan for a few games of scrimmage. He would show Millie and Harper the storefront in the morning.

When Harper mentioned how much she liked the vintage aesthetic, Peter was glad he'd decided to go ahead and furnish the short-term rental, as he typically did with these types of properties. But he was surprised to hear that she'd told Lucy to sell the little amount of furniture she still had in the Savannah apartment they shared. Why did she seem to be running away and cutting ties, when back at the engagement party, she was so hopeful? Maybe in time she would tell him.

"Sounds like the tie was not enough to deter her. Dude, you must've had some kind of a conversation with that woman." Declan's shot swooshed through the net.

Sullivan went after the ball and dribbled it several times, dodging his way around Peter. "I'm really going to have to see this tie."

Peter stole the ball and took his own shot. Three points.

Declan and Peter shook their heads. "Going to silence us with your signature three-pointer?" Declan took the ball and started dribbling.

"Whatever works." Peter lifted the hem of his shirt to rub the sweat from his forehead and crouched lower to get in position for defensive coverage.

Declan took a shot, but the ball bounced against the rim. "Can you start from the beginning with all this stuff? I'm getting confused. I mean, obviously I'm not confused about Harper. Or Lucy . . . unfortunately . . . but that's a story for another day. But you two lost me with all this satchel, wedding dress stuff."

Sullivan grabbed the ball and started dribbling. "We found those in an old house, and Peter thinks they might've belonged to his mother. Well, the dress definitely did, because she's wearing it in her wedding photos. But Peter says it's an antique, and there may be a reason his mother had it. Something we don't know about."

Declan stole the ball. "No way. So these could actually be the heirlooms in her box that went missing?"

Peter rolled his eyes. "I'm standing right here, guys."

Declan took the ball in both hands and grounded his feet. "You're right. So give us the scoop."

Peter recognized that look and knew their game had just come to a mutually acknowledged time-out. So he continued, eager to get the attention off himself. Talking about his stepfather and all that happened years ago wasn't exactly his favorite thing to do.

Peter raked his hand through his hair to push it away from his face. "You both know about my stepfather giving away my mom's stuff right after she died, right?"

They nodded.

"So those are the heirlooms I've been looking for. And obviously I found her dress, which was old when she wore it."

"You think the satchel is connected?" Declan passed the ball between his right and left hands as if trying on the idea. "That does seem to make sense." He hesitated, looking straight at Peter. "Here's one thing I've long wondered, though. How do you know the box of your mom's was important? I mean, obviously it was important because it belonged to her—but beyond that."

"Yeah, sure." Peter rubbed both eyes with his hands. The truth was, he didn't know. He'd been operating off hunches for years. "Isn't that the way with history? You're always trying to put together these leftover fragments in hopes they'll tell the full story that was actually lived. So I guess, even with my mother's history, I don't know for certain. But I do have this memory from when I was just a kid."

Sullivan unscrewed the lid of his water bottle. "You never told me this."

"Me neither," Declan said.

Peter leaned his head back, looking upward to the evening sky. "I remember she hung up the phone with somebody . . . back whenever people had landlines. My stepfather walked in upset, saying he didn't want my mother talking to that woman anymore and he wouldn't have his reputation compromised by somebody of her class. Mom was crying. I had no idea what any of it meant—just that I knew well enough to stay hidden in the hallway. When he walked off, I asked my mom what happened." Declan and Sullivan watched him intently, neither of them moving an inch. Peter continued. "She said she had a box of things that belonged to the woman on the phone and someday, when I was older, she would tell me the rest of the story."

Sullivan blew out a deep sigh. "Then the boating accident . . ."

"Exactly." Peter swallowed. Sometimes he could talk about her sudden death with ease. Other times, the grief pierced him with a fresh sting. This was a case of the latter.

Declan shifted his weight back and forth, a clear sign the game would start again soon. Peter was relieved to see it.

"You think it was your grandmother on the phone that day, don't you?" Sullivan took one more swig from his water bottle before replacing the cap.

Peter nodded slowly. "I always have. A hunch, I guess. I had no good reason to think that, except who else would it be? But then I found the satchel right there with the wedding dress." He glanced over toward Sullivan. "I didn't tell you this part earlier because I wanted to be sure. But when I got that satchel home and studied it, the colors of the thread were like this faint memory. Faded by time—sort of the way you remember little grooves in the wall from when you were a kid or your favorite television characters. A shadow of what used to be."

"Don't forget about the button," Sullivan added.

Peter pointed toward Sullivan, thankful he was here to get Declan up to speed. "Yeah, that's important. So the satchel described how its original owner, a young girl sold as a slave, was given two matching buttons by her mother when she was sold. I found one of the buttons on the wedding dress."

"Ah," Declan said. "And that's how you're hoping to find the rest of the story. Through the matching button."

"Improbable as that sounds, yes." Just hearing the words come out of his own mouth reminded Peter how small a button could be—and how often we pass them every day without so much as blinking. The very thing that might hold together the fiber of a long-sought-after story.

"Sounds like you're confident about it." Declan hit the basketball with his hand. "That these are the missing heirlooms."

Peter rubbed his hands together, ready to intercept the ball. "I just keep wondering if maybe my grandmother is still living."

Declan began dribbling. "Wouldn't that be something? She could be anyone. Just think."

Anyone, indeed.

NINETEEN

Fairhope, 1947

Rain fell in gentle sheets on the pier outside the boardinghouse on the day Franklin married Millie. And the whole earth, of course, waves at the start of a rain. The hem of her long, airy gown floated up like a cloud as the sunlight cast a glow like magic through the floor-to-ceiling windows at the back of the boardinghouse.

The holiday magic—the garland and ornaments and the candles —had been swept into boxes where they would remain until the following Christmas, and now a new year had begun. One that Millie hoped might bring its own sort of magic in its own sort of way.

Mrs. Stevens had given Franklin a Sunday suit that once belonged to her late husband and bought him a real nice hat and razor. Truthfully, Millie sort of missed the beard around his lips, but cleanly shaven, he was handsome enough to turn heads.

Millie wore a spritz of rosewater perfume, a wedding gift from Mrs. Stevens, and her hair was coaxed into rolled curls at the nape of her neck. The curls brushed Mama's butterfly buttons, and a trail of other buttons fell in place down her back.

Of course, Millie couldn't manage all these buttons herself, so Mrs. Stevens had helped with that too.

The woman had set to work getting the minister and making a little tea cake, even lending Millie her own pearls.

Millie felt as if she were a princess in a fairy tale. She clutched a small bouquet of pink and peach roses, and snuck a glance around the corner of the wall.

Franklin stood there beside the pastor and fussed with his bow tie.

Her heart tumbled down a meadow at the sight of him. Marriage for friendship—marriage to her only friend—was a prospect that she looked forward to. Sure, she had once fancied herself wearing one of those gowns she'd spied through the window of the Charleston shop and marrying for romance. What young woman doesn't?

But Millie was no fool. Franklin cared about her, would care *for* her, and she felt the same way. That was far more than many marriages ever managed, romance or none. Franklin would help her find a way to her dreams, and she would do the same for him.

One of the guests at the boardinghouse had offered to play the piano Mrs. Stevens kept in the lobby, and Millie clutched her flowers a little tighter as the "Wedding March" began.

Without hesitation, she stepped toward him. Franklin's expression washed with contentment, and for a moment, she wondered if he truly admired her. Love, of course, was out of the question.

But admiration—a cousin to love, perhaps—was something wholly desirable. As Millie took several steps to close the space between them, her stomach somersaulted, and she couldn't look away.

Franklin edged up on the toes of his loafers almost imperceptibly and willed her closer with his gaze.

What did he truly think of their marriage? Was he any less sure than she?

If she hadn't known any better, by looking at him now, Millie never would've guessed he was once a train jumper. Actually, looking at him now, he'd make for an honest-to-goodness husband—the kind you kissed before bed at night.

Franklin was a fool.

He'd known Millie such a short time, yet already, her every move captured him. She was grace upon grace in her movements, in her laughter, in the way she watched the stars come out at twilight.

The pianist led the group of five in a rendition of "Amazing Grace" and everyone else bowed their heads to pray, but all Franklin could think to himself was, *Dear God, how did I get so lucky?*

Toward the end of the song, he added for good measure, *Help me care for her well.*

He couldn't believe a woman like Millie would marry a hobo from Carolina, and he'd spend the rest of his life distracting her from the obvious.

Next thing Franklin knew, the preacher was sayin' something fierce about vows and commitment and divorce and all. His heart thudded, thinking of how they'd deceived Mrs. Stevens and how she'd been nothing but nice to them.

Franklin reached into his pocket for the ring he'd bought Millie yesterday morning. It wasn't real gold, of course, but he wanted her to have some token from the wedding. And he certainly didn't want any other men noticing her bare left hand. So he'd sold his cap and his one pair of suspenders in exchange for it.

Franklin left the ring in his pocket and took Millie's hand in his own. Her skin was as soft as petals, and Lord help him, all he could think of was the kiss that was coming.

He watched her, searching her eyes for what she might be thinking. He couldn't fault her if she wanted to run. Yet all he could see in her gaze was the same steady determination he'd first noticed on the train somewhere near Georgia.

She shifted her weight back and forth, and the bottom of her dress seemed to float with the movement. It was a very pretty dress. He'd never seen another one like it.

But then again, Millie was a very pretty woman.

"Repeat after me," the preacher said. "I, Franklin, take thee, Millie."

Franklin cleared his throat. "I, Franklin, take thee, Millie." He swallowed, his heart now thundering. Millie looked up at him, eyes wide and waiting. "To be my wedded wife."

One of Millie's curls fell loosely on her forehead as they repeated the rest of the vows from the minister, and Franklin reached up to brush it back.

He bit down on his bottom lip. Her gaze held him, steadied him. Millie had no idea how he meant this last part, after only a month of friendship. How he admired her. Longed for her. How he meant to commit himself. "To love and to cherish, till death do us part."

Millie turned ever so slightly to take the ring from the minister, and Franklin's focus trailed to the little butterfly buttons at the neckline of her dress. He recognized them as the buttons Millie's mother had given her the day she left Charleston. The day they first met.

Millie had seen fit to put her beloved buttons on that dress. Her wedding dress.

That had to bode well for him.

"You may now kiss the bride."

Franklin reached for her. It might be the only time he ever kissed her, and he intended to make it a good one.

Millie's eyes fluttered to a close as his lips found her own.

He told himself they were pretending, only pretending, and yet it felt so very real. He reached behind her waist, gently yet firmly drawing her closer to himself. He wanted to take the pins out from her curls and kiss the nape of her neck and tell her to let her hair down.

He was at once fully alive and keenly aware of the moment's passing, as the rest of the world blurred around them.

Against his better judgment, he inched his lips back and ended the kiss, trying to pretend his heart wasn't racing and his breath wasn't stolen as he looked into the innocent eyes of Mrs. Millie Pinckney.

Millie and Franklin spent the better part of their wedding night on the pier overlooking Mobile Bay, the planks still wet from an afternoon storm and the air still thick with humidity.

Starlight twinkled little lights around the old oak trees, and Millie leaned back onto the pier beside Franklin to watch. She still wore her wedding gown, for this was her one chance to enjoy it, and she knew it was the most beautiful dress she would ever sew.

She shifted her weight onto her elbows and reached out to loosen his tie. "You look awfully uncomfortable."

"That's 'cause I am." Franklin smiled his usual half grin, and his eyes caught glimmers from the light of the stars. "But anything for you, my bride."

Millie chuckled, then pulled off the bow tie. "How much mileage can I get out of this bride business?"

"Until dawn comes, you're practically Cinderella."

Millie tilted her head back at that and laughed, really laughed, wild and free for the first time in such a long time. She had done it—she had made a new life for herself and found a friendship that would last. Mama would be proud.

Maybe it was supremely practical, and maybe it wasn't romantic, but Millie had all the romance she needed in her dress shop dream and in the glittering details of this night, from the silk of her gown to the dimples of his grin, to the low-swinging sliver of the moonlight. She watched the waves gently lap against the pier and delighted in the smell of her own fancy rosewater perfume.

She might never tell Franklin her secret history, but that was all right. Some secrets were better kept quiet, just as Mama once warned.

"What'll it be, Red?" Franklin unbuttoned his collar.

Millie looked up into the sky, searching for a shooting star. She'd wish to remember this moment, this magic, for the rest of her life.

The way Franklin had searched her eyes when he'd said the words *my wedded wife*, it should've scared her senseless. But for some reason, it didn't.

The breeze over the water cooled her arms, and for a moment, Millie caught a chill. Franklin inched closer, slid off his suit jacket, then draped it over her shoulders.

"Honestly?"

Franklin nodded.

"I can't think of a single thing I want that I don't already have."

Franklin watched her. His jaw tightened. And the glimmer of the bay just beyond them played tricks with the pier so it looked as if he were suspended there—*they* were suspended there—floating in a space above the water where the moonlight and the stars scattered diamonds down on the tide.

It was the sort of moment he might have kissed her had circumstances been different, and she might have kissed him back.

It was the sort of moment he might've said he loved her, and she might have promised herself to him for the rest of her life.

But he didn't kiss her again that night. Instead, they sat together, two travelers become one, as the water pulsed toward the shore and the moonlight dipped into the dawn.

TWENTY

Charleston, Modern Day

Must have been the rosy glow of twilight. Either that, or the British audiobook Harper and Millie had enjoyed on the drive over. Perhaps a dangerous cocktail of the two. Because the light of morning proved Peter was *not* her own personal hero from Cornwall.

Peter, as it turned out, was a nerd. Just as she had initially suspected upon meeting him weeks ago.

Harper would be entirely unsurprised if he owned a NASA shirt.

All for the best, really. When Peter found out her dreams had come to a fiery halt, he wouldn't be interested anyway. What could she offer to a relationship right now when she wasn't even sure what she wanted in life? This morning, she'd even doubted her Starbucks order.

Still, she would be kind and pretend to be interested in this walking tour for Millie's sake, despite the fact Millie had conveniently found an excuse to get out of it.

Harper planted her ballet flats against the cobblestone street while the white bow at the back of her blouse flapped in the breeze. Flowers in pinks and purples caught on the breeze and floated over wrought-iron cemetery walls.

She tapped her foot against the ground and checked her watch.

Why was she the only one at the meeting spot? The tour was supposed to leave two and a half minutes ago.

Harper tensed all over again as a new realization dawned— she might be the only person taking the tour today. The tour had seemed like a fine idea when she thought she could blend into a group, but now she had to make conversation. And if things got awkward, they were still stuck with each other. Painfully so.

Millie had insisted on resting after the long travel day, prior to seeing the storefront.

But Harper had a feeling "resting" was the last thing Millie was doing right now. That woman was probably either enjoying tea at Charleston Place or snooping through Harper's stuff.

Harper tapped her other foot.

A man rounded the corner, a satchel slung over his shoulder and a grin on his face as if he'd intentionally taken his sweet time getting here.

Peter.

He wore a cardigan that was at once stylish and reminiscent of Mr. Rogers. Harper couldn't decide exactly which descriptor fit the man more.

As he came closer, the breeze ruffled his wild almost-curls, and she caught a glimpse of his green-blue eyes. Eyes that seemed to hold far more nuance than they had in her kitchen this morning, when he'd brought over cheap muffins and coffee. For the briefest moment, she felt a leap of sheer attraction to him—the same tumbling sensation in her middle as last night, when twilight painted the Holy City pink.

Then the moment passed. And she returned to sanity.

"I had a last-minute cancelation from the other family scheduled for today's tour, so it looks like it's just you and me." Peter gestured toward the cemetery behind the wrought-iron fence and to the ornate church just beyond. "I always like to start the tour at this Unitarian church cemetery. Though some other graveyards have many more famous headstones to boast about, this particular space draws up some very distinctly Charlestonian folklore. Have you ever heard the legend of Annabel Ravenel?"

Harper shook her head.

Peter seemed magnetized by the history. His passion quieted her unease. "Annabel was only fourteen when her father arranged for her marriage shortly before the Civil War. But much to her father's dismay, Annabel fell in love with a soldier named Edgar Perry who was stationed at Fort Moultrie. The story goes that the two began meeting secretly at the Unitarian cemetery, away from the eyes of her watchful father. But they were caught. In retribution, he locked Annabel in her room for months, and Edgar was transferred back to Virginia. Soon, she succumbed to illness, most likely yellow fever. But when Edgar tried to visit the gravesite, he couldn't find it. Her spiteful father left it unmarked to keep Edgar from paying his respects."

"Well, that's terribly sad."

Peter raised his eyebrows. "That's not the whole story."

Peter paused. Harper caught herself holding her breath, waiting for the rest.

"The soldier's real name was Edgar Allan Poe. He wrote a poem about the young woman, calling it—"

"'Annabel Lee!'" Harper covered her mouth as soon as she blurted out the words.

"Yes." Peter grinned. His eyes trailed to Harper's tote bag—emblazoned with a pattern of tiny Poe faces.

"You made that up because you saw my purse!" She started laughing. "Now I feel completely ridiculous."

"Actually, I didn't make it up." One mischievous corner of Peter's lips tugged upward as his grin widened. He had a certain confidence about him. "No doubt some of the story is embellished, but Poe *was* stationed on Sullivan's Island. There's much speculation he visited the city during that time. Who wouldn't have? It's possible that Annabel Ravenel, at least as folklore presents her, is fictional. She does not have a marked grave here.

But it's also possible that the story passed down from generation to generation . . . is true."

Harper took one more glance into the old cemetery where ivy and natural flora had been allowed to overrun. A swarm of bees buzzed past her ears and into the flowers, and she looked back at Peter. The more she listened to his passion, the more she felt the stir of her own dream. She'd tried to tell herself that dream was dead, but the stubborn thing was resurrecting.

With her cup of tea tonight, she would sketch a gown fit for one of those upscale bridal magazines, something that might appeal to a bride in this classy city. The gown wouldn't see the light of day, but her heart did quicken at the thought of the sketching. That was something.

"Where to next?" she asked him, surprised by how easily his zeal had sparked her own.

"How about the theater? I've got a great story to tell you about John Wilkes Booth."

Two hours later, Harper had a new appreciation for the city of Charleston. And tour guides—one in particular.

"Thanks for taking the time to show me the city. The history is far more interesting than I would've expected." She leaned up against the iron railing of the cemetery where they'd begun.

"I appreciate the compliment, but really, it's my passion, so you're probably the one doing me a favor by listening." Peter checked his watch. "I'm actually on my way to an estate sale now. Want to join me? We still have some time before we're supposed to meet back with Millie."

After the morning they'd just shared, Harper was convinced he could make a pencil sound interesting. She was intrigued by Peter's estate sales, to say the least. "I don't see why not."

Peter nodded toward the corner of the street. "Just a couple blocks' walk." He held out his hands as he started down the side-walk. "Such pleasant weather today."

Harper hurried to keep up with him. With each step she took, the bow of her blouse skipped along.

In no time, they reached the house. A handmade sign advertising *Estate Sale! Lots of Treasures!* was staked in the grass.

The cottage had been freshly painted in shades of grey and sage green. Its charm was the stuff of those home improvement TV shows. Harper imagined closets and basketfuls of dresses, linens, and buttons on the other side of the door. She followed Peter down the walkway.

He reached for the door handle. "Ready?"

Harper nodded.

As Peter opened the door for her to go first, she snuck a quick peek—anxious to see all that was inside. But to her surprise, there were no basketfuls of dresses, linens, and buttons.

The house smelled musty. The "treasures," as it turned out, were stained encyclopedias and half-broken stools.

Peter closed the door behind them. Harper turned to him and whispered. "Not quite as enchanting as I expected."

He shrugged. "It happens."

They passed through the hallway and then the bedrooms but soon discovered the encyclopedias were actually the highlight.

"Can I help you?" a woman asked from behind a stack of chairs.

Harper wanted to say, *Even if you could, I don't know how you'd get to us over all that furniture.* But instead, she ducked down a bit to see the woman through the curve of the chairs, then smiled. "I think we're okay, thanks."

"Let me know." The woman tapped a pencil against the desk where she sat. How in the world did she expect to sell anything with this kind of setup? Is this what Peter's estate sales always entailed? Harper could appreciate a good rags-to-riches story, but she couldn't imagine *anyone* who would consider these wobbly chairs riches. Except maybe an insurance company.

An old framed photo on the wall caught her eye. "Actually"—Harper spoke toward the heap of furniture as though she could see the woman clearly—"I am curious." She pointed to the wall. "Are those people the original homeowners? Along with the two kids pictured?"

"I'm sorry. I'm not sure." The woman shook her head. "I'm part of a company that liquidates items for these sales. I don't know anything about the history of the pieces. Wish I did, though. They sure make a nice-looking family."

"That's terribly sad. So their story is just lost? Forgotten?"

"I'm afraid so."

Harper turned to Peter. Chills ran down her arms.

Forgotten. The word sounded in her mind like an echo, the reality of the whole thing so strong. And she wasn't sure why she cared so much. These people were strangers to her. But maybe the point was more so that this same thing could happen to anyone. Including Millie. Including herself.

Peter gently took her elbow as they made their way out of the furniture maze and toward the front door. He opened it, and the two of them stepped outside. Harper willed herself to take in the fresh air and sunshine.

She rubbed her arms. "Are these sales always so sad?"

"Sometimes. You never know what you're going to find." Peter fiddled with a button on his cardigan.

Harper glanced down at the red geraniums growing in a row along the walkway. Such care in preserving the land, but such a mysterious history. The gravity of lost stories tugged her.

"How do you do it?" She caught Peter's gaze. "How do you go into a place and know the laughter and the tears and the stories may have all been silenced by the passing of time?"

Peter looked at her a long time. "Let me show you something."

"Okay."

The two of them walked several blocks to a neighborhood Peter called Radcliffeborough until they reached an old house with a little garden. Shutters hung lopper-jawed from the home, and one was missing altogether. The yard was overdue for a mow, and it was a wonder Harper's allergies didn't send her into a sneezing fit.

She looked over at Peter, who was watching her and beaming.

"What do you think?" he asked.

Harper raised her eyebrows and turned back to face the house. "Looks like it's seen better days."

Peter's grin widened. "This is my house."

"Your . . . house?"

She couldn't be sure, but Harper thought she saw a rat dart across the threshold. She faced Peter, telling herself it was just a baby squirrel she'd seen. She blinked, trying to keep up and forget about the . . . erm, baby squirrel.

"It's an old family home." He waved one hand. "Forgive the disarray of the shutters. I've been trying to find someone who can repair the originals instead of buying new ones. So I guess, to answer your question, *this* is how I go into house after house and salvage what I can of their history. Because you never know when you may find a history that's just now being told. Or in this case, restored."

Peter looked back toward the house. "As for this place, I don't know much about its history. I inherited it from my mother." He straightened his glasses. "But I'm going to find out."

A swallowtail floated effortlessly past them, swooping up and down over the weeds—rather early in the season for butterflies such as these, but in a few months, its descendants might populate the whole street.

Harper took a step closer. The house that seemed like an eyesore from the street was quite charming up close. She studied the property. With a location just off King Street, this lot alone had to be worth . . . well, a pretty penny.

Peter watched her. "What are you thinking?"

"Just that I think it's cool you invest in these properties."

Peter slid the key into the lock at the front door and turned the knob. He met Harper's gaze before he opened the door. "Real estate in Charleston has been on quite an incline, and I lucked out by investing when I did. The properties I started with were small, but you could say they were big enough to matter."

I'll say. Harper tried not to let the curiosity show on her face.

"You'd be surprised the treasures that can come from saving things." With this, Peter held the door open for her. "That's why I invested in the old dress shop you came to see. And on that note, Harper, tell me more about yourself."

She followed him into the home, but before she could answer, the smell of dust hit the back of her throat, and she started coughing. Harper covered her mouth with the sleeve of her shirt and looked over at Peter.

"Sorry, I didn't warn you the entryway is a bit of a Roman tomb right now." His eyes did a humored little dance at that. "I was doing some repairs to one of the bookshelves earlier. But it's exciting, isn't it?" Peter raised his hands in the air and took a turn around the room. "You just can't get details like this in modern construction."

You also can't get the flecks of lead paint and plaster dust from the ceiling I'm currently inhaling . . .

But Harper just smiled.

"You didn't answer my question." Peter came to a comfortable stance, arms crossed, in the living room. Standing like that, he looked as if he could withstand a hurricane wind.

Maybe, in his own way, he had. Holding on tight to these walls, trying to preserve their structure.

"Oh, there's not much to tell." Harper fumbled with her beaded coral bracelet, sliding it up and down her arm. She always fidgeted when she was the center of attention.

"I think you underestimate yourself," he said.

"Well, I do have a flair for adventure, I suppose." That was one way of putting it.

"How'd you end up here? In Charleston? With Millie?"

You, she wanted to say.

But she couldn't. Not now. Maybe never.

So she reminded herself not to get too close to Peter. Because the clock would strike midnight eventually, as the clock was prone to doing—and in this case, sooner rather than later.

Harper took a deep breath, directing her attention past Peter's shoulder and toward the window at the back of the house. A mockingbird perched on the ledge, peering inside.

"I followed my dream. Turns out, it was a dead end." She shrugged. "Millie was there at the right place and the right time. She offered to help me out, and here I am."

Peter was quiet a long moment. She geared up for the inevitable advice on staying true to her dreams, from this guy who seemed to have found all his own.

But instead, he simply watched her. "I'm really sorry."

Those three words—a stranger's heartfelt apology for her own shortcomings—were enough to flip the switch of her heart back on.

And the floodgates opened.

Harper walked closer to where Peter stood, then sat on the couch with her feet against the old floor. Without needing any prompting, Peter sat beside her.

Harper began to cry. Tears she had yet to shed from her last day in Savannah.

She could almost smell the air of the consignment shop, the familiarity of the come-and-gone dream. She covered her face at first, embarrassed to be fighting tears at a place like this and with a man she barely knew.

And yet this is what her heart had come to.

Maybe the Fred Rogers cardigan was to blame for her sudden sense of emotional security. Or maybe . . . maybe it was Peter.

She wiped away her tears and braved a glance straight into his eyes. She found him watching her, kindly, ready to meet her gaze whenever she offered it.

A noise startled her from another room. A dog's whimper? Then came a gentle scratching sound. "What's that noise?" she asked.

Peter shook his head. "Oh, that's just my dog. I shut him in the bedroom before I left to keep him from opening the pantry and eating crackers. He probably woke up from a nap and heard us."

Harper raised her eyebrows. "Your dog opens the pantry?"

"You seem surprised."

Harper laughed, and he urged her to continue her story. With a surprisingly steady voice, she spoke the words she'd been avoiding. "When I was studying dress design in Savannah, I actually thought I had a chance of being represented in a very prestigious show."

"That's right. I remember the dress you were wearing at the party." Peter absently rubbed his jawline with his thumb as he waited for more.

Harper looked at him. He remembered the dress?

"I take it things didn't go well the next day?"

"The woman told me I don't have what it takes to be successful. That I'm wasting my time, and that she was doing me a favor by helping me see this now rather than later." Harper shuffled her feet. "Totally blindsided me."

"And do you agree with her?" His words were the furthest thing from patronizing.

But Harper was so caught off guard, she stared straight into his eyes. "I mean, she's the department chair. She's had designs in major fashion outlets. Even magazines you'd recognize."

"Sure." He rubbed his lips together. "But that's not the question, is it?"

Harper shook her head. "Doesn't matter if I agree or not. I don't mean to complain—truly. I'm healthy and have a wonderful life. But I don't want to keep embarrassing myself. She was right." Harper nodded, hoping to convince herself by saying it aloud. "Better that I change course now before I humiliate myself even more than I already have."

"I don't think chasing a dream is ever a reason for humiliation," Peter said. "Dreams are hard to catch. For anybody."

"Well, the rest of the world wouldn't agree, Peter Perkins. I've got plenty of humiliation under my belt, and I'm only twenty-six. I don't think I could survive two, three, or no telling how many more decades of rejection and disappointment when my heart is so invested. And that's the thing. I had the dream right in the palms of my hands for a few months. I know how it felt to design those gowns alongside the best of the best. I just couldn't hold onto it." Her pulse quickened as she realized how close his fingers were to her own. "Sometimes, we have to do the hard thing and let go when passions turn to ashes and dust. Don't you agree?"

When she finished the question, Harper looked down, at the gashes and the scrapes time had worn into the floor of the old house.

But despite herself, she looked right back into Peter's eyes.

"Maybe," he murmured. "But maybe sometimes we don't."

TWENTY-ONE

Fairhope, 1948

Wind whistled through the cracks in the shutters and slapped the handmade wreath against the front door. Plenty of sunlight shone through the blinds, though the rain fell and the wind kicked up. Mama always said that meant the devil was beatin' his wife.

Sometimes weather like this meant rainbows. But sometimes weather like this meant trouble. Which was headed her way this afternoon?

Millie and Franklin were a mere six months into being the new owners and operators of the boardinghouse—ever since Mrs. Stevens fell and her kin decided she was better off living in their home. But Millie still couldn't shake the feeling she was staying here for just a spell. The thought of owning the place seemed too good to be true. To think she and Franklin were business owners. Franklin, a hobo, and she . . .

Well, she probably should've told him the truth by now. Lord knew she'd thought about it plenty of times. But how was a man with one whole heritage supposed to understand a wife with two half ones? She couldn't imagine Franklin would ever turn mean, but he might think of her as a liar or a runaway or maybe just as someone different from the woman he knew. She didn't want any of those things, not from Franklin. The truth was probably that a little part of her—okay, a big part of her—was absolutely terrified of what might happen to this beautiful life should anyone find out she'd also kept a beautiful secret.

And so she'd made excuses. Kept to the inn as much as possible. Franklin had begun to assume he'd married a shy woman who did plenty fine welcoming inn guests but preferred to spend most her time behind a sewing machine, alone.

But really, Millie hated being alone. And she sure wasn't shy. The fear of being recognized by the texture of her hair or the darkening of her skin in the summertime was just too much to risk. So instead of romping around Fairhope with Franklin, Millie busied herself with the customers at the inn. People who would come and go, taking any possible questions with them.

Regardless, on this particular late afternoon, Millie couldn't shake the feeling that this pop-up storm spelled trouble. But maybe that was just her imagination. After all, Mama always used to say Millie had an imagination that ran wild.

Three gentle but audible knocks sounded at the door. Millie put her patchwork down on the velvet settee and stood, straightening her cloche.

She rubbed her dry lips together and made an effort to smile despite the fear tightening her chest. She'd spent too much time thinking about her past, that was all. But she had a job to do now, so she would put that aside and be in the here and now as much as possible.

Millie opened the front door and then the screen door, which responded with a screech. A smart-looking woman fifteen, maybe twenty years her senior, stood at the doorway, with a little girl propped up on her hip. The two of them huddled together, protected from the rain by the porch.

The toddler looked up at her mother, as the woman eased a few stray onyx-colored hairs back into her own wavy hairstyle. She had the slightest bags beneath her green eyes, and Millie's heart pricked when she noticed something else there too—a tiredness beyond what sleep could heal. She recognized that look. She'd seen it in her own mirror many times.

If there was one thing she'd learned from Mrs. Stevens, it was that people often came to boardinghouses when they had something to hide. Question was, were these two running from something or toward it?

It was a question Millie often asked herself. If she was being honest, she still hadn't found the answer. Maybe that's why she enjoyed trying to sort through other folks' stories. Distracted her from her own.

The woman held out her hand toward Millie. "I'm Eliza, and this is my daughter. By chance," the woman said, "is this Franklin's place?" She moved her gaze around the doorstep, looking for him.

Millie's breath caught as she took the woman's hand. What was she needing with Franklin? The two of them were well-dressed, and Millie imagined they were probably fairly rich back wherever they came from. How did they know her husband? Would they see straight through the different identity she had created for herself?

But maybe the answer was simpler than that. Maybe Franklin met these people somewhere and told them about the boardinghouse. Wherever he went, Franklin was always making friends with the folks around him.

Millie did her best to hide her hesitation as the woman released her hand, waving them into the boardinghouse. "Please, come inside. I'll fetch Franklin for you."

"Thank you." Eliza brushed scattered raindrops from the sleeves of her jacket before crossing the threshold. Most of the inn's guests wouldn't think twice about coming inside as a dripping mess. Then, of course, the water warped the floors, and once the floors were warped, trying to get them lookin' nice again was an absolute disaster.

Millie's heels clacked against the hardwood as she hurried toward the kitchen, where Franklin was in the middle of eating a cookie. Half of it fell toward the floor, and he reached to catch the crumbs but wasn't fast enough. He started laughing, and Millie swatted at him, then crouched to brush up the pieces.

Franklin took her by the arm and pulled her up to standing. "I'll get that. My mess. Though we really should think about getting a dog."

Millie righted her shoulders. "Oh yes, I'm sure the guests would love having a dog licking their plates."

"Hmm." Franklin carried the crumbs toward the trash can. "Perhaps a cat then."

"No time for nonsense, Franklin—it'll be a fine day when inns let animals roam freely through their doors. Now, there's a woman here to see you."

"Don't pretend you wouldn't love keeping livestock in the sitting room if you had your way." Franklin kissed the side of her hair as he passed—the closest he ever came to a real kiss, yet he did this often. Millie didn't mind. In fact, it had become somewhat of a secret code between the two of them. Two people, married— more than friends but never more than whatever came beyond.

Okay, so she had a weakness for baby goats. Didn't mean she was about to let Franklin adopt all the strays in town.

"Here to see me, you say?" Franklin straightened his hat and new suspenders. "Give you a name, by chance?"

"Eliza." Millie dropped the cookie crumbs into the trash.

Franklin frowned, the sort of frown one gives when trying to make sense of a tricky puzzle piece. "Eliza, huh?"

Millie followed on his heels as he headed toward the entryway. "You know her, don't you?" She wanted more information and wished Franklin would fill her in privately. That way she wouldn't have to guess at the gaps. But Franklin wasn't the type to think like that, secrets and all.

Millie liked it about him. Usually. But not at the moment.

"Franklin," she whispered as he started turning the corner into the foyer. "Who is—"

"As I live and breathe," he said, addressing Eliza. The man had the focus of a fox and probably hadn't even heard Millie's last-ditch attempt at getting more information.

Eliza embraced Franklin, still holding her daughter on her hip. Unsure what to make of all this, Millie offered Eliza a smile.

She was surprised—unnerved, even—to find Eliza studying her. Intently. Chills ran down Millie's arms. What if this woman knew something?

"Please forgive me, but your hat . . ." Eliza began.

Millie's heart thudded in anticipation of what the woman might say next. *Franklin, why couldn't you have filled me in while we were in the kitchen?* A wave of fears tugged hard against Millie's calm demeanor and threatened to spill forth in a flood of emotion. What about her hat? How much did Eliza know? Did she recognize Millie from Charleston?

"Yes?" Millie asked, her fingers ambling upward on their own accord to take hold of the red wool.

"I believe I've seen it before," Eliza said.

Millie's mouth went dry. She darted a glance toward Franklin, who was too immersed in his own conversation with the child to have any idea what was going on between her and Eliza.

"I . . ." Millie took a deep breath, unsure what to say. What would Mama tell her if she were here right now?

"Now, you be careful. Mind for strangers, and keep your talkin' brief. We don't want nobody asking questions."

Avoid the question. That's what she would do.

"I doubt that," Millie said, "but thank you for noticing. I do enjoy wearing it."

And then—she didn't know why the next words left her mouth, maybe nerves or maybe fear or maybe something else—she added, "It was a gift. The hat, I mean. When I was a little girl."

Eliza's eyes softened, her grin widening. Her voice was gentle as she replied, "I know." And the unexpected response shook Millie down to her toes.

What does she mean, she knows?

Eliza watched her for a long moment, still with that steady smile, and then took a step closer toward the child and Franklin. Was that to be the end of the conversation, then?

Franklin turned to Millie and waved her closer. She hurried to his side, relieved to feel the warmth of him as he rested his arm over her shoulders. "Millie, I'm so happy to introduce you to . . . well, I guess I should start calling you Aunt Eliza."

"Aunt?" Millie looked up at him, bewildered. "But I thought you said your mother was your only kin." She drew in a deep breath, allowing her hand to rest against the banded waistline of her dress as her chest rose and fell. She was going to be all right. These people were not a threat.

Franklin bit down on his bottom lip. "I did say that, didn't I? It's . . . well, it's complicated. You catch my drift?"

Oh yes. Millie knew all about complicated.

Franklin glanced over toward the little girl, who was sucking her thumb. Did he know her as well?

"What the boy means to say is we've gotten into a pinch of trouble, and I was hoping you two could help us," Eliza said.

Millie eyes widened. "Trouble? Do you mean with the law?" She couldn't help but blurt it out. She glanced toward Franklin. She was going to need more information before agreeing to this, no matter how charming and no matter how close of kin.

Franklin—bless it—finally seemed to read her mind. He cleared his throat. "When I was just a baby, my mother and I fell on hard times. My family was known for having a good reputation in Charleston, but the truth was all of our wealth crumbled after the war. My uncle took care of us. Made sure we never went without." Franklin and Eliza shared such a poignant almost-smile that the emotion that passed between them passed through Millie as well. "His methods may at times have been a bit unorthodox, but he never hurt anybody."

Eliza ruffled her daughter's hair. "If it's all right, I'd like to get squared away in a guest room if you've got one. I can manage the luggage on my own."

"Of course," Millie said, Eliza's words still replaying in her mind. "*I know.*"

What did she know? *What* did she know?

"We would be happy to get all that sorted out. And don't bother with a rental fee," Franklin added. "After all, you're family." Silence. "Isn't that right, Millie?"

The sound of her own name brought her out of her thoughts. Millie nodded emphatically. Probably a bit too emphatically.

"Absolutely." Millie frowned. "But there's one thing I don't understand. Where is your uncle now?"

Eliza looked to Franklin, raising her chin ever so slightly. "That's a good question."

TWENTY-TWO

Fairhope, 1948

Millie settled into the settee by the window opposite the radio and straightened the full skirt of her dress as she glanced toward Eliza on the other side of the sofa.

Eliza smiled. The gentle but defined strokes of her eye makeup were reminiscent of flappers, and Millie supposed that was probably because Eliza was one, once upon a time. The corners of Eliza's eyes rose with the grin of someone who knows more than they're letting on.

Franklin was putting on a puppet show for the little girl, using two old socks with pinned-on fabric for their faces. It was all Millie could do not to blurt out to Eliza, *"Just what do you know about my hat?"*

The fact she had lasted the past quarter hour without saying a word was a testament to her willpower. But now that answers were imminent, her mind spun. The answers seemed to be coming too fast.

What if Eliza knew something she shouldn't about Millie's heritage? Millie's family? What if Millie had been recognized and her past had been compromised as a consequence? Or what if her future suffered much the same fate? What of Franklin?

Millie took a deep breath, willing her thoughts to slow down.

Eliza gracefully slid closer to the center of the velvet settee. Millie did the same. Eliza removed her gloves and rested one hand on Millie's knee, meeting Millie's eyes with her own unwavering gaze. Millie didn't so much as blink. What did Eliza see?

"You're wondering how I know about the hat."

Millie nodded, swallowing the knot in her throat as a nightly news program murmured from the radio.

"Anybody ever tell you the story?" Eliza asked, her lips rising like a mother in the midst of reading a Little Golden Book, pausing appropriately for each illustration.

Millie fidgeted with the taffeta of her dress. How much did Eliza know? How much did Millie dare tell?

"Only bits and pieces," Millie said. "Odds and ends, as it were." Like the little scraps of fabric one can either choose to trash or hold onto, waiting for a new project that may better suit them.

Millie knew a lot about that process.

"I see." Eliza patted Millie's knee decidedly. "Well, let's start at the beginning then, shall we?"

Millie's heart began to quicken. Was Eliza about to tell Millie her story? The one she'd run from? The one she'd been hiding?

Eliza straightened a ring with an intricate leaf-patterned band on her left hand. Millie watched the ring circle 'round and 'round and wondered at the leaf pattern, of her own roots, and what Eliza might know of them.

"Millie, I'm a watercolorist. I've painted many scenes from Charleston as well as many persons, and I did a series on Gullah tradition quite some time ago. I once painted a woman—a beautiful woman who told me a story about her ancestors getting tragically separated in the days of slavery, and how she and her brother and sister were doing all they could to preserve what they knew of that history for the next generation. She seemed to be madly in love with the most charming Italian man, and they had a baby." Eliza hesitated. "Cute as a button."

Millie shook her head as tears began to stream down. No. No, it couldn't be true. For so long, she'd lived as if that part of her story, her history, was gone, she'd begun to believe it herself. At least then, she wouldn't have to think about the people who killed her father and the people who would've hurt her too if he hadn't stepped in when he did.

Eliza waited until Millie dried the tears and met her eyes once more. "This little child absolutely adored my hat. I mean to tell you, I have never seen the likes of it before. I let her play with it." Eliza shrugged one shoulder up closer to her chin and offered a grin so charming it might as well have been a magazine photograph. The memory frozen in time—the past barreling into the present, when the long-ago moment could finally be told. Shared, even.

Millie's eyelashes pulled together with each blink, her mascara sticky with tears. She ran the edge of her finger along her eyes to collect the streaks of black trying to run down.

"I imagine you know the rest of the story."

"The little girl refused to give it back," Millie whispered, smiling. Yes, that's what her mama always told her—*"Ever since you was a baby, Millie, when you got a hold of something, you never did let up. No reason to start now."*

"That painting of your mother was one of my best works because I didn't have to look far for her story. She came to bring me a sweetgrass basket as a thank-you for your hat, and the next thing I knew, I was painting her." Eliza's gaze moved around the room, from the freshly swept floors to the fireplace and the new lamps and the odds and ends Millie had laid around. A doily here, a glass figurine there. Vases of flowers in as many nooks and crannies as she could fit them. Satisfied they were alone, still Eliza lowered her voice as she leaned her head closer. "Millie, how did you end up here?"

The words, so simple and yet piercing, stunned Millie.

How did I?

In all the secret keeping, the black-and-white clarity of her heritage had begun to grey so that she couldn't pull apart any longer what half of her belonged where.

"I wanted to own a dress shop." It was the only thing she could think to say.

Eliza lifted her chin as realization slowly dawned.

"The man you saw, my father, was killed not too long thereafter because he and my mama were together. My parents were married in the eyes of God, 'course, but some folks see only the law. Those men raged and raged that Blacks and whites shouldn't love one another, and their blood shouldn't be mixed. The men came after me for playing with their children, and in the process of his telling Mama to hide me, they took him. Hurt him real bad, and he died. Our story changed after that, mine and Mama's. She grew more cautious to keep me safe. Can't say I blame her after what happened with Daddy. We were both scared as we'd ever been."

Millie tried to hide her trembling hands under the skirt of her dress. "Mama told me to pass as white for my dream. She always believed I could catch the moon if I wanted. But now that I'm a bit older, I do have to wonder if the passing part was her tryin' to keep me safe so much as anything else. I guess she figured if I could pick just one heritage, I wouldn't have these two parts pushing and pulling inside of me, and people on the outside wouldn't be pushing and pulling with their threats, either. One heritage, one future."

Eliza's slender fingers slid along the velvet of the sofa. "Only there are two parts of your heritage." She reached out to straighten Millie's cloche. "Millie, what does that say about your future?"

What did it, indeed?

Two hours later, when they'd finished every crumb of their pie, Eliza sat at the bench of the boardinghouse's piano. She was going to start a new life in New Orleans, she said, far away from whatever chased them in Charleston. Her fingers seemed to fly across the keys and beyond as the jazz tune echoed deep within the room, deeper still within Millie's soul.

Melancholic, the words from Langston Hughes's poem "Harlem"

settled as a refrain within Millie, as she pulled a needle and thread from the sewing box she kept beside the settee. She thought of her own dream deferred. All the places it sent her, all the places the dream itself might go.

One stitch at a time as Eliza played, Millie told the story of Rose and Ashley and the little satchel with great provision. Preserving their history for the present and for the future.

She signed the satchel with the initials for Millie Middleton, the name her mother offered to keep her safe—a simple way to honor the stories of the women who'd come before. Women whose names would otherwise be forgotten by history.

With every stitch, with every letter, she tugged the needle through the fabric and bound the two together. She told the story of two histories, two ancestries, united.

And though Eliza had only been at the boardinghouse a few hours, Millie was thankful to have known her however briefly—a preservationist in every sense of the word.

TWENTY-THREE

Charleston, Modern Day

Funny how the house that initially seemed so broken now seemed so lovely. Cozy. Old bookshelves housed new titles, and current photographs sat propped on the mantel beside yellowing maps of the city.

Peter glanced at his watch. "Will you excuse me a minute? I need to give my dog his eye drops, pathetic as that probably sounds."

"No problem." Harper smiled.

Peter stepped into the other room.

As she was admiring the thick baseboards and elaborate windows, Harper heard a bark from the kitchen. The next thing she knew, Peter was yelling, "Rutledge, stand down." Some blur was charging toward her. Out of instinct, Harper held out her arms to soften the blow—but to her surprise, the animal jumped into them.

Rutledge, as it turned out, was an overly zealous beagle mix intent on making a new friend. Harper held the dog in her arms and laughed.

"You named your dog Rutledge?"

"He was one of the writers of the Constitution. The man Rutledge, that is. The canine version is just as feisty as the colonist. I'm really sorry. He's pretty dramatic." Peter squeezed one drop into each of the dog's eyes. "He gets dry eye—you know, like people do—if I don't do this twice a day."

Harper thought it was sweet he was willing to do something like that for his pet.

Peter's phone rang from his pocket. He set the eye drop bottle down on one of the bookshelves, then answered the call. "Yes, ma'am. We're done with our tour, so the timing works just fine." He paused, clearly letting her speak. "Yes, I'm sorry. I know you don't like being called 'ma'am.'" He shook his head at Harper, smiling. "Okay. Sounds good. We'll be there shortly."

Peter pocketed his phone. "Millie said she's done resting and wants to see the store. Maybe we can get this contract going. You up for it?"

"Absolutely." Except for the contract part.

A few minutes later, Harper followed Peter down the sidewalk toward the dress shop, imagining the history of each building they passed. Without his stories, she never would've considered how deep the history ran. Peter had inspired a whole new way of thinking. She'd never look at earthquake bolts or cobblestones quite the same way.

And though she'd probably never see him again after all this was done, his passion for history had changed something inside of her.

For the better.

Peter flipped on the lights, illuminating a room so old it could definitely be euphemized as historical. The door and windows showed a pleasant view of the antiques side of King Street, but the empty space had clearly been forgotten. Neglected, even.

"What do you think?" Peter asked.

"Hmm." Millie's fingers trailed over the old walls. She tapped her low orthopedic heel and looked up, holding her hat in place. For a moment, Harper saw her as a much younger woman, even a girl, back when this place was in its prime and maybe so was Millie.

"Would you believe I've never been inside? Only peered through the window and made up stories in my head about the brides who were shopping. I used to love imagining that sort of thing. Well, until I met Franklin. Then there was no need to pretend." Millie continued looking up at the slatted ceiling, as if the whole roof might open at any moment and give a glimpse of heaven.

"Why did you never go inside, Millie?" Peter asked.

Her gaze met and held his own. "I was but a girl when I lived here," she muttered.

Peter nodded and slipped his hands into his khakis.

Millie sighed. Her hips swung lightly to a rhythm Harper couldn't hear as Millie sashayed across the room as if she already owned the place. Maybe in some ways, she did. Long windows at the front of the shop let muted light stream in over the wood floor. The look on her face, the surrender to that beautiful moment, was striking.

"This room would be lovely for my bridal shop, Peter," Millie said, finally answering his question. She reached out and touched the shoulder seam along his sweater.

To Harper, this room was empty. Full of dust and the relics of decades long gone. But maybe to Millie, it was something more. Harper couldn't fault the woman for pretending their plans to open the store were real ones, just for a little while.

Peter smiled.

Harper's heart ached for him. Ached for the gentle respect he showed Millie. Ached knowing how badly he wanted to know his family secrets. Ached for the fact that *she* knew them.

Peter Perkins was clearly invested in the dreams of others, which in her book showed the quietest kind of strength.

Harper took a step forward, and a creaky board gave her pause. Ironic, really. She'd run from her life in Savannah straight into a dress store. Just weeks ago, a store like this was everything Harper wanted.

But that was before failure sent her on a wounded and frantic journey toward another dream. Now, it was just a façade. Oz at the end of the yellow brick road.

As Harper looked around the store, she saw something in the corner she'd missed before. "Is that a rack of dresses?" she asked.

Peter shrugged. "A handful I've found here and there inside the properties I've acquired. I didn't know what to do with them, so I've kept them in storage until now." He rubbed his beard mindlessly with his right hand. "I thought you two might want them. Sell them, display them—whatever you want."

Harper caught an excited giggle before it escaped her throat. Vintage dresses made her giddy. Even if they didn't belong to her, even if they were all part of the smoke screen this storefront represented.

They still had a story to tell.

Peter watched her and Millie with his blue-green eyes, framed by those tortoiseshell glasses he had on earlier. "Well, they're all up for grabs except for one. There's a wedding dress I was hoping you could give me some information about, being the dress experts you two are. It once belonged to my mom."

Harper tried not to all-out skip over to the rack. She always *had* loved these types of dresses. Millie followed closely on her heels.

But then something happened.

Millie stopped.

She stared straight ahead, her gaze fixed on the first dress of the rack. And then, like a magnet, the dress drew her closer.

The blush peach, silk dress was layered with cream lace over the bodice and hemline. Most arresting was the stunning cape that Harper imagined to be from the 1940s.

They just didn't make dresses like that anymore.

Actually, they didn't make dresses like it back then, either.

It was exquisite. One of a kind.

Harper stood in awe. This might be the most beautiful dress she had ever seen. And she'd seen a lot.

Millie took several steps forward. "I'll be," she said. "In this place, of all places."

She reached for the gown, and her fingers trailed the dainty lace until they reached a special button at the back neckline of the dress.

The button was faded blue, with the imprint of a butterfly.

Something borrowed, perhaps?

Something blue?

"Almost too delicate to be worn," Harper said of the button.

"What good are beautiful buttons if they aren't worn?" Millie's hands began to tremble as she gently touched the fabric. "We will live fragile lives, my dear Harper, if we avoid that which is delicate for fear it might break at the seams."

Harper frowned. She thought of her own dress and the negative feedback she'd received. Maybe she and Millie had more in common than she'd realized. Maybe they even shared a lost dream?

The spell broke. It must have been too much for Millie to process. The store, the memories . . . She dropped her hand from the dress and straightened her shoulders.

When she turned to them, she looked strong—for anyone, much less someone her age. But the red sting at the corners of her eyes was not lost on Harper.

"I'm sorry, Peter," Millie said, shaking her head. "I don't think I can give you any details except to say this dress is in splendid shape for its age. Whoever sewed it did a remarkable job."

TWENTY-FOUR

Fairhope, 1949

Millie came out of the bathroom with her dress zipped just past her bra line, and held both sides up with her hands. "Franklin?" she called into the bedroom. "Can you finish zipping me?"

She'd made several boatneck dresses in keeping with the trend, but each one required daily assistance zipping them up and then zipping them down. Franklin was always a perfect gentleman with his zipping duty, and Millie had come to look forward to these moments of closeness that bookmarked each day, beginning to end.

These past two years of marriage had been unconventional, sure. Yet they'd also been deeper and more satisfying than Millie had ever expected. Truth is, she had come to love him.

So much so, that she still held him at a distance when he winked at her one time too many or she noticed his gaze from across the room linger upon her. She wanted to gaze back—oh, how she wanted to. But that would mean taking steps toward trusting this man, and she just didn't have the luxury of trusting anyone.

That was the price of this life, wasn't it? Opportunities in exchange for an ever-guarded heart. Funny how lately, all she'd done to protect her secret felt a lot less like wisdom and a lot more like fear. But what choice did she have? She was too far in this thing now to turn back.

Franklin fiddled with the hook clasp at the back of her dress. "All set."

She shifted toward him and smiled. "Thanks."

He cleared his throat. "Really nice dress, Millie."

Millie stepped over to their dresser set where she kept her pearls, and fastened her earrings while she talked. "You think so?" She glanced at herself in the mirror above the dresser. The dress was a new favorite of hers. The creamy hue complemented her skin tone, and an everyday sort of lace ran along the neckline and waist. Her favorite part, though, was the three-quarter sleeves.

"Absolutely." He didn't know Millie could see him in the dresser mirror or that she noticed the way he looked at her. Her breath caught a moment, both from that look and the thought of them driving to the dress store. "You ready to head downtown?" he asked.

Millie adjusted the pearls around her neck. "Sure am." But the truth was, she wasn't really. Because there was only one dress store in downtown Fairhope. And if she jeopardized this opportunity, she could jeopardize the whole shebang. What then?

Franklin seemed to sense her nerves. "Remember, it's not an interview or anything like that. She just wants to meet you, is all."

Millie wiggled her toes inside her black leather heels. "Tell me again—how did I even come up?"

"Her son needed a ride over to her shop, and I was with him and talking about you."

Millie's heart warmed at the thought of having been talked about.

"Now, come on. Let's knock 'em dead." Franklin walked over toward the bedroom door and held it open as she stepped through, toward whatever might be coming.

Franklin and Millie strolled past the streetlamps and colorful flowerbeds in downtown Fairhope until they came to the dress shop.

The sign outside the store was hand-painted in cursive letters, *McAdam's Gowns*. Millie would just have to look past the misplaced apostrophe. The bell above the door chimed as she and Franklin walked through.

The wood floors had been recently polished, for they shone so clearly you could see your face in the reflection. Racks of beautiful dresses that looked like something Grace Kelly would wear lined the walls, and the smell of Chanel No. 5 floated around. Even the air the fragrance clung to was expensive.

A woman wearing a deep-purple dress appeared, her hair styled into a beehive. "You must be Franklin and Millie. I am Helen McAdams." She extended her gloved hand, which Millie and Franklin took turns shaking. "I'm so glad to have you in the shop."

She leaned closer, looking Millie up and down. Millie's heart quickened as she wondered—what did Mrs. McAdams find? Was she simply studying the homemade dress, or were there other answers she sought?

After a long moment, the woman crossed her arms. "Well, I have to say, Millie, Franklin wasn't exaggerating."

"You can tell all that just from looking at my dress?" Millie fussed over a wrinkle at the waistline.

"Your dress?" Mrs. McAdams frowned. "I'm sorry. I don't understand."

"Perhaps I misunderstood. Are we not meeting because you're in need of a seamstress?" Millie asked.

Slowly, the woman mouthed *oh* in the daintiest way as understanding dawned. "It's true, the other day I did mention I'm in need of a seamstress. But I thought we were meeting on account of my need for a model."

Millie's eyes widened. Panic shot through her veins. "A model?" she gulped. As in, for the eyes of everybody to look at?

"Yes, dear. Truly, you could stop a passerby in her tracks." The woman smiled. "Why, Millie, with your deep-olive complexion and green eyes, you're a knockout. I'd even venture that many a young woman would buy my dresses for the prospect of looking like you."

"Looking like . . . me?" But all this time, Millie had been trying to look like somebody else. *If Mrs. McAdams only knew . . . half of that* me *wasn't legally allowed to enter the doors of this dress shop.*

Mrs. McAdams nodded. "It's common for women of your beauty not to realize how stunning they are. I'm opening a new line of dresses in two weeks, and I want to display them on a real, live model during a little fashion show I'll be hosting here at the store. Get women's attention with the next big styles, yes? Tell me you'll consider it."

No one had ever called Millie beautiful before. Well, except for Mama, but that hardly counted. She'd always felt as though the two sides of her heritage were warring with one another, and she couldn't fully fit in, much less be admired. Yet here, in this moment, Mrs. McAdams seemed to imply that the blending created a unique kind of beauty . . . whether Mrs. McAdams realized she was implying that or not.

But Millie didn't need to consider the woman's proposal to know her answer.

"So gracious of you to ask." Millie gently shook her head. "But no, ma'am, I'm not comfortable modeling the dresses." She smiled, hoping the clarity of her next words would resonate rather than sound ridiculous. "You see, I'm a seamstress. And I'm far more comfortable behind a sewing machine than in front of a crowd, pretending to be something I'm not." There was no need to publicize the war going on inside her. And what if the wrong pair of eyes happened to see past the show she was putting on?

Mrs. McAdams folded her lips in the most serious expression Millie had seen on her yet. She looked Millie up and down again, only this time, she stepped closer to examine the seams of Millie's sleeves. Millie was silent, waiting.

"You made this?" she asked.

"Yes, ma'am." Out of old curtains, but Mrs. McAdams didn't need to know that part.

Franklin squeezed Millie's shoulder, and a rush of encouragement flooded her at his touch. "I'm going to get some fresh air while you two ladies do business." Millie grinned at him, and he returned her smile as he pushed open the door.

"He's a doll." Mrs. McAdams looked back toward Millie. "How long have you been sewing?"

Oh goodness. How long had she been breathing? "Long as I can remember. I was just a child when my mama taught me with a needle and thread."

Mrs. McAdams made a clicking noise with her tongue as if she were thinking. Hope rose up within Millie like a cloud floating along, and she was glad she'd turned down that modeling offer or else this conversation never would have happened.

"Your experience shows." Mrs. McAdams lifted her chin. "In addition to the dresses I design for the store, we also make custom gowns and offer dress repairs. It's in the latter two categories I need help. We have some high-end clients, Millie. Actresses and musicians and the like. So I will need you to be efficient and make no errors. Do you feel yourself capable?"

"Quite." Millie touched the pearls at her neck.

The woman leaned closer, looking around to see if anyone might be in earshot. "We also have some . . . delicate . . . situations we must work around. I've recently been contacted to design a dress for a famous scat singer."

Millie's eyes widened.

"A *colored* scat singer." Mrs. McAdams whispered the word. "Now, I don't know how you feel about segregation. It's my belief we ought to have the same schools and stores and all, but not everybody thinks like me, and the law's the law."

Millie's stomach turned as her stomach often did when white people who thought she was white too talked about Black ones. And though it was true she didn't know to whom she belonged, she found herself at times like this belonging in two spaces, pulled by the two opposing sides. When really, why did they have to oppose at all?

"What I'm saying is," the woman continued, "I need a seamstress who will not alienate my clients. Who is flexible and sensitive to the needs of customers and will put those above any personal beliefs on the matter. Can you handle that part as well? Because I would love to have your help on the gown."

"I can assure you, ma'am, blending in to address each client's needs will not be a problem."

After all, blending in was one thing Millie did well. So well, in fact, that sometimes she woke at night with dreams of sweetgrass baskets and Mama's recipes, and she would miss that part of her heritage so fiercely that she would get up, go to the kitchen, and make a big pot of red rice, Gullah style. And she wondered in those moments—was she ever really meant to blend in?

"Very well. Though the position is part-time, I hope to make it long-lasting," Mrs. McAdams added.

As she reached to shake Mrs. McAdams's gloved hand knowing she was one step closer to her dream of dressmaking, Millie couldn't get the thought of Mama's red rice out of her mind.

TWENTY-FIVE

Charleston, Modern Day

Harper watched Millie hover over the wedding dress and wondered what the shop must've looked like back in its heyday—what it must look like through Millie's eyes even now. Were wealthy patrons buzzing about, wearing expensive hats and fiddling with their kidskin gloves? Were the lace and the silk and the rows and rows of gowns as enchanting in their prime as Harper found them in their maturity?

Millie reached to touch the fabric of the other gowns on the rack.

Peter walked over to her. "Are you feeling all right?"

Millie patted him on the shoulder. "Just fine. It's strange, you know." She looked up at him. "Being in this space again, only this time, from the other side of the glass. Never thought I'd see the day." She warmed them both with one of her winsome smiles.

Harper knew the feeling of a love affair with dresses, and she knew what it was to lose that love too. Well, maybe not lose it, exactly, because you never really *lose* your dreams. But over time, maybe a person grows more realistic or just more discouraged, and the dream that should inch closer and closer actually blasts out of reach. Harper's heart ached for Millie.

Perhaps, at least, the nostalgia would be enough to tug Millie toward telling Peter the truth. Then they could have the conversation they all so desperately needed without actually leasing Peter's space. What a ridiculous thought.

Why was Millie so comfortable with secret keeping? The band of Harper's skirt felt tight. All the secrecy was suffocating her.

"Let's sit, shall we?" Millie started toward the center of the room where Peter had opened three folding chairs for them in a little circle, reminding Harper of the musical chairs game she'd played as a child.

Peter and Harper both followed Millie and sat, as the breeze sent a flurry of leaves outside the window scurrying down the sidewalk.

Here they came—the words that would change everything.

Millie folded her hands. "I've decided I want to rent the property. It's perfect for my needs."

Harper blinked. So not the words she was expecting.

She glared a hole through Millie, daring the woman to break eye contact with Peter and instead glance her way.

Millie didn't.

Harper wanted to groan. Wanted to run outside and grab a gelato from the place down the street and bury her sorrows in a rack of cheap sunglasses at Forever 21. She didn't care if she was past twenty-one—that was the point of the store, wasn't it? Better yet, she'd turn to Etsy. She would hurry upstairs and cover herself with blankets and hide away from the world, save her phone and the lovely portal it offered into the world of cyber consignment.

But instead, she was brave. Or maybe just in shock. Either way, she stayed and confronted the thing. She said the words that would be equally surprising. "Sounds great, Millie. Why don't you go ahead and give him the first payment?"

Millie's eyes widened, as she finally turned her attention to Harper.

Sweet victory. That did the trick, all right. Harper looked back at her. *Want to call an audible? I can do that too.*

She needed to get out of here sooner rather than later. Before the history of the place and the romance of the gowns and the whole silly dream of a dress store got to her. Again.

"Sounds lovely." Millie's grin all but glowed. "Harper Rae, be a dear and fetch my pen."

Un-be-lievable.

"Oh, there's really no hurry." Peter stood. Harper did too. Meanwhile, Millie—bless it—Millie just sat there, still grinning. "So long as I get the money within the next week. I know you're good for your word."

Oh. My.

Harper held the palm of her hand to her forehead. What in high heaven was Millie thinking?

Neither of them had discussed this as an option. It was too outlandish. Too impulsive. But something had shifted in Millie roughly fifteen minutes ago. Around the time she first saw . . .

The dress! Of course. The dress Peter found must be connected to Millie. Why hadn't Harper put the pieces together before now?

Harper had been fortunate to land this job with Millie. She truly enjoyed helping, even traveling, despite all the Broadway soundtracks Millie had insisted they listen to on the drive over in between audiobooks.

But this was something else entirely. Millie was getting far too close to the fence Harper had used to secure her old dreams.

Harper needed that part of herself contained. Off-limits. Bygones and past failures from which she had learned. She was moving on with her new life.

Running a dress store with someone as gifted as Millie wasn't exactly the easiest way to leave past dreams in the dust where they belonged. Maybe working for Millie wasn't such a good idea after all.

Just as Harper opened her mouth to say something, she caught Millie's gaze drifting to the dress rack—to the peach silk little number that must've stunned in its day, because it certainly stunned on this one.

The look on Millie's face could've stopped a train in its tracks.

And Harper knew then she would do it. She would do whatever Millie asked.

Not because this was her dream, but because it was still Millie's.

Harper used to lie in bed at night, eyes open, dreaming new dreams. Windows cracked to hear the crickets, and the whip-poor-will if she was lucky. Whip-poor-wills were funny about comin' and goin' as seasons changed—no way to tell when, but one night once the weather warmed, you'd hear them singing.

She was oh so tired of the dreaming. It was an awful thing to think, when this dream had made her heart leap in the way that only sheer and perfect hope could. But it was the truth.

And yet, even still, she saw dresses when she closed her eyes in the evening. And she knew she had to get them out on paper if she was ever going to get a wink of sleep.

So later that night, Harper cradled her sketchbook in her arms and tiptoed into the living area, ready to make a pot of tea for her own company.

She had decided she would tell Millie she'd stay on board to help with the dress shop only until Millie could find a reliable manager. Then she would head back home. Whatever *home* might mean.

A hiss of steam came from the kitchen. The kettle was already brewing.

"Millie?" She kept her voice low and walked over to where the woman sat by the window that overlooked King Street.

No response.

"Millie?" Harper tried again. Panic began to stir. In the lamplight, it was nearly impossible to see. Was Millie . . .

The woman turned. Harper breathed a sigh of relief.

"You'd think I was dead or something with that sort of reaction. Calm yourself, child."

"I thought we agreed you'd call me 'sugar.'" Harper set her sketchbook down, then stepped over to flip on the light near the refrigerator and busied herself removing the pot from the stove. She poured the water from the kettle into teacups, then dunked a decaf tea bag into each.

Charleston Tea Plantation. Hmm. Millie had done some shopping, probably while she was supposed to be "resting" during the walking tour. But Harper wasn't complaining, not after the undrinkable beverage Peter tried to pass off this morning as coffee.

She put a spoonful of sugar into her own and half a spoonful into Millie's. Hadn't taken long to learn how Millie liked things. Her pillows, her slippers, her tea . . .

"Millie, what are you doing? It's well after midnight." Harper took a seat across from Millie, just a coffee table between them. She held out the cup toward her.

"Oh, confounded." Millie tossed her hands in the air, completely ignoring the tea. "I may as well tell you."

"Tell me what?" Harper set both cups down on the little table.

Millie took her time leaning forward. "You've got to swear to me you won't tell a soul."

Wonderful. Another secret to keep from Peter.

Harper frowned. "Millie, you know I don't like swearing."

"Then give me your word."

Harper cleared her throat. In this case, she didn't want to give that, either. But Millie seemed like she really needed to talk to somebody. And to be honest, Harper was curious. "You've got my word."

Content with that, Millie took her teacup from the table and rested back in her chair. "That wedding dress this afternoon—"

"The one with the beautiful button?" Harper tried sipping her tea. Still way too hot. So she wrapped her hands around the mug and blew to cool it.

Millie hesitated, then sighed.

Harper's eyes were adjusting to the dim lighting, and she

watched as Millie's gaze trailed out the window onto the street below. She blew on her drink and tried another sip.

"It's mine." Millie gripped the plush blue armrest of the chair with her free hand. The memory, whatever it was, seized her. Millie turned her head away from the window so she looked straight at Harper. It was a look that arrested attention. A motherly sort of look from which you dare not look away.

"I know." Harper offered a gentle smile. "I put the pieces together. Did you sew it yourself?"

"I did." Millie set her cup down and folded her hands in her lap. "I wore it on my wedding day."

Her wedding day? Now, that was something.

Harper took a sip of her tea. There was one other thing she'd been wondering all evening. Now seemed to be as good a time to ask as any. "Millie, what is it doing here? Does Peter know it's yours?"

"That seems to be the million-dollar question."

And like that, Millie was quiet once more. The two drank the rest of their tea in silence until Millie saw the sketchbook Harper had brought into the room.

"What's that?"

Harper waved the question away with her hand. "Oh, nothing. Just some dresses I've sketched here or there." She picked up the empty teacups and carried them toward the kitchen sink.

"Mind if I take a look?" When Harper returned from the sink, Millie had turned on a desk lamp and was already flipping through the sketches.

The thought of Millie looking through her creative work was unnerving, to say the least. No one had seen her sketches since her department chair proclaimed her dress worthless. What good could come from a dead dream? No use feeding the thing. On to bigger and better things.

"Just a little hobby of mine." Harper filled in the silence, resisting the urge to snatch the drawings from Millie's grasp.

Millie closed the book and set her hands on top of it. "You're quite good, Harper. You always have had a gift for this."

"I'm average."

Millie watched her a long moment, then stood with a wobble until she got her bearings, using the chair for stability. "I'm going to sleep now. Thanks for finishing the tea."

She handed the notebook back to Harper and kept walking, leaving behind a wake of questions. Hope began to bounce around Harper's heart like a child's ball, and she had the hardest time catching the thing.

She'd already had a chance at the big-picture dream, and that world didn't agree with Peter or Millie's hope-filled take on things. She finally stilled herself with the memory.

As she'd told herself, bigger and better things.

Strange, though, how she kept finding herself talking about the same old dream.

"Oh, and by the way, I've decided I am definitely going to rent the dress shop from Peter. Lest you think that was all for show this afternoon." Millie turned and spoke this over her shoulder, as casually as if she were asking Harper to turn off the lights from the entry. "Sleep tight."

"Not so fast," Harper said.

This was her chance to explain she would commit to helping with the store only until it was up and running. But her heart tugged with the prospect of losing this connection with Millie. Before they had that conversation, there was another thing she needed to ask.

Millie waited.

"You knew all along, didn't you? You were planning to rent it out from the beginning. You act as if you've even researched how much the lease will be."

Even in the dim light, Millie's eyes sparkled. "I said I didn't like the Internet, Harper." She raised her chin. "Never said I couldn't use it."

TWENTY-SIX

Fairhope, 1952

"I'm sweatin' like a sinner in church." Millie fussed with the curved collar of her emerald blouse. "It's hot enough to melt sugar in tea out here."

Franklin smirked, offering her one of his sly half grins. "It's January, Red."

Five years into their marriage, and the nickname that first night had stuck.

"Oh, hush."

She was fond of him—very fond of him, actually—and though their lips hadn't so much as brushed since their wedding day and they'd faithfully slept with an invisible barrier between each side of the bed, she was beginning to long for him in a way she had never quite longed for anyone.

And over time, that little nickname had begun to stir a new set of feelings toward Franklin, so that when she heard it—her own special name—her heart came alive, garnered by his full attention toward her.

He could've called her anything, and she would've felt the same.

He was, of course, her husband. Only, he wasn't. Not in all the conventional ways. So she would go on pretending her heart was as steady as ever, that she saw him as a helper and her dearest friend, for she certainly didn't want to upset the balance of their perfectly beautiful life.

But some mornings, like this morning, she did look at him for a long stretch of time before he awakened—studying his jawline, his neatly trimmed beard, even the way his chest rose and fell with breaths full of relaxation, and in those moments, she longed to be closer to his breaths, closer still to his heart.

Oh, she was in for it now. All kinds of trouble.

She had fallen for him, that's what.

"I realize it's only January, but you could swim through the humidity after that storm last night. Do you not feel it's unseasonably warm? Why, even the azaleas are blooming early."

Certainly he wouldn't argue with the azaleas.

He studied her a while. "Fetch your hat," he said, finally.

Millie hurried over to the hat rack and started to reach for the new hat she'd made last week. Brightly colored flowers framed one side of the small hat and led down toward several inches of netting. But then she thought better of it and grabbed her red cloche instead.

She all but leapt to his side, calming herself lest she look like a child. But she was simply dying to get out of the boardinghouse for a few hours, and adventures with Franklin were her favorite thing.

He took the keys to his old truck from the hook by the entry, then opened the door wide enough for Millie to pass through.

She rewarded his good manners with a wide grin and a swoosh of her skirt, the outer layer made of dotted Swiss lace she'd salvaged from some old gowns Mrs. Stevens had given her years prior. They walked toward the truck, and Franklin helped pull her up into the seat, which sat far too high above the ground for a woman in heels.

Mrs. Stevens's kin brought her to visit from time to time, usually for breakfast, and she never missed the chance to tell Millie and Franklin how proud she was of the way they were running her old inn. Millie's heart warmed every time.

"Where are we going?" She was settled near him and fidgeting with the radio before she thought to ask.

"Do you trust me?" Franklin turned the ignition of his truck and leaned forward, his plaid button-down pressed to the large wheel as he checked for oncoming traffic.

With his hair slicked back and his thick-rimmed glasses, he could pass for a successful businessman. And maybe he was.

Maybe somewhere along the way, he and Millie had stopped pretending to be innkeepers, both running from one thing or another, and had actually come into a new life. Together.

Another five years, and they'd be rollin' in high cotton.

"Should I?" Millie straightened her skirt and grinned at him. But something within her stirred with greater meaning.

Should I? The question offered a quiet refrain. Franklin still didn't know why Millie boarded the train that day. Oh, she'd thought to tell him. She'd thought to tell him a million times.

But secrets are funny things in that sometimes you reach a point in life where they're easier to keep than to break. Such was the case with Millie's past.

"I'll leave that up to you." Franklin winked, sending a tickle of happiness down her arms. "But in this case, the answer is frozen and full of sugar."

Millie grinned from ear to ear. "Ice cream!" She could kiss him right now for how excited she was. She hadn't enjoyed a sundae, her favorite treat, in ages.

She and Franklin fell into a comfortable quiet as they bought their ice cream and ate it at the little shop downtown. But on the inside, a swell of gratitude and anticipation overwhelmed her. All she could think was how far her life had come since that ice cream on King Street five years prior. She had fallen deeply in love. She had married the man. Just not in that order.

This was the life Mama had wanted for her. A life full of opportunity. And yet, she still felt something missing. The tug of a past that used to be. A silent part of her identity that longed to speak. The colored part of her that she was still proud to be. All of that was the reason she hadn't opened her heart to Franklin more fully. Every time she started to tell him, she thought about what happened to her daddy. Maybe Mama knew best when she told Millie to keep it all hushed.

And there was the tug of another thing too—her dress shop dream that had still not come to be, despite her hard work at the store in town and all the mending she did at the inn. She would like to think every stitch brought her closer, but sometimes she wondered what exactly she was sewing.

A good half hour later, after the sun had set full and good and the moon was a smile from the sky, Franklin pulled into the driveway of the boardinghouse. A blissfully pensive Millie made her way to the little porch swing at the back of the old honeymoon suite. The deck, overlooking the bay.

The air was thick as ever with humidity, but the ice cream had done its trick, and Millie had finally cooled down.

Franklin, as he often did, came to sit beside her. "Mind if I join you?"

She never minded.

Back and forth they rocked like that, in the easy quiet that only time and trust can bring. The water lapped against the grassy shoreline, and the oak trees stretched their limbs but a yard away from the ground. So many stars were out that night, as far as Millie could see, and you could hardly make out the stars from their reflection on the water.

Franklin looked at her and stretched his arm around her shoulder. He did not often do that part.

"Happy anniversary, Millie."

Her heart did a dance then, and when she met his gaze, she saw the fire in his eyes and wondered how long he too had felt the insatiable pull she'd come to experience.

Her pulse quickened, and she had the strangest sensation of floating—up from the porch swing, up toward the stars and moon.

For she knew this was a night she would remember, a night when she fell in love with her husband of exactly five years, and a night that love was returned.

"Millie," he whispered, searching her gaze as she had just searched his own.

I love you.

The words need not be spoken aloud—for any sound, however sweet, might take the sanctity of what passed between them.

She simply nodded her affirmation and wondered if even the moonlight might not hide the warmth of her cheeks.

He needed no further invitation.

Franklin drew her closer, traced the curve of her chin with his finger, then pulled the pins one by one from her hair, gently tossing her hat to the wooden deck beneath their feet.

He kissed her with the light of a thousand stars, and though her eyes shut from bliss, she could still see light as she'd never seen. The light of a future, the light of a passion, and the light of a fire Franklin hadn't lit until she was ready.

But now . . . here . . . everything had changed.

Millie slipped off her shoes and slid into his arms, and he carried her over the threshold that evening, willing and oh so ready.

For the next five years. For the next fifty.

TWENTY-SEVEN

Charleston, Modern Day

Harper lined the two fabrics together at the seams—one a true vintage, daisy print, and one a new lining. Lucy had brought Harper's sewing machine over from Savannah last week, and the cool metal of the machine warmed her heart with the comfort of familiarity. She ran the fabrics through the vintage machine, careful that the blending of the two different fabrics didn't cause any puckering.

Lucy had asked about the rest of her furniture, but Harper told her she planned to drive over in a couple of weeks and sell it to other SCAD students.

The front door to the storefront creaked open.

Harper released the pedal of the machine but kept her hold on the fabric. Peter stepped inside. She straightened the thick headband that tamed her curls and offered a smile.

He rubbed his five o'clock shadow and slipped both hands into his pockets. Then he looked down to the stacks of boxes and gestured toward one with his loafer. "What are these?"

Harper cleared her throat. In retrospect, she probably shouldn't have taken the liberty to pile them like a fortress around the repair supplies he was using to get the storefront ready. But those suckers were *heavy*.

"Shoes."

Peter pulled his glasses from the bridge of his nose and wiped them with the hem of his sweater.

"I'll move them." Harper filled the silence.

"Nonsense. I'll do it." He reached for one of the boxes. "So, shoes, huh? Your own or for the store?"

"Very funny." Harper rolled her eyes but grinned.

"Is the whole business owner thing starting to sink in? Or does it seem surreal?"

More surreal than you can imagine, considering there was no actual plan to run a real store until Millie's sudden announcement.

Harper finished the row of stitches, then loosened her grip of the fabric.

"It hasn't sunk in." She shook her head. "But then again, it's not my dress shop. It's Millie's."

Peter crossed his arms. He took one step closer, toward the sewing machine. "Seems like a cop-out to me."

Harper just stared at him.

"Why are you being so evasive?" he asked.

"I'm not . . ." Harper ran her turquoise necklace back and forth along her collar. Peter was not going to let this go, was he? She didn't break eye contact. "I've been disappointed before."

He waited for her to continue, unflinching.

She fought a compulsion to fill the silence. She lost. "I came here with the intention of helping Millie. Not running the dress store."

"And yet here you are, repairing an old . . . whatever that thing is." Peter pushed a couple of the boxes closer to the brick wall. "This is about your stupid professor, isn't it?"

"The piece is fine. The sort of thing I could get from any Anthropologie."

The words echoed from the empty chamber of her heart once filled by her dream.

Before she could say anything, he continued. "What if she was wrong, Harper? Have you considered that? You're going to allow her words to keep you from following a career that matters to you?"

Harper fiddled with her earrings. "On the contrary, Peter. I am readily and gladly working alongside Millie to get this dress shop ready. But I am not going to be foolish about it." She shuffled back and forth on her feet. "And I am certainly not going to pretend the dress shop is my own. This is about Millie."

Peter kept his arms crossed over his broad chest. He didn't seem persuaded in the least. "And yet *you* are the one ordering and sorting items to sell. You're the one at the sewing machine."

Harper pointed down to the blouse she was repairing. "Oh, this isn't for the store. This is for fun. I'm taking a break from the real work before I sort through the shoes and start tagging them so they're rack-ready. I got a ton of them at deep discount from a store that was closing."

Peter blinked. "Do you hear yourself right now?"

Harper laughed.

"Seriously. Do you realize how ridiculous you sound? You're taking a break from shoes by sewing a shirt."

"That's right." Sewing had always been the way she expressed herself, ever since she was twelve and got her first machine. She couldn't imagine *not* sewing. Connecting seam to seam, button to button, fabric to dream, was how she made sense of the world. She might hesitate to run a dress store after all the years of struggling, but she would never, never, give up creating.

It was the whole interacting-with-the-outside-world part that she couldn't do anymore.

Harper reached for the blouse and straightened the fabric to begin the next seam. But before she touched the pedal, she looked up at Peter one more time. "I just don't think I could handle the heartache if this thing fails and I own it. You can understand that, can't you? I'm holding it loosely."

He looked down at the floor and slowly nodded. When he raised his head, he met her gaze with a sigh. "I do. But I think you've got more fight in you than you admit. Just ask that blouse." His grin unraveled her for more reasons than one.

By the glow of the streetlamps and the stars above, Peter, Millie, and Harper strolled down Queen Street to get some supper. Back when his mother was alive and he saw Millie every year or two, they'd eat at Poogan's Porch when she came to visit. Peter could never bring himself to order the fried chicken outside of her company.

But if they didn't speed things along, nobody would be getting fried chicken tonight. They were already fifteen minutes late for their reservation because Millie insisted on going back upstairs and changing her scarf and earrings.

At least Peter had talked her into comfortable shoes. The walk from their rental to Poogan's Porch was a relatively short distance, but still, cracks in concrete and cobblestone were inevitable.

He was nervous enough about their loft being on the second floor of the building, but Millie kept insisting that women all over Europe spent their entire lives climbing flights of stairs in big cities, and she could easily manage the few steps up to their rental.

And she had Harper to help.

Peter grinned just thinking of Millie's tenacity. Most people her age were happy to be sitting in recliners and playing sudoku. Not Millie.

It seemed that, simply put, Millie never stopped living. He knew no one else who would have the courage to start a store at this stage in her life. And he couldn't help but wonder if Harper only *thought* she was the one doing the helping.

Perhaps Millie had a greater plan in this all along. Peter suspected she was trying to give Harper the experience of owning a store, despite that professor's criticism. He could be wrong, of course, but . . . well, he knew Millie. And Millie was always up to something.

"Isn't that window box darling?" Millie stopped outside a pink single house—the iconic Charleston style—framed by black shutters and wrought-iron planters.

Harper stopped too. "Oh, it is. I love the little pops of red."

Peter's eyes were about to roll back into his head. At this rate, the two of them were on track to see every flower in the city by midnight.

Millie bent slightly to take in the perfume of the blooms. She looked very royal, and appropriately so for Queen Street. But then her red cloche fell.

As if on instinct, Millie reached for her hair with both hands and patted to secure her hat, but it was too late. The red cloche Peter remembered her wearing since he was a boy began to roll down the sidewalk toward the street.

"I've got it!" Peter yelled over his shoulder, having already closed half the distance between himself and the runaway hat. He scooped it up just before it plopped straight into a pool of water that had, ironically, drained from a window box full of flowers.

Peter pulled a small stick from off the wool exterior as best he could, careful not to damage anything.

That's when he saw the button.

He brushed a smudge of dirt from it with his thumb, until the image of a butterfly came into view. The design was a perfect match to the button on his mother's wedding dress. Two halves of the same story.

Peter nearly dropped the hat all over again for the way his shock affected his grip. His heart began to race as he pieced it together.

M.M.

It's Millie.

All this time, it had always been Millie.

He glanced up toward her and Harper as the two stepped closer. Joy flooded his soul with such force that he could've wept in the middle of the street.

Peter had long felt an overwhelming sense of pressure to fill in the blank spaces on his own. He was the one, and had always *been* the one, who did the looking. No one came looking for him in return.

Or so he'd thought.

But maybe he'd been wrong. His mother's friend—Aunt Millie, they always called her—had been a steady presence in his life growing up. His stepfather never liked the woman. Said she spoke her mind too freely and lacked the sophistication with which a woman should carry herself. Funny how those two characteristics were precisely why Peter liked her so much.

Sometimes he and his mother would pay a visit to the boarding-house Millie ran. He hadn't been there in years. But he'd never forget the solace he found on Millie's pier in the weeks following his mother's death.

His fingers trembled around the rim of the cloche and the button that had been there all along, much like Millie. He started to run to her, and hug her, and tell her he knew everything.

The two of them could finally have this conversation, and all the questions would be answered. He started toward her, but stopped himself. Why had they never talked about this before?

For some reason, Millie must not want him to know.

Millie and Harper stepped closer, both smiling about his hat rescue.

He needed to make a decision quickly. He could feel his heart beating faster and faster.

A growing flood of anticipation threatened to overwhelm his good senses. Her blood might flow through his veins, but he was now in his late twenties and in all that time, Millie had never told him the real story.

Why hadn't she?

Was it his stepfather? He wouldn't put it past his stepfather for setting limits on what everyone was allowed to say. If it *was* because of that man, Peter should take the initiative.

And why had she suddenly returned to Charleston . . . even more, to his storefront? Was this all really about the dress shop, or was something else going on behind the scenes?

Millie was in arm's reach now. Indecision pulled, threatening to rip him in two. At once, he wanted to fold her up in his arms yet also run two blocks ahead before she could see straight through him.

Surely his mother would have told him more about her ancestry eventually, had circumstances been different. How would she handle this if she were here?

"You can't turn back time, even if you move the dials."

His mother's old idiom, so quick in his mind, sobered him. If he did say something, there was no turning back now.

Peter pushed back his nostalgia over his mother and all these years of loving Millie. If he really loved her, he would honor her by waiting until she was ready to tell him herself. It was, after all, Millie's story.

In the meantime, his focus would be keeping the two of them in that loft rental as long as possible. Maybe the short-term rental could turn into a long-term arrangement, just like the store would be. Because being a landlord gave him a far better excuse to show up unexpectedly than simply owning the storefront property.

And maybe if he bought enough time, Millie would explain.

She and Harper stopped a foot away. Peter gently sat the cloche back on Millie's head where it belonged, and she dipped down as if being crowned. When he met her gaze, he recognized the same amber flame around her pupils as his mother once had. Why had he never noticed that before?

Millie smiled at him. If she noticed anything out of the ordinary about his reaction, she didn't show it. "That's my Peter." She ruffled his hair. "Always saving something just in the nick of time."

TWENTY-EIGHT

Fairhope, 1952

Millie had been waiting all year for the strawberries to bloom.

In her enthusiasm, she'd chosen to wear a day dress she'd adorned with several little strawberry buttons. Her rounded stomach was becoming harder and harder to hide.

Day and night, Millie tussled with whether she'd made the right decision marrying Franklin—well, really, not in the marrying so much as letting herself love him.

Mostly because of the dreams.

Sometimes she woke with the clearest image of a light-toned baby. And sometimes, with a darker one. Two images of two different futures, representing one singular family she loved so very much.

She loved her Italian father in what she remembered of him and she loved Mama deeply still, and what was more, she was proud of them both. And the people before them too, all the folks whose stories made a space for her own.

But despite her resolve and her love for her heritage, the world wasn't so simple. And sometimes Millie wondered what life would look like should her child be born white, and what life would look like should the baby be born Black.

Either way, she felt as though only one half of her heritage could win out, and even now she grieved for the other half. Would she always have to choose one or the other? Could she ever publicly claim her mixed blood with the pride she felt inside her heart?

Something had happened the day she realized she carried life within her belly.

Her father's murder took on a whole new meaning now that she herself was responsible for a new generation. And she loved this invisible baby with every fiber of her being so much that she was terrified, absolutely terrified, of what might happen. She understood now why her own mother sent her away to Alabama, and it wasn't just to encourage her about the store.

In other words, Millie was becoming a mother.

So the strawberries, they were a big deal because Franklin's mother had come down for a visit and Millie had been asleep when she got in last night. The strawberry pickin' would be their first outing, and their first time meeting for that matter.

Franklin was always talking about how his mother loved strawberries, and Millie loved them too, so she supposed they had that to start with at least.

"Millie?" A woman stood several feet away wearing a beautiful but modest day dress, a tentative look, and a smile like Franklin's. "I'm Hannah." She reached out her hand.

Millie returned her grin, her nerves immediately settling amid Hannah's warm presence. She pulled her mind from all her frettin' and instead focused on the present—the woman standing in front of her. She stepped closer and took Hannah's hand. "So nice to meet you," Millie said. "You've raised quite the charming son."

"He's everything to me." Hannah's gaze clouded, and Millie wondered what memory had come and why. The woman shook her head slightly, and her eyes were clear again. "You've made him so happy, Millie. I haven't seen him this way since he was a child."

Millie patted Hannah's hand. "Would you like some tea and a biscuit or two while we wait for the aforementioned party?"

Hannah giggled. "The boy always did take life at his own pace. I see some things haven't changed."

"Just as tardy as ever." Millie grinned, leading Hannah into the kitchen. She took the kettle from the stove and poured her mother-in-law a cup of tea, then offered a biscuit from the pan that'd come fresh out of the oven.

Hannah took one of the biscuits, pulling off a bite then blowing off the steam, and something about the way she did that reminded Millie of Mama. Millie felt both comforted and grieved by the familiarity.

"I'm so happy for you and Franklin," she said, reaching for her tea. "Raising a child is such a rich experience. It requires sacrifice like nothing else, but oh, how it's worth it."

Millie poured her own cup of tea from the kettle. "That's what my mama always said too. Though I have to admit, I'm not sure I really understood what she meant before." Millie rested one hand on her ever-widening belly. "Or that I understand even now."

"You will." Hannah met her eyes with gentle kindness, and Millie knew then where Franklin got it from. "When the time comes, you'll find your instincts and trust them, beyond what you want for yourself. You'll always figure out what's best for your child. Even when you want nothing more than to keep them fittin' in your arms for longer than time allows."

Millie nodded, trying to smile, but all the while wondering what exactly that might look like and whether or not her own heart would really know what's right.

"Franklin tells me you've got a new house. Someplace South of Broad?" Millie took a slow sip from her tea. "He's really proud of you and all you've accomplished despite the hand you were dealt. He said your family disowned you?"

"That's right. The house used to belong to my brother William and his wife. Really beautiful garden, full of bluebirds, like something from a painting." Hannah looked down into her teacup. "My family is quite wealthy and when I got pregnant . . . well, I wanted to do things a certain way, and they didn't like that. So my parents said enough was enough, and they never looked back. I don't think I could've done it without William's help. I guess that's one reason why it's always been so important to me that Franklin knows no matter what, I'll accept him and never stop loving him."

Maybe it was the hormones or the conversation or the promise of strawberries, but for that moment, Millie desperately wanted to tell Hannah everything. But she hadn't even told Franklin. She had promised Mama she'd keep it a secret. And now that Millie was becoming a mother herself, she was only beginning to realize how important it was to her own mother that she stayed safe.

Millie took another sip of her tea.

TWENTY-NINE

Charleston, Modern Day

Peter sat across from Sullivan at a Starbucks that'd been converted from an old bank, complete with an original safe. Sullivan's idea. Peter would just as soon have taken an old park bench. He jabbed a straw into his iced tea.

"Any update on the code stuff? What are you going to do about the repairs? The clock is ticking on it, right?" Sullivan asked.

Peter groaned and stretched the tension from his neck. "Don't remind me."

"Dude. You've got a sweet old lady and beautiful young woman moving a store into the place."

"Yes, I know." Peter shook his head, slurping his tea. "That's the problem."

Sullivan picked up his iced coffee. "I'm not following."

"If I kick them out to fix it up, they may get spooked about the extent of the repairs and leave town."

Sullivan watched him for several moments as if trying to figure out what Peter wasn't saying.

Peter set his cup down on the table between them. He had yet to speak the words out loud and, silly as it seemed, was nervous. What if he was wrong? "Millie is my grandmother."

The coffee grinder kicked up behind them, and Sullivan turned to look. "Are you sure? It's not the first time you've thought you located—"

"This is different. I found the button." And as it turned out, Millie had been like a grandmother to him all along. The memories flashed through his mind like an old-fashioned photo reel.

Sullivan stilled. "Now you've got my attention."

"She was at my mother's funeral. And my college graduation. Even some of my soccer games in high school. I always thought she was a friend of my mom's. I just . . . well, I never realized the connection." *Never recognized the deep wrinkles that frame her green eyes like a road map of her life experiences—eyes like my mother's.*

"But she has the matching button."

Slowly, Peter nodded. "On her hat."

Sullivan exhaled a deep breath, then tapped against the edge of the table. "You think that she came back here to check in on your mom from time to time." Sullivan's words were a statement, not a question.

"That's exactly what I think."

"Maybe. I guess it's possible." Sullivan's phone beeped with a text, and he set it to silent.

"I just can't figure out how Harper is connected to all of this." Did she know about the buttons and artifacts, even now? Or did she simply think she was coming to Charleston to help Millie? Selfishly, he still hoped their first meeting had something to do with Harper's reasons for returning.

The store buzzed with activity. A woman in a white dress walked by, carrying a drink tray full of coffees, just as a man entered the store with a service dog. The hum of the store blurred into Peter's periphery as he thought about Millie. He couldn't risk her leaving. Not this time.

Sullivan slid his phone into his pocket. "I just don't think it's a good idea to put off the repairs indefinitely. I mean, code enforcement is going to return, right?"

"In ninety days."

"So you've got three months."

Peter nodded. He didn't know why Millie was taking so long to admit her identity, but now he'd gotten himself into a predicament. He'd planned to explain all the code problems with the building as soon as she and Harper arrived, but then he realized the gravity of what their arrival meant. He couldn't very well turn them away.

"Why don't you just fess up and get the repairs done quickly?"

Peter looked through the window, out onto King Street. A mother clutched her little son's hand as cars rumbled down the street. "I've thought about that." He shook his head. It was just too much money. "My rental properties are doing well, but a building like this one? The cost of it would decimate my savings. This whole ramshackle building could keep deteriorating. What if it's a money pit, man?"

Sullivan raised his eyebrow skeptically. "You think I believe you're going to run away from this thing and give up that building? You, who once hand-pulled antique wallpaper from old walls like it was some kind of sticker sheet? Who saved an entire block of historic homes from demolition by proving the historical building codes protect them?"

"This is different." This was Millie. The woman he'd been looking for as if she were a ghost in every old house from here to Beaufort. His favorite relative long before he realized they were actually related. The stakes were so much higher now.

Peter's best hope at this point was that the extra projects he'd planned would provide enough for him to make the repairs little by little, in a way that was mostly undetected by Harper and Millie *and* would satisfy the folks over at code enforcement.

"You'll find a way," Sullivan said.

Peter shook the ice in his tea. "Well, I'd better hurry."

Sunlight streamed through the window as Peter sat at the foot of his bed and pulled on his socks. Maybe today would be the day

Millie told him she was his grandmother. Now that he thought about it, her reaction to the wedding dress made more sense. . . . It'd been hers, hadn't it?

Why had she come all this way and not told him the true reason? Was she deliberating whether he was worth claiming as family?

As his mother used to say, beggars can't be choosers. And in this situation, he was definitely not above begging.

Peter tied the laces of his loafers and combed through his hair before walking the short distance to their loft. He had tried to start each day over breakfast with Millie and Harper, and now that he knew Millie was his grandmother, he had all the more reason to meet with them.

But when Peter climbed the steps and knocked on their door, he only saw Harper. "Good morning!" He straightened the cuffs of his grey button-down. "Where's Millie?"

Harper held a teakettle. Strange. He didn't usually keep tea in the pantry. "You startled me." She was still wearing pajamas. More specifically, a grey sweatshirt and pants with little penguins holding hearts. She held the door open wider so he could step through. "Come inside."

He decided not to mention that he noticed the pajamas. "Want me to put on a pot of coffee?"

"No thanks," she said.

"Suit yourself." He set his wallet and keys down on the coffee table, then went to the fridge and grabbed a bottle of the water he'd brought over yesterday.

"Wait." Harper set her cup down on the kitchen island. "You're not drinking coffee either."

"No, I typically only make it for company."

"But you're drinking water."

"What's wrong with water?" Peter unscrewed the cap and took a gulp.

"Uh . . . it has no caffeine." Harper stood staring at him, gaping.

Peter shrugged. "Who needs caffeine when you've got fresh air outside?"

Harper groaned. "So you're one of *those* people."

"Why don't you come with me today, and I'll show you what I mean?" He didn't know why he said it. He certainly hadn't planned to invite her. But somewhere in the recesses of his mind, it seemed like a good idea.

Harper took her tea mug between her hands. "No offense, but I've had my fill of old houses for the week."

Peter set his water bottle down on the counter. "Oh, I don't know about that."

"Hmm?" She took a tiny sip of her steaming tea.

"This one provides some rather different scenery." He stepped closer to the sitting area beside the door, then grabbed his wallet and keys from the coffee table and pocketed both. "I've got to do a reclamation pickup this morning and afternoon, but I'll be done around six. Think about it, and if you want to come along, you're welcome. You can see how the experts do it." He grinned at her, then opened the door and took the steps two at a time.

Six o'clock finally came. To say Peter was surprised to see her ready and waiting at his house would be an understatement.

He'd given her declaration about old houses some thought and realized he needed to do better about remembering that few people shared his passion for old stuff. Harper had her own thing going on, and that was fine. Not everyone wanted to listen to him drone on and on about earthquake bolts and why Spanish moss didn't grow along the Battery.

Yet here she was.

Looking beautiful. Her hair fell in loose curls, and she had this natural grace that could make even a T-shirt and jeans memorable. He had no doubt she could run a dress shop if she wanted. She had an eye for fashion and putting unlikely pieces together. Why had she believed there was nothing special about her? If only he could help her realize what a lie that was. Peter walked over to the closet opposite the kitchen and slid out a heavy box of antique tiles.

"You're here."

"I am." Harper walked over and bent to help him. Without a word, she took the opposite side of the box, and together they lifted it. The extra pair of arms made for lighter work. He nodded toward the door and started walking backward. She followed him.

Together, they carried the box of tile toward the driveway. "So, we're delivering these tiles to a home on the Battery, and I'm also taking some measurements while there. I don't think the owners will be home. The two of them are in this ridiculous reality TV show."

"Really?" Harper laughed.

"Wish I was kidding." The people were embarrassing themselves and the great city of Charleston with their pseudosignificant weekly scandals. The ancestors whose last names they were capitalizing on would call that kind of behavior shameful.

"How are we getting inside, then?"

"I have a code."

They reached the bed of his truck and set the box down.

"A *code*? What kind of place is this?"

Peter smiled. "My old neighbor's house."

THIRTY

Fairhope, 1952

A room full of boardinghouse guests sat on the green floral furniture—ladies with their legs crossed at the ankles and men with elbows perched on their knees—all leaning toward the television set and watching a new episode of *I Love Lucy*. Millie grabbed the wall for a moment of relief until the gripping feeling in her gut settled enough that she could keep walking.

The picture came in and out, so Franklin stood to adjust the knobs.

Millie patted the pin curls escaping her red cloche. She had recently added a strand of velvet ribbon—one of the most precious items she'd inherited from Mrs. Stevens, who'd worn the ribbon on her own little hat every day for years.

When she and Franklin had shown up so young, fresh off that train, Mrs. Stevens must've wondered what in tarnation they were thinking. But she never let on. Not once. She did for them what she did for everyone, just brought them right inside.

Even then, Franklin was stately, in his own way, with his charm and those fetching eyes, always looking for adventure.

The roundness of Millie's belly had far surpassed her ability to hide her condition with a wrap dress. Typically, of course, women in her state had long been tucked away at home, outside the public eye. But Millie's home was the boardinghouse.

The wind brought a slight breeze and the smell of Confederate jasmine through the open window, and Millie breathed an almost imperceptible sigh of relief. For that moment, for that one moment, she could breathe.

Such injustice, such a crying injustice, that at seven months, Millie's stomach was already the size of a full moon. And to think, she'd even forgone her slice of pie each night while Franklin snacked away blissfully. Yet somehow, she'd still all but lost her former figure.

While the rest of the room laughed at Lucille Ball and passed around the new *Peanuts* comic strip, Millie could think of only one thing: the pain. The intense pain that was altogether and unexpectedly familiar. She knew it was false labor, but it sure didn't seem false when it doubled her over.

Clemence turned the corner into the sitting room, carrying a tray filled with teacups and cookies. The young woman's eyes rounded, the color of chestnuts and nearly as wide too. "Millie," she whispered, clutching the tray. "You're unwell."

Was she? Come to think of it, Millie was unsteady on her feet. The pains had been coming more regularly, but she still had so much time left in her pregnancy. She'd never considered the contractions might be productive.

Clemence set the tray of tea and cookies on the table and hurried to Millie. "Let's get you to your room now, Mrs. Millie."

Millie wished the girl would stop with the *Mrs.* business—the only thing worse was being called *ma'am*. What was so wrong with using peoples' names, anyway? But Clemence wouldn't hear of it. And when Millie tried to insist there was no sense in it whatsoever, all Clemence said was, *"There's sense enough—don't be ugly."* So for some reason, Millie listened.

She stuck by Millie's side as if half scared that Millie might fall and be unable to get back up. Together they walked slowly through the hallway.

The hallway. That's where it happened. That's where the water began to pool under Millie's feet. And a familiar question returned with force—would the baby look like Mama, or like Franklin? Truth be told, Millie wasn't even sure what she hoped for.

Maybe she hoped for both.

Clemence clutched Millie's arm. "I'll tell Mr. Franklin to phone the doctor."

But Millie grasped her like a falcon. "You'll do no such thing."

The two stood there, both holding onto one another but both for different reasons, except one commonality. Utter fear.

Not panic, mind you, for Millie prided herself in having a steady head about her. But something altogether deeper, something that couldn't be brushed away as nerves or the hormones of maternity.

Millie tried to swallow, even as the tightening around her belly came again, and she couldn't breathe.

"Ma'am, you need a doctor."

As if Millie didn't know such a thing.

But it was a risk she simply couldn't afford. Millie herself had no idea about the life growing inside her own body, whether her future would look like the past she missed dearly or the other heritage she'd stepped into, which she loved too. How was a doctor to understand?

She wasn't even sure Franklin could. Or would.

Or that she'd find the courage to give him the chance, if circumstances led.

She tried to breathe in the moments between the pains, the moments when breathing was easy. "You've delivered children before," she whispered—half question, half statement.

"Yes. Four of my siblings," Clemence said. "But never a white baby."

"Very well." Millie steadied herself by the frame of the bedroom door. "Then I have every confidence in you."

Clemence simply stared. The poor girl, scared silly.

"Clemence, you promise me one thing."

"Ma'am?"

"Promise me," Millie grimaced as another contraction grew in strength, "that no matter what happens with this baby, you'll say nothing."

"What does that mean?" Clemence's tone was sharp, sharper than she had used in this home before, and secretly, Millie was glad for the display of strength. Millie needed to summon someone else's strength, for a little while at least.

Millie slipped off her shoes and leaned her arms, palms out, against the bed as another contraction came.

She wiped the sweat from her own forehead and forced herself to breathe deeply. "We will see."

The baby's cry pierced heaven and earth, and for that miraculous and wondrous moment, all the space in between filled with the fullness of every good thing.

You know, the type of moment that inevitably leads to grief, because life this side of heaven cannot stay so full or perfect or so entrenched with meaning. And no matter how hard you try to grasp at it, those glorious, almost golden moments turn to dust as soon as they hit your fingers.

"Millie, wait." Clemence's voice grew troubled.

Coldness settled into Millie's veins, chilling her blood.

"What's wrong with the baby?" Her voice was a rasp.

"Nothing." Clemence swiftly placed the beautiful baby in Millie's arms. "But I'm going to need you to push again."

Millie cradled her innocent babe. The little girl's dark hair framed milky skin and beautiful green eyes. Millie gently rocked her back and forth, entranced by the newness of her child's first moments.

Sharp pains brought her back to reality.

She felt as if she were being stabbed in half, or worse, dying.

So she pushed. Out of instinct. Out of fear.

Why it took until that moment for Millie to put the pieces together, she didn't know. But the sudden emptiness of her womb, the sudden relief of pressure, sent the fiery sensation spreading.

Another baby.

All this time.

There was another baby.

"Heavens, Millicent!" Clemence shrieked.

Something was wrong.

Millie's breath grew shallow.

"One last push, Mrs. Millie. Make it a good one." Clemence's tone grew clipped.

Millie clutched the daughter in her arms as tightly, as gently, as could be.

"You're bleeding. Awful badly. Stay with me. Millie?"

It was the last thing Millie heard before the room began spinning.

THIRTY-ONE

Charleston, Modern Day

Peter's story was surprising, to say the least. Raised in a mansion along the Battery? No knowledge of his charming grandmother? And to think that he left all the opulence to reclaim that old house where he was living, that he made such a heroic choice without even seeing the connection to Millie.

Harper couldn't get the gaps in his family history out of her mind, and she was beginning to realize why Peter found history as a whole so fascinating. She wished it were as simple as telling him what she knew. But she'd promised Millie.

The slightest sea breeze clung to the air as Peter and Harper walked the pathway along Charleston Harbor. A few dolphins played in the not-so-distant waves, and sunlight fell like glitter in shades of orange and pink against the water. And this—*this*—was Charleston.

All they needed was a front porch painted haint blue and a proverbial glass of sweet tea.

Harper crossed her arms over her middle, wishing she'd slipped on a light sweater now that she felt the subtle chill of the breeze. The ends of her hair whipped this way and that as she faced the water.

"Windy day." Peter laughed. A labradoodle tugged his owner

down the sidewalk, and Peter reached to pet the dog's head as they passed.

"So, where is the house?" Harper shifted her body to face Peter. "Much further?"

He turned and pointed. "Past this green space, see the pink three-story with black shutters?"

"You're kidding."

He wasn't.

Several minutes later, they'd crossed through the park and approached the historic home. Harper's shoe caught against the cobblestone, and on instinct, Peter steadied her elbow. His touch was warm, gentle, and not exactly unwelcome.

"Head over heels for the place, are you?" he joked, then stepped forward and punched a code into the security system. The plan was to take the measurements he needed, then go back to the truck for the tiles since they'd parked a block up for their tour of the Battery.

To Peter's credit, he'd resisted overwhelming her with historical information on the walk and had managed to limit himself to one pirate story and a nod toward Fort Sumter. Actually, she hated to admit it, but Harper was beginning to crave his little historical tidbits.

She could ask him for more, of course, but she wasn't *that* desperate.

As if he could read her thoughts, Peter held the iron gate open for her to pass through, then motioned once more toward the Battery. The smell of jasmine caught on the breeze. "Hard to believe that all this grandeur sits on man-made land. You know what's under here?" He tapped his shoe.

"No clue."

"Rocks, dirt, and oyster shells." Peter led Harper through a garden courtyard spanning the width of the ornate house. Flowers bloomed in every color and variety, and bees hummed, happily searching for the last nectar of the evening.

Harper breathed it all in as best she could. The beauty of the place was striking.

"Follow me." Peter waved her toward the front door of the home, then typed another access code into a keypad by the entry. When he opened the door, Harper stood in shock.

She had never stepped foot in any home like this before.

Lavish, narrow-slat wood floors led through the entryway toward a stairwell on the right side of the house. On the left, an antique brick fireplace shimmied up the wall.

Harper tilted her head up. Overhead, an ornate chandelier hung from a decorative mount on the ceiling. The place smelled like history in a whole different way than the house in Radcliffeborough. And yet, Peter's reaction was the same.

He was something else, wasn't he? He stood unaffected by the details of wealth, details that pulled a person in like dangerous fingers curling come hither, into the trap of never-enough.

Harper couldn't take her eyes off the chandelier. "I can't imagine having this kind of money."

Peter let the tape measure retract abruptly. "Oh, around here, it's not about the money. You know that, right?"

Harper frowned. "What do you mean?"

"In Charleston, you don't get into the inner circles by being rich. Anybody can be rich. That's the easy part." He grinned. "You can buy a house here, sure, but for better or worse, you can't buy a history."

"Then how do you get into Charleston's elite?"

"You're born into it. Ideally, for ten-plus generations. Some of these families have kept their homes for decades and even centuries. That's why it was such a big deal for my stepfather that I take his last name." Peter pulled a tiny notepad and pen from his pocket. "You'll see what I mean when you open your store."

Your store.

The words brought a flutter of anticipation, quickly resolved by Harper's determination to remain level-headed.

One purpose drew her to Charleston—to support Millie. Once the store was up and running, Harper would help Millie find a new manager and move on. Otherwise, she might get caught up once more in her ridiculous, unrealistic fancies.

"We need to talk about Millie." The words tumbled out of her mouth.

Peter raised his eyebrows. "What about her?"

She's your grandmother, for starters. Harper tucked several wisps of her hair behind her ears. "How are we going to help make this store a success for her?"

Peter locked his jaw, lost in thought. Birds on the long, gabled porch outside chirped a background medley. "I think I have an idea. A friend of mine is hosting a wedding expo next month."

"An expo?" Harper slid her heels back and forth along the polished floor. "You mean for vendors?"

"All sorts of vendors. Brick-and-mortar stores participate. We could rent space for a booth and get a buzz going about the place."

Harper nodded. "It could work."

"It would take a lot of effort getting things ready in just a month. But maybe you could do something with the vintage dresses?"

"Peter, that's perfect! We can repair them and use the gowns as a display to catch people's attention."

"Sure, and to help spread the word about the new store. By the time you open, folks will be lined up outside." Peter slid the tape measure into his pocket. "It's settled, then. I'll give my buddy a call."

Harper's heart did a flip-flop, suspended upside down like a toddler trying to learn how to tumble. She didn't know where she belonged in any of this.

This was not the long-term plan. But then again, Harper didn't have a long-term plan. So maybe she wouldn't recognize it if it came.

But she did know one thing. Peter was making it all very easy.

Two Weeks Later

A jazzy tune crooned from Harper's phone as a cinnamon espresso candle flickered on the table beside her. Midafternoon sunshine streamed inside the dress shop, which was empty save for that table, the velvet sofa where Harper sat, and the rack of vintage dresses Peter had given them. And of course, the rows of Harper's shoes, tagged and sitting in the corner waiting for the dresses they would accessorize.

Harper threaded gold beads into the fabric of a 1920s Gatsby-style gown. She rocked her head back and forth shamelessly and sang along with the music, completely immersed in imagining the story behind the gown. Perhaps a young woman had worn this dress to her first social party, outfitted with a long flapper necklace, and maybe even a feather in her hair. Harper sighed, smiling. The fabric seemed alive with a forgotten story to tell.

Whatever happened to the woman who wore it? Where did she go and who did she become? Harper felt strangely connected to these questions as she sewed new beads on, one by one.

Footsteps gently rapped down the stairs, and Harper recognized the two-steps-at-a-time rhythm. Her heart skipped at the sound of it. She turned from the sofa just as Peter was taking the last step toward her.

"Hello!" Still watching him, she pulled the needle the rest of the way through the fabric. "Did you know Fitzgerald thought *The Great Gatsby* was pretty much a failure?"

Peter ran his hand through his hair. He wore a grey polo that brought out the amber flecks in his blue-green eyes, even under his glasses. "Well, that's depressing."

Harper used the needle to collect another bead from her open palm. "I know, right?"

Peter took a few steps closer and leaned over the back of the couch to see what she was working on. "Suddenly, your Fitzgerald comment makes a lot more sense."

Harper shook her head slightly, moistened her lips, and looked down to find the exact spot she should pierce the fabric. "Some people consider it the best American novel."

"Personally, I've always been a Longfellow fan, but—"

"I mean, can you imagine it?" Harper set the dress down in her lap. "I'm sorry. Did I interrupt you?"

One corner of his lips rose in a uniquely Peter way. Was he flirting?

No, that was ridiculous. Peter didn't flirt. Peter didn't need to.

He cleared his throat. "Millie wants you to know her muffins are ready." He came to stand at the opposite side of the sofa. "Apparently, I'm a message boy."

Harper smirked.

"Cool dress." Peter gestured toward the golden gown in her lap. "You're fixing it?"

"Yeah, for the expo." Harper dropped several spare beads from her palm onto the little table with the candle. "I was actually entertaining the idea of wearing it."

"I'm sure you'd look beautiful."

She glanced up at him. He didn't fidget or pause. Just looked back at her, like he had the confidence of Cary Grant. Like this flattery was the most natural dynamic in the world, and he hadn't been a sheepish historian just hours ago.

Her heart fluttered under his attention, as a dress with layers and layers of tulle floats with every spin. She felt remarkably comfortable around him for having known him such a short time.

A comfort that, perhaps, came from the utter impossibility of anything romantic forming between them. After all, he was Millie's grandson, and she was keeping Millie's secret. No telling for how long or if that time was even coming, but a promise was a promise.

"So, the uh . . ." He tapped his foot against the wood floor, the laces shaking rhythmically as a Billie Holiday song started streaming. "The muffins."

"The muffins." Harper nodded, a slow grin growing. "Message received."

He turned from the sofa to leave.

"I'll just be a minute."

"Hey, if you're comfortable with the prospect of me and Millie eating all of them, suit yourself."

Harper laughed. "I'll take my chances."

But instead of leaving, Peter took one step closer, and the world around her seemed to still with his gaze, so directly in tune with her own. He hesitated at the edge of the sofa. "Can I ask you something?"

Anything. So long as it doesn't have to do with your grandmother.

THIRTY-TWO

Charleston, Modern Day

Peter started to sit on the velvet sofa beside Harper, then noticed her plush tomato full of straight pins and gripped the armrest to stop himself from getting stabbed. She should've warned him she was in the habit of keeping sharp objects scattered around when she made dress repairs.

She pointed toward the tomato. "You can move that."

His eyes widened as he used two fingers to move the pincushion closer toward her. "Any more sitting hazards you need to tell me about first?"

She situated the gown in her lap and laughed. He continued to study her eyes, and she wondered what he saw there. Did he see the fear?

Peter crossed his arms in a way that communicated he was anything *but* closed off. "Forgive me if this is too forward, but why the sudden interest in tragic literary figures?"

Harper sighed so deeply, her shoulders fell with relief. He hadn't mentioned Millie. Still, she had a feeling he was going to ask more. He had a way of seeing into her as no one else ever had.

She jabbed her needle into the plush tomato and set it all down on the dress in her lap. Where did she even begin?

Peter waited.

Harper ran her tongue along her teeth, trying to find the words. She shifted toward him. "Okay, I guess it all started when I was fourteen."

"Can't say I expected that, but please continue."

Harper looked away from him, toward the window and the busy world outside. "I had recently lost my mother, and my aunt and cousins came to visit—probably to provide a distraction. We drove over to the beach in Gulf Shores, and one of my cousins and I took my daddy's kayak out on the water. She was around eight or nine at the time, and my fourteen-year-old self didn't think we needed life jackets. My aunt and my other cousin thought we were safe because they were on the beach the whole time."

Peter stretched one of his arms along the back of the sofa. "Oh man."

"Yeah," Harper nodded. "You see where this is going. A wave hit, the kayak started to flip, and my cousin fell out. I jumped to save her and threw her back in the kayak. But then the tide . . ." Harper cleared her throat.

"You got sucked under."

The panic that had gripped her underwater returned in that moment. Harper's next breaths were shallow as she remembered the strong pull. "Rip current." She looked up at him. "You have to realize, I was a certified swim instructor at that point. I taught children's swimming classes. I knew all the right things to do in my mind, but I guess the fear took over." She shook her head. "My impulse was to fight the water, but I wasn't strong enough. The harder I tried, the farther the tide carried me away from shore. My cousin was screaming and crying and flailing around from the kayak, trying to get my aunt's attention, but it happened so fast. They were sunbathing and making sandcastles and had no idea."

Peter swallowed. He didn't move an inch from where he sat. "Harper, what happened? How did you make it out without drowning?"

"Well, I fought for a long time, exhausting myself." Harper

mindlessly twirled the ends of her hair around her finger. "Then I finally did the only thing I could do. What I should've done from the start." She thought of the waves sweeping over her, spinning her so she didn't know which way was up and which way was down, and her heart sank with the memory of hopeless disorientation. "I swam parallel to the shore until I got out of the rip current. I stopped trying to push against the tide and instead let it carry me."

Peter stared back at her. "Wow."

Harper picked up her needle from the pincushion and started back to work on the dress in her lap. "That was the first time I realized that sometimes, the harder we fight for something, the further we get carried by it until ultimately"—she shook her head—"it drowns us."

Peter lowered his arm from the back of the sofa. "I don't mean to sound like I've got all the answers because Lord knows I don't. I mean, you lived it, and you sure know more about dressmaking than I do." He leaned forward. "But Harper, have you ever considered whether fear—rather than your dream—is what you're holding onto?"

Harper pulled the thread through the fabric until the stitch was tight. "What do you mean?"

"Just that sometimes, we all hold tighter and tighter to the very things that are drowning us. We think we're keeping ourselves safe, but we're not. We're just trying to control the stuff that scares us rather than to feel the fear and move on."

Harper hesitated, her needle poised for the next stitch. "That's always been hard for me." She wouldn't have considered herself a particularly fearful person in the past, but maybe Peter was right. Maybe she'd all but convinced herself the store would be another failure as Savannah was a failure because it was easier on some level to fear failure than to risk dreaming again.

"It's hard for everyone, Harper." He stood, glancing toward the stairs. "How about if I bring one of Millie's muffins down?" Peter walked over toward the stairwell.

"That'd be great. And tell Millie I'll be up there soon for another one." Harper picked up a handful of beads to finish out a row of beadwork before taking a break. But first, she allowed herself another glance at him.

He hesitated on the second step, turning his shoulders. "Harper?"

"Yes?"

"You and Millie . . ." He cleared his throat and rested his fingers along the handrail. "You're not going to be F. Scott Fitzgerald."

"Or John Keats?"

"Or Emily Dickinson," he added.

Harper smiled. She did love Emily Dickinson. She watched him over the slope of the velvet sofa. His words were a balm to her broken heart. So light, so pure, they swept her hope up from the floor and into the sunshine.

"But how do you know?" She felt as though he would have an answer, as though she could trust him.

"Because sometimes faith comes before the bridge to the other side."

Harper had just hung up with the new-business-permit people and was hanging twinkle lights from the window display when a postwoman pushed a trolley full of large boxes toward the front door. Harper hesitated mid-string. Strange. She wasn't expecting any deliveries.

The woman peeked through the window at Harper and waved, then pointed toward the front door. Harper nodded, set down the lights, and hurried over.

The postwoman smiled. "Lovely window display you've got there. Are you turning this into a dress shop?"

"We sure are. And thank you." Harper slid her hands into the pockets of her dress.

"Forgive me for being nosy, but will you sell vintage pieces like the one in the window?"

"In the window?" Harper turned to check the display and realized the woman was referring to Millie's dress. "Oh no, I'm sorry to say that one isn't for sale. Belongs to the owner. But we will have many lovely gowns."

The postwoman began unloading the boxes from the trolley. "I appreciate it, but I'm looking for something that's true vintage. You just can't replicate a piece with a story."

Harper helped push the boxes inside the door. "Sure can't, can you?" She was just about to verify the woman had the correct address when Millie came slowly ambling down the stairs, holding a Tupperware container with muffins.

Uh oh. Harper was going to be in trouble for never coming when Millie sent Peter after her earlier. But she needed to get this work done on the shop.

Millie took one glance down at the pile of boxes and brushed a curl of her hair back into place. "Oh lovely. I see the packages have arrived."

"Are you Millicent?" The postwoman held out a tablet for Millie's signature. "I just need you to verify these have been delivered."

Millie handed the Tupperware to Harper and reached for the tablet stylus. "Not a problem. Thank you, ma'am."

"Y'all have a nice afternoon." The postwoman offered a dainty salute before pushing the empty trolley away.

Still holding the Tupperware, Harper looked down at the stack of boxes at her feet. "Um, Millie?"

"Hmm?" Millie walked over toward Harper's sewing supplies and rifled through them until she found a pair of scissors.

"Did you order a lifetime supply of tea or something?"

Millie chuckled. She opened the scissors and went to work on the tape along the top of the boxes. "See for yourself."

Harper started to rip the boxes open, then realized they were postmarked from Paris. "You know someone in Paris?" The woman would never cease to surprise her.

"So many questions, dear. Just open the box and see."

Harper loosened the flaps of the first box, then unwrapped the protective plastic surrounding the contents. Inside the box were neatly folded, silk gowns.

Harper gasped. She reached for one of the delicate dresses and held it up for inspection. "Absolutely stunning."

Millie tilted her head. "They are, aren't they? I have a . . . friend . . . in Paris who offered to send a few things to get us started, but I didn't know what she would be mailing. These certainly exceed expectations."

"Indeed." Harper's mind spun. Paris? Silk dresses? What was happening?

Millie started over toward the window display and stood straight in front of her wedding gown. Her smile held the light of the sun.

Harper set the Parisian dress back down inside the box and joined her. "Everything okay?"

"Yes. Absolutely. I just never imagined I'd be standing on this side of the window." Millie shook her head. "That means nothing to you. Forgive me for rambling."

"It really is something, Millie." Harper watched Millie, even as Millie watched the gown. "Your wedding dress, I mean."

"Thank you, dear." Millie brushed the fabric with her fingertips. "I agree."

Harper wanted to know more, so she decided to try asking. "Tell me. Were you head over heels in love? Was your wedding day a dream?"

Millie smiled, still staring toward the window and lost in memory. "I wasn't in love with him yet, no. That came later. Times were different then, right after the war, and even though the desperation from the Depression had faded, the impression it left on all of us was still fresh as ever. Franklin and I knew we could help each other through a marriage of friendship. I was very young, you see, as was he."

Millie turned to her. "Though looking back, I see that I fell in love with him far sooner than I realized at the time. It was the little things that captivated me. The way he sat so tall in a boat or the way he laced his shoes."

Harper's heart swelled just imagining the two of them.

Millie shook her head as if coming out of a reverie. "I'm sorry—what was your other question? Oh yes. It was magical."

She whistled low, and her eyes glimmered. She held Harper's gaze, and slowly, she spoke the memory. "Sometimes life gives us those moments. Like the very first flutter of a butterfly's wings. Moments that are so profound and so purely beautiful, you try to capture them so you can come back to them later."

Millie touched the French address scrawled across the boxes as if it were something precious. "But no matter how hard you try to scoop up every detail of the thing, it's never quite the same because a memory isn't living and breathing." She met Harper's gaze. "Sometimes life is just magic."

Magic. Harper knew the feeling with the familiarity of a best friend's voice. But she and magic had parted ways in a department chair's hallway back in Savannah. She'd grown up from the naïve girl who believed naïve things about dreams, and it was for the better, really.

Harper chipped at the grey nail polish on her fingernails. Millie spoke about the passion that had been missing from Harper's own life, and she wanted it for herself—to love someone that deeply. The only person she knew who had that kind of passion was . . .

Peter.

Harper turned her attention back to Millie.

"You can imagine what seeing that gown again means to me. So, thank you, sweet girl." Millie squeezed her hand. "Thank you for finding me, thank you for bringing me here, thank you for everything."

The sentiment startled Harper in its transparency. All she could do was squeeze Millie's hand in return. She should be the one thanking Millie, for letting her know the dress's history. And more importantly, for letting her share part of Millie's story.

In that moment, everything that had happened in Savannah was worth it. All the tears and self-doubt and loathing and extra pounds from Leopold's ice cream.

Because without it, without it all, she never would have found Millie, Peter, or their story.

Or for that matter, all she was beginning to discover about her own.

THIRTY-THREE

Fairhope, 1952

The air was thick with humidity and the smells of birth as Millie came in and out of consciousness. Clemence roused her by the arm and waved salts beneath her nose, bringing her back to a fragmented reality.

But the pain of childbirth had no comparison to the searing fire ripping through her heart as Millie remembered what had just happened.

"Mrs. Millie, you gave me a scare there. I very nearly fetched the doctor."

Millie tried to turn toward Clemence from the bed, but pain pierced her empty womb. "You didn't call him?"

Clemence shook her head. "No, ma'am." Gently, she set both babies into the crooks of Millie's arms.

But the babies looked different. One had thin blond hair and the other, tightly curled locks like Mama's, with a head full of them to show.

Two tiny, angelic faces stared back at her, and Millie's innocence broke into a thousand pieces at the sight—for the time when the three of them had shared one body was now over, and never again would she be able to shelter them from the rest of the world.

Two different hearts, two different futures.

Clemence cleared her throat and stared at Millie.

"What's the matter?" Millie asked.

"Forgive me for bein' forward, but Mrs. Millie . . . one looks like Franklin, and the other . . . well, that hair. Her complexion's bound to deepen in the next day or so. Who does she look like, Mrs. Millie? You tell me."

But Millie didn't say anything.

Clemence shuffled her weight between her feet and straightened her cotton day dress. "You know you must choose one child, don't you?

Millie looked up and met her eyes. The proposition was a dagger to her lungs, and every ounce of oxygen, every ounce of breath, rushed from her body. She was a body with no soul, skin with no heart. For to choose between two daughters was to choose a grief that would hollow one-half of her for the rest of her life.

And Millie knew—oh, how she knew—that Clemence was right. Racial violence was rife through Alabama, just like it'd been in South Carolina. Violence not unlike her own father's murder years prior or the harassment she and Mama had experienced from the likes of Harry and his family.

And keeping the babies together, side by side, would be the most dangerous possibility of all.

Millie trembled as one baby yawned and the other nuzzled against her chest.

The one-two tug Millie had carried on for decades had materialized in human form. She had chosen to live as a white woman with Franklin. She'd been happy here, but she had never forgotten Mama. Never forgotten the life she left behind.

Never stopped aching with pride for the family, the heritage Mama had told her to leave behind.

Now she had to choose all over again.

Maybe she could run.

But no amount of running would loosen the curls, darken or lighten the skin of a child. She could tell everyone her father was

Italian, and the darker-skinned baby favored him. But would they believe her? Would she ever be able to escape deceit? And would her daughter come to resent her for teaching the denial of her heritage along with pride? Would she understand it was safety that prompted Millie's lies?

She still struggled for breath, and she thought for a moment that she might faint all over again.

Would she live with such breathlessness for the rest of her life?

"Are you ready for me to call Mr. Franklin?"

Millie's mouth was dry, but she feared even the slightest drink of water might turn her stomach.

Slowly, she nodded. What the heavens was she going to tell him?

But for her daughters' sake, she had to be strong.

For the longest time, Franklin just stared at them. All of them. Stared with his hands in his pockets, at the foot of the bed.

Millie loved another man. His Millie loved another man. Though he had loved her since their vows.

It was the only thing that made sense. The only reason why the babies looked different from each other.

Franklin desperately wanted to reach for the children. Wanted to touch them, hold them, and kiss his wife for birthing the most beautiful babies in the world.

But he didn't know what to do now. What to think, for that matter.

He didn't know if these were even his babies. They had come early, after all, and he needn't be a fool about the timeline.

But on the other hand, they were small.

Franklin tightened his fists in his pockets. Life had been much less terrifying when he jumped trains and had only himself to think about.

Millie watched him as tears streamed down her face.

His trance broke when he saw her cry.

Franklin hurried over to her side and crouched beside the bed. Then with his thumb, he wiped the tears one by one from her eyes.

"The children are perfect." His voice was hoarse. He locked in on Millie's gaze, and something in the fiery ring around her eyes shook him down to his core.

She was terrified.

He could feel it from her eyes.

Franklin brushed the hair back from her sweaty forehead. "Red, what . . . why . . ."

"My mother was Black." She blurted out the words, never once looking away from him. "My father was Italian. That's why they killed him. They were after me for playing with their children, and he shoved them away to protect me. They grabbed him, and . . ." More tears streamed down. "After that, I learned to be more careful."

Killed him?

Franklin struggled to understand. It was all happening so fast. The floor spun beneath him.

He knew this kind of thing happened. Everybody knew this kind of thing happened. That people out there would kill somebody just for their race or culture. In body, yes, but in other ways too—in soul and spirit, with words and hate, and maybe by instilling fear most of all. But Franklin realized with sudden clarity how lucky he'd been that he had never seen it or felt it or really *known* it. Until now.

He reached for her hand.

Millie's body looked weak, lying there in the bed, and he worried over her condition. But her voice was strong. She told the story as if she were telling the whole thing for the first time. In a way, maybe she was.

"When we met, you assumed I was white, and I wanted people to think that. I thought it would give me a better chance at my dress shop. My mama made me swear I'd never tell anybody the truth because she wanted to protect me from what happened to my father." Millie leaned her head back against the bed pillows, and both babies squirmed in her arms. "But the truth is, Franklin, I'm only half white. And in my own way, I think I loved you from the moment we met."

Franklin closed his eyes as his body clenched from top to bottom. He turned from the bed and shook his head. "Millie, how could you?" he rasped.

"I thought if you realized the truth, it might all come crashing down beneath my feet. This life we've built together." She whispered the words.

Franklin's attention snapped back. He rubbed his eyes with his hands. "Is that what you think?"

"Isn't it why you're mad? Why, even our marriage papers wouldn't hold up by the law."

"Millie." His tone was firm. She had just given birth, and he needn't be too harsh. He didn't want to weaken her further by traumatizing her. But she should know. She should know how he cared for her, what she had done to change his life. "For years, I have loved you day in and day out. To me, you're the same woman today that you were on that train. The same woman who saved me from living and dying on those trains. Whatever your heritage is, Millie, I'll love that too—because it made you who you are."

Millie gently shook her head and began to tremble badly. Had the aftereffects from birth caused this reaction, or were his words to blame?

He tried to calm her with his hand on her arm, but the shaking only grew worse. Even her teeth chattered. "What I can't believe, Red, is that you didn't trust me. All this time."

Millie's face and arms and hands were sweating, so Franklin reached for the towel at the other side of the bed. The sheets were still drenched with blood, and the sight of it sobered him. For some reason, he hadn't noticed it until now.

For the first time in a long time, Franklin began to cry.

He could've lost her today. That's what Clemence said. He could have lost her.

Franklin couldn't stop himself. He leaned down and kissed her as he had waited to kiss her all afternoon long. He kissed her as the girl on the train, he kissed her as the mother of his children, and he kissed her as his bride.

"What about now?" She looked up at him.

"We raise them," he said. "Simple as that."

Millie paled and looked as though she might be sick. She looked down to the babies sleeping in her arms. "We can only choose one."

Franklin balked. "No." He would sooner give his right arm.

"I know this reality as you do not." Millie moistened her chapped lips and struggled to sit up in the bed. "Franklin, there's far too much violence to raise them together. And that's to say nothing of different seats at the theater, different drinking fountains, different schools. I realize you are enchanted with them, but you must think of this with logic. For their sake, you must be strong."

Franklin was trying to be strong. But his heart was racing along with his mind, and he wasn't sure he could be trusted to think straight right now. He was too in love with both babies already to know how to do right by them.

"I'm not afraid, Millie," he said.

"Well, you should be!" she snapped with a fury he'd never seen before. "There's no amount of wishful thinking on our part that can deny reality." She looked down at the babies. "*Their* reality. All they will face." Her expression grew wistful. "If others see our girls together—twin sisters—who look so very different . . . people will talk. People will make assumptions. And the consequences for our marriage, our family . . . their lives will both be in danger. My entire life, I have tried to find a way to hold both parts of my identity. The world hasn't let me."

Franklin sobered.

Millie had been forced to hide half her past . . . a past it was now so obvious she loved. She wasn't acting out of selfishness—if she were, she'd want to keep both daughters here under one roof just like he did. Who would want to separate their heart, their future?

Certainly not Millie. She was trying to keep them safe in the best way she knew how. Franklin didn't know what the answer was, but he did see that much clearly now.

"Maybe someday things will be different. Maybe someday we can hold them both side by side. But for now, doing so would only bring harm upon them. We can take the lighter-toned child to your mother in Charleston. She will have opportunities there that we could never give her here. And I want to raise the curly-haired daughter ourselves. The tips of her ears are a little darker, and in coming days her color will deepen. This way, I can look after her myself as that happens, and in the days and months and years beyond. Keep her safe from harm."

Millie spoke as if it were so simple, as if her mind were made up.

"What about when people ask questions?"

"We'll notate their birthdays a week apart so no one suspects they're twins. As for the darker skin and features"—Millie stroked the hair of one baby, then the other, with her thumb—"my father was Italian. We can say that."

"Will people believe it?"

"Time will tell," Millie murmured.

Everything within Franklin screamed that this was wrong. Screamed that there must be something they could do, some way they could raise both children.

But he was quiet.

Because for the life of him, he couldn't think of *any* way to make it happen.

And he knew then, looking at Millie, that her mind was made up. He knew then why she trembled, and he knew their family would never be so whole as they were right now, when his wife held both fragile daughters in her own fragile arms.

"I'll phone my mother," Franklin said. "Maybe we can take both babies around the city, try to come up with another plan. Some way to keep them together. We'll even visit the train terminal where we first met."

But Millie shook her head. "Mama said the train terminal on East Bay Street burned clear down. No going back now."

THIRTY-FOUR

Charleston, Modern Day

Harper sat out on a wicker rocker on the second-story porch over-looking King Street and made a mental checklist of all that still needed to be done before the expo in a couple days.

Farther down King, toward the college, the hustle and bustle of youth would keep the streets vibrant late into the evening. But on this side—the antiques side, as Harper liked to call it—the busyness of the day had dimmed to a glow of streetlights and the occasional passersby holding hands or enjoying an ice cream.

She sighed.

Peter rapped his knuckles against the porch door. "Got a minute?"

Harper shifted in her chair to face him. "Sure."

He opened the door and stepped into full view. A whiff of the pecan pie Millie was baking accompanied Peter outside.

He wore that familiar grey button-down with black pants, a black tie, black socks, and black shoes. His pants fit like he bought them at Pacific Sunwear ten years ago. "What do you think of this?" He gestured toward his ensemble. "For the expo?"

Harper opened her mouth to speak. Then she closed it, tilting her head slightly to the side. She pointed her finger toward him. "That is, uh . . . yeah, are you sure you want to go with grey?"

Peter made no effort to hide the smile on his lips. "You think I look ridiculous."

"No way! Not ridiculous at all."

"Hideous?"

Harper crossed her legs and bounced the heel of her foot in and out of her pink sandal. She cleared her throat and used her hands while she spoke. "It's just that you're such a . . . vibrant . . . person, and all the grey is maybe a tad dreary?"

"You think I look dreary." Peter looked down and pressed his shirt with his hands. "But I wore the skinny tie."

Harper folded her lips to keep her laugh contained. "Yeah, skinny ties aren't really a thing anymore."

"What?" Peter adjusted his glasses and feigned shock. "And here I was, thinking I'm so fashion forward."

Harper did laugh at that. "You know you don't have to attend this thing, right?"

Peter pocketed his hands, hesitating like a guilty toddler. What was he hiding? Did he actually *want* to go for some reason?

"It's no trouble," he said. "Besides, I want to be there in person to thank my friend for waiving the entrance fee."

"I can appreciate that." Harper nodded. "Do you want me to look through the rest of your closet to see if there's anything else I can put together?"

Peter gestured toward his clothes with both hands. "I can definitively say this is as good as it gets."

Harper took a good look at him. Her attention caught over his broad shoulders and blue-green eyes. Yeah, that outfit was definitely *not* as good as it was going to get.

"Sometimes—" The wind blew a wisp of Harper's hair into her eyes as she stood to go inside. Less than a foot away from Peter, she raised her chin and looked up at him. "Well, it's like your old houses. You've got an eye to see the beauty beyond the dust. With the right restoration, something really special can happen."

Peter met her gaze, his dimples showing. "Did you just compare my clothes to a condemned building?"

Harper rested her hand on his shoulder and returned his smile.

"I absolutely did, and in case you didn't read between the lines, we're going shopping tomorrow."

Clearly humored, his expression softened, and he made no effort to remove her hand from his shoulder. "Are you going to fairy-godmother me?" He opened the porch door wider.

"How do you feel about pumpkins?" Harper slipped under his arm, through the doorway.

The next morning, Harper brushed the Callie's Hot Little Biscuit crumbs from her lace-overlay skirt while she stared at the dressing room door, waiting for Peter.

"This is embarrassing," he mumbled.

"I'm sure that's not true." It'd taken a solid ten minutes to get him past the sticker shock of how much a well-fitting pair of pants cost.

"I look like that guy from *The Notebook*."

Harper crossed her arms and tapped her kitten heels. "That guy from *The Notebook* is named Ryan Gosling, and women all over the world adore him, so you could do much worse."

"Okay, then I look like Ryan Seacrest."

Harper rolled her eyes. "The pants are slim fit. It's what everyone wears now." And had been wearing for the last decade.

"I'm not feeling the skinny jeans. What's next? You're going to take me to buy a fedora and a European coffee roaster?"

"So many things are happening in that sentence, I don't know where to start." Harper watched his socked feet and the hem of his pants shuffle back and forth under the door. "Would you please just let me see?"

Slowly, he opened the door.

He wore a crisp white shirt, unbuttoned at the top, a fitted black blazer, and the aforementioned slim-cut pants. He slipped his feet into the old-fashioned brown saddlebacks she had found for him.

And Harper's mouth dropped. *Hello, Ryan Gosling.*

"You seem flustered. Are you okay?" He raised an eyebrow.

She swallowed. No, she was not okay. She didn't know what she was expecting. But it was definitely not this. This was . . . surprising.

Yes, that was a good word for it.

Heart-leap-into-your-throat-so-you-can't-breathe surprising.

Peter even smelled delicious.

Harper took a second to compose herself. Her toes were tingly. And her toes only got tingly when she was smitten by someone.

She blinked.

Unfortunately, it did nothing to close her nostrils to the smell of sandalwood and anticipation.

"So, what do you think?" He inched down ever so slightly so he could meet her eyes. Lord have mercy, if he could read what was going on behind them. But Harper feared she could only hide her attraction so long.

She gently pulled the chain of her necklace back and forth. "I think it's a definite step in the right direction."

She liked him.

Peter could feel it in the way she checked the fabric of his coat, her fingers lingering on his elbow. Her gentle touch shook him right down to his feet.

He took a glance at himself in the mirror of the dressing room. He could be this man—for one night, at least. The kind of man Harper Rae wanted to see.

Peter slid his arms out from the coat jacket and placed it back on the hanger. He was careful not to get dirt on anything. This store probably charged money to breathe. And he'd been saving all his extra cash flow for the repairs that needed to be done on the dress store.

He didn't even care about the building anymore. He just wanted it for Harper and Millie.

And he had a plan for that now, at least. The wealthy client on the Battery. He'd be working lots of extra hours on the restoration project, but that money—combined with some of his savings—should be enough for the repairs. He wouldn't even have to evict Harper and Millie, just tell them some maintenance was needed on the building as he tried to coordinate with their business hours.

Peter followed the buttons from his collar down, careful not to loosen them as he unfastened each one. He was ready to shimmy back into his T-shirt. Expensive clothes made him nervous. He was a whole lot more comfortable in his walking tour uniform, which consisted of a faded polo and khakis.

But if it meant Harper looked at him like *that* again, he'd buy a three-piece suit and all of Pemberley.

Twilight fell on the twinkling city streets the next evening as Harper and Millie waited in the living area of the loft. Millie wore her signature red cloche, red lipstick, and a velvet navy dress that was every kind of classy. Harper had decided to wear the antique dress she'd been repairing, and she liked to think the golden tones of the skirt brought out a little sparkle in her cheeks.

Harper fidgeted her hands and stared at the front door, where Peter would appear any moment. She wondered if the butterflies she'd felt yesterday were just a fluke, a consequence of her surprise at seeing him all dressed up.

Then Peter opened the front door, and her heart fluttered a thousand times over.

Definitely not a fluke.

"Ready, ladies?" He held his arm out widely toward the door as if he were on a game show and teaching a contestant to play Plinko. He was such a nerd, and though she'd never admit it, Harper loved that about him.

"You clean up nicely." Her voice was hoarse, so she cleared her throat.

"I could say the same about the two of you." Peter simply grinned, adjusting his tie. "How are you tonight?"

She was nervous around him. She'd never felt nervous around him. She shifted her weight between her heels, suddenly wishing she'd spent more time on her hair. "Yeah, I'm fine. Great, actually."

"Well, that's . . . great. Shall we?" He offered his elbow, then leaned closer to her ear and whispered, "You do look beautiful tonight, Harper."

It all seemed to feed his confidence—her awkward manner, her inevitably palpable attraction. He stood a little taller, and his gaze lingered just a little while longer on her lips.

But no, Harper was wrong. It wasn't so much a matter of confidence as attention. He was, perhaps for the first time she'd seen, undistracted by the glitz of someone else's history—and completely immersed, for a few moments at least, in his own.

The dashing-date role suited him quite nicely.

Just as Harper's heart was melting to a satisfying swirl, Millie swooshed between them. She reached for Peter's tie and tightened the knot, then gave it a satisfied pat. "Let's not forget the old woman in the room, shall we?"

Peter just chuckled, then looked her straight in the eyes, grinning with the sweetest look of admiration. "You're not so old, Millie."

Millie patted him once more on the shoulder. "You are charming, Peter Perkins. I will give you that much. Your mannerisms . . ." Millie sighed. "Well, you remind me of a person who meant a lot to me."

Peter stilled at that, and Harper watched him, wondering. Was Millie finally going to summon the courage to tell him everything?

But in a moment's time, the spell was broken. Millie draped her beaded purse on her shoulder and looked toward Harper. "Go on now and fetch your purse. There's no time like the present."

You're telling me.

THIRTY-FIVE

Charleston, Modern Day

There was something different about Peter tonight, under the light of the city streetlamps. Harper was superficial for noticing, but there was a word for how Peter looked, and the word was *fine*.

But the difference was so much more than looks alone. Peter was one of those few people who become vastly more attractive the longer you know them. He was the opposite of entropy, the bettering of what was good.

But he could never know the feelings that were beginning to stir in her. No one could. She'd kept his long-sought-after grandmother a secret for weeks. Millie was the one person that Peter would give anything to find, and Harper had kept her from him. Not on purpose, sure, but there was no telling if Millie was ever going to come out with the truth. Besides, Peter represented a dream that Harper needed to cut all ties with if she was eventually going to find closure.

A jazz band settled down behind their instruments as expo guests donning colorful hats and various sizes of pearls mingled with one another. The dresses—oh, the dresses—ranged from floral prints to off-the-shoulder, lacy details. And the band, with their penchant for old swing songs, was sure to book new gigs because of the expo. Even Harper had taken their business card, though she didn't have an occasion.

They started up with a nod to years past with "Rockin' Robin." Peter held his hand out toward Millie. "Care to dance with me?"

Harper's heart pitter-pattered just hearing him say the words. And she didn't even like dancing. Oh, she was done for.

Millie's olive skin warmed with a blush, but she played coy as he patiently led her out toward the dance floor, offering his arm as support.

To keep from staring, Harper busied herself straightening the several gowns they'd displayed in front of the booth. To keep from swooning . . . well, she didn't have an answer to that one.

She would just focus on the dresses and the event. What better way to advertise a new dress shop than going straight to the source with an expo designed for bridal parties? If all went well, the contacts they made tonight could become customers in the coming weeks.

"Excuse me?"

Harper jumped at the woman's voice behind her. She turned to greet the would-be client.

"I'm so sorry to startle you." The woman held out her left hand, flashing a diamond the size of the Aiken-Rhett mansion Harper had toured with Peter last week. "Do you have a card or something?"

Harper hurried to grab one from the folding table in the middle of the booth. Millie thought it would be cute to add buttons and flower petals as table arrangements, so Peter and Harper did as they were told and followed through.

Harper handed the card to the bride-to-be, then reached for the plate of cookies. "You're welcome to one of these if you like. The owner of the dress shop made them. She ran a boardinghouse for decades and is an amazing baker."

The woman smiled and slipped the business card into her clutch. "Wish I could, but I already gained two pounds last week from my cake tasting."

Note to self: When and if you someday have a wedding, plan ample inches within your wedding dress to accommodate the side effects of cake tasting. You do not want to be turning down cookies.

Harper set the plate down. "Well, we look forward to seeing you at our grand opening next month."

"I plan to be there with bells on."

Harper smiled. "Thanks for your support. It means a lot, really."

The young bride waved her left hand, scattering tiny prisms all over the vintage dresses and the little booth.

Harper looked toward Peter and Millie, then reached for a cookie.

All evening, a steady line of people had come over, grabbed the cookies Millie had insisted on making, and gushed over the vintage gowns they had repaired. All the customers promised to visit for the grand opening of Dresses by Millie. They were fooled by Harper pretending she belonged here.

By all accounts, the opening was guaranteed to be a success. That much was sure.

But Harper couldn't seem to still the nagging voice inside her head. It echoed through the empty spaces her confidence had once stood guard over.

She'd never been one to feel sorry for herself, never been anything but stubborn. But her department chair's words had come on the heels of a decade of work, a decade's worth of failures.

At some point, even the strongest lose hope.

And even dreamers must sleep.

Millie laughed and held on to her hat as Peter acted as if he were about to dip her. Harper took another bite of the cookie. Was it bad that she found herself jealous of Millie right now? She knew she shouldn't feel this way, but she would do anything for a few moments in Peter's arms.

The band slowed the song to a close, and Peter and Millie returned.

Millie took a seat in the padded chair they'd brought along for her. "Well, I'm plumb wore out." She looked up toward Peter. "Sorry to say, you'll have to find yourself another dance partner."

Peter's gaze drifted to Harper's, and she fell into the blue-green tide behind his tortoiseshell glasses. She could not tell him the truth, and it wasn't fair to flirt until he knew the whole story.

You promised Millie. You promised Millie. You promised Millie.

"You did help me with this ridiculous suit I will probably never wear again. So in exchange, I'd love to offer my mediocre dancing skills and very possibly step on your toes. It's only fair."

Harper moistened her lips, dry from the dark lip stain she had used, and didn't let go of his gaze. "I'm not much of a dancer." She wasn't.

"I don't care." He didn't, did he?

Peter took her hand, and Harper's low heels clacked against the cobblestone until the two of them made it to the corner of the makeshift dance floor.

His touch was gentle, but his fingers were roughened by the work of saving old things. They'd known each other such a short time—just weeks, really. But sharing a dance was a funny thing— touching a person's hands and leaning on their shoulders. Learning the details of where their feet rise and their posture falls. Somehow, in the midst of all the movement, the racing thoughts inside your mind still long enough for you to really know somebody, when you both do your part in rhythm.

And in Harper's case, well, she was smitten. Warmth tickled her skin, and nerves fluttered in her stomach as the realization sunk in that he would touch her hand like this, gently, decidedly, and not let go.

The band counted off, then started into a rendition of an Ella Fitzgerald song she had always loved.

Peter seemed to be following the tempo in his head. "I think we can rumba to this," he murmured. "Do you know how to rumba?"

Does an extensive knowledge of competition dance shows on TV count for anything?

Harper just shook her head.

Peter leaned a little closer. He placed his free hand at the small of her back and explained the slow-quick-quick rhythm as her heart began to outpace the music.

She was going to make a fool of herself, wasn't she?

Peter pulled her toward himself, leading the pace of their steps and even adding a turn or two for variety. Harper had *no* idea what she was doing, but she melted into his hold and into his lead and found herself very nearly floating over the dance floor.

He was good at this. Very good.

He smiled down at her as if he knew his own skill.

But of course he did.

Because if there was one thing Harper was learning about Peter, it was that he did everything with passion. He did everything well.

Why should she be surprised that he would dance well too?

Peter inched her even closer as she gained familiarity with the steps. He leaned down to whisper, "You're not so bad, Harper."

Chills ran down her spine at the mention of her name on his lips. She looked up at him, her face inches from his own and her eyelids suddenly heavy, begging to close from the breath of his kiss.

But she was getting ahead of herself. It was only a dance, after all.

A very well-executed rumba with a surprising amount of hip sway from the historian. Only a dance, she told herself again, but darn it if Peter wouldn't stop looking into her eyes.

His nearing, then, was almost imperceptible. Harper could feel it—the charge in that space between them.

Peter bit down on his bottom lip, his hand pressed to the small of her back, and she almost leaned in those last two inches. And she would have, but what if she were misinterpreting?

The song ended with a drum flourish, and Peter's Adam's apple warbled. He seemed stuck in that place of in-between, unwilling to close the gap between them, but equally unwilling to move away. "Thanks for the dance, Harper."

When he dropped his hand from her waist, she all but groaned for it back.

She had very little dance experience, but she didn't need it to know Peter had been about to kiss her. And she would have welcomed it wholeheartedly.

The expo went late into the night. Harper still hadn't recovered from their almost-kiss when Peter returned from loading the vintage dresses back into his car.

"Hey, where's Millie?" Peter stretched his shoulders and looked above the dwindling crowd.

"She told me she's parched and they're all out of water, so she's getting a bottle across the street."

"By herself?"

"Yes, I know." Harper shook her head, leaning against the display table of their booth. "I tried to go with her, but she insisted I stay, and you know how ornery she can be. I did manage to convince her to take her cane, though I doubt she's using it."

Peter didn't smile at this attempt at humor. Suddenly, Harper felt much more worried. "You don't think she's unsafe, do you?" She swallowed hard and adjusted the pearls around her neck. "I thought this was a good part of town."

Peter rubbed his hands over his eyes and started toward the exit, onto the street. Harper followed.

He glanced over his shoulder. "Downtown is safe, but this street is also full of tourists and college students who may've been partying at this time of night."

Harper should've thought of that. If something happened to Millie . . . but she was supposed to be just across the way. It shouldn't be hard to spot her.

Wait. Was that Millie?

Two men surrounded her at the exit of the convenience store. One of the men held her red cloche in his hands.

Millie raised her cane and began swinging.

She made contact with the man's shoulder. He dropped her hat.

Peter began to run. He stripped off his jacket and tossed it to Harper who caught it midair. "Get away from her!" he yelled.

He unbuttoned and rolled up his sleeves. What did he think was about to happen? Harper's pulse began to race. She willed herself to help but didn't know what to do.

The other man—whom Harper now saw as scrawny and old, but intoxicated and uninhibited by reason—grabbed Millie's hat from the ground. A smarter thief would've run.

But instead, his pride apparently threatened, he turned back to Peter and waved the cloche around. "I'd like to see what you're going to do about it." The man slurred his words.

"Give the woman her hat back." Peter's voice took on unwavering authority. Harper grasped his jacket. The streetlights cast a glow upon them and turned their forms into shadows. She could smell the liquor even from where she stood.

Millie shook her cane toward the man. "You heard him, fool."

Not helping, Millie. Harper sent her a sideways glance.

The drunk did not respond well to Peter's command—or Millie's, for that matter. He yanked Millie by the arm and spat at her feet. This guy could hurt her if the situation continued escalating. Realization set in.

Harper began to panic, arms tingling and nerves burning. With two strange men involved, how would she and Peter manage? They had to do something, and quick. There wouldn't be enough time for police to arrive.

But then she saw the fire in Peter's eyes. Fire enough to light the street and send the shadows back under it. And for reasons she couldn't explain, she knew Peter was capable. He would take on the world if he had to.

Peter pulled back his arm, his shoulder muscles tightening as his fist connected firmly with its target. The drunk man dropped his hold of Millie's arm. He staggered and wiped the blood from his nose.

Peter shook out his hand, getting ready for another punch.

Harper felt as if she were watching it all play out on a screen, fast-forward and surreal. The other man, the forgettable one, tugged Millie's hat from the thief's hand, then tossed it to the ground.

"Let's get out of here, you idiot," he mumbled to his companion.

Peter angled his body in front of Millie, a human shield from harm, until the two were out of eyeshot. Satisfied by their disappearance, he turned to Millie and cataloged her from head to toe. He put two gentle hands on her shoulders and looked into her eyes. "Did they hurt you, Millie?"

Harper bent down and reached for the cloche. She brushed dirt from the rim and repositioned the hat back where it belonged. Guilt seized her. How could she have let this happen? She had one job—to take care of Millie. No matter how Millie had insisted, she never should've let the woman go alone.

Millie trembled from Peter's embrace, and he pulled her closer. "It's all right, Aunt Millie." He rested his chin above her hat. "We're here now. You'll be all right."

Tucked beneath the safety of Peter's arms, Millie shook her cane once more.

Peter drew in deep breaths as he held her, his chest heaving with each one. Adrenaline, Harper imagined. And then he began to laugh. "Millie, would you put that cane down?"

"Confounded fools were going to take my hat," she mumbled.

Peter held her a little tighter and made eye contact with Harper, rolling his eyes and offering a relieved grin.

The sight of Peter holding Millie changed something in Harper. He was no longer the searching grandson, the nerdy historian, or even a Gosling doppelgänger.

He was strong. Unrelenting and calm. No threat was too large to stop him from protecting Millie. Of that, she had not been surprised. What she had *not* anticipated was how very capable he had been. She would have expected the bravery, but Peter had offered something far more.

Peter had become Millie's hero.

Peter, whose golden heart was beginning to quicken Harper's own.

THIRTY-SIX

Charleston, 1952

Millie hadn't planned this part.

The leaving.

The trees browned with the colors of fall. With one baby discreetly nursing from the crook of her arm, Millie looked out the window of the yellow Plymouth as the tires caught traction against the gravel, smashing the pebbles deep into the dirt, and the bricks of that house grew smaller and smaller until their individual pieces faded into a blur.

She didn't cry at first.

She was far too weak for tears.

For it was almost as though someone had taken a scoop to the heart of her, leaving her hollow. And so alone.

She glanced over at Franklin, who wiped tears from his eyes in the driver's seat.

Poor Franklin, much as he loved the babies, could never fully understand.

Not in the way of Millie's arm reaching for her absent child, or the milk that already leaked.

Her body had bulged with two babies. Her arms had carried two babies.

And yet this—this grief, this emptiness, this parting—was the only way the two girls could both have lives filled with opportunity.

Still, everything within Millie ached and screamed, as one wakes in the night to the swelling of a broken bone that's been wrapped and set and still cries out.

Grief enough for both babies.

In her pocket was a note from Hannah. *You will always be her mother,* it read, *but I promise to raise her with love.* Millie had given Franklin's mother a letter for Rosie, a letter she'd written just before leaving, and Hannah had given her this in return.

Millie didn't know what to make of this. Didn't know how she felt. Thankful, she supposed. Yes, thankful. That's how she ought to feel. If only it were as easy as *ought to.*

The drive away from Charleston was entirely different from the last time they had departed the city by train. They were entirely different too.

Once two kids themselves, they had all the possibilities of life ahead, however bleak their reality.

Now, Millie and Franklin were grown. Stronger, perhaps. But more broken. And Millie, for one, was definitely more alone.

As they drove south through Georgia, Franklin parked at some little town on the coast. Millie didn't know what the place was called, but it had a lighthouse, so that was good for something.

Franklin flipped off the ignition and turned to face her, his arm already resting on her shoulder.

"There's nothing I can say, is there?"

Millie bit the inside of her lip and shook her head slowly.

"I loved her too."

She wanted to say—*not as I did! Not as one-half of myself!*—but she realized, quite unexpectedly, that she didn't really know that about Franklin, did she? She didn't know his pain any more than he knew hers.

And love was not a yardstick to which she ought to be comparing. Loss was loss, and grief was grief.

Something to acknowledge, something to cherish, something to which they might cling. Something that would altogether shape them and their future by the absence it had rounded out in their beings.

Millie reached into the backseat for the picnic basket she'd packed earlier with sandwiches. She handed Franklin his food, then sipped water from her thermos.

They both chewed numbly. Millie knew she had to eat, had to drink, for the sake of her other daughter. But the will for all of it had left her.

And for that reason on that day, perhaps her other daughter saved her.

They sat like that in silence for an hour, the two of them looking in tandem at the lighthouse and then at the sea, looking for hope while drowning.

Lord—Millie watched the top of the light turn 'round and 'round—*someday, let me see her again. Somehow, let me know she is safe and happy. And let her know she is always, fiercely loved.*

Wasn't it Hemingway who said the sun also rises?

Millie only wished she could rise so faithfully.

She had changed her mind.

She, Franklin, and Juliet had been living as a little family for six months. Juliet's skin tone had continued to deepen as the days passed. So when folks at the pharmacy or the hardware shop asked, Millie told them her own father was Italian. They smiled kindly in return, and Franklin smiled back. But Millie never missed the sideways, skeptical glances they gave as they walked by.

Sometimes she considered telling guests at the boardinghouse that she and Franklin had decided to help the young child, and the biological mother was devastated she couldn't keep her baby. That way, people wouldn't ask any more questions.

Neither answer would be a lie.

But she couldn't stomach the thought of telling anyone that Juliet wasn't her own flesh and blood. It was bad enough she had to do that with one daughter. But both of them?

For the longest time, she blamed her volatile state on her body's transition into motherhood. She had frequently forgotten to eat, and would often wake in the night in sweat and panic, thinking that one of her two daughters had been taken from under her roof. And then Franklin would calm her, tell her it was going to be all right and his mother was taking care to give Rosie the best life she could. And for a few moments, for a few hours, Millie would sleep again.

But the dreams, as it turned out, never faded—never blurred as she anticipated they would.

Franklin didn't seem all that surprised when she woke him a little after two o'clock and told him they needed to go to Charleston, and soon.

She watched by the moonlight as he rubbed his eyes with his hands. His voice was hoarse from sleep. "What is it you want to do, Millie?"

"I don't know." She shook her head as she clutched the sheets. Her nightgown was damp with the sweat of the dreams. "I just want to hold her, Franklin. I want to kiss her forehead and smell her hair, and when she's older, teach her to read. I want her and Juliet to know one another. If the world won't permit them to be sisters, perhaps they can at least be friends. It's better than nothing."

Millie's gaze trailed to the dark window behind Franklin. Outside, a cloud slowly floated in front of the moon, so that the moonlight cast an ethereal glow all around its perimeter.

"Okay." Franklin laid his head back down on the pillow.

"Okay?" Millie's heart leapt with anticipation. How could he go back to sleep at a time like this? "Really? You'll take me to Charleston?"

"Millie, if it will bring you back to yourself once more, if it will give you some peace, I would take you to the moon."

THIRTY-SEVEN

Charleston, Modern Day

One month after the expo, Harper situated Millie's gown over the display mannequin in the front window, careful to raise the hem of the old silk so it floated in a smooth cloud toward the ground.

Millie busied herself behind the antique cash register they'd found last week. She'd swooned in the thrift store over the sound of the bell as she repeatedly opened and closed the drawer, marveling that the antique was still operational.

Peter's single rack full of dresses had multiplied with the arrival of Millie's mysterious boxes, and now, four long rows of wedding and evening gowns made the store seem complete. If all went well today, Harper would work on sewing some more custom dress samples. Twinkle lights hung from the exposed brick walls, and a large, whimsical chandelier gave just the right rosy glow to the space.

They were ready for the not-so-grand opening of Dresses by Millie. This soft launch would give them a chance to recognize and improve upon any potential business hiccups prior to the actual grand opening next month.

The bell above the front entry chimed as Peter pushed open the door. He held a white box in his hands and wore his new slim black pants with a dusty-blue sweater.

"Morning, ladies." He walked toward the back of the store and set the box and a stack of napkins on the counter beside Millie.

Harper hurried over, her kitten heels clacking. "Please tell me those are from Glazed Gourmet."

"These are from Glazed Gourmet." He opened the lid to reveal a variety of specialty flavor combinations. The scent of sugary glaze filled the air. "I've got a mocha donut for the coffee lover, a lemon old-fashioned for Millie, and a raspberry one for myself."

Harper and Millie each took a napkin and snatched their donuts from the box.

"This was super sweet of you." Harper took a bite, then heard the pun in the words she'd just spoken. She began to laugh at herself, and Peter joined in.

Millie pinched the smallest bite off her donut as if she didn't quite trust all the hype. "I don't get it. What's funny?"

"Sweet . . . like the donuts." Harper talked with her hands, still holding the mocha donut.

"Right." Millie simply raised her eyebrows and took another bite of the lemon pastry, which had apparently passed her test. "I get that part. Just don't understand why it's funny."

Peter turned to Harper then, and she couldn't help herself—her laughter got the best of her. Peter's too. Harper tried to hush her laugh, but her failed attempt only made her laugh harder.

Peter was more successful. He took his own donut from the box and wrapped it up inside a napkin. Then he checked his watch, an old-school relic in the age of digital timekeeping. "Hate to deliver these and run, but I'm scheduled for a private tour on the Battery in ten minutes." He reserved a humored twinkle in his eyes just for Harper.

He took a step closer. Just close enough that Harper could smell a hint of his sandalwood shampoo. Just close enough for her to notice the strength of his shoulders and think back to the expo, to that dance and his very heroic display.

She breathed in the smell.

"Hope everything goes well for y'all today."

Harper smiled at him. "Have a great time teaching strangers about history."

"I intend to." He turned then, donut in hand, and grinned right back. Then he waved and headed out the door.

Harper took another bite of her donut, savoring the glaze, and sighed. If Peter kept this up, she was tempted to make the short-term rental a long-term situation.

"Well, isn't this an interesting development." Millie put one hand on her shoulder.

"What's that?" Harper bit her tongue as she chewed.

"Oh, sweetheart. I may be old as dirt, but I'm not blind. You're falling for him."

Harper started to protest—that she had no such feelings and he wasn't her typical type. But then she snapped her mouth shut. Because they both knew Millie was right.

Too bad there was nothing she could do about it.

Seven hours later, Harper flipped over the *Open* sign on the door to read *Closed* and twisted her key in the lock.

A grand total of twelve customers had come to the soft opening, two of whom had only walked inside to ask if the dress in the window was for sale. Millie sat on the sofa that still anchored the center of the room.

Harper moved to sit beside her. "I just don't understand. People seemed so interested at the expo. What happened? The whole point was to walk through a typical day in the dress store so we could know what to expect and what to improve. Is *this* what we should be expecting?" Failure? The added word hung unspoken in the air.

Millie smoothed her embroidered cardigan with her wrinkled hands. "Maybe it was just a fluke."

"The expo, or the opening?"

Millie didn't answer.

Harper shook her head, looking around the shop. She had imagined she'd have stacks of gowns in the dressing rooms to return back to the floor. But instead, all the racks remained pristine, the dresses largely untouched. There was little or no work to be done because there were so few customers.

She'd stayed up late making sure the store was ready. She'd climbed into the window display, accessorizing the mannequin again and again until she had it just right. She had remembered all the details. Swiffer-swept the floor. Tested out the Bluetooth speaker and made the perfect playlist that wasn't too trendy but also wasn't too Celine Dion.

Why had no one come?

Why did she keep readying this fantasy again and again, when no one had ever come? Her dream had become like an elusive blind date, only in this version, she was Meg Ryan in the coffee shop again and again and again.

Harper blew out a deep breath. She shouldn't overreact. It was only the first day, after all. But she couldn't seem to silence the voice inside that kept whispering, *"Your dreams will never amount to anything. You should stop embarrassing yourself."*

Peter would say she was listening to fear. Maybe he was right. But she didn't want to feel the sinking disappointment of failure again.

Millie set her hand on Harper's knee. "Come now, it's not so bad. See, I'm in good spirits, and I've waited much longer to own a dress shop than you have."

Harper released a sad sigh. She shifted so she faced Millie more directly. "So, we just keep planning, and hope the real opening goes better? Maybe we could increase our marketing efforts."

Millie nodded, patting Harper's knee twice before moving her hand. "More advertisements. Maybe Peter can make some referrals." Her red lipstick framed her beautiful smile.

"I bet he wouldn't mind. He's certainly well-connected in the city." Harper thought back to some of the projects he'd told her about.

"We'll see." It was Millie's way of ending the conversation. Harper had begun to recognize the strategy.

Preparations in the dress shop continued to be discouraging the following week and brought much of the same doubt that had begun to hover like a looming shadow over their dwindling optimism. Harper could probably also call it *naïveté*, honestly, but she was avoiding that thought. So she and Millie decided at the close of the business day, they would take action to spruce up the place. Get their own enthusiasm raised in hopes that it would spread to would-be customers. The store decorations were minimalistic, after all, and perhaps all they needed were a few more things to jazz up the place.

Millie followed closely behind Harper as she reached for the door, and the little bell chimed with a ring very familiar to the streets of the Holy City and all its steeples.

Together, they walked down King Street, past the charming storefronts and under striped awnings, toward an eclectic antique shop that sold everything from vintage clothing and handbags to lampshades.

Millie ambled toward a framed poster of Katharine Hepburn while Harper made her way to the rack of dresses and browsed through them.

Harper's fingers lingered over the hanger of an emerald-green gown. The fabric was stiff but vibrant. She lifted the hanger and tucked the dress safely over her arm, then headed toward the curtain at the back where she found the dressing room.

The fit would be tight, at best, especially with no stretch to the fabric. But she had to try anyway. The dress was stunning.

Harper swooshed the curtain shut and unzipped the dress, careful to mind the seams so as not to catch the fabric. She shimmied into it but stopped abruptly, mid-waistline, when she confirmed her love of pralines from Savannah Candy Kitchen had finally caught up with her.

But as she slipped the dress up and over her head, a sea of old emerald brought waves of fragrance.

The smell was familiar and immediately elicited every manner of flashing memory—from a vintage dress Daddy bought her to the torn fabrics she'd found at estate sales and repurposed, and even the lonely nights spent in Savannah, trying to perfect her work.

The smell was an open door to a hallway of memory. She would never know the original dress owner, this woman who had probably zipped the waistline with ease, or what the pockets carried. She would never know her, and yet the fabric was the same. A shared intersection of this mystery woman's story and her own. The thought of all that meeting at the seams gave Harper chills, as emotion pulsed through her veins.

Hope, namely. Fascination and determination and the bliss that only comes from one's deepest dream.

Dust mixed with old fabric.

Not a particularly complicated sort of smell. But a powerful one.

It was the smell of old books. Of old houses like the ones Peter loved. The smell of untold stories leading up to the next chapter, and the smell of home. Fabrics that have been worn day by day, sometimes accumulating dust, until the day by days begin to take on the scent of one another, a scent that is as recognizable as fabric, sewn stitch by stitch into a gown.

When Harper zipped the dress back onto the hanger and tugged her own stretchy jeans back on, she knew she had to buy it, even though her own waist was a good three inches beyond the allowance. She thought of the rack of clothes Peter had given her and Millie for the shop, and somehow, for some reason, this dress just seemed to belong.

It was a silly impulse, but she couldn't shake it. She had the strangest sense that leaving this dress at the store would mean leaving part of her own story behind.

Harper opened the curtain of the dressing room to find Millie waiting, several long strands of pearls draped from her arms.

"Find something to purchase?" Millie took the fabric of the dress between her finger and thumb. "This is lovely. I had one just like it once . . . but that was a lifetime ago."

Harper hesitated. Millie's hand along the old fabric seemed to jump-start a time machine, blurring decades and chronology, until the only thing left was life as it is lived before it becomes memory. The fabric between the seams.

THIRTY-EIGHT

Charleston, 1955

Millie pulled back the floral curtain and peered through the window. Franklin pressed behind her, so close her heart leapt at the smell of him—coffee and firewood and water—a smell he must've brought to Charleston all the way from the boardinghouse in the small suitcase she'd packed for him. He wore a tie with his white button-down, and the shirt tucked into a pair of pleated trousers, Millie's favorite outfit of his.

"Are they here yet?" Franklin asked. "Is that their car pulling up?"

Millie turned to him, putting her hand on his face as Juliet carried an old doll by the arm. She'd wanted to bring Rosie too, but then realized that would set a dangerous norm for when the girls grew older. It was one thing for the three of them to make visits and then leave, but quite another for them to publicly take Rosie around town. Rosie was to believe she had been adopted by Franklin's mother, which, in her mind, would make him her much older brother. As she grew older, she would question why her brother would take her to his wife's family's house, would she not?

Complicated, yes, but they must think this through. And Millie had spent plenty of nights doing just that. They had to be consistent. So for now, Millie, Franklin, and Juliet would keep their visits to his mother's place, much as that hollowed out her heart.

She turned her attention back to Franklin. "Are you sweating? I've never seen you like this." He was adorable. But she wouldn't say that part out loud and embarrass him all the more.

"Mama," Millie called. "They're here."

Mama hurried over from the kitchen and lifted the curtain of the opposite window to watch as Aunt Bea stepped out of Uncle Clyde's automobile.

"Oh, Lord have mercy," Mama murmured. "They've done brought the whole show."

Millie laughed. Aunt Bea carried a huge sweetgrass basket-in-progress on her hip as if it were a baby, and Uncle Clyde carried his old guitar. She hadn't heard him play in ages, but he could strum the blues like no other. They both wore their Sunday best, Uncle Clyde in his crisp suit and Aunt Bea with a wide-brimmed hat that might not fit through the door.

"Don't you worry now." Mama ruffled the front of Franklin's hair. "They may talk tough, but they'll love you. How could they not?"

Millie caught a glimpse of Juliet playing behind them, and her heart tugged with nostalgia—not for the past, but for all the future memories they wouldn't have together.

Rosie should be here.

How could something that hadn't happened, that wouldn't happen, feel as weighty as regret? Millie's next breath was heavy. She needed to get her head on straight before her aunt and uncle came through that door.

It was the first time she'd had the courage to invite them over while she was visiting Mama. They'd never met Franklin or either of the girls, and Millie didn't know much of what was happening in their lives except for what they sent in postcards.

She had no idea what to expect.

Millie scooped up Juliet from the path of the doorway, and the toddler let out a shriek and kicked her little legs like a frog scuttling along. If Rosie were here, she would've just stared at the reaction, like she'd done to Juliet all weekend long. Funny how two girls born at the same hour could react in such different ways.

The door opened then, and Aunt Bea had to duck her head to fit herself and her hat and that basket through the door, just as Millie had predicted. Uncle Clyde held his guitar upright in front of him and dipped his own news cap as he caught sight of them. His smile widened.

Juliet stopped her wailing as she studied the strangers in the room, but her legs kept to kickin'. Millie held onto her, laughing. "Well, if that isn't a welcome, I don't know what is."

Aunt Bea took several purposeful steps toward Franklin. He held out his hand, and she shook it.

"Ma'am." He lowered his chin to pay her respect and raised his other hand to cover her own. "I'm Franklin. Pleasure to meet you."

Aunt Bea let him hold her hand a hot minute as she cradled that basket against her hip with her other hand.

Franklin tapped the toe of his oxfords almost imperceptibly. So subtle was the movement that anyone else would've missed it. Anyone but Millie.

And she *did* worry for him because Aunt Bea had a way of speaking her mind, and Millie had no idea what the woman might say. But regardless of all that, it was important to Millie that they know Franklin, all of them. Even if their marriage was unconventional. After all, through it all, she loved him.

Uncle Clyde stepped forward, and Aunt Bea pulled back her hand to carry the sweetgrass basket over toward the sofa where she settled in.

"Son, you just call me Clyde, ya hear?"

Franklin nodded and enthusiastically shook his hand. He couldn't hide his grin, and his joy made Millie smile too. At least she could count on her uncle to play nice.

"So, Millie. Seems congratulations are in order." Aunt Bea took the long stalk of sweetgrass and jabbed it into the next portion of the basket, sewing the strands together as she talked. Millie couldn't tell from her tone if she approved or disapproved, but one thing was clear from all that fidgeting. Aunt Bea was keeping something to herself. Because the woman never fidgeted unless she was holding something back.

Millie set Juliet down. She decided the best course of action would be to keep the conversation moving forward. "Thank you, Aunt Bea." Millie glanced at Franklin, then toward their daughter. Indeed, she found herself both heartbroken and fully alive, and she didn't know how to explain that except to say thanks in reply.

"Y'all excuse me," Mama cut in. "I gotta get to the kitchen to stir the macaroni before it sticks to the pan."

"Glad to hear it," Uncle Clyde teased. "After last Christmas, nobody wanted to eat your macaroni again."

"Oh, hush it." Mama dismissed him with a wave of her hand, but Millie saw her smile as she disappeared down the hall.

At the mention of last Christmas, it was all Millie could do not to cry. Because she'd missed last Christmas. And she missed her mama. And even being here right now with Franklin and Juliet . . . well, they had to be discreet because if the wrong neighbors saw, that might be dangerous for them all.

"Your mama tells me you and your husband run a boarding-house." Aunt Bea pulled the stalk of sweetgrass tighter, sewing a pattern of color into the basket.

"That's right. On the bay there in Fairhope, Alabama."

Clyde sat down beside Aunt Bea, stretching his arm along the top of the sofa so his frame suddenly seemed larger than life. "Sounds real nice."

"It is, sir," Franklin added. Millie held back a chuckle at the thought of Clyde being a *sir*. She wished Franklin would feel more comfortable, but maybe that would come in time.

"What's your story, Franklin? How'd you end up in Alabama, married to my niece?"

"If I said the luckiest day of my life, would you believe that?"

Franklin grinned at Millie, and she was glad to see him loosening up a little. Juliet handed him the doll, and he wiggled the arms so it appeared to reach out and hug her. Franklin looked back up toward Aunt Bea and Uncle Clyde. "Actually, when I was just a kid, we'd fallen on real hard times, and so my mother and I took to train hopping. One day, she fell off. So I had to find a way to send money back to her here in Charleston while she recovered. Train jumping and looking for temporary jobs seemed as good a way as any." He shrugged. "Kept saying I was going to stop and settle down like everyone else. But I got so used to it, so good at it, the truth is I didn't know if I'd be good at anything else or brave enough to try, until I met your niece. Sir."

Millie blinked in surprise. He'd never told her that part of the story before. In fact, he'd seemed plenty brave enough from where she stood. Always had.

She stood beside him and slipped her hand into the crook of his elbow. He planted a kiss on the top of her head.

"Well, girl, I'm glad you found yourself somebody who sees you for who you are." Clyde cleared his throat. "It's good seeing you happy. Isn't it, Bea?"

But Aunt Bea's weaving grew increasingly agitated until finally she set the basket down and wiped the little remnants of sweet-grass from her hands. "I'm sorry. I just can't do this." She shook her head and stood upright, her hands on her hips. "I can't pretend."

Millie squeezed Franklin's elbow, frowning. "Pretend what?" That she liked Franklin? Was excited to meet Juliet?

Aunt Bea blew out an exaggerated breath, looking Millie straight in the eyes. "Isn't it obvious, child?"

Millie shook her head.

"Why, you act as if you're ashamed of us all. You weren't raised like this." Aunt Bea's throat warbled as she swallowed. "You're Gullah, girl. And you have every reason to be proud."

"Ashamed?" Millie's voice was a hush, so in shock was she to hear the accusation. How dare Aunt Bea say such a hurtful thing?

Didn't she know how it tortured Millie to hide? To hide half her heritage—half her future and half her past?

"Where is your pride for *our* family? For all we've been through and all we've overcome? If you have any pride left, you sure haven't shown it to nobody. And all for what?" Aunt Bea straightened the sweetgrass basket with her hands so it wouldn't fall. "You ever even get that dress shop?"

Millie's eyes widened. "I—" Her voice caught, just as Mama reentered the room.

Mama smiled and rubbed her palms against her pale-blue dress. "What'd I miss?" Slowly, her countenance fell. She must have noticed the tears pooling in Millie's eyes.

Aunt Bea watched Millie, waiting for her to finish the sentiment. She must'a imagined Millie didn't have an answer. That she was right and Millie was ashamed and couldn't defend herself.

Oh my, how she was wrong.

"That's what I thought." Aunt Bea hitched the basket back up on her hip, then reached over to tussle Juliet's hair. She glared at Uncle Clyde to hurry up and stand, so he grabbed the guitar he hadn't even played yet. Franklin and Juliet would've loved to hear him. Millie just knew it.

"You do have a beautiful family, Millie, and I am glad to see you happy. I just wish you didn't have to leave us behind for them and your so-called dreams." She turned to Millie's uncle. "Come on, Clyde."

But before he followed Bea out, Clyde walked over to Millie and hugged her with those long arms of his—arms that as a kid, she once thought could shelter her from anything. Had she been wrong? "Give her some time. She'll come around." He stepped back, righted his hat. "You gotta admit, it's a lot for all of us to process."

Millie nodded as the tears welling in her eyes began falling down.

"Don't you believe for a minute she doesn't love you, or Franklin, or the babies—or that she isn't proud of you, girl."

"You promise?" The desperation in Millie's voice was pathetic. But she needed her uncle's reassurance right now.

"Sure." Clyde nodded. "She just needs to know you're still proud of her back, is all."

How could she ever doubt that?

He reached out to shake Franklin's hand again, and the two nodded at one another before he headed out the door.

The four of them, even Juliet, stood in silence for a moment that seemed to stretch with expectation and deflate with disappointment, as the reality of what had just happened hit home.

Mama put her arm around her daughter, the gesture bringing a welcome comfort for which Millie was more grateful than Mama might ever know. No matter how she aged, no matter where she moved, Millie always had a sense of belonging here with her mama.

"Who wants some macaroni and cheese?" Mama smiled.

THIRTY-NINE

Charleston, Modern Day

Harper had spent last night waiting for dawn. She kept wondering about Millie's hidden past and why all the secrets from Peter. Then she began to consider all she already knew about Millie, particularly how long the woman had been waiting for her dream of owning a dress shop. And as Harper sat in the little living space of their loft last night, dunking her tea bag in and out of her cup, she stared at the door leading to Millie's bedroom and discovered a determination she hadn't met in Savannah.

Come hell or high water, she would make the dress store a success. Oh, she'd been committed to her own dreams and to SCAD. She'd given it her all. But when her *all* emptied out and she still met resistance . . . well, that was a different story.

But this time, she would not give up. She would fail repeatedly if she had to, then would press in and work harder. She would get on Pinterest and browse Hobby Lobby for inspirational quotes. She'd play Taylor Swift in the car.

She would hustle as much as it took to keep this whole store afloat for Millie, even if she never found her own Jubilee tide.

Harper checked the clock above the register and frowned, glancing at the glass door. Lucy was five minutes late, and Lucy never missed an appointment.

Was everything okay?

She'd give her friend a little bit longer before texting to check in. Maybe Lucy was just stuck in traffic, trying to find a good parking spot.

Harper stepped out from behind the register and decided to start pulling sample bridesmaid gowns that might match the color Lucy had texted her earlier.

After a few minutes, the bell above the door chimed. With her own arms full of dresses, Harper looked up to see Lucy huffing through the entryway.

Harper laughed. "What in the world?"

"Thank goodness for your kind face." Lucy stepped over and engulfed her in a hug, dresses and all. "You're never going to believe who I just ran into."

Harper shook her head. "Reese Witherspoon?"

"Declan." Lucy massaged her temples. "That man is exhausting."

Harper held back a half grin. "Exhausting, huh?"

"Yes, exhausting." Lucy crossed her arms over her chest as if the reiteration of the word should make it final. "Why did you ask like that?"

"Like what?"

Lucy tapped her shoe against the heart-of-pine slats of the floor. "You think I'm into him."

Harper sidestepped to hang the dresses up on a separate rack. "I didn't say that."

"You might as well have." Lucy let out a big sigh, then made a face and quietly moved her mouth like she was imitating someone.

Harper gently lifted the hems of the gowns so the fabric would seamlessly float into place. "You're repeating the conversation to yourself, aren't you?"

"Maybe." Lucy took several steps toward the dresses. "These gowns you picked out are gorgeous. How am I going to choose?"

"We'll try them on as soon as you tell me what happened."

Finally, Lucy made eye contact. "He stole my parking spot because he's an entitled jerk."

"Wow. Well, did you have your blinker on?"

"Very funny." Lucy rolled her eyes. "Do you know me at all? Of course I had my blinker on."

Harper took one of the dresses she'd gathered for Lucy and held it up to her friend's shoulders to get a better idea how it might look on her frame. "You want to tell me why you're talking about him like the time you went to New York and got off on the wrong subway stop and missed that sample sale?"

"Harper, *all* of the good dresses were gone by the time I got there. It was infuriating. So much potential."

"My point exactly." Harper set the dress back on the rack and reached for a different one. "Is this the color your sister wants? It looked like a match from my phone, but you know how it's hard to tell with screens."

Lucy removed a swatch of fabric from her purse and held it up to the dress. "Perfect match." She put the swatch back inside. "So we went on that date, you know? And it turns out, there's history between us."

"History, hmm?" Harper teased.

"Not that kind of history." Lucy reached out to touch the dress. "Actual history. Between our families."

"No way." Harper stretched the fabric around Lucy's waistline. This dress looked to be about the right size and wouldn't require many alterations. "What are the odds?"

"Right? It all goes back to this thing . . ." Lucy talked with her hands. "My ancestors and his ancestors feuding over missing silver back in the Civil War. No one ever found it."

"Ever?" Harper draped the gown over her arm and started toward the dressing rooms.

Lucy followed. "That's right. My family always blamed his family, and apparently his family did the same to mine."

"This is all sounding remarkably like a Shakespearean tragedy."

Harper swept open the curtain of the dressing room with her free arm, then hung the gown inside. "Try this one on."

"How did you know which was my favorite of the stack? I didn't even tell you yet."

"It's what I do." *Well, for the time being.* Harper grinned.

They spent the next hour trying on a whole host of other dresses, but none compared to the first one Harper picked out. She carried it up to the antique register for Lucy and scanned the price tag.

"Thanks for letting me vent about Declan." Lucy pulled out her debit card.

"What are friends for?" Harper shimmied a garment bag over the dress to keep it safe in transit. The words *Dresses by Millie* were scripted along the front, and Harper smiled seeing Millie's name on the bag. She handed it to Lucy. "But just to be clear—are you or are you not into him?"

Several hours later, Millie peered out the window of Harper's car and read each street sign they passed. "Ann Street. Harper, turn!" This sudden notification of their whereabouts was as startling as Harper's favorite messaging app and nearly caused its own sort of disastrous crash.

Harper barely made the turn. The car behind them honked.

Millie grabbed hold of the passenger-side door frame. "Are you trying to kill me, driving such a way? You know, when I was your age, women didn't drive. And though I'm usually the first one to advocate for women having equal opportunities, every time I get in your car I wonder if you might need a few more lessons."

Harper laughed. "I like how you're implying your navigational skills have nothing to do with it."

Millie straightened her cloche and raised her chin. "I don't know what you could possibly mean." She pointed to a large brick building that looked like some kind of warehouse. "That's the place, so keep a lookout for parking and try to avoid slingshotting us around the car again, would you?"

Harper noticed clusters of mothers gripping the wrists of young children, and she squinted to read the sign, "Children's Museum of the Lowcountry." She turned her attention back to the road before Millie could offer another quip. "You're taking me to a children's museum?"

"Don't be ridiculous." Millie settled back into her seat. "I'm taking you to see a replica of the first steam engine in America to pull a train of cars."

"Yes, that makes a lot more sense." Harper grinned. She noticed an empty spot where she could parallel-park, so she flipped on her blinker and reached her arm behind Millie's seat to look back at traffic.

Together they walked into the train museum adjacent to the children's area and looked up at the train. A toddler still unsteady on his feet ambled around back and forth beside them, clearly mesmerized by the size and vivid colors of the locomotive.

Harper read several of the signs posted about the train's history, waiting for Millie to explain why she'd requested to come here, of all places.

Millie clutched the beaded handle of her small handbag, her gaze fixed on the train as if it were about to move at any moment. "Did I ever tell you I married a train jumper?"

Harper's eyes widened. "As in . . ."

Millie turned to her and nodded. "Yes, he actually jumped trains. Real dangerous work, but a lot of people had to do it back then. In the years following the Great Depression, you didn't have the luxury of staying put somewhere. You went where the work was. So my Franklin did just that. And then in the years that followed, after the war, most people settled down and stopped jumping the rails. And it took Franklin longer to settle than most. He used to say that until we met, he had trouble keeping a steady job, but I always suspected he liked the thrill of it all."

Harper tried to imagine all this. No doubt, Millie could see her surprise. "Wait. Does that mean *you* were a train jumper?"

Millie puckered her lips as if she might as well have asked whether Millie's biscuit recipe came frozen. "Do I look like the sort of person capable of tossing myself onto a locomotive?"

Harper started giggling. She couldn't help herself. "I'm sorry. It's just the thought of you . . ." She waved her hand in front of her face to try to keep her laughter under control.

"Yes," Millie nodded, smiling. "I am well aware why that's funny. Because if I ever tried to jump a train, the thing would probably run clear over me." The wrinkles around Millie's eyes pulled gently, and her expression sobered as if lost in sweet memory. "Back then, though, riding the rails didn't have the connotation it does now. Plenty of honest people jumped trains—tryin' to find work, not trouble."

Harper hesitated. "What was Franklin trying to find?"

Millie straightened her hat. "Well, I can't speak to what he was trying to find, but what he did find was me, and I'll tell you, that changed things for both of us."

Harper put her hand to her chest. "Millie, that has to be the sweetest thing I've ever heard."

"Do you see a bench?" Millie glanced around the museum, then pointed, and the two of them sat down. "My mama gave me some heirlooms before I left Charleston. See, I met Franklin on a train because I was leaving here to head toward a different life." She fidgeted her hands.

"Why did you have to leave to do that?"

Millie sighed, looking right into Harper's eyes. "Because being biracial in those days meant I had next to no chance of owning my own store. Being a woman made that venture hard enough. The heirlooms were passed down to my mama from my grandmother, who was sold at the age of nine."

Harper imagined the little girl holding the satchel Peter found, and sadness seized her heart. "Nine?" Harper mouthed the word, the air sucked from her chest. She thought of her nine-year-old cousin, who still played with paper dolls.

"Hard to imagine, isn't it? So young." Millie took Harper's hand and patted it. "That's how I got the heirlooms, and I took them with me on this big adventure to Alabama. I could talk about my Franklin for days, but the long and short of it is that I was a fool for the man, and several years into our marriage, I got pregnant."

"You passed the heirlooms down." Harper was beginning to understand now. "And your wedding dress . . ." The thought of the artifacts traveling through time together gave her chills. "Peter's mom was the reason you never opened your store?"

"Yes." Millie held on to Harper's hand. Harper didn't mind. On the contrary, the motherly affection did wonders for her heart. "But I don't have one ounce of regret about that part."

Harper squeezed Millie's hand. "Why all the secrets from Peter, then? You know he adores you."

Millie looked up at the still train. "Because sometimes we put a halt to the very things that would free us—we stop them, push them away, because our fear becomes too strong. We have no guarantee what will happen, so we make sure nothing happens at all."

Millie took the hat from her head to straighten one of the pins in her hair.

Harper's gaze suddenly pulled toward the beautiful butterfly button at the rim of Millie's cloche. "I've seen that pattern before . . ." Only, where? Wait a minute. Of course! "This button matches the one on your wedding dress."

"The buttons are part of the heirlooms my mama gave me." Millie touched the fabric of her hat gently. A slow smile rose from the corners of Millie's lips, blurring the wrinkles and the settled pigment of her pink lipstick. "There are two of them."

FORTY

Fairhope, 1958

Yesterday, the hummingbirds disappeared from her window.

There had been two. Always in a battle for food, their rapid wings a deceptively gentle hover around Millie's nectar-rich basket of flowers. One would come, only for the next to knock it to the ground. Over and over they did this, those dainty little birds, providing hours of fascination for six-year-old Juliet through the other side of the kitchen window. She pulled the little toy train Franklin had made her back and forth over the windowsill, saying *all aboard!* and *choo choo*.

Yesterday, Millie mailed her mama a letter. It read:

Dear Mama,

I know you always said early to bed, early to rise, but sometimes I look outside my bedroom window and the clouds stick like marshmallows to the dark starry sky, and I just get to wondering where they've been and where they're going, and then I get to wondering about myself.

Did the good Lord know I'd be Alabama bound, or did I mess up His plan somewhere along the way?

I really thought I'd have that dress shop by now. I've been working so hard between seamstress jobs and mending folks' clothes here at the inn that I'm tired as a lark. Sometimes I think I'm so busy in the preparation that maybe I wouldn't recognize the opportunity when it does come. What I mean is, when I finally do get the money, will I still have the time? And when I have the time, will I have everything else? Guess I thought it would all be simpler. But as it turns out, my dreams still feel far. Is it just like dreams to feel that way?

Will they ever come?

I miss you, Mama. Love you always.

Millie

Millie was reaching into the barrel full of flour she used for the morning biscuits whenever she heard the door shut behind Franklin. She always mixed the ingredients straight inside the thing like the old-timers did.

What drew her attention to the door was not the sound but the smell. When the winds shifted, when the tide brought a storm, there was always a particular aroma of leaves blowing the wrong way and air thick with tiny drops of water. It wasn't a real bad smell so much as a distinctive one, plants and soil and the sea.

Beyond the kitchen windows, the morning clouds clustered into billowing grey sheets, blowing closer and closer toward the boardinghouse. But Millie didn't pay them much mind.

She put the kettle on the stove, grabbed her gingham kitchen mitt, and set the biscuits in the oven to bake. All the while, she thought of the hummingbirds—where they were going, where they had been. The two of them so small, so fragile to be halfway across the States, or halfway across the ocean.

Awakened by the sunlight every morning to another day's search for nectar, another day's search for beauty. She couldn't get her mind off it. She nearly forgot to close the stove.

Such were her thoughts when Franklin stepped closer and she realized his trousers were dampened and the hair beneath his cap was strewn all about.

The kettle whistled as she looked at him. "Franklin, what in Sam Hill—"

He crossed his arms as the leaves began to smack against the window.

Millie's heart lurched to a stop. "Franklin?"

"Stevens came down to warn us. Said he couldn't bear anything happening to his mother's boardinghouse and we better hunker down." Franklin's face washed pale as flour. And if Franklin was concerned . . . well, that wasn't a good sign.

Millie shook her head. "I don't understand. The storm?"

"It's a cyclone, Millie. Mr. Stevens was out on the water at dawn and says he scarcely made it out alive."

Millie held up her gingham-mitt hand. "Should we leave? Go someplace with higher ground?"

Franklin removed his cap and ran one hand through his messy hair. "Ain't no place we could go, Millie. That's what happens when you live in secret, like some kind of outlaw."

"Oh, that's real nice, Franklin." Millie yanked the mitt from her hand and tossed it down on the counter. "You act like you hadn't any part of the plan to live here."

His sigh was deep with frustration—or was it remorse? "I'm sorry, Millie." He took a step closer. "Shouldn't have said that. But my point being, there's nowhere for us to go. And even if there were, roads aren't fit for driving. The storm is comin' anytime now."

Millie locked her heart with his eyes. His gaze was her anchor, her green-blue steadfast against the bobbing of the clouds.

"We don't have any guests coming until tomorrow." Millie knew this would be his next question.

Franklin nodded, scanning the kitchen as if seeing it for the first time. "We need to get everything up off the floor in case the house takes on water. The roof will hold just fine, but these windows are old, and the house isn't as far from the shore as I'd like."

The wind began to whistle outside. Millie's mind flashed with images of all her favorite parts of the boardinghouse. The pier out back and the rose trellis she'd grown from Mama's clippings and her favorite mockingbird who lived in the bush outside her window.

"After we get this stuff up, Millie, I need you to grab Juliet and gather any valuables you don't want takin' on water. I'll lock and barricade the doors as best I can, and then we'll need to get comfortable in a room with as few windows as possible. Better avoid any parts of the house where tree limbs might fall as well. Don't want any surprises."

Millie bit down on her bottom lip. "The honeymoon suite?"

Franklin smiled, stepped forward, and slipped one hand behind her back. "If I'm going to die in a cyclone, I can think of no better location."

Millie picked up the oven mitt and swatted him with it. "Don't you dare say such a thing! Surely you don't think we're in real danger?"

Franklin kissed the top of Millie's head. "No, but our boardinghouse may well be. So find Juliet, and I'll get to work on everything outside."

A half hour later, the grey clouds had grown greyer, the whip of the wind against the house had grown harsher, and Millie's calm demeanor had been replaced by the unsettling reality that a storm was rolling to the shore.

Outside, a sudden thud shook the house. Juliet shrieked and cowered into Millie's arms.

"Hush now, it's okay." Millie covered the girl's hair with her hand. She looked to Franklin and mouthed her question above Juliet's head. "Tree limb?"

Franklin nodded. He glanced over to the window at the other side of the room, for he was far braver than Millie, who dared not take a single look. "We're okay," he mouthed back.

Millie nodded, the contents of their valuables scattered across her lap.

She held tight to her daughter and husband, tight to the stitches of the satchel and all that the words meant to her heart. She hummed softly to keep Juliet calm.

If only the rain would stop. If only the whistles of wind would cease growing louder, screeching against the side of the boarding-house like a locomotive at full speed toward its station.

Fear collided with the future in an intersection of startling clarity.

Millie realized, as the bushes scraped against the side of the inn, that what terrified her the most was her missing daughter. Who would hold Rosie during cyclones? Who would tell her all would be okay and stroke her hair with a mother's particular touch?

Someday Millie would pull the buttons from her wedding dress and give each of her daughters one. Maybe one of her daughters would even want the dress itself. But all that wasn't enough. She looked down at the satchel, the dress. Why didn't she see it before now? If the satchel would only survive this storm intact, she would give it to Rosie, since she couldn't give her more than that.

Rosie, her hummingbird who had disappeared one morning.

The electric lights flickered off with a jolt.

"That's all right." Franklin was quick with his match. "I got a candle for that."

"Daddy, you think of everything." Juliet snuggled closer to her father as the candle cast their shadows up against the wall.

Millie watched them, those shifting shadows, and tried to make sense of how they rose and fell. Franklin told some jokes to keep Juliet laughing, but Millie—with that dress and satchel and half of her little family—was somewhere else entirely.

She was transfixed by those shadows when she heard the boom. When the windows blew out, and the water began to pool into a flood.

When Franklin jumped to standing and Juliet grabbed the heir-looms and ran down the hall.

Millie watched the little shards of glass float across the room, oddly beautiful from the glisten of the candle. An oddly fragile means of keeping the storm outside.

She was going to tell her the whole story.

Juliet stood in the doorway as Millie swept shards of broken glass into piles.

The storm had come to an eerie and sudden stop, but Franklin said that probably meant the eye was passing over and the winds could pick back up at any moment, so they'd better stay good and ready. Loud pounding sounded from the hammer as Franklin hurried to nail boards across the open window. Rain was sure to slip through the little gaps between the seams and flood the floor with storm water, but they would do what they could to minimize the damage.

Innocent fear flickered from Juliet's eyes, and she dared not take a half step closer into the room, for Millie had forbid the child lest she get hurt.

Juliet tightly clutched the satchel and the dress, though the fabric of the latter was double her size, easily.

What was Millie thinking? She couldn't tell Juliet the truth about her sister. Not under these conditions. Not with the girl so afraid.

The glass clinked as Millie brushed several tiny pieces into the dustpan. And that's when she saw the little train Franklin had made for Juliet blown off the window frame, cracked and soaked with water.

Millie dropped the broom. She hurried over and picked up the pieces of the train. The splintered wood pricked her thumb, which in turn started bleeding.

"Drat," Millie muttered. She flicked her wrist and held her bleeding thumb up to her own lips.

"Mama, are you okay?"

Millie bit down on her bottom lip and held out her hands, still

275

holding the broken train for Juliet to see. "I'm so sorry, sweetheart. But I bet your daddy can fix it."

Juliet finally set the dress and satchel down on the dry hallway floor; her shoulders drooped from the weight she'd carried.

"That's all right, Mama. Besides, I don't like that train anymore anyways."

Millie looked down at the broken pieces in her hands and choked back the emotion threatening to rise. "What do you mean?" Come to think of it, this morning *was* the first time Juliet had played with the train in a while.

Juliet shrugged. "Now that I'm almost a grown-up, I like grown-up toys. I only play with that anymore because Daddy made it and he likes trains so much."

"He does like trains." Millie nodded, smiling. "Grown-up toys, you say? And what does that mean?"

"Oh, you know. Dolls and dresses and thread and string. Like you play with every day." Juliet leaned against the door frame, her toes wiggling in the rainwater that had sloshed through the room.

Millie stepped closer and set the train down, away from the pile of broken glass. If only she could sweep all the water into neat piles as well; if only the tide would pull the water out as it'd pulled the water in.

One week after the storm, a parcel from Mama came in the mail. Millie brought it inside and set it down by the window where she used to watch the hummingbirds. The house was still humid and too warm from the storm damage and the broken window.

Carefully, she unwrapped the brown paper, running her fingernail under the tape that bound the package together for safe travel.

Millie gasped when she saw the neatly folded pile of lace fabric inside. She felt the respite of her mother's arms despite the many miles, a comfort that was so welcome it brought tears to her eyes.

Sugar,

As usual, you're thinking too much. Hush now with this talk like your dreams are too hard. You've made a life for yourself, haven't you? Which is no simple business, and that seamstress job isn't small potatoes. Stop looking at all that's going wrong and consider all that's going right. You don't need to fix the world in one night, child. Give it time. Wait for the right shape of the moon to come, and it'll pull in your tide.

I put this lacy tablecloth up for you ages ago, but I think it's high time I send it. Consider this an investment in your dress shop. Keep it safe until the day you can use it, and keep it in your heart too. Dream about all the dresses you can make, then sketch them out and make plans.

Hold onto your hope, my girl. Always hold onto that.

All my love,
Mama

FORTY-ONE

Charleston, Modern Day

A month after the expo, an Etta James track played over the speaker connected to Harper's phone as she pulled three large cardboard boxes from the storage closet. Peter helped her carry them into the middle of the dress shop. He didn't know the first thing about inventory, but he'd missed her, so here he was.

Trying to find the courage to tell her about the need for repairs.

"Didn't expect manual labor at a dress store, did you?" Harper showed him where to set the boxes.

"I don't mind." He might've seemed as if he were being polite, but it was the honest truth. "I do need to tell you something."

Harper shifted toward him. "Oh?"

Nerves turned Peter's stomach. Why had he waited so long to admit the state of this building? Why had he been so scared she and Millie would bolt?

"It's not exactly convenient."

Harper crossed her arms over her chest. "I'm listening."

How should he put this?

"The building needs some maintenance on account of its age." He swept his shoe along the floor. "Nothing to worry about, but I've got a couple companies scheduled to come next week."

Okay, so he'd made it sound like the repairs were something

a half hour trip to Lowe's could fix. But did that really matter, so long as she knew the repairmen were coming?

Harper ran her hand over her forehead. "But we're supposed to open next week." Her gaze moved through the store. "Everything is nearly set."

Peter realized he'd been holding his breath. Slowly, he sighed. "I know. And I'm sorry about that."

"Can't you hold off for a little while, until business gets settled?"

Not unless you want to be evicted.

"I can't put it off any longer."

Harper hesitated. "Do what you need to do, then. We don't want the walls collapsing in on us." She laughed as if this part were a joke.

"No, we wouldn't want that."

Harper reached out and touched his elbow. "Wait. The walls aren't actually in danger of falling down?"

Her touch stirred him more than he cared to admit. "Far as I'm aware, the walls are structurally sound." *In fact, they might be the only thing that is.*

"Well, that's a relief." Harper pulled a small utility knife from the pocket of her red skirt and cut through the packaging tape on the boxes. He liked a woman who came prepared. "I was thinking that I've never asked about your first architectural salvage project. When did you know that's what you wanted to do with your life?"

Peter removed his glasses and rubbed a fingerprint from the lenses with the hem of his shirt. He knew the answer instantly—it needed no consideration.

"I started college as a pre-law major. Then my mother died."

Harper looked up from the boxes. Sad lines of understanding framed her gentle eyes.

Peter nodded. A wave of nostalgia tugged him back to the memory he was recalling. "Long story short, my stepfather has always made me work for his approval, but he took that to the extreme after my mother's passing. I remember, I was at Millie's boardinghouse, actually, sitting out on her pier when it hit me. I wanted to change my major to history."

Harper suddenly covered her mouth with her hands.

Did he miss something? "Is my change of major really that surprising?"

"No, that's not it." She laughed softly. "It's just that . . ." She looked straight into his eyes as if she could see clear through him. "Well, I remember you."

Remembered him? But what could she mean?

Peter blinked. "I don't understand." Had they met at some point prior to the engagement party? She did say she grew up in Fairhope.

"I used to live across the bay from the inn. One night, I was sitting outside having dinner with my dad, and I remember seeing this guy around my age who was standing out on Millie's pier." Harper took a half step closer. "I asked my dad about you."

Peter's next breath caught in his lungs. "What did he say?"

"He told me about your mother and that you'd come to stay with Millie because of something that happened with your stepfather." She brushed her hair behind her ears, never breaking eye contact with him. "It's strange to say out loud, but I felt this connection with you because of what I'd just gone through with my own mother. I prayed for you." She shook her head. "I never imagined we would meet someday."

Peter rested his hand on her shoulder. He wanted so badly to pull her closer but hesitated. He wasn't even sure if she cared for him as he'd come to care for her. But the thought of her company that night—along with the fog that settled over the water— overwhelmed him, to say the least. The evening was still so clear in his memory. "Thank you."

Harper broke eye contact, then slid a row of bracelets up and down her arm. "So you told me why you changed your major, but what about the old houses?"

Peter let his hand fall from her shoulder. "My stepfather and I were on bad terms ever since he gave away my mother's things.

Then he pretty much disowned what little relationship we had left when I told him I was leaving the lawyer plan to pursue history."

"Yikes."

"Yeah, but transitioning to a boxed-mac-and-cheese kind of lifestyle was easier than I'd expected. Because for the first time in my life, I felt like I could breathe. Just not financially." He raked his hand through his hair. It still felt like a punch in the gut to think about. "My mother had inherited a home, and then she passed away and that house went to me. Thing is, when I moved in— thinking I might learn more about my mother or find those missing heirlooms inside—I discovered the place had long been neglected. Nothing there to help me understand why my mother had inherited it."

Harper frowned. "What did you do? Did you consider selling?"

Peter rubbed the back of his neck with his hand. "Of course I considered it, and back then I really could've used the money. But in a different way, I couldn't afford to sell it. It was a link to my mother that I would've lost. And if I sold it, a property developer probably would've bought and demolished it to build something new."

He met her eyes. "That's when I realized if I wasn't going to sell history, I needed to start saving it." This time, he didn't look away. "Thankfully, Charleston's booming tourist industry has been favorable to my rental investments. I realized I could make a vocation out of all that before I was forced to sell the house."

Harper fidgeted with her pearl necklace, tugging it this way and that. "Peter, can I ask you something?"

Anything.

"Sure."

"You have trouble letting go, don't you?"

Peter rubbed his jawline with his hand. "I think that's a fair assessment."

"You came into my life at a good time, I guess, because the truth is"— she took two steps toward him, and his pulse raced as she neared even more—"I was about to give up."

Peter nodded. He knew that about her. And he also knew Harper wasn't typically the type to quit when things got hard. Just look at her now, with Millie.

She shook her head, clearly troubled by the tug of dreams and disappointments. "For so long, I thought owning a dress store was what I wanted to do with my life. I planned it all out. Practiced stitching for hours, got into SCAD, even had internships and odd jobs. But the thing is, Peter, and this is the real kicker—time after time after time, I have come up short." She searched his eyes as if he should have the answers, as if he should understand. "Do you know what it's like to have this dream that you breathe for, this dream you're so passionate about, and then life keeps saying you're not ready or you're not enough?"

He had a feeling he'd better not answer that.

She inched up taller on her fancy shoes. "Sometimes I feel like I walk around with two selves. The outside of me lives in the real world. But the inside of me is itching to sketch dresses late into the night. The inside of me flickers with this impossible dream, and I can't put the candle out. At different points in my life, I've tried to fully commit one way or another. I've given up hope on my dream, as you've seen firsthand, or I've given up on boring, old, regular life. But I cannot—*I cannot*—seem to reconcile what to do with these two halves, which one should win my future." She settled back down on her heels. "What do you think, Peter, as someone who doesn't give up quickly?"

He thought a long while. "Well, you obviously need money to eat, so there's that." Although he would gladly ditch their rent payment if it meant she and Millie would stick around.

"Yeah." Harper straightened the dresses on the rack so there was plenty of space to see each one of them. As she did, her shoes sent tiny dust bunnies scuttling across the floor.

"But you also can't ignore the thing that keeps your soul alive, because I believe God puts that sort of stuff in us for a reason. That He speaks to us through it. God is faithful, and when He calls you to something, He will also give you the means, even if it doesn't look as expected."

"You sound like my dad."

Was that a compliment? Peter rested his hand on her shoulder. He meant it as a gesture of comfort, but in an instant, his mind went back to the expo—to that ridiculous, trendy suit and the moment he almost kissed her. He swallowed and shook his head before the memory showed in his eyes. "It's a hard spot you're in, for sure. But I guess my advice would be that if you sense this push and pull within yourself, the problem isn't that you need to choose a side."

Harper stared at him. "It's not?"

"The problem is, something about your story hasn't been told yet. The something that connects the two halves."

"Very profound of you, Peter." She tightened her ponytail as she leaned down to gather another dress from the box.

"Well, to be fair, there's something I haven't told you." Peter watched as she stood with the dress in her arms, gazing boldly back into his eyes and waiting. "The house in Radcliffeborough?"

"Yes?" Harper hung the dress on the rack and gently trailed her fingers along the fabric.

"It once was Millie's."

FORTY-TWO

Fairhope, 1963

Millie was wiping the rim of her favorite mixing bowl with a damp dish towel and setting both back on the counter when she heard Juliet call out from the living room.

"I'm coming." Millie hurried over. A few seconds was all it took to reach her daughter, but in those few seconds, boarding-house guests had already crowded around, looking toward the television.

Walter Cronkite was talking. And some journalist named Patterson.

Millie parted the small group of guests to take Juliet's shoulders firmly between her own two hands. Her gaze scanned her daughter but came up with no visible blood, scrapes, or bruises. Only a fixed stare at the television set.

What was going on? Juliet had sounded so concerned.

With Millie's touch upon her shoulders, Juliet's rigid posture softened. She turned toward Millie and rested in her mother's arms, still saying nothing. Millie held her tightly. And it was only then Millie registered the nightly news must be why the crowd had gathered. Snippets from Cronkite and Patterson's exchange filtered through the haze of worry blurring Millie's mind.

We stand in the bitter smoke and hold a shoe. If our South is ever to be what we wish it to be, we will plant a flower of nobler resolve for the South now upon these four small graves that we dug.

"Mercy, what's happened?" Millie asked.

One of the women staying at the boardinghouse explained there'd been a bombing at the church on Sixteenth Street where Dr. Martin Luther King Jr. was arrested last spring. Four little girls getting ready for church had been killed. Maybe more injured, as rubble fell in every direction—brought destruction and hate and death—blowing a stained-glass depiction of Jesus into shards so that what once served as an image of love had been weaponized.

Dear God, Millie thought. *What have they done?*

With Juliet still in her arms, Millie managed a nod toward the woman explaining the scene, then looked back up at the television as Cronkite took over the coverage. She held onto Juliet even tighter.

"That girl I met downtown last month . . ." Juliet choked. She looked up at Millie, and Millie knew exactly what she meant even before her daughter said more. "The one I've been writing letters back and forth with. She lives in Birmingham. That's her church they just showed. What if she was . . ." Juliet froze. "What if she is . . ."

Many responses passed through Millie's mind.

I'm sure your friend is fine, she wanted to say. *I'm sure she wasn't one of those little girls they found amid the rubble, dead. I'm sure she ran out of the sanctuary so fast that she never saw it fill with smoke, never saw the dust settle like ash, never even heard the cries.*

But the fact was, Millie wasn't sure of any of that. Millie wasn't even sure what she was doing, raising Juliet as though they were white when in reality Juliet probably identified with her pen pal in more ways than one.

And in one fell swoop, Millie remembered the girl's most recent letter to Juliet. She'd invited them all to come visit for a long weekend. No doubt, that included Sunday service. Sunday school and pretty hats and hair bows and the whole nine yards.

Maybe even getting ready in the bathroom.

Suddenly, Millie felt as though all the air was gone from the room. She looked down at her daughter's hair, pinned behind Juliet's ears with a curl, and she closed her eyes and breathed in the feeling of her living, breathing daughter as the little girl cried against her mama.

In that moment, all the fear came back with a roar. And as Millie acknowledged she had, indeed, made so many decisions from a place of anxiety, something unexpected happened.

The fear got worse.

She saw Juliet's face in that church. She saw the lace of Juliet's dress bouncing as the little girl ran with the others through the door. She saw Juliet stand from a pew to shake someone's hand, then fall to the floor with the rest of the congregation as the dynamite exploded.

And with sickening clarity, Millie's stomach turned.

It could've been *her* daughter.

After all, it'd already been her father.

Millie closed her eyes. There was no need to trouble the child with her own fears. Millie would pretend, if she had to.

"Mama?" Juliet was murmuring, and Millie opened her eyes to find her daughter looking up, watching. "Mama, you okay? You look like you're gonna be sick."

Millie hesitated. "You don't worry about me." She brushed her daughter's cheek with her thumb. "But how about you and I go to your room for a little while and talk about what's happened?"

Juliet nodded. Millie took her by the hand and led them down the hall. They sat beside each other on the quilt of faded fabrics that covered Juliet's bed, each with one arm holding on to the other.

"Mama, I'm scared." Juliet looked straight into Millie's eyes.

Millie looked back. "Keep doing what we talked about, and you don't have any reason to be frightened, sweetheart."

Juliet bit her bottom lip and looked up at Millie with eyes as wide as a little child's. "There's something I haven't told you."

Millie's heart stopped. The image of Harry ripping her sleeve in that soda fountain flashed through her mind.

"Last month, when that big family with all the kids was staying here . . ." Juliet fiddled with the threads of the quilt. "They were playing games outside, and I thought I'd ask if they wanted any lemonade, being hospitable and all."

Millie waited for a long time. "Go on."

Juliet shook her head. "Well, the oldest boy asked me why a colored girl was living with white parents. I didn't tell him about passing or any of that. I told him like you and Daddy said I should, that my grandfather is Italian—but he didn't believe me. He just started laughing and called me something awful."

Millie rubbed her face with both hands.

Why didn't you tell me before now? But then she thought of how she hadn't told her own mother about Harry until she had to.

Juliet searched Millie's eyes once more, still holding onto the fabric between her fingers. "He said if I ever have a brother or sister like he's got, then they'd probably be white, and everybody would see what he already knew—that either my mother had something to hide or my daddy wasn't really my father."

Millie groaned. She wanted to reach her arm across the inn, across the bay, across the state line until she could grasp that ignorant boy where he thought he lived so securely and pick him up by the collar. She would give him a what-for until he regretted the day he ever met her daughter.

But that wouldn't change anything, would it?

"He told me that colored people don't belong beside white people, and that I shouldn't live here because someday, someone would find out, and they would hurt me or they would hurt you, or they would light the house on fire. I tried not to think about the whole thing, but when I saw the news . . . well, was he right? It could have been me, couldn't it, Mama?"

Yes.

No.

Maybe.

Colored people don't belong beside white people.

These words, their echo, shook Millie to her core. Because all people belonged side by side, and she should be allowed to say so. And her own kind of fire kindled in her soul—of grief, namely—to think that in separating Juliet and Rosie to keep them both safe, maybe she had played into this wrong, evil ideology of segregation, however unintentionally.

But what else could she have done?

Juliet waited for an answer.

Millie waited for one as well.

Hours later, Millie sat in that room again—this time, alone with her thoughts.

Only she wasn't alone, exactly. Because after the conversation with Juliet earlier, she kept hearing another echo in her mind. Aunt Bea, years prior, saying, *"You're Gullah, girl,"* as though Millie had forgotten, as though she didn't care about that anymore. As though she didn't remember at every waking moment the half of her heritage that screamed to be shared with the world.

She was trying to make sense of everything that happened this afternoon, and why her heart always seemed to trip over the same old worries.

And it occurred to Millie in that moment the reason for all the fear she'd carried. The load that'd grown from year to year to year as the girls grew taller, like old blankets shoved into the closet one upon the other.

The problem was not that keeping both her daughters safe and loved was too heavy a load to carry on her own trembling shoulders.

The problem—the real fear—was the deep-seated, buried knowledge that despite her best efforts, she was incapable.

Her gaze moved across the room toward the sweater hanging from the door of Juliet's closet.

She had made the sweater weeks ago from a Simplicity pattern, but Juliet had come home disappointed when the sweater snagged. Millie had a hunch her daughter faulted the craftsmanship, though snagged and flawed was the furthest thing from Millie's design. She meant, of course, for her daughter to have a covering. Meant for the fabric to last as long as Juliet had need. But something happened in between.

A sharp corner here. A stumble there. A rip and a tear, that sort of thing.

So Millie held together each torn piece, and stitch by stitch she reinforced the garment's seams.

Let me mend you. Let me take the load you were never meant to carry.

The words came unexpectedly. Not in writing or an audible voice, but in a place within Millie's heart so very deep one might call it her soul. And she could've wept for the truth of it, echoing through her being.

Because the truth was, somewhere along the way, somewhere hidden deep inside of her, she had ceased believing God is good. Begun instead to trust her own ability to keep her daughters safe and happy. And every time she read a news story or thought about the harm the world might bring, it seemed to confirm her worst fear that God was far less capable than she. And the fear only worsened and worsened, until some nights she could hardly sleep, and when she awoke she'd had terrible dreams.

But now, faced with news of the Sixteenth Street Baptist Church bombing, the trauma had come a little too close. The fear, a little too real. A little too strong for Millie to pretend she was in control any longer.

She needed saving. For years, she'd run away for security instead of running toward Jesus. To peace. And she didn't want to do that any longer.

Sweet Jesus, she prayed, opening her palms toward the heavens. *I can't do this any longer. I choose to trust You have a plan for me. Be my Savior. Be their peace.*

She might not know what tomorrow would bring, but she did know the One who made the morning. And no matter what happened next, she was sure deep in her soul that was all she would need.

FORTY-THREE

Charleston, Modern Day

Harper tapped her fingernails along the railing of the stairwell. She still couldn't believe Peter owned and lived in Millie's childhood home. She'd been so sure yesterday that he was about to say he knew Millie was his grandmother, that he'd put the pieces together and she didn't have to keep the secret anymore. But Millie had interrupted them.

Lost in thought, Harper hesitated at the turn of the stairs.

What was that sound? Almost like a whoosh.

She frowned.

Her skirt spun as she turned the corner. And then she saw the flood. A good six inches of water floating through the store, pushing through a soppy hole in the wall by the door.

She hitched up her skirt and ran. Clouded water splashed around her legs as she rushed toward the inventory. Racks of delicate dresses that now dangled in the murky water, their hemlines sinking down.

Ruined.

All of them.

No. No, no, no . . .

The sound of a gasp behind her arrested her before she could do more.

Harper turned.

Millie stood at the end of the stairwell, one hand gripping the railing and the other hand covering her mouth as tears ran down her face and her shoulders trembled.

Millie didn't seem to notice the destruction to the building. Or the inventory. Instead, she stared off in the distance, toward the window.

The window!

Harper splashed through the water as quickly as her feet would take her.

"Child, be careful!"

Harper could hardly make sense of the words. She had to get there in case the water rose further. If that leaking pipe burst . . .

She scrambled up into the window display. Several people were walking down the sidewalk and turned to watch her. She didn't care.

Harper fumbled to unfasten Millie's gown, then gently lifted it up over the mannequin.

The walls of this space might crumble and the floor might flood, but she would not let anything happen to Millie's dress.

"It's okay!" Harper folded the dress and covered it with her own cardigan so a rogue splash of water wouldn't stain the silk.

If only she could get her own words to sink in.

It's okay, Harper. It will be okay.

But would it?

Wasn't this—this store, this dream, Peter, and Millie—already her second chance at okay? She couldn't bear to lose her dream all over again.

She splashed toward the stairs and carefully handed the dress to Millie.

"Take it upstairs." Harper breathed the words. "Call Peter."

Millie clutched the gown and swallowed visibly. She nodded. Harper worried for how shaken Millie seemed.

Harper set to work. Though truthfully, she turned in circles, trying to figure out where to begin.

She splashed her way over to the front door and opened it so the water had someplace to flow. Then she opened each one of the front windows to let the heat in.

The water tunneled its way toward King Street. Her initial panic subsided into an aching realization of the damages.

"Harper."

She turned, and he was there at the door as though her thoughts had summoned him.

Peter was going to be shocked.

Peter was going to be horrified.

But Peter didn't look all that surprised.

He stepped into the water as it flowed out the door, and he came to stand beside her. He rubbed his forehead with his hand, his silence deafening.

"I should have done something sooner." He all but whispered the words.

Even the tiny tide of the water came to a standstill.

Harper tilted her chin, trying to understand his meaning. Then she realized.

He knew.

He knew the plumbing was bad, and he hadn't told them. She could see it in the tightened lines around his eyes and feel it in the drop of his timbre. During their last conversation, he nonchalantly mentioned the repairmen as if a ceiling fan needed replacing. But this. This was no ceiling fan situation.

Peter. Her heroic, larger-than-life Peter had let this happen to her. Let this happen to Millie. Even let this happen to the building.

"Why?" Her voice was a rasp as she searched his gentle eyes for answers.

He closed his eyes and shook his head. "I was so scared she would leave me too."

Harper grabbed him by the arms, and his eyes snapped open to lock with her frantic gaze. "Peter, what is that supposed to mean?"

The set of his jaw said it all.

He knew Millie was his grandmother.

"How long?" She didn't let go of his arms. "How long have you known the truth about Millie and me?"

"From that night we went to Poogan's Porch. I saw the button on her hat." Peter kicked at the water. "Don't tell her, okay? I promise I will say something soon, but I need to get my thoughts straight on all of this."

Harper gaped. "Peter Perkins, what's the matter with you? You left me in agony while I waited for Millie to tell you the truth. To think, all of this could have been avoided if you'd just been a little braver." Harper gestured toward the rows of dresses, the hems now soaked from the flooded floor.

He winced slightly. The accusation must have stung. Harper hadn't meant to be cruel, but it was true, wasn't it?

"And when was that going to be, Harper? When was Millie—or you, for that matter—going to tell me the truth? What reason have you given me to trust you?" He freed his shoulders from her grip and stared at her. "You thought I couldn't figure this out? My own flesh and blood? I'm a historian."

Harper held up one finger and opened her mouth, but Peter wasn't done.

"I should've been more up-front about the repairs. Admittedly." He took a half step closer and looked deeper into her eyes. "But isn't it plain, what's in front of you? My feelings . . ."

About Millie.

His unspoken words hung in the air. The rest of the sentence was clear. For as much as she wished he might have said *for you, Harper*— that was not what he meant, was it? She'd caught the nuance to what he'd said before, that he was scared Millie would leave him.

Maybe things would have been different under different circumstances. If she were just Harper and not Harper, keeper-of-secrets. But now any prospect of a happily-ever-after was as soiled as the hemlines.

The hollowed-out hope within her ached as she realized something with certainty: the depth of her feelings for him. And in this blending of newly realized love and grief, the world around her spun with the vibrancy and speed of a tie-dye machine.

Peter bent down to the hole in the wall and pushed on the wet spot around its radius, determining the extent of the damage. "The real question, Harper, is why are you still sticking around?" Peter waded over to the rows of dresses and lifted them from the water so they could begin to drip-dry. "Disaster has come. That's your usual cue to bolt, isn't it?"

The one thing King Street lacked was a fetching secondhand store. If it had one, Harper would be there already. She would be living there. Buying all the vintage heels as they came in the door.

But as it stood, her current ranking on the pity scale was somewhere between a Target run for cheap cosmetics and ice cream, and all-out sobbing her way through old J. Lo movies.

In other words, she had lost herself. And as she climbed the external stairs to the second story of the loft—because Lord knew she wasn't going back through the dress shop while Peter was still inside—she sighed down to the bones of her being. She sighed because she was oh so weary.

"God, I don't understand," she mumbled on her way up the steps. "I thought this was it. I thought the dream You gave me was finally happening." Harper shook her head and gripped the handrail as she neared the top landing.

The whole building suddenly seemed unsteady, ready to crumble under her feet. Wasn't that the way of things?

She took the final step and stood beside a pot full of red geraniums in bloom. Millie would be inside, resting or reading as she always needed to do midday.

Harper would not take her own pitiful attitude inside the walls of this loft. Millie deserved better. After all, the store was Millie's. The dream was Millie's too.

So until Harper could get a handle on herself, she would stand here. Fuming.

She had spent the last half hour at the coffee shop up the street, searching the Internet for every article she could find on flooding in historic buildings.

Sure, that might've been a little like searching a cough on WebMD.

But when it came to historic structures like this, she knew nothing except for her emotional attachment and Millie's own history with the place.

The prognosis was not good.

At best, the space would have to be aerated, and the walls could take months to dry completely. There was no telling how long the old pipes had been leaking.

It could be a good thing, the Internet said, when the flood finally happened—with visible evidence of decay, repairs could be made. Even if it meant deconstructing walls and insulation.

But it didn't seem like a good thing.

Especially considering Peter had known the building wasn't up to code. Could he even afford to keep it? Because she and Millie certainly couldn't.

"Peter," she murmured to herself. His name was as sour as lemons on her lips.

How dare he suggest she ran whenever things got hard. Peter, whose dreams had been handed to him on a lucrative real-estate platter. Peter, who conveniently lived his dream job daily.

Peter knew nothing of the silent rise and fall of dreams. A rise and fall not at all unlike breathing.

Harper shuffled her still-wet feet over several fallen flower petals and started to reach for the door handle. But then she dropped her hand. She was still too angry, too shocked, and she didn't want to upset Millie.

The dresses were largely unsalvageable. She would try. Of course she would try. But with an array of silks and delicate lace . . . well, it was highly unlikely her efforts would make any difference.

For the dresses. For the store. For her dream.

And here she had promised herself after Savannah that she would not invest her heart this way. Not again. She'd known she could not take another failure, not when her hope was already so weak.

But this time was worse by far than before. Because this time was about more than just her dream. This time she had Peter.

Peter, who had been so irresponsible. Peter, who despite herself, she was falling in love with.

Harper sighed with frustration and looked up into the sky.

What now?

She shook her head and covered her face with her hands. None of it made sense. Why would God let this happen? Why would Peter let this happen too?

Harper clenched her hands hard into fists. Maybe Peter had a point when he mentioned her leaving. Not because she wanted to run this time, but the contrary. Because she wanted to stay so badly, a fairy tale had clouded her vision.

The time had come to move forward. She would get Millie settled and the dresses squared away and the mess cleaned. And after she had done the hard work, she would do the harder.

She would finally give up the one thing in her life that held the power to pronounce her a failure. The dress shop. The dream. The sketches she had begun as a child.

She would put them aside and find a steady, realistic, less embarrassing pursuit to follow with her life. Then people would respect her, and work would be easy. Because work came easy when you didn't care about what you were doing.

And after she closed this chapter, she would pay a visit to the one person who had never led her the wrong direction. Her father.

Maybe Millie would even come along.

FORTY-FOUR

Charleston, Modern Day

Two weeks after the flood, the storefront that had changed so much through the decades was empty once more. The dresses were gone. And today, just as Peter predicted, Harper left—this time with calm insistence there was no place for her here any longer. She offered to take Millie back to the boardinghouse, but Millie said the inn was in good hands and for now she would like to stay in Charleston.

Peter woke in the dark that night, gasping for air and sweating.

He had the dream again.

The one where he couldn't find his shoes.

And he walked all around the city of Charleston, into his home—Millie's childhood home—until the dust of the place covered his feet so much they became invisible. He couldn't feel his feet, then his legs, then his lungs.

The dust was suffocating.

When he opened his eyes, he was having a panic attack. He knew it, through clenched teeth.

The suffocation was a telltale sign.

What he didn't know was how he would ever tell Millie the truth. That he'd known she was his grandmother. That he had played the part, helped with the dress store, as he waited for her to admit why she left his mother as a baby.

And in Charleston, bloodline was everything. Bloodline and history. Peter should know.

He gulped back the emotion in his throat. He couldn't fight the sinking feeling he was a nobody with no history. Even with a stepfather from one of the most prominent families in Charleston, a stepfather who disowned him simply because Peter wouldn't play along any longer.

Why hadn't Millie claimed him as her own by now?

The dream's echo was a lie, and he knew it. But for so long, he had studied other people's stories, thinking that maybe, eventually, he would find where he fit in. He never expected to discover his own story had been there all along—that his dear Millie would be the one for whom he was looking.

Peter took several practiced deep breaths and reached for the bottle of water he'd left beside the bed. After several gulps, he pulled the sheets over his head, hoping to hide until morning.

When he awoke once more, it was from a different sort of dream. He was standing in the water beside the pier at Millie's boardinghouse. He looked down at his hands and noticed a small cut that was bleeding. From the scrape flowed multicolored threads, all twisted up together like DNA. Peter reached for them, tried to pull one thread, then another, to see them distinctly, but the threads were so tightly woven that he couldn't loosen any. Then a pelican flew overhead, and the cut was washed by water from the bay.

Peter blinked, trying to remember the rest of the dream as he looked down at his hands. The dream seemed surreal—all he could see now was the skin, not the blood underneath.

And in that half-awakened frame of consciousness where his breaths came quick and his heart raced and he was maybe more alert than during daylight hours, his mother's voice came to him, singing a verse she always used to hum before he went to sleep.

There is a river whose streams make glad the city of God.

The clarity of her song was so striking that for a moment he wondered if she were in the room with him, even looked for her, and then he remembered she couldn't be. He grew more and more awake as the music faded, but for the first time in his life, he realized why she always sang that song and really what it meant. That a bloodline was like a river—changing, branching, ever flowing—until grace upon grace sweeps across history and the past begins to pull with the tide of the now.

So the stories mingle together, multicolored threads woven like little streams through the Lowcountry, in all the blood we cannot see. In all the blood and all the threads that are redeemed.

By the light of day, Harper was still gone. Millie, meanwhile, was going about her usual routine, sitting at the breakfast table with a slice of cinnamon toast, when Peter entered the loft to check in on her.

He didn't know what he'd expected. Millie didn't seem the type to panic or burst into hysterics. He had a feeling she was always strong, even before life made her stronger. But still, this polished picture caught him off guard.

Millie broke off a piece of crust and took a good look at him. He was a mess, and he knew it. He hadn't shaved, his long-sleeved shirt looked as if it'd been folded in a ball for months—truth be told, it probably had—and he was all but certain the sleepless night had left him with tire tracks under his eyes.

Millie, meanwhile, was dressed to the nines and looked as if she were ready for tea with the governor. She ate the crust of her toast and took a slow sip from her teacup.

"You're in love with her." Millie set her cup down on the table and shook her head. "I don't know why I didn't see it sooner."

Peter crossed his arms and leaned against the kitchen counter, several steps from the table. He tried to play it cool, but his foot was rapping against the floor so fast, Millie surely caught the nervous movement before he could think to stop it.

Hope and disappointment whooshed in and out of him with the rise and fall of his breath, and though he'd rather not talk about Harper, he knew there was no hiding his feelings for her any longer.

"Does she know?" Millie squared the red hat on her pinned hairstyle. "What am I saying? Of course she knows."

Peter turned toward the top cabinet and reached for a glass he could use for water. He filled it from the tap and took a seat beside Millie. "What is that supposed to mean?"

Millie tapped her fingers against her teacup. "Perhaps I shouldn't have said anything." She was baiting him, and Peter was playing right into it.

Oh, she was good. She could charm the queen's guard into a grin if she wanted.

Peter leaned closer, his elbows on the salvaged table. "Millie."

With a wave of her hand, she smiled at him. She lifted the teacup to her lips and took another slow sip from it. An eternity seemed to pass before she set the cup back down on the table, and meanwhile, Peter's pulse rushed with an optimism he hadn't felt since Harper drove away.

Millie rolled her eyes. "You young people have the advantage of every type of technology at your fingertips, but you've forgotten how to simply talk to one another. She loves you too, Peter. Anyone with half a wit of sense about them can see it."

Peter hesitated. Could this be true? He rubbed his five o'clock shadow with his hand. "Are you sure, Millie?"

"Have I struck you as the type of person to make up these things?" She took another nibble from her toast, then looked up at him. "I am quite sure, Peter."

"Wait." *Wait.* Surely he misunderstood. "She told you she loves me?"

Millie tilted her head to the right, then to the left, mulling this over. "Not in so many words, but we did discuss it."

"And you're sure?"

"Heavens to Betsy. How many times are you going to make me say it?"

Peter grinned, and he could've sworn the sunlight from the kitchen window floated up higher and higher through the room. "She loves me?" He could hardly wrap his mind around it.

Millie nodded, and he caught the corners of her grin rising as she lifted the teacup once more to her lips.

"I have to find her." Peter considered jumping from the kitchen chair and running down the stairs. "I'll tell her hope isn't lost for the store, that I'll do whatever it takes to restore the place for the two of you."

"Now don't have a conniption, but—" Millie's cup rattled against the saucer as Peter stood. "I get the feeling that's a lesson Harper needs to learn for herself."

Peter stilled.

"She'll be back. Mark my words." Millie reached across the table and covered his hand with her own.

Was this the moment? Was she finally going to tell him about being his grandmother?

But Millie's mind seemed still fixed on Harper. "When she returns, may I humbly suggest you tell her that you love her too?"

Peter nodded. Millie was right about everything. He knew it.

What he didn't know was how he would manage the coming days waiting for Harper.

FORTY-FIVE

Fairhope, 1968

The boardinghouse had proven the perfect place for Millie to keep her promise to Mama by hiding her heritage for so many years, always talkin' with guests, but never quite addressing anything. But in times like these, with Franklin ill, Millie wondered if she had made the right choice by hiding away from the rest of the world.

It was the coughing, the rasp, and then the little bit of blood in his handkerchief that worried her.

Franklin told her not to worry, that he had simply caught a fever and would recover just fine. But she had read something in the paper. *Mesothelioma*, the headline called it, "The Invisible Death of the Railman." The article said how it affected railway workers. Cancer caused from breathing all that smoke, even years and years ago.

Like seeing a mosquito in the bedroom and imagining the bite, she couldn't get it out of her mind. Had she created a mosquito from a shadow, or had the bug vanished among the air of the night?

His wheezing woke her in that dark hour just before dawn.

She turned to him, brushing the wisps of hair from his sweaty forehead, and stroking his back until his chest found that soft rise and fall once more.

Millie didn't go back to sleep after that. She pinned her hair and made her face and even set the kitchen timer for a sheet of biscuits. She did everything as she would on a normal day, knowing this day wasn't normal at all.

When dawn finally came and Franklin didn't rise, her concern grew. Millie sat in the chair beside their bed and watched his chest continue to rise and fall, interrupted here and there by the wheeze of his cough. His body sought the rest he so desperately needed.

It was near afternoon by the time he woke fully. He sat up in the bed, sheet around his middle, and his voice was a rasp though his eyes danced at the sight of her. "You're beautiful, Red."

"High time you woke up." Millie smiled. "I'm canceling our trip to Charleston. You aren't well enough."

Franklin shook his head, but a sudden bout of coughing betrayed him. "My mother is getting weaker. You have to go, for her sake and for Rosie."

"Let's concentrate on getting you better, then. Sooner you recover, the sooner we can make the trip." Millie watched him a long moment.

"You need to go without me, Millie." His blue-green eyes searched her own. What did they see there? Resilience? Fear? Love? "My mother won't last long. You're right. I'm not strong enough for the journey. But you can go for both of us."

"I won't leave you." She leaned closer until her hand could reach his own.

"But oh, sweet Red, it's what I want."

Millie's heart slowed at the familiar endearment. Still, she stood by what she said. She wouldn't leave him.

"What if I promise to make a full recovery before your return?"

Millie laughed. "Only you, Franklin, would concern yourself more with others than your own well-being in such a state."

"Oh, but I'm being plenty selfish. I'll worry myself sick over Rosie if you don't go to Charleston and bring that girl home. Just imagine what might happen to her after my mother dies." He started coughing once more.

"I'll go to her when you're stronger." Millie took his hand.

"That'll be too late. She needs us now." He pled with his eyes.

Millie's heart wrung, yanked in both directions without provision enough for either of them. She watched him long and hard and finally broke the silence.

"If I do go, will you promise to fetch a doctor in my absence?"

"If things get bad off, sure."

They both knew what that meant. A resounding *no, I do not promise anything of the sort.*

"Besides," he said. "I've got Juliet. She's plenty old enough to help if I keel over."

Millie swatted her hand in the air. "Do not make jokes like that at a time like this. My nerves are about to give me a fit as it is."

Franklin raised Millie's hand and lifted it to his lips. "Did I ever tell you, Red, I loved you from that first moment on the train? When you saw me through the window."

Tears began to stream down from Millie's eyes.

"I love the life we have together. I love *you*, Millie."

"I love you too, Franklin. Oh, how I love you too."

He squeezed her hand. "Now, go check on my mother and take care of our girl."

With her thumb, Millie wiped the tears from her eyes and memorized everything about him. The faint scent of pine from his soap, the symmetry of his jaw, and the arms that held her through the storm. She memorized it because she knew she would return to it in Charleston tonight, when she missed him terribly and wanted to hurry home.

But Franklin was right, of course. His mother was dying—there was no other way to say it—and Rosie needed guidance now that she was nearly done with school. She and Juliet had become the best of friends through their letters and twice-yearly visits and the occasional long-distance phone call.

Millie would simply be strong for her daughters' sake and Franklin's too. When she returned, Franklin would be well once more. Her wild imagination could be put to rest.

She bent to reach for the shoebox under the bed, then opened the lid and began removing the cash she'd been saving.

Franklin shook his head. "Not that, Red. Not your dress store money." He covered his cough with his hand.

Millie winced at seeing him so weak. "I'll spend as little of it as possible, but if Rosie and I are to travel alone on the journey back, I will need to plan ahead."

She pulled several stacks of money from the box and could feel Franklin watching her.

"Not so much you'll delay buying the store. You've nearly got enough again now, after all those repairs from the cyclone derailed us for years. All your work matters, Millie. All your dreaming and all your saving. You matter."

Millie stopped what she was doing to walk over to the bed. She kissed him and kissed him well. Then she reached for her red cloche, set it atop her head, and began sliding the bills into her carpetbag, trying to hide the tears she couldn't keep from her burning eyes. "Some things matter more." She stood to look at him and hurried to press one more kiss to his forehead. "Rest now, and I'll see you in a few days, Train Jumper." She hadn't spoken the nickname in years, but it seemed to humor him.

And the smile that passed between them shook the walls with its echo.

Millie set her carpetbag down on the stoop and looked up at the beautiful house as she rang the doorbell.

Rosie jerked the door open and threw her arms around Millie. "Thank heavens you're here."

At precisely 2:05 in the afternoon and for no particular reason, Millie felt as if the air had been sucked away from her chest. She ached with longing, with emptiness, as the cord that binds one to another in love tugged and tugged hard.

And she knew.

She knew then he was gone.

FORTY-SIX

Fairhope, 1968
One Month Later

The bay was especially hazy that morning, the low-hung clouds touching the water. The surface of the little waves reached up toward the heavens and the heavens reached back down, and both blended together so Millie couldn't quite make out where the horizon ended and eternity began.

As a child, Millie had always wanted to dance and jump and lie among the clouds. Always imagined what it might be like to hop from one to the next in the sky, weightless and free.

Never imagined the pull of gravity that sunk the raindrops deep into the ground.

Millie sat on the pier behind the boardinghouse, legs pulled up and arms around her knees, as she watched the pelicans gracefully swoop into the water.

Today, one month after laying Franklin and his mother to rest, was the first day she felt brave enough to read the letter he'd left her. Juliet said he'd insisted Millie mustn't read it until she was good and ready.

Took her a full month's time to realize she would never be good and ready again.

Her stomach knotted as she replayed their final conversation over and over in her mind. She never should have left him alone with Juliet. And yet, he was right. Who would have been there to look after Rosie? His mother had died the day after Franklin, of heartbreak as much as anything else.

And Millie's heart, as Millie's heart had long been, was split. A chasm, a gap, too big for her to know what to do.

She used to think of it as split in halves, as if the two parts of her were portions of her identity. But maybe that was wrong.

Maybe, rather, she was split in two wholes—two full hearts she was forever trying to merge together but couldn't seem to blend. Two separate fabrics, layered one upon the other so that one must always be the underlay and one, the top layer.

And in this case, she had chosen Rosie because to do so was to pick both the child and Franklin, and wasn't that what it meant to be a parent?

Yet the other whole heart she carried would never be the same. And she would never forgive herself, though were she to do it over again, she would choose no differently.

She loved Franklin as the color of wildflowers on a summer's day. She may be Red, but he was all the others and she would see him every time she saw the blending blur of brightly colored petals waving in the breeze.

Millie slid her finger along the corners of the envelope until the seal released.

My Millie:

I have a confession to make.

I knew I wasn't long for this world when I told you to leave. A man can feel these things in the way his sleep grows deeper, harder to climb out from. But I needed you to be there for Rosie.

Don't be mad, Red. Don't be mad at me for dying, or for what I've done.

You know I long believed we should tell both girls the whole story. Now that I'm gone, consider it my last wish that you talk to them. Well, that and one more thing. I can be greedy and take two last wishes, can't I? Promise me you will do whatever it takes to own that dress shop.

You need to know how you changed my life. Took me from a boy on a train to a business owner at the boardinghouse. But more than that, you took me from a lonely soul to a man who could say he found love, richly, in all its forms.

Don't cry for me, Red. Don't cry for what's gone. Lift your chin, look out the window, and just imagine what's yet to come. You'll get that dress shop someday. I just know you will.

Until next time, love.

Franklin

Millie pressed the letter to her chest and hoped the thin parchment would warm her. Her lungs had frozen, and her skin had gone cold even as the swallows fluttered in the yard.

But her heart. Oh my, her poor heart had never been more alive. Beating, throbbing with all of her emotion. At once fullness of joy over Franklin's gentle words, as well as fullness of grief with their finality.

So long as she'd kept the letter sealed, she'd felt as if a small part of Franklin were still with her. Who knew what possibilities the yet-to-be-read words held? But now. Now it was truly over.

As she reread the lines again and again, one in particular stood out.

Don't be mad at me for dying, or for what I've done.

And she felt as though her feet had been swept up into a rip tide, turning her in circles again and again and again, with nowhere to go each time.

What did Franklin mean by that? What exactly had he done, and why in the same breath did he urge her to talk with Rosie and Juliet?

There was only one way to find out.

Millie knelt in the garden, her fingers sore and splintered from pulling up the ground and thorns and what didn't belong—all to make room for something new.

As gently as she could, she scooped the dirt out of little holes so that everything underground took a deep gulp of air before the new roots went down.

One at a time, she held the pots upside down and wiggled the plants out of their temporary place of residence so they could be planted.

And one at a time, she set the flowers inside. Brushed the soil in little mounds to cover all the cracks and then gave them each several gentle pats to cover any crevices still left over.

Soon it would be spring, and the butterflies would arrive at these abundant little blue flowers.

Forget-me-nots.

Millie brushed the leftover soil from the hem of her day dress and then stood to admire the garden.

Franklin's garden.

Oh, but that he were here to see it himself. And to help her with what she had to do next.

"Lord, give me strength," Millie said. Not as a trite or casual expression, as a child asking for treats, but as an earnest prayer. Because Millie saw stars every time she thought about the conversation she needed to have with her daughters, and she didn't know how she was going to manage it.

The screen door flapped open, then screeched shut. Franklin would've fixed that screen with WD-40 by now.

Millie didn't know where he kept the can.

Rosie and Juliet stepped out, one after the other, into the shadows and sunbeams. "You wanted to talk with us, Mama?" Juliet asked.

Millie swallowed so hard her throat hurt. Slowly, she nodded and pointed to the porch swing, suspended below the haint blue slats of the ceiling that almost looked like the sky.

Lowcountry tradition said haint blue keeps the ghosts out.

Millie never did believe in ghosts, but she did know a thing or two about haunting and a past that follows no matter where you go. Maybe ghosts were just a fictional version of that real, honest-to-goodness ache you feel whenever your heart wants something that's gone, or at least might as well be.

Millie climbed the porch steps, then snuggled up into the swing. Rosie and Juliet took the wicker rocking chairs, one on each side of her.

And as they gently swung up and down, weight suspended among the arc of their chairs, Millie's resolve did the same until she knew she must all but spit out the words if she was ever going to have this conversation.

Millie closed her eyes, and one of her daughters took hold of her hand. She opened her eyes to see it was Rosie who'd touched her.

"Are you missing him?" Juliet asked.

Millie nodded. "I will miss him with every breath for the rest of my life. Though I suspect I will learn to do a better job of smiling in between breaths."

Millie rubbed her face with both hands, realizing only afterward that the soil had sunk deep under her fingernails and likely streaked black marks like train tracks along her skin. She didn't make any move to wipe them.

Instead, she looked to Rosie, once again taking her hand. "Sweetheart . . ." Millie hesitated. "I don't even know where to begin." Her gaze trailed to Juliet, then back again. Both girls stared intently at their mother, as if concerned for Millie's own heart. Little did they know they themselves had composed it since the day they were born. Her future, in two parts.

Millie opened her mouth to speak, hoping the words would follow. "The truth of it is, Rosie—I am your mother."

Rose's eyes widened just like Franklin's until the whites at the corners filled with floods of tears, and the tears turned to streams rushing down.

She came to Millie on the porch swing and clung to her, and the two of them heaved with sobs. Maybe it was a minute or maybe it was a lifetime, but all Millie knew was her daughter knew the truth now and hadn't run.

"Don't be mad at Franklin," she whispered into Rosie's hair as she held onto her. "He always wanted to tell you. If you must rage, let it be at me. I'm the one who was afraid." Millie gulped. "I've always been the one who was afraid, if we're being honest. It's kept me so many times from all that mattered—"

"Millie, stop," Rosie interrupted.

Millie frowned.

Rosie looked up at her, hesitancy tightening her expression, and yet she continued. "I already knew. Dad told me last year."

Millie shook her head, even as her hands trembled. "What?"

"You don't be upset at him, either. I was droning on and on, and I think he could just tell I needed to hear it as much as he needed to say it."

"But we had agreed. We did it to keep you safe, and your sister too." Fury and relief and disappointment and joy all flooded Millie's soul. "Why didn't he tell me?" she whispered.

"I'm sorry. I'm so sorry." Tears slipped down Rosie's cheeks. "I think he felt guilty for saying it so suddenly, and he didn't want you to have to keep the secret from Juliet." Rosie's gaze trailed to her sister.

"So somebody did actually think of me. Between all the lies, I mean." Juliet's words, like daggers, were a comfort to Millie—a strange relief to feel the sharp pain she deserved for a few moments rather than the deep ache of loss. And one thing was certain. Millie did deserve the reaction. Every bit of it.

"Why would you do that?" Juliet's eyes flashed with fury. "Why would you send her away?"

"I didn't send her—"

Juliet stood from the rocking chair before Millie could finish, her feet hitting hard against the ground beneath them. "That's exactly what you did, and we all know it. And then you lied to us, all those years. How could you be so cruel?" Juliet crossed her arms and looked off along the horizon of ancient oaks and the fog that'd rolled in along the water.

"Juliet!" Rosie chided. "Enough."

But she shook her head, looking toward Rosie. "Easy for you to say. You just got a new mother." She clenched her jaw as she met Millie's gaze. "Was anything you told me true?"

The words rushed like a tidal wave into all the weakened crevices of Millie's heart until the fragile walls she'd pieced together with masking tape began to crumble down, down, down.

Juliet turned on her heels, and Millie knew what she was going to do next. But Millie was not going to let that happen. She would not lose one of her daughters. Not again. She would fight for her with a fight she had reserved for fear in the past. She would be strong for her daughter's sake, or at least, stronger.

She stood and grabbed Juliet by the arm. Spun her around to face her. "We will sit on this porch until you've heard every word. I will tell you about my father's murder when I was a child and the lynchings in the papers when we moved to Alabama and the reasons I know so well what can happen in these times if a person isn't careful, if a person isn't guarded." She tightened her grip on her daughter's arm. "But you will not leave this porch, Juliet. I'm the one who taught you to run, you know. But I want us to do better. For your father's sake as much as anyone's."

That got her attention. Juliet's expression softened ever so slightly at the mention of Franklin. "Why? Why did you keep me and not Rosie? Why couldn't you raise both of us? Why did you have to be so afraid?" Juliet held up her free arm for inspection. And in the motion, in that moment, Millie traveled back in time to Charleston when she herself was Juliet's age and really just a girl, and her mama said she must go to Alabama and never tell anyone she was choosing just one part of herself in the process.

But Mama never told her how she'd grieve the other half.

"Well?" Juliet rap-rap-tapped her shoes against the ground.

Millie blew out the deep breath she'd been holding. Rosie was still sitting on the swing and wringing her hands. "I separated you two because I loved you then, even as I love you now. I was so scared one of you might be hurt if I kept you together." Her shoulders heaved with the weight of her heart. "And so, in a decision that has wrecked me every day since, we took Rosie to live with your daddy's mother because we knew the world would be kinder to you both."

"Well, that's not fair. To either of us." Juliet's forehead wrinkled in anger.

"No, it's not. But neither were the times. I did what I had to in order to keep the two of you safe. And at least I can say I did that much." Millie tried to take a deep breath. Her resolve, like her hands, was beginning to shake.

Had she and Franklin made the right choice all those years ago? She still didn't know, and she probably never would. How does somebody make the right choice when there is no *right choice* available?

"What good is safety," Juliet blurted, "if you live as a glass figurine on a shelf?"

Millie understood her point. But Juliet hadn't known the trauma of racial violence like Millie had. Millie had made sure of it, always softening a would-be threat or distracting Juliet from a racial slur. But Millie was no fool. She knew that kind of violence. Saw firsthand what it did to her mama, to her own family. And the fact Juliet would even ask that question showed just how good a job Millie had done at sheltering her daughter from the pain, from the grief she herself knew all too well. Because a guarded life was better than a dead one.

She thought of that book—what was it? *The Glass Menagerie?*— and how that part with the shattering was so real in her mind's eye she could still see every single shard falling like little crystal cymbals to the ground.

"Come with me." Millie rubbed her hands against her dress as she looked to both daughters. "I need to show you two buttons that may help you understand."

FORTY-SEVEN

Gatlinburg, Modern Day

"I thought everything was going to be okay. How could I have been so wrong?" Harper rocked back and forth in the large wooden chair, looking off into the Blue Ridge Mountains. She was so tired that the peaks of the mountains seemed to touch the valleys with each swing of her chair. She held the fabric of an antique blouse in her lap and pulled the thread in and out of the tear at the neckline.

She thought of the bench beside that train with Millie, and how Millie spoke of fear and trusting God. But Harper's own heart was taking on water, and she just didn't think she could dream the dream any longer.

Her father turned to look at her. His hair had greyed, and his love of Five and Dime ice cream showed more than it used to around his middle. But he still took a long swig from his coffee cup, just as he always had. He caught her gaze and didn't dare turn away.

"Don't you remember what I told you back when you were a girl?" Daddy reached toward the wicker coffee table between their chairs and set his cup down. "You may not know the how, or the why, and you probably won't like the when."

"Jubilee doesn't come all the time." Harper whispered the

words, as they returned to her like the tide. "But when it does, get your nets good and ready."

He picked his cup of coffee back up and held it for a long moment without saying anything. "What makes you think you've failed?"

"Isn't it obvious? I got the dress store I always wanted." Harper rapped her chipped fingernails against the armrest of her chair. "Still couldn't make it happen."

"You remember that story in the book of Ezekiel, Harper? The one about the bones and the dust? The one about the army."

Harper stilled her chair and leaned closer to him. Her heart quickened for reasons she didn't quite understand, but she wanted to hear more. "What about it?"

"Well, you were always troubled as a kid that the bones didn't just *poof!* and come alive. You'd ask me over and over why Ezekiel had to prophesy twice, like I was some kind of pastor and knew the answer."

Steam pulled up from Daddy's coffee and dissipated into the mountain air.

"Because God obviously could've done it the first time," she added.

"He didn't, though, Harper. The bones came together from the dust, just like your dress shop. But the life . . ." Daddy shook his head. "Life didn't come until Ezekiel spoke to the breath."

"What does that mean?" Harper hesitated. She had the strangest sensation of breathlessness, like after a long hike into high altitude just before cresting a mountain.

"Well, it's resurrection. From the ashes. From the dust. From the dead things. Your problem is, you're looking at the bones instead of breathing." Daddy sighed. "Maybe your dream was never about a shop at all. Maybe there's a second command, Harper Girl. Another place where you're supposed to breathe life."

Harper looked down to the blouse in her lap. To the thread and the needle.

She thought of Millie's buttons.

And then hope—glorious and beautiful hope—filled the landscape of her heart as the sunrise scatters new light over the mountaintops.

Of course! Why hadn't she seen it before? All this time, she had been focused on the store. But her gifting, her dream, was so much more than that.

Her gifting was repairing the broken places. Mending forgotten tears and weak seams. Breathing life back into the fabrics that told stories, into the buttons that bind them.

Taking up the discarded pieces of life as if they were the living ones.

Harper leapt up from her chair. She needed to make a phone call.

"You okay?" Her father's eyes widened.

"Daddy, you are a genius." Harper kissed him on the forehead before she hurried inside for her laptop.

"Do you want to talk with him?" Millie asked from the other end of the phone line.

Harper leaned back against the headboard in Daddy's guest room and picked up the damaged blouse in her lap, fiddling with the seam. "Not yet. I don't know what I'll say exactly."

"But you are returning?"

"Soon." Harper stuck her finger through the open seam under the arm of the shirt to better inspect the work she still needed to do. "Very soon."

"I knew you'd come around eventually."

Harper laughed. "Good-bye, Millie."

She ended the call and set her phone down so she'd have both hands free to pick up her thread and needle.

To think, through every failure and every detour to her plans, *this* had been the big picture all along. If the store had been successful from the get-go, or if she'd gained acclaim from SCAD . . .

Harper shook her head. She might never have found this perfectly tailored dream.

Repairing beautiful, broken things.

Still, Harper sensed there was something more to discover, a peace she hadn't yet found. She gently tugged the fabric to check for other weak seams, of which she found several.

Then she closed her eyes, her hand still on the fabric, and took a slow inhale. That's when it hit her.

The breath of it flowed well beyond the air. Well beyond her lungs, into her heart in a way that was entirely unexpected, so free and so strikingly clear.

For a moment, it was as if her very breath came from an altogether separate place. A sanctuary. The words resonated so deep within her, she knew they could only come from one place.

From the beginning, I have been working between the seams. Where you have ripped, I have mended. When you have torn, I have sewn you. Stitching death to resurrection, failure to dreams, hurt to healing. I never throw out a fabric because it needs repairing.

You've spent your life on the other side of the seams, thinking all the if-only's. But there will always be another section to piece. Another hole that needs mending. So long as you live, you will have loose stitches— don't avoid them. Come and exchange them for strong seams.

Keep the fabric of your dreams.

FORTY-EIGHT

South of Broad, Charleston, 1992

Millie grazed the palm of her hand along the rail separating the shore from the Charleston Battery and looked out toward the harbor, the meeting point of two rivers. The low tide brought gentle waves to shore as the sun dipped closer to the horizon.

Millie turned toward the park and the line of mansions along the Battery, feeling thankful even though the path to this point had broken them all a little, and sometimes a lot.

Rows of mature oak trees framed the gazebo central to the park, as the last light of day came through the branches. Millie nearly didn't recognize them without the iconic Spanish moss. Rosie had written that Hurricane Hugo washed all the moss from the limbs and botanists couldn't figure out why it wasn't growing again. But my, what a strange sight to see.

Spanish moss was funny that way, how with the right conditions it grew like a weed and dripped down to the grass below—a perfect nesting material for hummingbirds. But in one fell swoop, the storm took it away. And sometimes, conditions could not be replicated for its return. Sometimes it was simply gone.

Spanish moss didn't grow on just any old tree, after all.

Millie took a deep breath and gripped the railing as she took the stairs down from the pedestrian wall along the Battery. She continued walking and crossed the street, turning toward Rosie's new mansion.

The estate was something. That's for sure. And Rosie's new husband didn't seem at all deterred by her tragic loss last year. He had helped her grieve, even accepting the baby as his own, and seemed comfortable when she used terms like *heroic* in reference to the boy's father or the Gulf War.

Millie opened the wrought-iron gate and stepped between two stone pillars, then walked through the garden. Night-blooming jasmine transported her senses to another time and softened the sinking feeling in her stomach that Rosie's husband did seem deterred by something else.

Her.

The man opened the front door before she could reach it. "Millie, you're back." He cleared his throat. "Would you like to have a seat?" He motioned toward two chairs set up along the porch that wrapped around the side of the mansion.

"Sure." Millie raised her chin. She refused to be intimidated, no matter the way this man reminded her of Harry in her childhood—and all the other Harrys ever since.

She chose one of the wicker chairs and sat with her ankles crossed like Mama taught her as a girl. He took the chair opposite her.

Millie looked at him—my, he was such a young boy, wasn't he?—and smiled to soften whatever conversation may be coming. "Something on your mind, Weston?"

He shifted in his seat and folded his hands as though getting ready to lean onto the table where he drew up his legal documents. "I don't know how to say this, exactly. I appreciate you being here for Rose and helping with the baby."

Millie nodded. "But you want to know how much longer I plan to stay."

He scratched the back of his neck. Was he uncomfortable with how direct she was being? Well, if he was going to have the boldness to suggest she leave, she was going to make him come out with it. None of this hemming and hawing around. "Rose is your daughter. Obviously. And the truth is, I think highly of you, Millicent. But we come from very different worlds. My father and grandfather have made sacrifices to maintain a certain position in Charleston society, and with that role comes . . . certain expectations."

Millie blinked. "Wait. You mean you're saying this because you think I'm poor?"

Weston shook his head and blew out a deep breath. "No, I don't think you're understanding me. I have no problem with you or how you make your livelihood. You seem to have lived a rich life in your own way. But you are very forthright with your thoughts, and I fear I'll have to do the same in this case. So here's the truth. I'm completely comfortable with you maintaining regular contact with Rose, but I want to raise Peter in the same social circles my own family raised me. I want him to take over the business someday, maybe even this house, because I think he could be somebody in Charleston's elite. What I do not want is for Peter to know you are his grandmother."

At the mention of the word *grandmother*, the world seemed to simply stop turning around Millie, save for the song of a mockingbird and a large magnolia blossom that fell from a tree toward her feet.

She tried to find her next breath, her next thought, her next heartbeat. She tried to follow the logic, but all she could do was look back at Weston, blinking.

"You want me to pretend I'm of no relation to him?"

All over again?

Weston leaned backward, crossing his arms. "It may not be pretty, but the reality is, my family's reputation and status could be ruined by the smear of illegal marriages and a baby given away. We can't have scandal following the family name. I don't care about your race or anyone else's, but I do care about scandal. I can provide a good life for Peter, but as he grows up, I don't want him asking questions. Whether we like it or not, people will talk if the past doesn't stay gone. And the last thing I want is for Peter to live a life preoccupied with dredging up old history."

Millie had half a mind to slap that fool clear out of his ignorance. She didn't care a lick about his last name. But the anger pounding in her veins slowly gave way to grief, as she remembered that this man was Rosie's husband, and this was the life Rosie had chosen to lead. After all, Rosie had grown up believing Franklin's mother to be her own. So what say did Millie have, really? She had already made the heartbreaking choice to leave.

She could only hope that despite all odds, her grandson would someday develop an interest in history.

FORTY-NINE

Charleston, Modern Day

With a spatula, Peter pushed half the scrambled eggs onto Millie's plate and the other half onto his own. Steam rose from their breakfast even as the electric kettle whistled.

After a month of breakfast dates with Millie, Peter had picked up the habit of drinking hot tea, as if he were some kind of Englishman. The whole thing had started as a way to help Millie keep her routine, but now that he'd grown accustomed, he was actually starting to like it. He had picked up Millie's discriminate taste for the expensive stuff.

Peter put a tea bag into Millie's favorite large, red mug and poured the boiling water in. He grabbed a spoon from the drawer and slid the sugar container over the bar toward her. No matter how hard he tried, he never seemed able to figure out just how much sugar she liked.

Harper knew. But Harper wasn't here, was she?

Millie took the mug in her hands and dipped the tea bag up and down as it steeped. "You look nice."

Peter straightened the collar of his faded grey polo and reached for the ball cap with his personalized walking tour logo. "Thanks. I've got a tour in an hour."

Millie dunked half a spoonful of sugar into her tea and began to stir. "I don't have any plans today, and with the racket those repair guys put on yesterday, I intend to stay as far away from this place as possible until the close of the workday." She took a cautious sip of the boiling liquid. "Perhaps I'll accompany you."

"If only I could be so lucky." Peter poured water into his own mug for tea and plopped in some sugar. He was far less fussy about the amount so long as it tasted sweet. Then he handed a plate of eggs to Millie and jabbed a fork into his own. "But are you concerned about all the walking?"

He winced a little hearing the words come from his mouth—she needn't be reminded of her age, did she?—and yet he didn't think it was a good idea. The walking tours were hours long, no matter the weather.

Although the temperatures today were exceptionally pleasant.

Gracefully, Millie took a forkful of her eggs. "You act as if I'm an invalid."

Peter shook his head as he chewed. "You know you're always welcome. I just don't want you to get tired, is all."

Millie sipped her tea. "The only thing I tire of, my dear Peter, is this conversation."

Peter kept his smile to himself. "You'll at least wear comfortable shoes?"

"You know, Harper was never this obnoxious." Millie took a couple more bites of eggs. "But she also didn't cook this well, so I guess you're even."

Peter did laugh at that. "Is that a yes or no on the shoes?"

An hour later, Peter and Millie stood at the Four Corners of the Law at the intersection of Broad and Meeting Streets. Peter wore his walking tour cap, polo, and khakis, and Millie wore a fashionable pink dress with her always-present cloche and one-inch heels that she no doubt dug out of her closet just to spite him.

Two couples had already joined them for the tour, and a family with two teenage daughters looked right and left as they crossed Broad Street. Peter waved to them, then stretched out his hand to make introductions as they approached.

He took a step backward to address the whole group. "I'm Peter Perkins. My family has lived in Charleston for generations, and I'm looking forward to sharing some of my favorite history with you. Happy to have you all along today." He grinned at Millie. "So, let's get started."

The quiet group simply stared at him in response. He could already tell he had his work cut out for him if he wanted to get them talking.

Well, all except for the oldest teenager, who was currently looking at him as if he were Ed Sheeran. He had a hunch she wouldn't mind talking.

"Anyone know what this particular intersection is called?" Peter gestured toward the streetlamps at the corner as another tour group shuffled past.

After a long hesitation, Millie cleared her throat. "I believe it's referred to as the Four Corners of the Law."

"You are correct." He pointed to Millie, then looked to the rest of the group. They appeared relieved someone else knew the answer. "We in Charleston use that term because here at this intersection, we see representation by a church, a courthouse, city hall, and the post office. We have God's law, man's law, and the ability to write home about each. We like to say that here, you can get married, divorced, taxed, and jailed all in one place." Peter straightened his glasses at the bridge of his nose and nodded down the block. "Our next stop is going to be the Old Slave Mart, then Rainbow Row—which, if you can believe it, was not painted those vibrant colors until the 1930s and 1940s. The saying goes, folks before the preservation movement were too poor to paint but too proud to whitewash."

Peter turned and led his group across the street. Soon, they had reached the front of the Old Slave Mart building. Many people assumed that the City Market was where slaves were bought and sold, but in reality, that space was historically used as a marketplace, just as it still is today. Prior to the Civil War, the market gave some persons of color the opportunity to sell enough handmade goods that they could purchase their freedom.

The dirt of decay washed the archways, the old bricks of the building that stood like an immovable blight upon the historic cobblestone street—barred gates that once held persons in slavery but now held the ugliest sort of history.

An eeriness settled over Peter every time he made this stop of the tour, every time he considered the echo of the screams.

But now, standing here beside Millie . . . he wanted to run to the next stop of the tour. He didn't want to put Millie through the pain of seeing this building where Rose had passed, exchanged as if she were an item rather than a human being.

And now, knowing she was his ancestor too. Though his skin was a different shade and his birth over a century later, this was his bloodline. This was his family.

This was his origin story within this city.

Peter took a deep breath, daring a glance over at Millie, who looked up at the building with one hand over her opposite elbow and her face awash with . . . was it memory?

"What's this building?" the teenage girl asked.

"This is the Old Slave Mart." Peter pointed up toward the archways. "Where people were bought and sold into slavery."

The young woman's eyes widened. "In this building?"

Peter nodded as a horse carriage ambled past. "I'd like for you to all take a moment and imagine what the scene must have looked like. Children taken from their families, the strongest among them auctioned to the highest bidder." Peter shifted his feet and glanced down. "The struggle, the hope for a different sort of life that would never come to be. The screaming, the weeping, and the lifetime after spent wondering."

When he looked back up at the group, Millie was fixed on him. She stared at him in understanding, her mouth parted slightly.

Yes, Millie, I know. I have known for months.

"This landmark is particularly chilling for me, as I've recently learned my own ancestors were sold here. Among them, a little girl named Ashley. She was nine years old when she was sold, and she never saw her mother again."

Peter never broke Millie's gaze. She stood steady, even as her hands began trembling. Her eyes spoke a thousand emotions, but her lips couldn't seem to say a thing.

It's all right, he hoped his expression said. *I understand why you didn't tell me.*

He could see now that she wouldn't have visited Charleston for all those years if she didn't care for his mother. And she wouldn't have come now if she didn't care for him too.

Though Peter still didn't know what had happened to his family generations prior or why, he did recognize one thing.

Millie had lived her life stuck at the seams of the in-between.

And he could only assume she had done so because she belonged a little too much to both to ever fully forsake the other.

Someday, maybe she would explain it all, and he could tell her that she didn't have to choose any longer. Her future, her history, were all important parts of her story.

"Does anyone have any questions?" Peter asked.

The teenage girl pointed to him and then Millie. "How do you know each other?"

Before he could think of an answer, Millie reached for his shoulder.

"Peter is my grandson, and I couldn't be prouder of him."

FIFTY

Charleston, 1967
One Year Prior to Franklin's Death

With one hand on the worn stairwell, Franklin shuffled down the stairs of his mother's house toward the kitchen in search of a glass of water. He had the most nagging cough but didn't want to wake Millie or the girls.

He made it to the kitchen and felt his way through the dark until he opened a cabinet and heard a glass clang.

Strange, to be in a place so achingly familiar and yet to know it belongs to another time. The single house south of Broad Street had once belonged to his uncle William, back when Franklin and his mother still used an icebox.

Well, just look at Mama now. Bright green fridge for an icebox. And for that matter, look at him too.

He reached for the handle of the fridge to pour himself some water, and that's when he saw her, sitting on a barstool and sipping from a bottle that, judging from the fridge contents, could only be Coca-Cola. It had better be Coca-Cola.

"Rosie?" Franklin set the water pitcher down on the counter and blinked until she came into clearer focus. He couldn't be sure, but the sixteen-year-old seemed to be smiling.

"My dear brother." The name stirred him with remorse every time. Couldn't he have been more? Couldn't he have been her world, at least for a while?

Franklin poured the water in his glass, returned the pitcher, and sat on the stool beside her. He took a long slurp, which immediately soothed his cough.

"It's midnight, young lady."

"Midnight for you too, you know." She took a sip of her Coke, then set it back down, completely unfazed by his reproach.

"Couldn't sleep," Franklin said.

"Yeah, me neither." Rosie shifted on her stool to face him. He noticed now that her hair was pinned up in curls. No wonder the child couldn't rest, all those pins jabbing her head.

"Any reason?" Franklin reached for her bottle and took a swig. *Yes, definitely Coke.*

"Franklin!"

"Consider it a tax for not ratting you out."

She put both hands back on the bottle and giggled. She wore button-down pajamas that looked far more comfortable than Millie's dainty nightgowns. Yes, she was certainly his daughter.

After a long pause, she looked back up at him. "There's this guy."

"Uh oh." Franklin held back his groan.

"Forget it. You already hate him," Rosie said.

Franklin chuckled. "But you've hardly said a thing about him, dear one."

"I don't need to. I can already tell you hate him." She shook her head, and her curls didn't budge one inch. "It's not so much about *him*, anyway, as the dance tomorrow." Rosie put her hand on Franklin's arm and turned all her attention to him. "Oh, Franklin, it would be the dreamiest."

Then, of course, came her contented sigh.

"*Would* be?" Franklin asked. Live with Millie long enough, and a man learned to read between the lines.

Rosie reached for her Coca-Cola and took another long swing.

"If I didn't have two left feet. I dance like an elephant, honest to goodness."

Franklin rubbed his jaw. "Come now, that can't be true." He glanced behind his shoulder and scanned the room.

"What are you looking for?" Rosie enjoyed the last sip from her bottle, then set it down on the table.

"How loudly does sound carry through the house from this floor?"

"Sound?" Rosie slid off the bar stool and stepped over to the basket they used to collect bottles for recycling. From the amount of soda he'd seen her consume, Franklin suspected a hefty portion of her weekly allowance came from bottle returns. Rosie looked up at the ceiling. "I'd say it's insulated pretty well."

"Good." Franklin took one more drink from his water and walked toward the radio. Took him long enough to find it. His mother had moved the thing to an opposite corner of the room since his last visit.

But this way worked better for his plan. He always had a plan.

Franklin opened the side door that led to a long and skinny porch, with a garden just beyond. What the house lacked in width, it made up for in height and charm.

The place even smelled like home, from his mother's constant baking and the little white flowers that trailed on the patio outside. One open window, and the fragrance of those flowers would fill up the room. And he was so glad to be sharing it with his daughter, even if he couldn't tell her that.

Franklin pushed the coffee table with the radio closer and closer toward the patio.

"What are you planning to—"

But Franklin turned on the radio before Rosie could finish.

She rushed over to him even as he took two steps through the doorway.

"Franklin!" Her whisper was louder than her speaking voice. "You can't turn that on. Do you know the heap of trouble we will both be in should someone wake up?"

She always called him and Millie by their first names, for as far as she was concerned, he was her much older brother. The imbedded deception tugged harder upon his heart, reached deeper inside of him with every year that passed—just as it did for Millie.

The station on the dial was halfway through a jazzy tune, and Franklin reached out his hand to her. "Then let's take care not to wake them."

Rosie laughed as softly as a teenager could manage, then quickly took his hand.

"Dancing's simple, really, Rosie. You've got to stop thinking so much and enjoy yourself."

"How am I to enjoy it when I very nearly make a fool of myself every time?" But despite her words, Rosie was rocking back and forth to the music with ease.

"There you go. Keep at it."

The music slowed to a stop, and Franklin recognized the first beats of "Rockin' Robin" before any words were sung.

"I heard a song like this on *American Bandstand* yesterday! Rock and roll, right? But"—her sigh was so heavy, her shoulders slumped—"I haven't the slightest idea how to swing-dance."

"Just follow my feet. Only a few steps to master if you're the lady. The fella, on the other hand, has to learn the tricks and dips—and keep from getting distracted by how pretty his partner is. I'm sure your mystery guy will prove himself well." Franklin took both Rosie's hands and spun her into several moves Millie had insisted upon teaching him. Despite his resistance.

Franklin smirked by the shadow of the night. Millie never paid much mind to his resistance, did she? One of the many things he loved about her.

"Now the fun part," Franklin said, "is when you hear that stop in the music. You've got to jump. Stomp. Do whatever you like, but make it count."

Rosie's grip on his hands tightened. "But how will I know when?"

"It's like jumpin' a train, Rosie. You can count it out and get it in your own head, but at some point you've just got to feel it when the moment comes."

Seconds later, the music broke, and Rosie jumped, perfectly in time. She burst into laughter, then glanced toward the stairwell and quickly quieted herself.

Franklin smiled. "Now you see why we didn't do this on those wooden floors inside."

Rosie soon found her stride, and three songs later, her yawns grew too persistent to ignore.

"Better get some sleep if you want to feel good for that dance tomorrow."

Rosie simply stared up at him. He hadn't seen her make that expression before and didn't know what to make of it.

"I was just thinking." She blinked several times, then fiddled with the buttons of her pajamas. "Times like this make me wish I had a father. A real one, you know?"

"You do."

Two words he hadn't meant to say. He certainly didn't have a plan now. Millie would be fit to be tied if he told her. He knew that much. But maybe . . .

"What?"

Frank Sinatra crooned in the background, filling the silence between them.

"Rosie, I know this is going to be hard to get a hold of, but I'm your father, and Millie is your mother. Juliet is actually your sister." He reached out to gently take her by both arms, hoping that the touch would somehow ground her beyond the shock.

"But"—she shook her head—"I don't understand. How?"

"Let me put it like this. You ever notice how when we come to visit, we spend most of the time inside the house?"

She hesitated, then nodded.

"You're plenty old enough to know what would happen if you were out on the town with Juliet, yes? You've heard the ugly stuff and know the laws about the theater, and the drinking fountains, and everything else." He closed his eyes, the memory still fresh with regret and pain. "There was this one time when the two of you were much smaller . . . I hope you don't remember. The four of us were walking down toward the Battery to play chase through those oak trees, and some men called your sister a horrible name. I stepped in, and Millie grabbed me—terrified those men would hurt me like the men who killed her father."

"I do remember. Not the part about the name. I think that went over my head. But I remember you defending Juliet and that I felt really scared." She looked down at her hands.

Rosie's tears began to stream down. His always-talking girl had suddenly lost her words. He kept talking in hopes she might find them again.

"When you were born, the country still followed the one-drop rule. We knew the two of you would face a lot of hate and a lot of ignorance and a whole lot of cruelty if we tried to keep you together. Because it's side-by-side together that seems to be the problem, bringing out the violence in people whether in body or in words." Franklin faked a gentle smile, doing his best to keep his grief hidden behind it. "We wanted to give both of you the world."

She studied him, maybe trying to determine if this was true. Maybe trying to determine if they hadn't just changed their minds when two babies were born instead of one.

"But all I ever wanted," she whispered, "was you." She shook her head, as the tears fell harder. "How could you do that to me? To all of us?" She looked into his eyes. "Did you even miss me?"

"We missed you more than you could ever know." Franklin's heart shattered. "Sweet girl, being together as a family was all your mother and I ever wanted too. We began taking these trips to Charleston because the pain of being apart was too great otherwise. Been that way since the moment we left you." Franklin stepped over to the radio and turned the dial until the Sinatra song faded into a memory. "Rosie, can you ever forgive me?"

She fell silent, but he wouldn't push her for an answer. He didn't need one. Her feelings and her grief belonged to her alone, and she would need time to process them. But he knew he'd made the right decision to tell her the truth.

Franklin wrapped his dear Rosie into a hug then, resting his chin on her pointy-pinned curls as she shook with tears from within his arms. And he knew he'd done the right thing because his girl needed a father just as much as he had fiercely needed his other daughter. Also, he had an eerie feeling he might not get another chance.

He took a deep breath of the night air as he hadn't breathed in the last fifteen years of his life.

And finally, finally—he felt fully alive.

FIFTY-ONE

Charleston, Modern Day

After the walking tour ended, Peter asked Millie how her feet were holding up and told her he had one more surprise for her. Sweet Peter's demeanor had buzzed to life in the last half hour since her confession. His smile was the spitting image of Franklin.

His gumption too.

Millie should've told him sooner, but she just couldn't bring herself to say the words before now—not after the promises she made when his mother was living.

"Close your eyes." Peter held tighter to her hand.

"What am I, a child?" Millie liked to know where she was going. But Peter just laughed. "Oh, I suppose I've got nothing to lose." At that, he gently turned her in a circle, her eyes still closed, until she couldn't tell which way she faced any longer.

By Millie's count, they should be in front of the Ashley River. But after a few steps and a corner turn, Peter stopped her. "We're here," he said.

Slowly, Millie opened her eyes.

The sight before her was too much to take in. Her hand flew to her mouth as her fingers began to tremble. She tried to whisper *thank you*, but her lips were putty.

All she could do was look at him, wide-eyed with surprise.

Peter's grin broadened.

Tears began to fall. Tears she didn't know she had left. Tears for all the moments of *have not* and *could be*, and the hope—thank God—that, despite her age, she still carried with every breath.

The hope for the next.

Millie took his arm gladly this time. She could scarcely wind her way through her own thoughts, let alone wind her way down the sidewalk.

Millie looked up at the house—the house where Mama had raised her—as she held tight to his arm. "How did you know?"

Peter hesitated as they neared the front porch. He straightened her cloche. "I inherited it after my mother passed and have been gradually restoring the place. Hoping to find the stories between the walls." He looked up at the home. Though modest, its charm couldn't be denied. "Then I realized that story was yours."

Millie stepped toward the front door and placed her hand against the bricks she hadn't seen in decades. Still as sturdy as she remembered them. The feel of the house, the walls, triggered a memory of Uncle Clyde and Aunt Bea here after Mama's passing. *"Sweetgrass Millie,"* Aunt Bea had called her. *"You always did weave beautiful stories."*

Peter slid the key into the lock and looked at her, eyebrows raised, as the door swung wide.

Millie stepped into the foyer and closed her eyes.

Her old feet were suddenly strong by memory. Her old heart, held by the walls. Her old dreams took flight from the floor, and this—this was the feeling of homecoming.

Peter flipped on the lights, and Millie opened her eyes.

"Welcome home."

Her gaze swept the room as chills swept her arms. The floors had been polished and repaired—they were old when she'd lived here, and she couldn't imagine what shape Peter had found them in. The windows had been replaced, but the fireplace was just the same.

"Why would you do all this?" Millie spun to face him, tears welling up again in her eyes. "Just to save it . . ."

Peter shrugged. "Same reason you and Harper love dresses, I guess. The house was in a bad state when I got it, but it meant a lot to me. I was determined to do the repairs one way or another."

She didn't know what to say.

Peter gestured toward the plaster ceiling. "Besides, you can't get these kinds of craftsman details anymore." He shifted and caught her gaze. "But if you want it . . . I mean, if you've considered staying in Charleston . . . well, I just thought as the saying goes, there's no place like home."

Millie smiled and rested her head on his chest as she hugged him. "No, Peter, there certainly is not." When she glanced up, her heart turned wistful.

"What is it?" Peter asked. "You all right?"

"Oh, absolutely." Millie fiddled with the sleeves of her dress. "I was just thinking, it's funny how sometimes life takes us away. But other times, life brings us back."

"And maybe that was your story all along."

Peter and Millie had just turned the corner of King Street when the rain began to drizzle. "He was seriously a train jumper?"

Millie raised her chin. "I wouldn't fall in love with someone dull, would I?"

Peter took a long glance at her and shook his head. "No, Millie. I guess you wouldn't."

He pointed to the nearest antique store. "Why don't you go inside so you don't get wet, and I'll run up the block to get my car?"

"Always so chivalrous." Millie patted his arm. "Well, thank you, calvary, but I do intend to walk the rest of the way and am quite certain I won't melt."

"But I really don't mind."

She put one hand on top of her hat to keep it from falling as she looked up at him. "Nor do I."

Peter smiled. He angled his elbow toward her. "Then at least take my arm. We can help one another avoid tripping over any cracks in the sidewalk."

Millie swiftly reached for him. "Are you always so accommodating, or only with your long-lost grandmothers?"

Peter gave a half grin. The rain continued falling—gentle but persistent—and in no time, the cotton shoulders of his shirt were sticking to his skin. He was ready to hurry back home and get some dry clothes on, but he wouldn't trade this conversation with Millie for anything.

He wanted to know more details, like how the train smelled or what happened to Franklin. But he knew all that would come in time, and he didn't want to overwhelm her with the memories she'd only just begun to speak about.

"It's come full circle, hasn't it, Millie?"

She grinned up at him. "What's that?"

"Well, you left Charleston chasing a dream for a different life, and I'd like to think you returned for much the same reason."

She patted his arm with her free hand. "Why, when you put it that way, yes. I suppose you're quite right."

Peter sidestepped around a huge puddle and took care to help Millie avoid getting splashed. Knowing her, the shoes she was wearing were probably as old as him.

A storefront offered a welcome awning, a sudden reprieve from the rain, and they both hesitated under it. Millie turned to face him. It was a natural sort of movement, but he suspected she knew what he was about to ask next.

Peter removed his glasses and did his best to wipe the raindrops from his lenses with the hem of his damp shirt. Then he squared them at the bridge of his nose and looked back at her clearly.

"I understand now why you left Charleston on the train that day. But why did you leave my mom?"

And why had she taken so long to tell him the truth? She must have known how hard he'd searched for answers.

Millie blinked, and he couldn't tell tears from raindrops, but he assumed the moisture in her eyes must be the latter because he'd never seen Millie cry.

"I was trying to keep them safe. Both of them."

Peter frowned. "Both of . . . who?"

Millie wiped her eyes with her fingertips. "You have an aunt. Juliet is her name. She and your mother had very different complexions. Put them together side by side, and they would have been targeted just as I was when I was a child. She came to the funeral."

Peter tried so hard to recall that day. He remembered Millie there as a friend of his mother's, but the rest was blurred by grief.

"She lives in New Orleans. Owns a dress shop in the Garden District. Although she's in France right now, gathering ideas for new inventory and studying under some of the biggest names in the industry. Can you imagine? She isn't deterred a bit that they're half her age, and her dedication has taken her a block away from the Eiffel Tower." Millie glowed with pride. "She's the one who sent me the initial inventory for the store."

Rain fell behind the lenses of Peter's glasses once more. "A dress shop?"

"Apple doesn't fall too far and all." Millie grinned. "She'll be back in New Orleans soon, so maybe we could arrange for the two of you to meet properly."

"I'd really like that." Peter's mind spun with all this new information. In one fell swoop, Millie had filled in blank spaces he'd researched for years. To think that all this time, he had an aunt. His gut clenched with the thought of time lost, but he willed himself to remember the opportunity ahead.

"Let me be clear." Her unwavering gaze arrested him. "The day I left your mother in Charleston, I left half of my heart behind. I was never the same until we all reunited after Franklin's death.

The girls came to live at the boardinghouse in Alabama for a while, and then I paid for their college and your parents' wedding—"

"With the savings you'd accumulated to start your dress shop." Peter let go of a deep sigh. It all made sense now. Of course Millie would give up her own dream for the sake of helping her children, especially with Franklin gone. She was their mother, after all. "And you couldn't raise them both because one looked white and one looked Black. Would've been dangerous back then."

Millie nodded. Even now, the memory tightened the wrinkles around her eyes. He imagined it would never let her go, this loss she had endured. Choosing, at every turn, one part of herself. One part of her past, one part of her future, and never really getting that dress store.

Until now.

"There were so many times I questioned the decision of asking Franklin's mother to raise Rosie. Hearing my own daughter call someone else *Mom*." Millie swallowed. She looked straight at Peter. "How do you do right by your child when you don't even know what that is or looks like? At times, I was convinced I'd allowed fear to make all my decisions and done everything wrong. Other times, some awful act of racial violence would be in the paper, and I'd feel justified."

Peter reached out and folded his grandmother into a hug. She didn't need to say any more. He understood now—at least, as well as he could understand. From the beginning, Millie's every choice had been for her family. She must've feared how he would react just as she feared how his mother would've.

But she clearly wanted to know him since she traveled all the way to Charleston. A city to which she wasn't supposed to return. Not for his mother Rosie, and not for him either.

Peter rested his chin on top of her red hat. "I'm glad you're here, Millie. And I know the boardinghouse has been a home for you, but I do hope you'll consider staying here for a while."

"You'll be itching to get rid of me like a head full of lice." Millie ducked ever so gently from under his arm. She held out her elbow, as if she would be the one to steady him this time.

And perhaps she would.

By the time they made it up the block from his house, a drenched Peter clenched his teeth against the breeze despite the otherwise pleasant temperature. Millie, meanwhile, strolled down the sidewalk completely composed, as if there weren't the faintest cloud in the sky. Typical.

They turned the corner toward the loft, and that's when he saw her. Wearing one of the dresses he'd salvaged from the closet of an old house, along with golden shoes and her hair in those curls that drove him mad.

"Harper." All the breath rushed from him at the mention of her name. Peter tossed his ball cap to the ground and ran to her.

She ran to him as well. "I didn't see you upstairs, so I thought you might be out on a—"

His fingers met the underside of her hair as his other hand pressed her waist against him. He looked down at her, little raindrops on the tips of her blinking eyelashes, and he couldn't wait any longer.

"Harper." This time, her name was a whisper.

He lowered his chin far more confidently than his rational mind would've allowed until his parted lips slowly met her own. Attraction pulled him, floated higher and higher until he feared—as with air balloons—the heat might push him to the sky. But to be lost among these clouds.

He pulled back, held her by both arms and noticed she seemed as breathless as he.

"Don't mind the old woman over here—I'll just be inside getting dry." Millie's voice might as well have been miles away from how focused he was on Harper's blue-grey eyes.

"You came back."

"We had an unfinished conversation," Harper said, never breaking his gaze. The rain continued to fall, but he wasn't cold any longer.

Peter tucked a stray piece of Harper's hair back in place, and let his thumb linger on her ear. She smelled like flowers as always, only this time, from this close, it may as well have been a field of them.

He had dreamed about her last night. He could almost reach out and touch her, and when he woke, he realized she was gone. He hadn't fallen back asleep for hours.

"Are you sure you're real?"

Harper laughed. "My rumbling stomach would suggest I am indeed."

Peter leaned closer, a half grin on his lips as he said in her ear, "Perhaps you'd like a cup of coffee while we decide what restaurant."

Harper angled her head so she could see him over her shoulder and grinned. "Cheap coffee has never sounded so appealing. Although I have to confess, I think Millie threw away the stuff you got us. She said it might attract weevils."

"How romantic." He turned her to face him, the two of them laughing, and kissed her again. His pulse pounded as he backed away, her berry lips inches from his own. "Harper Rae?"

"Hmm?" Her eyes had fluttered shut, and she waited for him to say more.

"I'm in love with you."

She opened her eyes, and they seemed to glitter in the puddled reflections of sunlight all around. "I love you back."

Peter grinned, spinning her around until her feet splashed shallow water and came up off the ground. Then he set her back down and slid his arm around her waist, drawing her closer to himself. Side by side, they started toward the stairs leading to the loft.

"It was the Poe story that won your heart, wasn't it? Tell the truth." Peter reached to hold open the door for her.

Harper flashed him a smile as she stepped inside. "I can definitely say it was not the Poe story."

"Maybe my Ryan Gosling clothes."

"Now that . . ." Harper bit her bottom lip, and the admiration in her eyes shook him down to his core. He wanted nothing more than to spend the day with her, and then tomorrow, and then all the tomorrows thereafter.

She had ruined him for any hope of enjoying life without her. So he didn't intend to let that happen. He was certain, in fact, he would love her for the rest of his life.

FIFTY-TWO

Fairhope, 2008

Millie was scooping flour from her biscuit barrel and mixing dough with the firm roll of her palm when the phone rang. She brushed the flour from her hands onto her floral apron and reached toward the phone.

"Hello?" Millie turned her back toward the dough and leaned against the counter to get a better view of the wall clock shaped like a teacup. The phone cord would only let her go so far, so she squinted. Still so early in the morning for calls.

"Hi, Mrs. Millie. This is Jane." Pause. "Unfortunately, my daughter Stephanie and I won't be able to make it to your sewing lesson today. Something has come up. I'm so sorry for canceling last minute. I do hope you haven't made preparations for us."

Millie closed her eyes. After a moment's hesitation, she sighed and mustered up as much grace as she could. "Oh, don't worry yourself, Jane. These things happen." Millie smiled in a sad sort of way and hung up, replacing the phone on its receiver.

She shook her head, turning once more toward the biscuits. She'd made enough to feed a Sunday school class even though Jane and Stephanie were the only two scheduled for lessons that day.

The boardinghouse was empty for two nights, near empty for more than that. Juliet was in New Orleans; Rosie, in Charleston. And the family heirlooms had been split among them, including

Millie's wedding dress, which Rosie wore in her wedding to Peter's father, Jack.

Millie was alone. Her joints ached from arthritis, and her heart ached from everything else. She lived among beautiful memories here at the boardinghouse—stories that a steady stream of new customers gave her. She loved that every year, the same smell of magnolias caught on the breeze birthed by water. That the wooden planks on the floor still held familiar grooves made by dancing, and that the view out her bedroom window still brought a new sunrise every morning.

But sometimes it caught up with her. That her dream to own her own dress shop had never actually come true. Every time she'd gotten close to saving enough money, one of her daughters had a need—first the family trips to Charleston while the girls were growing up. Then with Rosie's wedding; then Juliet's own store opened. And then, of course, Rosie's baby and the extended time Millie stayed in Charleston after the tragic death of Rosie's husband.

Now, both her daughters had long passed the age of needing help. But something unexpected happened in the meantime.

Millie had long passed the age of being able. At some point, in all those years of providing for the two of them, providing for everyone who came through the inn for that matter, Millie had developed stiff joints that made extended dressmaking no longer possible. It'd been years upon years since she quit her seamstress work at the bridal shop downtown. She now had the money, the time, and the resources to start her own store but little interest in finagling a mortgage, and not enough energy to work long hours.

So while it wasn't entirely true that she'd stopped dreaming about the shop, it *was* true that somewhere along the way, she'd stopped seeing it as possible.

She would admit that, of course, to no one but herself. When her daughters asked, from time to time, about her long-held dream, Millie simply said she was busy with the boardinghouse and *maybe next year.*

Offering sewing classes to young women seemed like a nice way to pass along her skills without the rigor of being an independent business owner. But of course, that too had fizzled out before even starting. She couldn't shake the feelings of isolation and anonymity that had settled into her bones.

Millie sat down at the kitchen table, flour still under her fingernails. She started feeling sorry for herself—but no. No, that wouldn't do. She stood back up and opened the door to step outside.

The early morning carried with it the gentlest, low-lying fog that blurred the bay into the pier and the rest of the horizon. Enchanted by the surrealist effect, Millie walked out toward the pier. She was startled from her thoughts when a fishing boat pulled out of the fog.

"Mornin'!" the man said, lifting his ballcap from his head to wave it toward Millie. She recognized him then—the fisherman who lived with his family across the water.

"Good morning to you." Millie nodded, smiling, though she wasn't entirely sure he could see her through the dense fog.

"How are ya, Mrs. Millie?"

"Not too shabby," she said, then decided for whatever reason to keep going. "Though this morning's turned into a bit of a disappointment. I'm going to have to cancel my sewing class before it's really even begun."

"Sewing class, you said?" He righted his ball cap backward on his thick head of hair. "Why, my Harper would love that. She's always cuttin' up old fabric from sheets and napkins to make little clothes for her dolls. How much for the class, Mrs. Millie?"

Hope warmed Millie's clenched chest, and for the first time, she saw the scattering of sunbeams glistening through the fog along the water. "Oh, it's no charge. The class is nonrefundable, and the other student canceled, so Harper could simply take her spot." Actually, Millie would teach the child for free but didn't want to offend by straight-up saying so.

"I'll get these fish inside and tell my wife. Harper will be thrilled. What time?"

"Say . . . ten o'clock?"

"Works for us." He docked his boat along his pier and carried both his cooler and the invitation inside.

Millie turned from the pier toward the table where she'd laid out the lacy tablecloth her mama had mailed decades ago. She'd found in an old drawer, tucked away for safekeeping.

Looked like she would be using it after all. She would go ahead and set the table, then return to the kitchen to finish the biscuits. After that, she'd prepare the tea and carry her sewing machine outside. Yes, this was all working out.

Millie took the tablecloth by two corners and shook it in the air. Dust floated up, up, up from the fabric as she held tight to both corners—as if they were the beginning and ending marks to a forgotten story, and if Millie just held tightly enough, it would all come unfurled.

As she clutched and the wind caught, the space between the corners became a flag and the fabric settled on the table, waving an announcement to the world that sewing lessons were about to begin.

Millie hurried around the table, tugging and straightening the lace until it laid just so. And then she looked up toward the heavens, happy about this opportunity to teach Harper but still heavy with melancholy.

"Why did my dream never come?" she murmured, straightening the lace further with her wrinkled hands.

Then, through the fog, as muted sunbeams shimmied through the tree limbs, she sensed the reply with startling clarity from the heavens: *I'm not done.*

Nor, it seemed, was she.

Little Harper sat at Millie's kitchen table, her shoulders turned toward the window. The storm outside whistled through the closed door beside them.

Millie folded the lace tablecloth into thirds, setting it on the kitchen table and pressing each seam so the fabric would be ready for its next use some other day.

Harper's mother came beside Millie and took a liking to it. "How beautiful," she said. "Is it vintage?"

Her eyes met Millie's. Millie chuckled under her breath. "It's vintage, all right. It's old as me."

The woman held Millie's gaze. "So lovely. It seems to have a story to tell."

"That's because it does have a story." Millie straightened her cloche and took a deep breath. She hadn't planned what she was about to say next, and yet, she had the strangest sense it was the right thing to do. "I'd be honored if you'd take it home with you."

The woman's eyes widened, and her hands fluttered to her faded blouse. "I couldn't."

"You could, and you will." Millie waved toward the tablecloth. "I've loved it many years but rarely get use out of it anymore. It'd make me happy knowing someone still sees value in it."

Harper's mother trailed one finger along the lace, as if that one finger was all she dared use to touch such delicate fabric. But Millie knew the lace was stronger than it seemed.

Millie picked up the folded tablecloth and held it out toward her. "Truly."

The woman reached for the lace as tears welled in the corners of her eyes. "Harper and I will use it for tea parties."

Millie smiled. She glanced through the windows. Wind swept the rain so it pulled like waves along the sidewalk, rushing closer toward the house and whipping water against the windows.

Elbow against the table, Harper rested her chin on her fist and turned to them. "Why did it have to rain?"

The oven timer buzzed. Millie hurried over, tugging a cat-shaped oven mitt onto her hand. "We can still do the lesson inside."

Harper sighed. "Thank you, Mrs. Millie, and I *am* excited about that, but it's just not the same."

Millie held back her smirk as she reached into the oven. She remembered clearly from Juliet's childhood that Harper's age was about the time melodrama set in.

Still, she understood the disappointment. Even felt it too. The three of them had scarcely moved her sewing machine back inside before the dark clouds rolled in and the heavens parted. Little Harper had grabbed the lacy tablecloth and run, and it flew like a cape behind her.

The biscuits were ruined. So was the sun tea Millie had brewed yesterday for the occasion.

So instead, they'd set up the sewing machine on the kitchen table and were about to eat cut-and-bake snickerdoodles, with powdered lemonade to drink.

Millie set the cookie sheet on top of the stove. She waved her patterned oven mitt over the cookies to cool them.

"You know, my mama always said you can't have flowers without some rain." Millie shimmied each cookie up with her spatula.

She'd caught Harper's attention. The little girl turned her head. "Guess I never thought of it that way."

"Sure, because nobody likes plans changing. We want things to happen just the way we dream them, just the way we expect." Millie held her spatula in the air. "But what I've learned in my years is that the same water which brings us Jubilee goes up into the clouds then rains back down. Without the rain, eventually, we wouldn't have any tide."

This time, Harper's mother was the one to turn. Still holding the tablecloth to her chest, she let out a sigh so deep that Millie felt it too.

Millie set the plate of cookies in the center of the table and reached for the ceramic pitcher of lemonade. It may be powdered, but at least it was pretty. She poured three glasses while looking at Juliet's photo on the fridge, then started to pour a fourth out of habit. Juliet loved lemonade. But Juliet had returned to New Orleans last week, their visit far too short for Millie's liking.

Millie put the empty glass back inside the cabinet. Harper's mother helped her with the other three.

Millie sat down in the chair beside Harper and folded her hands on the table. "So, sweetheart, tell me. Why do you want to learn how to sew? Clothes for yourself or even your dolls? Embroidery? Quilting?"

Harper blinked. "You're going to think it's silly."

Millie leaned closer, reaching for the plate so Harper could take a cookie. "Try me."

Harper took one bite and covered her mouth with her hand. "These are delicious."

Millie grinned. "Thank you." She waited until Harper was ready to continue.

"I want to own a dress store someday." Harper took another bite of her cookie.

Images flashed through Millie's mind like a picture book blown by the wind. Herself at the ice cream shop. Mama at the train station. Meeting Franklin. And then, of course, the babies.

And with each memory came a different sort of fabric—some soft, others coarse, some floral, others with predictable stripes and patterns. But life had sewn each of them, stitch by stitch, together.

Maybe, in her own way, Millie *had* gotten her dress store after all. Though nothing was for sale here, she was surrounded by a lifetime of fabrics, literal and otherwise, she had worn for various occasions and in different seasons. Each dress, each sweater, lining her drawers and her closet racks and, more than anything, lining her memories, so that stitch by stitch the one central pattern in it all was redemption. And she wouldn't trade her unconventional, unexpected dream-come-true for anything.

Not even the dress shop on King Street.

"Dear one," Millie said, standing to pull fabric from the drawer for their first lesson. "It would be my joy to help you."

And she meant it: she meant it with every fiber of her being.

FIFTY-THREE

Charleston, Modern Day

Harper watched as the morning sun streamed through the window, casting a shadow of the wedding dress against the wall and an even greater shadow of Millie.

From the shadow, Millie looked taller. As if she possessed the power to achieve anything by simply standing in the path of the sun. Refracting its beams by positioning herself in the here and now, looking at once toward the darkness that might scare others and beyond it, to the sunlight that pierces through clouds.

Harper once read an article about hummingbirds, and how with certain kinds, the sunlight becomes a prism through their wings and the prism becomes a rainbow. All that's left is the shadow of the little bird in the photo and the rainbow wings that carry it through gardens. Moving from beauty to beauty, of kept promises with each open, living flower. Everlasting hope. Everlasting covenant.

Even dead seeds make roots, and roots underground sprout blooms, and the rain falls, and in due time and in due season the hummingbird returns, looking for nectar and hoping to find a harvest. Carrying her story in her rainbow wings, from generation to generation.

And as Harper watched Millie and that shadow on the wall, she couldn't shake the feeling she was standing on holy ground.

She breathed in the smell of the place—gardenias and jasmine. Like the prettiest bridal gown turned into a scent. She'd never been able to pinpoint whether the fragrance was perfume, room spray, or candles. But it was distinctly Millie, and now, distinctly hers too.

On the drive back to Charleston, she'd come up with the perfect name and location for the new store.

Second Story.

Instead of fancy gowns you could find any old place, they would specialize in vintage pieces that had been restored, each one coming with a tag that told the piece's story.

For the past few weeks since she'd returned from her father's house in the mountains, Harper, Peter, and Millie had been working long hours labeling each garment with the information they knew about the previous owner. A whole set of 1950s cardigans belonged to a woman who lived in a cottage on Edisto. A pair of heels were once worn by the first female student at the College of Charleston. They'd even found some jewelry dating back to the Civil War at an estate sale.

Each purchase offered the customer a chance to be part of a story that had started long ago. That was the enchantment of vintage clothing. The power of stories restored. Harper didn't know why she hadn't thought of it before.

Second Story was nearly ready to open but still needed one more addition.

Harper stepped toward a rack at the front of the shop to hang up the dress she'd submitted for the Senior Show months ago. Her fingers lingered over the embroidery. When she looked at it now, she didn't see failure or even flawed stitching. She did see a hint of Anthropologie, but she would take that with flattery. Funny how the things that seemed like the biggest failures could open up the wildest dreams.

"That dress is stunning. Truly remarkable." Millie stood in front of the dress with admiration.

"There was a time I thought it was proof my dreams were shattered."

Millie stepped over toward her wedding gown and held out her hat so the buttons showed as a perfect match. "For a long time, I thought this dress was gone as well." Millie's eyes trailed the delicate fabric of the gown. "But God has taught me here in Charleston"—Millie held on to Harper's gaze—"that our stories, *His* stories, are never really gone."

Harper stilled from straightening her dress on the rack.

"When I was a young girl," Millie said, "I spent so much time afraid of shadows. I imagined them to be the figure of whatever villain seemed larger than me at that point in my life. But as I grew, I realized something." The sunlight shifted through the window and threw the silhouette of Millie's wedding dress upon the floor. "No matter how hard we try to avoid them, we'll spend half our lives living in the shadows. Because the thing of it is, we were never supposed to run."

Harper moistened her dry lips and shook her head slightly. "I don't think I understand."

Millie took several slow steps closer to the window until she stood in the shadow of the gown. "The secret, my sweet Harper, is we stop fearing shadows when we see the sun that makes them. Instead of cowering, we shift into the sunlight, and the shadows shift as well."

The truth of it ran in chills down Harper's arms, seeping down into her heart. She thought of her favorite verse as a child. The "Father of lights." Every perfect gift coming down from Him above.

Millie reached out, inviting Harper to close the space between them. Harper did, readily taking Millie's warm grasp into her own.

Millie's sniffle was the only tell she was about to cry. She raised her chin slightly as her hands trembled. "Let me tell you what the Lord has done in this shadow, Harper."

So it began. The story of Millie's life and the story of Millie's love. Of dreams with disappointing reality, and the splitting of futures that Millie had settled long ago as an inevitable break in her heart.

And all the while, Harper stood transfixed in the shadow of the buttons, in the shadow of the wedding dress, until Millie spoke, and Harper's gaze lifted.

"I always did say, there's no sense in beautiful buttons just sitting around."

"You're right, Millie." Harper smiled. "You're absolutely right."

"There's one more thing I want to tell you." Millie situated her hat on her head, securing it with the pins. "Surely you saw it coming."

Harper shook her head. She never had the slightest idea what Millie would say next.

Not when Millie turned. Not even when Millie stepped toward the wedding gown. But then Millie reached for it, laid the fabric between her arms, and held it out toward Harper. "The dress is yours."

Harper's eyes widened. All the sounds of the street outside faded to a blur, and all she noticed was the flicker of anticipation in Millie's eyes.

"I couldn't."

"Oh, hush. Of course you could, and you will." Millie nodded once, definitively, as if the matter were settled. Perhaps it was.

But Harper chided herself—she couldn't dare consider taking Millie's gown! The piece was an heirloom. Who was she to deserve such a thing? Such a story?

She had come to believe her designs were ordinary. That *she* was ordinary. There was nothing about her as exquisite as this dress. And yet God had reminded her of the value of her dreams. By taking the safe route, she was actually taking the harder one, allowing fear to trump faith in her heart. Pushing healing away from herself and others, telling God His plans for her weren't worth her time because she'd been too afraid to make the steps.

And now, here she was, standing inside the store she was meant to start all along. Somehow, God had used all those attempts to bring her where she was now. Tears began to well up in her eyes as validation rose deep within her heart.

"I'm not even engaged," Harper whispered, looking off at the inventory.

But Millie set the dress in Harper's arms. She raised her own finger to Harper's chin and gently nudged until their eyes met.

"I want you to have it. No one else will love it as you will. No one else will see the story as you have. And if my hunch serves me well, as it usually does, you'll be wearing it soon enough as my granddaughter." Millie didn't so much as blink, and Harper dared not blink, either. "The story is yours now."

At that, the rock Harper had so carefully used to close up her hopes and her dreams and her soul began to roll, and fast. In its place, she found beauty, she found freedom, she found purpose streaming forth.

But most of all, she found her own second story.

Millie reached to brush the fabric of her mended cardigan.

"Harper," she said, "it's time to fasten the buttons."

And Harper knew she was right.

Buttons may be tiny. Delicate, even. But they fasten together the fabric of an entire garment. The fabric we wear day in and day out, the mundane cotton blouse and the lacy wedding dress. The fabric, the seams, that cover us, warm us, protect us. Binding dream to dream, story to story, but mostly, death to life.

With a particular kind of beauty that rises from the dust. The resurrection life of a second story, of the breath that mends us.

Harper took Millie's hand in her own and together, they stepped toward the door to open the store for the first time.

NOTE ON HISTORICAL ACCURACY

Millie represents many men and women of her time who made the agonizing decision to pass as white and hide part of their ancestral history in an effort to secure safety and opportunity. It's my hope that I've clearly portrayed the complex struggle this choice creates within Millie, and the unrelenting pride she holds for all aspects of her heritage—a pride that ultimately prompts her to embroider the sack and effectively render it a historical, artistic, and cultural heirloom whose narrative will be preserved.

The satchel referenced in this novel is based on a true story about a sack purchased at a flea market in Nashville that would later become an integral artifact for African American cultural history in Charleston and beyond. Ashley's Sack is on display at the National Museum of African American History and Culture in Washington D.C., and was originally filled with a dress, pecans, and a braid of hair. I fictionalized the buttons for the purpose of this story. The actual embroidery on the satchel reads:

My great grandmother Rose
mother of Ashley gave her this sack when

she was sold at age 9 in South Carolina
it held a tattered dress 3 handfulls of
pecans a braid of Roses hair. Told her
It be filled with my Love always
she never saw her again
Ashley is my grandmother
—Ruth Middleton, 1921

Ruth Middleton was likely the granddaughter of Ashley and was well known in affluent households within Philadelphia for her remarkable fashion sense. By embroidering the satchel in this way, Ruth ensured Rose and Ashley's tragic story would continue to be told, and their sacrifice honored for generations to come.

AUTHOR'S NOTE

Dear Readers,

Thank you for taking this trip with me to the dress shop on King Street. I hope you enjoyed reading Harper and Millie's story as much as I enjoyed writing it. Millie represents such a different set of experiences from my own that during many stages of this process, I felt intimidated to write her story justly, but she soon became my favorite character in a decade's worth of writing. I felt her struggle for the freedom and safety to express her identity as though she were a dear friend. With that said, I would love to give you a little behind-the-scenes glimpse of how the book came to be.

I've always been interested in postmodernism, and it's fair to say I hope this book provides an alternative to the cultural unraveling of "truth"—instead pointing toward a greater hope, a greater redemption, a greater Truth beyond any binary construct of power or identity, even those of our own making.

I first began writing novels ten years ago. Like Harper at the beginning of the story, I was so sure this was what God had called me to do, and while I expected I would have to work hard at my craft and face rejections, I never expected those obstacles would come repeatedly for a decade. But you know what? God never left me alone on that journey, and without every one of those rejections, I would still be writing subpar attempts at rom-com. I certainly would not have written *The Dress Shop on King Street.*

Did Harper and Millie's story resonate similarly with you? Do you have a God-given dream within you, that maybe you've believed is dead because you have worked at it but haven't seen anything happen? Maybe you gave it a good-faith effort, only to fail, or perhaps you've found yourself immobilized by fear or loud voices speaking insufficiency. Let me tell you something—the author of creation is the author of your story, and where He calls, He equips, even when manna provision doesn't look as we'd expected. Whether you've dreamed of being a writer or an artist, a teacher or a foster parent, it's time to look straight at that dead dream and allow God to breathe life into it. I pray you will find your own vision resurrected and stronger for the beautiful in-between, just like Harper and Millie.

Thanks for reading, and I can't wait to tell you more about Lucy and Eliza's story in the next HEIRLOOM SECRETS novel!

—Ashley Clark

BOOK CLUB QUESTIONS

1) What experiences do Harper and Millie have at the dress shop on King Street? How does the store itself change through the course of the story? What might these changes represent?

2) Both heroines believe life has disqualified them from following their dreams. What has happened to make them feel this way? Can you relate?

3) Millie's racial identity has a profound influence on the choices she makes, as does the trauma of what happened to her father. Do you fault Millie for these choices? Why or why not?

4) Though the novel is primarily about Harper and Millie, their love stories with Peter and Franklin play a key role in shaping their dreams. What was your favorite romantic moment, and which hero did you find more swoon-worthy?

5) My one-word theme for the book is resurrection. How do you see this theme play out in the story? Can you think of

any specific moments? Also, how do you see this theme playing out in your own life—or how do you want it to?

6) Water plays a key role throughout the story, as both sustaining and destructive. Can you think of any examples? How do those moments change the characters, and how do similar moments change us within our own lives?

7) Where would you rather visit—Millie's boardinghouse in Fairhope, or one of Peter's rentals in Charleston?

8) Millie carries two heirloom buttons throughout the book that help unravel long-held family secrets. What is significant about these buttons as a symbol, both for the characters and for your own life?

9) Do you think Harper and Millie are ultimately successful or unsuccessful? Why or why not?

10) Sparks are flying between Lucy and Declan for all the wrong reasons. What do you think may be coming for their story—as well as Eliza's—in the next HEIRLOOM SECRETS novel?

ACKNOWLEDGMENTS

Like threads weaving in and out of embroidery, so many people have graciously touched this work and left it more beautiful for their investment—some when the story was only a dream, others in its final stages, but all with the commonality of helping make *The Dress Shop on King Street* the best version of itself. I am thankful for each of you.

Raela Schoenherr, sometimes I still pinch myself to think you're my acquisitions editor. Thank you for believing in this story—and me!—long, long, long before it ever saw the light of day. Readers may not always know your name, but they should because you better the world of Christian fiction for all of us. You also have excellent taste in television shows.

Elizabeth Frazier, you've tirelessly and patiently worked to make my story shine, and I'm in awe of all the catches you find as well as your valuable big-picture feedback.

Amy Lokkesmoe, Noelle Chew, and all the team members who have diligently, creatively, and faithfully worked to place this story in front of all the right channels—you are so incredibly appreciated. Thank you for all you do!

Bethany House family, I am constantly gushing over you. You are amazing. Every one of you is intentional about producing quality fiction that embodies the hope of the gospel, and I am humbled to partner with you.

Karen Solem, you believed in me from the first day we met and never let me settle for anything less than the best fit for my stories. Thank you for never wavering and for offering such wise counsel. You are a wonderful agent.

Alley Cats, I remember the day you asked me to join your blog. I had no idea that we would become like sisters in this writing journey, and I cannot imagine walking this path with anyone else. Pepper Basham, Angie Dicken, Cara Putman, Amy Simpson, Sherrinda Ketchersid, Laurie Tomlinson, Julia Reffner, Krista Phillips, Mary Vee, Casey Apodaca, and Karen Schravemade, I adore you all. Let's be best friends forever.

Angie Dicken, where would I be without you? In every season, you have been faithful, helpful, and understanding, from chapter critiques to celebrations. Thank you for always cheering me forward.

Cara Putman, there really are no words to acknowledge the many ways you have invested in me over the years. You are the kind of person I can go to with anything, and I wholly trust your advice. God knew I needed you from the start! You are a gem.

Betsy St. Amant, your early edits of this story were such a huge help, but even beyond that, you gave me the courage on a fundamental level to tell a story that felt intimidating and bigger than myself. You are a wonderful human being, and I am so thankful for our dear friendship and mutual love of *Gilmore Girls*.

Joy Massenburge, your name suits you. You are a gifted author and an absolute delight. Thank you for graciously offering a much-needed lens on my story.

Ed Grimball and Sue Bennett, the two of you are an embodiment of class, charm, and the culture of Charleston. Your walking tours inspired not only this story, but also my love for your great city. I am so thankful to know you both and will forever cherish our friendship.

Matthew Clark, when I told you I felt God was calling me to write, you believed me, and you never looked back. You've come to writing conferences, celebrated my milestones, and have been there when it felt as though it was all crashing down. You are my best friend, and I would marry you all over again.

Nathanael Clark, being your mother has changed my life. Your kindness, creativity, and spunk brighten my days, and I have your fierce love of trains to thank for inspiring the train-jumping portion of this novel.

Steve and Laurie Young, you taught me never to give up on my dreams and continue to bring encouragement, strength, and joy into my life. I am beyond thankful to have you as my parents.

One of the reasons I'm so drawn to multigenerational, southern stories is because I've had the privilege of knowing my grandparents well. Ernie and Melody Rippstein, and Jim and Dolores Young, I am so thankful to have grandparents like you and for the heritage of faith you have given me.

And I feel I'd be remiss if I didn't mention my dogs, Maddie and Schroeder, who have offered a whole lot of moral support, cuddles, and doggie high-fives, as well as concerned looks whenever I was going through line edits. As they say, don't shop—adopt!

Ashley Clark writes romantic women's fiction set in the South, and *The Dress Shop on King Street* is her debut novel. With a master's degree in creative writing, Ashley teaches literature and writing courses at the University of West Florida. Ashley has been an active member of American Christian Fiction Writers for over a decade. She lives with her husband, son, and two rescued cocker spaniels off Florida's Gulf Coast. When she's not writing, she's rescuing stray animals, dreaming of Charleston, and drinking all the English breakfast tea she can get her hands on. Be sure to visit her website www.ashleyclarkbooks.com.

Sign Up for
Ashley's Newsletter

Keep up to date with Ashley's news
on book releases and events
by signing up for her email list at
ashleyclarkbooks.com.

◊ BETHANYHOUSE

 Stay up to date on your favorite books and authors with our free e-newsletters.
Sign up today at bethanyhouse.com.

 facebook.com/bethanyhousepublishers @bethanyhousefiction

 Free exclusive resources for your book group at bethanyhouseopenbook.com

More from Bethany House

When deaf teen Loyal Raines stumbles upon a dead body in the nearby river, his absentee father, Creed, is shocked the boy runs to him first. Pulled into the investigation, Creed discovers that it is the boy's courage, not his inability to hear, that sets him apart, and he will have to do more than solve a murder if he wants to win his family's hearts again.

The Right Kind of Fool by Sarah Loudin Thomas
sarahloudinthomas.com

Reeling from the loss of her parents, Lucy Claremont discovers an artifact under the floorboards of their London flat, leading her to an old seaside estate. Aided by her childhood friend Dashel, a renowned forensic astronomer, they start to unravel a history of heartbreak, sacrifice, and love begun 200 years prior—one that may offer the healing each seeks.

Set the Stars Alight by Amanda Dykes
amandadykes.com

Determined to uphold her father's legacy, newly graduated Nora Shipley joins an entomology research expedition to India to prove herself in the field. In this spellbinding new land, Nora is faced with impossible choices—between saving a young Indian girl and saving her career, and between what she's always thought she wanted and the man she's come to love.

A Mosaic of Wings by Kimberly Duffy
kimberlyduffy.com

◊ BETHANYHOUSE

You May Also Like . . .

In this epistolary novel from the WWII home front, Johanna Berglund is forced to return to her small Midwestern town to become a translator at a German prisoner of war camp. There, amid old secrets and prejudice, she finds that the POWs have hidden depths. When the lines between compassion and treason are blurred, she must decide where her heart truly lies.

Things We Didn't Say by Amy Lynn Green
amygreenbooks.com

Secretary to the first lady of the United States, Caroline Delacroix is at the pinnacle of high society—but is hiding a terrible secret. Immediately suspicious of Caroline, but also attracted to her, secret service agent Nathaniel Trask must battle his growing love for her as the threat to the president rises and they face adventure, heartbreak, and danger.

A Gilded Lady by Elizabeth Camden
Hope and Glory #2
elizabethcamden.com

As Chicago's Great Fire destroys their bookshop, Meg and Sylvie Townsend make a harrowing escape from the flames with the help of reporter Nate Pierce. But the trouble doesn't end there—their father is committed to an asylum after being accused of murder, and they must prove his innocence before the asylum truly drives him mad.

Veiled in Smoke by Jocelyn Green
The Windy City Saga #1
jocelyngreen.com

BETHANYHOUSE